T0146543

FOR MORE THAN FORTY YEARS, THROUGH MANY WARS, ACROSS DESERT AND OVER MOUNTAINS, THEY'VE BLAZED A TRAIL OF *FIRE AND STEEL*

THE LEGACY OF LATRUN: During the 1948 War of Independence, in the wheat fields below the Latrun fortress, half the 7th Armored Brigade is killed and their precious few vehicles are picked off by the Arab Legion. On the lips of the survivors, a vow is born: "Never Again."

LIGHTNING IN THE SINAI: In the 1956 Sinai Campaign, outnumbered and on unfamiliar turf, the 7th Brigade burst across the Sinai, crossing nearly 100 kilometers of desert— every inch fiercely contested.

ONSLAUGHT INTO EGYPT: Launching a surprise blitz- krieg against an enormous army of Russian-built battle tanks, officers of the 7th Brigade choreograph an unstoppa- ble charge—carrying the 1967 Six Day War.

THE VALLEY OF TEARS: Desperately short on ammuni- tion, live crews, and time during the 1973 Yom Kippur War, the Brigade decisively crushes Syrian offensive capabilities in the northern Golan.

Books by Samuel M. Katz

The Elite
Fire and Steel

Published by POCKET BOOKS

ISRAEL'S 7TH ARMORED BRIGADE

FIRE & STEEL

FOUR DECADES OF VICTORY
AND COURAGE — THE STORY OF
THE MOST AWESOME TANK
FORCE IN THE WORLD TODAY

SAMUEL M. KATZ

POCKET BOOKS
New York   London   Toronto   Sydney   Tokyo   Singapore

An *Original* Publication of POCKET BOOKS

 POCKET BOOKS, a division of Simon & Schuster Inc. 1230 Avenue of the Americas, New York, NY 10020

Copyright © 1996 by Samuel M. Katz
Foreword © 1995 by Brigadier-General (Ret.) Avigdor Kahalani

ISBN: 978-1-5011-0041-3

First Pocket Books printing June 1996

10 9 8 7 6 5 4 3 2 1

POCKET and colophon are registered trademarks of Simon & Schuster Inc.

Cover photo © Michael Zarfati

Printed in the U.S.A.

Dedicated to those who
have donned the black beret
and never made it back
from the battlefield

Foreword: The 7th Brigade—
The IDF's Spearhead

The epic saga of the 7th Armored Brigade in Israel's wars is an inseparable part of the history of the Israel Defense Forces and the State of Israel in its plight for survival. It is not by coincidence that the brigade placed a spear into the center of its unit emblem, as it has served as a spearhead, an example, by which to shape the IDF into what it is today.

From the battles of Latrun in the War of Independence to the battle for Umm Katef and Abu Agheila in the Sinai War, from the breakthrough at Rafah and El Arish in the Six Day War to blocking the Golan Heights from being overrun in the 1973 Yom Kippur War, and to its fight against the Syrians in Lebanon's Beka'a Valley, the brigade has presented itself as the Armored Corps' leading and central force. The brigade established new standards of excellence in tank warfare and established in Israeli military thought the inescapable fact that it is the tank that leads on the battlefield. The Armored Corps' battle doctrine, in fact, was deeply influenced by the battles that the brigade fought and the lessons its commanders learned. Professionally, the brigade was the cutting edge to the Armored Corps and to the IDF in general. Its battlefield exploits were not only studied by commanders in Israel, but in military academies throughout the world—the brigade's battle doctrine of maximizing the potential of a tank force, sometimes beyond expectation and the realm of possibility, would become commonplace in the IDF.

It wasn't in the professional aspect of tank fighting that the 7th Brigade established new levels of excellence that would define armored warfare. It was on the basic human level, on a simple soldier's level, that the brigade became a symbol of the Israeli youngster conscripted into military service and a proud statement of how he was brought up and raised. The 7th Brigade's means of training and preparing a soldier has often been imitated and has personified the modern Israeli warrior. And it isn't by coincidence that so many Israeli eighteen-year-olds, upon their conscription into the IDF, volunteer into the brigade. Through its epic and heroic battles, the soldiers of the brigade have proven that it is the friendship and comradeship of the soldiers in the tank and in the unit that is ultimately the true stepping-stone to victory. The image of the commander as the man fearlessly leading his soldiers into battle is a stoic symbol that also draws on the commander's personal example as a man, a soldier, and a professional officer. The essence of the tank soldier, as an integral element of a crew, whose committed professionalism and limitless loyalty has been a fundamental element of all the battles that the brigade has fought. On the path of blood and sacrifice that the brigade has traveled over the course of Israel's wars, this immortal bravery shines as a beacon. It is a limitless love of the nation, and the love and faith in the soldier's tank, his crew, and his commander that has left an indelible stamp on the IDF and the history of the State of Israel. Everywhere the brigade has fought, it has been the soldiers' souls and spirits that have been shown to be made of steel, a soul and spirit passed down through several generations of soldiers and commander.

The history of the 7th Armored Brigade is one paid with heavy price with many dead and many more wounded. The families of the fallen and wounded are an inseparable essence of the brigade's existence, an essence that the brigade and its soldiers hold dear to their hearts. It is these soldiers, who have seen their best friends die in their arms, that are the ones who pray in their hearts for peace. It is the courage of these soldiers, and their presence on battlefields past and present, that is the sole force powerful enough to have elevated the State of Israel to negotiate for peace from a position of strength. Only when peace comes will the dreams of these soldiers be realized.

As a proud son of the 7th Armored Brigade, as a witness to its most desperate battles and its heights of courage, I am confident that this book will serve a young generation of men as an accurate history of all the heroism and awe that is the 7th Brigade.

> Brigadier-General (Ret.) Avigdor Kahalani (MK)
> Tel Aviv, October 1995

Author's Note

In this age of high-tech commandos, of special forces warriors bursting through doors and windows to rescue hostages or rappelling down from space-age helicopters to raid an enemy fortification, the notion of conventional war waged by simple soldiers inside 60-ton vehicles has lost its sex appeal. Readers of history, and specifically the history of warfare, have noticed over the past several years that fewer books are being written about major campaigns in major wars (there is intense debate among many if "Operation Desert Storm" can be considered a major war in the pure meaning of the word), fewer unit histories are being published, and the stories of average fighting men in extraordinary combat situations are being drowned out by headline-grabbing, obscenity-filled manuscripts of special forces operators tasked with fulfilling a personal or political agenda rather than telling a tale of historical note. Special forces commandos may start wars with spectacular raids, but it is the conventional fighting men, the tank soldiers on the whole, who fight these wars and win them. Their stories, without the laser sights and balaclavas hiding faces, are as terrifying, spellbinding, and dramatic as those of any commando. According to one Israeli tank officer, "Anyone can jump from an airplane, anyone can lunge from a helicopter. It takes a brave son of a bitch to sit inside a box, filled to capacity with fuel and eighty very explosive shells, while that box is the simultaneous target of tank cannons and infantry-held missiles alike."

This book is about one small group of those courageous SOBs who *do* perform their tasks inside a steel box while warheads and ordnance are fired at them from ranges of 2,000 and 3,000 meters—or at point-blank ranges. People tend to believe that sitting inside a tank during combat is the safest place to be, but nothing could be further from the truth. A tank is a target. A moving target, pure and simple, that attracts the most destructive types of ordnance that could be found anywhere: high explosives, armor-piercing, armor-penetrating rounds that slice through 152mm of sloped armor and turn the insides of a turret into a death vault of ricocheting metal interspersed with exploding shells and mangled flesh. Tanks do not just get hit and halt—they burn a slow and horrible death. Fire is the tank soldier's greatest enemy. Once a tank is hit, it erupts into flame that turns a 60-ton tank into a 60-ton oven. The flames roast through the crewmen's Nomex flame-retardant coveralls, and soon the heat burns everything inside its terrible wrath. Infantrymen can hide behind rocks and other bits of cover should they come under fire. Tank soldiers have to frantically escape a burning death trap by sliding through passages and holes that reach well above 500 degrees (F). Once out of the tank, the survivors usually find themselves under murderous artillery and small arms fire—there is no easier target than the dazed and injured crew of a burning tank. These burned and blackened tank crews must then transform themselves into expert infantrymen to survive and reach friendly lines only to be issued a new tank and endure the hell of armored combat one more time. Anyone who does not think of a tank soldier as an elite fighting man is seriously uninformed about the horrors of war. These men are not Rambos and they are not caricatures. They are strikingly real and down-to-earth. Avigdor Kahalani, perhaps Israel's most famous—and decorated—tank warrior and the man most connected to the 7th Brigade, is a soft-spoken gentle man who has come to personify the meaning of "above and beyond the call of duty."

This book is about one brigade of these brave and battle-tested tank soldiers that have fought in seven major wars in less than fifty years. It is a story of how a tank force was created by an infant state by hook and by crook, and how this fledgling armored combat unit has managed to build itself up from nothing to become the premier tank unit in the world. Military men in other countries might disagree with that statement, but no other tank force in any army in the world has found itself in the combat situations that the 7th Brigade has endured, and few military units anywhere in the world have persevered and excelled under such battle-field odds as have the men of the 7th Brigade. This book is, in fact, the story of the modern State of Israel, told through the wars, battles, and developments of the 7th Armored Brigade. Most importantly, this book is about the men who have donned their crewman's helmets over the past half century, who fought on the desolate hills of Latrun and Jordan Valley, and who have waged brutal close-quarter tank battles in Sinai and on top of the Golan Heights. This book is about those men who sacrificed their lives in battle, and about those who have given new meaning to the words courage under fire.

It is hoped that this is the *complete* history of the 7th Armored Brigade—a study of the brigade's creation, maturation, and manifestation in battle. Yet it is also hoped that this work is a complete history not with the stories told of the various battles fought by the proud and mighty force, but in the desperate prayer that this fighting unit will have to fight no more battles, and add no more names to the long list of its fallen.

Many people have assisted me in the research and production of this book, and I would like to take this opportunity to thank them. I would like to offer my sincere gratitude to Lieutenant-Colonel Irit Atzmon and Major Natan Rotenberg of the IDF Spokesman's Office for the faith that they have shown in this project, as I would like to thank Captain Hanni Yeshurin for her kind assistance. I would also like to

AUTHOR'S NOTE

thank Colonel Y. and the staff at the 7th Brigade for their kind help; Member of Knesset Brigadier-General (Res.) Avigdor Kahalani and Member of Knesset Major-General (Res.) Orri Orr for the generous time they afforded me (both have forever changed my perception of the Israeli politician for the better); Major-General (Res.) Avigdor Ben-Gal for his unique and personal insight into the 7th; Major-General (Res.) Shlomoh Shamir for his generous time and insight into the creation of the brigade; Colonel Benny Michelson, the IDF Chief of Military History and a one-time officer in the 7th, for his brilliant memory and access to previously inaccessible files; to Brigadier-General (Res.) Elyashiv Shimshi, a highly decorated officer and best-selling author in his own right who was kind enough to bestow upon me his time and friendship; Colonel (Res.) Moshe Givati for his generous time and friendship; Colonel (Res.) Eliezer Granite at the Armored Corps Memorial and Museum at Latrun for his invaluable insight and assistance; Dr. Reuven Gal, one of the more analytical and sincere thinkers in Israeli military circles; Marty Ostertag and Kurt Sayanga of the Discovery Channel and the entire staff behind the *Fields of Armor* television series, working with whom I found a most enlightening and enjoyable experience; Joseph S. Bermudez, Jr., and Mike Eisendstadt for their brilliant insight into the Syrian military machine and the 1973 War; Mike Green; and Steve Zaloga, this country's greatest tank scholar. I would also like to thank Lieutenant-Colonel Shai Dolev at the IDF Military Censor's Office for the fair and prompt review of this manuscript, as well as Mr. Nissim Elyakim and Shiri Elyakim for their kind—and absolutely invaluable—legwork on my behalf. Their devotion to this project and kind sacrifice of their own time was instrumental in the production of this book. Lastly, a special thanks to my wife, Sigi, for her patience, understanding, and unflinching support.

Samuel M. Katz
May 1995, New York City

Introduction

The evening chill comes quickly to the Golan—especially on a November night when the crisp clear skies assume a foreboding shade of amber. As the sun set on the volcanic plateau that has served as crucible for war and bloodshed between Syria and Israel, the harsh northern winds from Mount Hermon and Lebanon bite through to the bone of any man or beast unlucky enough not to find shelter. Yet even shelter cannot offer protection from the Golan's elements: ice-cold air, sweeping winds, and the threat of full-scale war. The Golan Heights, from both the Syrian and Israeli sides of the fortified frontier, is an armed camp bristling with the tools of war, the soldiers of war, and the possibility of war. Should a seventh full-scale Arab-Israeli war erupt, it is most likely that the bloodletting will transpire on the Golan Heights. Should Middle East peace negotiations fail, Syria will almost certainly once again attempt to retake the heights, *its heights*, by launching its half-million-man army across the "Purple Line" boundary separating the two warring nations.

The men and machines of the 7th Armored Brigade are determined to stop them.

The whining howl of the frigid winds slamming against the exposed plains of the Golan is muted by the clanking percussion of tank treads rolling hard on the volcanic turf, and by the grinding hydraulic gears shifting inside armored tinder boxes; the chatter of field radios hissing in the night is incessant. Attempting to make sense out of a cold and moonlit night atop the treacherous Golan is Colonel Y.,[1] the *Ma'Hat,* or brigade commander. With the Golan substituting for a second home away from home for most of his seventeen years in the Israel Defense Forces (IDF), Colonel Y. is not fazed by the elements; even though many of his officers are wearing insulated cold-weather suits over sweaters and long johns, his Nomex fire-resistant coveralls have their sleeves rolled up to a tight fold around his biceps. As he gazes through high-powered field glasses, the full moon affords a deep and revealing view into Syrian territory. Beyond the endless coils of barbed wire fences and minefields, Y. could see advanced elements of the Syrian Army in position—T-72 main battle tanks, and enough BMP armored personnel carriers (APCs) to make anyone *this* side of the Purple Line just a bit anxious. As an act of second nature, he glances down to make sure that his Kevlar body armor and Glilon assault rifle are within immediate grabbing distance. The fact that over 3,000 men had died on the ground he was standing on was not lost to the 7th Brigade commander. It was a haunting edge to the importance of the night's activities.

Colonel Y.'s men had not slept properly in approximately 48 hours. A day earlier, they had endured a day-long, cordite-filled firing practice on the plains of the southern Golan. Perched atop a small volcanic hill, Colonel Y., the brigade's deputy commander, operations, intelligence, and communications officer, as well as all battalion commanders, stood underneath a camouflaged net substituting as a tent. Inside were half a dozen field radios, squelching a deafening hiss throughout, as well as maps, charts, and female NCOs, eighteen-year-old conscripts in very flattering one-piece Nomex coveralls, yelling instructions at captains, lieutenants, and sergeants. Target practice 7th Armored Brigade style takes place in a vast field of wild thorns and rock formations hedged in by volcanic boulders the size of apartment buildings. At the far-off edge of the range are several old Russian-made T-34 tanks, formerly of the Soviet Red Army, and then passed on to the Syrian military in the late 1950s. These veterans of Kursk and Stalingrad are also defeated veterans of the Golan Heights. They were captured on June 10, 1967, and have served their purpose ever since as battlefield targets.

Each Merkava Mk II main battle tank participating in the exercise will race its engines to the maximum speed of 45 kilometers per hour and settle to the starting line. Then, for the next ten minutes, the tank will advance slowly and simulate a fire-and-roll exercise: it will acquire the target, and destroy it as it advances across the battlefield. For good measure, the tank commander, affectionately known by the Hebrew acronym of *Ma'Tak,* will pepper the smoking and flaming remnants of a target with a belt-emptying burst of 7.62mm fire from his cupola mounted FN MAG. The range for the 105 is approximately 1,500 meters, and each tank is expected to hit the target—the center of the T-34's turret—on the first shot! Anything less is considered unsatisfactory—in fact, it's considered downright unacceptable. During war, hitting the target on the first shot means the target won't kill you on its first shot. During live-fire maneuvers, not hitting your target on the first shot means the waste of the cost of a 105mm round. It is neither a price that the financially limited IDF can ill afford nor a failure the brigade tends to tolerate. Today, the majority of the battalion being examined scores on the first or second shots. The unfortunate T-34s are obliterated in earsplitting explosions of 105mm armor-piercing and SABOT projectiles, racing through the thin air at over 6,000 feet per second and impacting into their thinly armored targets with awesome explosive force. As the hulking tank churns its path toward the target, the commander signals the end of his run by firing off his belt-load of 7.62mm ammunition.

The brigade's brass, standing anxiously in their camouflaged tent, monitors every nuance of every tank operating in the field. A giant tally board lists the success and failures of each crew, each company, each battalion. For the tanks who do score well in this display, there is no praise. Perfection is what is expected if these tank crews, serving as a line of steel in northern Israel, will be able to make another defensive stand in the Valley of Tears and survive it all. The Valley of Tears looms large in virtually every aspect of the 7th Brigade's current existence. According to Colonel Y., "We (the brigade commanding officers) refer to the Valley of Tears on a daily basis, with the young soldiers of the Seventh Armored Brigade, as one of the symbols, by which we educate the Seventh Armored Brigade's fighting generation, which is prepared to do the same mission, of defending the Golan Heights."[2] The "Valley of Tears" is an appropriate name for a small incline into the volcanic landscape that proved to be a tank soldier's death trap during the frantic first days of the 1973 War atop the Heights. It was here that the Syrians pushed the might of their armor against the IDF's vulnerable northern flank, and it was here that the tank soldiers of the 7th, with the shit hitting the fan and their backs literally to a wall, put up a frantic and close-quarter last defense. Syrian and Israeli tankers died facing one another; many died side-by-side in the close-quarter hell of indistinguishable tanks, targets, and corpses. The sight of steel beasts fighting it out at point-blank range was a horrifying sight to all who fought in this epic fight. They were battles, described by many veterans (both Syrian and Israeli) as Hollywood-Western-style quick draws, although here six-shots were replaced by 105mm smooth bore cannons.[3] For those who fought in the Valley of Tears, the small wedge of flat territory surrounded by the protruding Booster and Buqata hills, it is an icon of national resolve. For those who weren't there in 1973 but are there now, the Valley of Tears is a calling card of resolve. Just as Pearl Harbor is a tangible expression of America's resolve never to be caught by surprise and just as Stalingrad served for five decades as a point of Soviet determination never to succumb to foreign invasion, the Valley of Tears is a symbol of how a successful surprise attack can truly turn a military unit, a force of scared eighteen-year-old kids-turned-soldiers and a few experienced officers, into an entire nation's final line of defense.

Colonel Y. did not fight in the Valley of Tears in the 1973

War. He was a sixteen-year-old high-school student filling sandbags during the war, but he knows every inch of the Valley of Tears as if it were the back of his hand. He knows where the tanks (on both sides) moved about, where tanks were hit, and where tanks made their final stands before being overrun by overwhelming numbers and obliterating firepower. In fact, every 7th Brigade soldier is taught the history of the Valley of Tears: They study its battle and sanctify its significance. Gazing across his brigade's positions this November evening, Colonel Y. cannot help but juxtapose the present with the past. Imagining what it must have been like for the Centurion tanks of Lieutenant-Colonel Avigdor Kahalani's 77th Battalion to face such overwhelming odds, Lieutenant-Colonel Yair Nafshi propelling his mechanized force of APCs and infantrymen against a gauntlet of Syrian armor, and Lieutenant-Colonel Yosef Ben-Hanan, who reached the Golan Heights via a honeymoon in the Himalayas, leading a charge of battered tanks to save the remnants of the 7th Brigade from being overrun. Colonel Y. cannot help but remember the memory of Colonel Ben-Shoham and the destroyed 188th Barak Brigade, the 7th's flank to the south, that was annihilated by superior Syrian armor in the first two days of the war. Even though Colonel Y. was not there that fateful autumn atop the Golan he cannot look at his forces of Merkava MK II tanks, stricken against the autumn's moon, without conjuring up images of what it was like for the brigade in 1973.

The Golan Heights is ideal real estate for war, and ideal real estate for tank combat—the flat plateau of volcanic rock and ash serve as combat playing field wedged in by hills and mountains that act as reviewing stands and borders. In fact, according to many experts, the Golan Heights is one of the ideal tank battlefields in existence anywhere in the world, and, in the land of the Bible, it appears as if its flat plateaus, protective boulders, and rolling and protective hills were deigned as such by the powers that be. Biblically, in fact, it is where Armageddon is to take place, yet nothing can compare to the Armageddon that takes places when tanks face off against one another atop the Heights—especially on the narrow battlefield where there is little—if any—room to maneuver and outmaneuver the opponent, and opposing armies

5

are forced to slug it out. According to one American tank officer visiting the Golden Heights from Fort Knox, "It is a merciless battlefield, one that requires the right tank, the right crew, the best of officers, and the luck of the devil."[4] Colonel Y. will not rely on the luck of the devil the next time that the 7th Brigade is fighting in the Valley of Tears. With his Merkava MK II as the unit's primary tool, he is confident that he has the best tank in the world in his hands. Looking at the eighteen-year-old conscripts milling about, cocky nineteen-year-old tank commanders, and twenty-year-old officers, he knows that his chariots of iron and steel are maintained and crewed by the finest tank soldiers in the world.

There is a sense of urgency in the drills and exercises this November. War is not expected—it wasn't expected in 1973, after all. Even though the border is quiet and peace talks with Syria are currently (at the time of this book's writing) underway in Washington, D.C., and other backdoor channels, if past Middle Eastern wars have taught the IDF one thing it is to always expect the unexpected. Quiet today could mean a full-scale invasion tomorrow. The Golan Heights, the volcanic plateau so strategic to two warring nations, is as volatile a piece of real estate as exists anywhere in the world and can become the scene of the world's next major conflagration in a combustible second. Israel captured the Heights in a lightning strike in 1967; Syria attempted to reclaim her ground in a similar, albeit far more ferocious, lightning strike in 1973. The only means for guaranteeing that the long columns of Syrian T-72s and BMP-1s, posed across the fence and adorned for war in their blending shades of green and brown, will not burst across the frontier is for there to be a long and lasting peace treaty between Damascus and Jerusalem. Until that happens, the 7th Brigade must stand at the ready, prepared for any type of contingency. Deployment exercises atop the Golan Heights are meant to simulate a realistic alert and responses at a time when the threat of full-scale war is imminent.

As an alert is on, the brigade does not sleep well—they wear full uniform to bed, boots and all, and have their web gear, flak vests, and Glilon assault rifles wrapped up inside their sleeping bags and blankets—never more than a grab away. Their corrugated tin huts are Spartan conditions, but it is home. Posters of speed cars, motorcycles, and, of course, the obligatory pinups adorn the tin walls. There are also armor recognition charts courtesy of the Intelligence Branch and a bit of outdated graffiti proclaiming *"Tachana Ha'Ba'ah Damesek,"* or "Next Stop Damascus!" Another gift of graffiti is fresher. It simply states, "If you love your tank, your tank will love you back!" Close to 4:30 A.M., when the sounds of snoring mouths fill the room, the platoon commander, Second-Lieutenant Eli, bursts through the door, already in full battle kit, ordering his unit, a platoon in "M" Company, one of the best in the 82nd Battalion, to be inside their vehicles and ready to go in a matter of minutes. It is a mixed bunch scurrying about the barracks racing to their positions: Sabras born and bred in Israel whose fathers and brothers served in the brigade, Russian immigrants, and Ethiopians rescued from starvation in Operation Solomon, and now full-fledged soldiers defending their new homes. The soldiers race about their quarters and compound putting on their gear, including their specially designed chest pouches that allow them to carry a full battle load of magazines, grenades, and canteens while sitting comfortably in their constricting confines for many hours. Kevlar crewmen helmets are donned, and groups of men, in fours, head out to their vehicles parked in rear dug-out pits. The vehicles are virtually indistinguishable from the real estate—the brown-gray khaki scheme allows the Merkava to blend in to the bleak topography and color of Golan perfectly, especially in the foggy haze of a November's dawn. The crews all climb onto their hulking steel vehicles with absolute speed and dexterity—after all, they have done this countless times before—and remove the khaki canvas cover from their turrets. The driver enters his compartment and fires up his massive engine, the gunner and loader ready their seats, and the commander, standing upright in the turret as every Israeli tank commander is taught to, goes through his checklist and orders the vehicle *"Kadima"*—'Forward!" A puff of black smoke emerges from the exhaust and the tank proceeds down its path toward its forward firing position; the entire parking area is soon covered in a cloud of choking black smoke. Colonel Y. is already in his command and control M113 APC, coordinating the movements, making sure everything on the practice deployment is perfect.

The conscripts know that this is just an alert, but on one cloudy morning in 1973, an alert suddenly became full-scale war. All crews are equipped for full-scale war. Operation Desert Storm brought the realities of a full-scale war being fought with chemical and biological weapons to the threshold of implementation in 1991,[5] but Israel had been preparing for such a contingency for many years. It is no secret that the Syrians produce their own chemical agents, and there is little doubt that Damascus would not refrain from using these "poor man's weapons for destruction" should a war not go in Syria's favor. As a result, each soldier in the 7th this cool and fresh predawn carries a gas mask strapped to his leg even though the Merkava does offer the crew full NBC (Nuclear, Biological, Chemical) warfare protection.[6] Fighting a conventional battle is hard enough—artillery and air strikes, infantry-held grenade launchers, and the 120mm SABOT shells blazing toward you at 6,000 feet per second are daunting enough. But inside the confines of a tank, even one protected by NBC defenses, engaging in full-scale combat while yellow clouds of poison gas are dispersed into the clean atmosphere above can make the hardest soldier shake in his boots. He knows that should his tank get hit, he will be forced to expose himself to the toxic elements and have to fight and survive in a cloud of death. These tank soldiers, hunkered down in their giant Merkavas in full battle kit, Kevlar flask vests, and crewman ballistic helmets, hope that any future conflict never comes down to the deployment of gas or nerve agents. They are, in fact, trained to fight a full-scale war quickly. Get it over with in haste before Syria— or any enemy—will panic and deploy weapons of mass destruction. For tank warfare to succeed, especially in an Arab-Israeli context, war must be fast. Timing is everything.

Reaction time for an armored fighting force is crucial if they can perch themselves in defensive firing positions in time to withstand and repel any enemy invasion—get there too late and your firing pit is under "new management." It could mean the difference between waging a close-quarter armored fight to regain the high ground, regain the initiative, regain the advantage. Armored warfare, especially in this high-tech disposal age when a foot soldier armed with a tubular device with a cone-shaped warhead can turn a beast of steel into a flaming death trap for all those inside, is all about timing. It is a quick draw of man versus machine that can have only one victor; an armored piercing RPG projectile bouncing *inside* a turret is a ghoulish and horrific sight. In its purest form, however, tank warfare is nothing but a question of timing: which gunner will locate the target first, who will fire accurately first, which tank will recover, recoup, and recalculate its trajectory first. According to Major-General (Res.) Orri Orr, one of the more famous Israeli tank officers to emerge from the 7th Brigade, "Tank versus tank warfare is like a shoot-out in a good Hollywood Western. Whoever is quickest on the draw, whoever has the most accurate firing skills, is the one who survives the exchange of death."[7] Colonel Y., who was a simple private when "Colonel" Orri Orr commanded the 7th Brigade in 1974, is a student of Orr's; he is also a student of history, and a student of the IDF's elite tactical school, known by its acronym of *"P'um" (Pikud U'Mateh,* or Command and Staff), knows the art of tank warfare, the art of moving man and machine in a coordinate blaze of gunfire and movement, better than anyone. He is well-versed in the importance of timing. The stopwatch fastened securely inside the pocket of his Nomex fire-retardant overalls is not for running the mile. The gunners in the 7th Brigade are expected to hit their marks on the first round fired, loaders are expected to read the minds of their commanders and have the exact type of shell ready for insertion into the breach of the Merkava's all-powerful 105mm cannon.

To achieve the timing and split-second reaction that separates a tank brigade left discarded on the battlefield in burning hulks of steel from one moving on its target without hindrance, a tank force requires a stringent application of discipline that exists in very few other military formations. Tank soldiers, more than any other type of soldier, must be able to take orders and obey them to the letter without thinking or flinching. Infantrymen and paratroopers, for example, must innovate, improvise, and use their wits in order to survive on the battlefield. Although part of a brigade, battalion, company, platoon, and squad, when foot-slogging it through a rice paddy, desert ravine, or burnt-out shell of a town, he is a lone figure who must be able to react quickly with his assault rifle. If something moves inside his field of vision, he hits the dirt, finds cover, and aims through the sights of his weapon. A tank soldier, a driver, a gunner, or loader, can only react to the tank commander's orders; reacting to anything else means only one thing: that their hulking tank has been hit! A tank soldier is not an individual, he is a limb of a four-person creature that in unison allows the tank to be such a devastating and lethal battlefield predator. To achieve that intercrew coordination, to achieve that interpersonal level of reaction among one another, tank soldiers must be well-trained and extremely disciplined. Discipline, the dreaded *"Mishmat"* that all tank soldiers fear in the IDF, is unflinching, unforgiving, and demanded permanently inside the IDF Armored Corps. In basic training, it is harsh and new. In the tank crew's course, it is harsher and a code the young soldiers, physically and mentally honed, must live by. In their operational settings, at their brigade and battalion homes, discipline is the currency by which they live. According to official statistics, more tank soldiers are sent to the stockade in the IDF than from all other corps combined. Armored Corps Master-Sergeants, the professional "lifer ball busters" who make sure that berets are worn, uniforms tucked in, and salutes saluted, are considered the meanest in all of Israel. Discipline among the different tank units differs as well. A tank brigade based in the Negev is not as tightly strung as one on maneuvers and joint-security duty along the Jordan Valley. For those based on the Golan Heights, discipline is razor sharp. There is a saying in the IDF's main "Conscription and Absorption Base" which, loosely translated, goes something like this: "If you have been a good boy for your eighteen years, you'll go anywhere but the Armored Corps. If you've been bad, you'll end up in the 7th Brigade." That statement, in fact, is a badge of honor that a 7th Brigade soldier wears proudly from day one of the soldier's service in the Armored Corps—the day he realizes that the 7th and the Golan Heights will be his home for the next three years. In reality, however, it is a unique honor and privilege to serve in the brigade. Any conscript worth his mettle knows that being assigned to begin basic training with the 7th, the brigade that saved the nation on two separate occasions, is an award for being a cut above the rest.

The human aspect of the tank soldier is even more important than the vehicles they fight in. Commanders in the brigade know that they have to be tough with their men, and sometimes that rigidity in discipline does not come easy in the field—especially in Israel, a small country where everyone knows everyone else, and where egalitarian ideals are a driving force behind the very existence of the Israel Defense Forces. But tank soldiers are not just human beings, they are the tools, like a gear or a spring, that make the tank function. The tank is a fighting system, operated by a team, equaling an infantry platoon on its operation ability, and the same or more in its ability to destroy. Virtually any soldier can be taught to operate the tank, however, but it is the intangibles, the morale and patriotic reasons behind the hard work, that officers attempt to cultivate.

For many years, the Armored Corps held its swearing-in ceremony at the ruins of ancient Israel at Metzada, the desert fortress where Jewish zealots held off the Roman Legion for more than three years. Through tenacity, holding the high ground, and sheer "Jewish ingenuity," the zealots were able to mount a dedicated defense of the old Herodian palace. When Roman forces began to overwhelm the beleaguered defenders, they opted for mass suicide rather than succumb to slavery. *"Metzada Lo Tipol Shenit,"* or "Metzada will not fall a second time," was the slogan of the Armored Corps during these dramatic hilltop ceremonies, and the tank soldiers were supposed to guarantee this promise. When the young eighteen-year-old soldiers swore their allegiance to the State of Israel and the IDF, a wooden sign with the words *Metzada Lo Tipol Shenit* was set ablaze to illuminate the darkened desert night. The ceremony was intended to be high on drama. There was nothing light about the defense of a nation that has fought seven major wars in less than fifty years of existence.

Today, however, Metzada is no longer used as the stage for the Armored Corps to instill Zionism, history, and esprit de corps into its future generations. That honor and distinction now belongs to Latrun, a hilltop overlooking the Ayalon Valley, approximately halfway between Tel Aviv and Jerusalem that was, ominously enough, the scene of some of the fiercest battles ever to take place in biblical Israel; it was here that, according to legend, the sun stood still, and it was in the valley that both King David and Judah Macca- bees fought and won significant and large-scale battles.[8] The British built hilltop Taggart police fortress atop Latrun and King Abdullah's Arab Legion turned it into a fortified an- chor controlling the ultrastrategic link from Tel Aviv to be- sieged Jerusalem during the 1948 War. Latrun was a mass grave for the men of the 7th Armored Brigade, Israel's first armored force. It was there that an infant brigade was blood- ied beyond recognition and, many believed, repair in the thorny hills of the Ayalon Valley as professional British-led soldiers of the Legion pulverized a force of ragtag conscripts, some Holocaust survivors straight off the boat from deten- tion in Cyprus. Latrun was the first battle of significance for the IDF's Armored Corps and the Corps' first unit, the 7th Brigade.

It would not be the brigade's last.

The history of the 7th Brigade is, in fact, the history of the Israel Defense Forces and the State of Israel. Few military formations in any army in the world can boast of being in existence at the moment of their nation's birth, and partici- pating in every subsequent war since, in battles that have decided a nation's fate. The 7th Armored Brigade is one such formation. There is a certain pride that military units possess that transgresses even nationalistic feelings, and fam- ily loyalties. A sense of being part of a military formation that is considered elite, or special in its talents and capabili- ties, is a catalyst that promotes unit cohesion and effective- ness. Not performing up to one's standards of excellence is not a mark of individual failure but rather a mark against the regiment, the brigade, the division. In elite fighting units, soldiers "pick up one another," strive to be the best so that others will emulate them. The 7th Brigade is such a fighting unit. No other brigade in Israel's history has pro- duced the number of generals as has the 7th—men who at the age of eighteen sat underneath a tent to learn how to operate a Sherman or AMX-13 and continued on to be- come legends. No other brigade has produced as many

medal winners as has the 7th, and no brigade has produced as many casualties. No other brigade in the history
of the State of Israel has played so crucial a role in the
defense of the nation, and no other brigade has sacrificed
so many of its ranks in battle.

This is their story.

1

From the Hell of Latrun to the Sands of Abu Agheila: The 7th Brigade 1948–1958

To most Israelis, the word *Latrun* has little significance—to most, it is an expressway interchange on the bustling highway connecting Tel Aviv and Jerusalem where a gas tank can be filled and some of the best wine in the country can be purchased from the adjacent St. Joseph monastery. Yet Latrun is much more than a geographic landmark and a roadside service station. It is a symbol of a nation's genesis, and a symbol paid for with the blood of nearly 1,000 Israelis. To Shlomoh Shamir, a kind-looking gentleman of eighty-one years of age who still possesses the vigor and determination of a twenty-year-old, Latrun is a shrine of courage, sacrifice, and national preservation. As a forty-six-year-old colonel in the newly created *Tzava Haganah Le'Yisrael* (Israel Defense Forces), Colonel Shlomoh Shamir was ordered to take an armored brigade that had no tanks and very few soldiers and assault a fortress defended by well-equipped Arab Legion troopers, commanded by British officers, and supported by 25-pounder guns, in broad daylight when the enemy was expecting an attack. That hundreds died at Latrun does not surprise Major-General (Res.) Shamir—that

15

anyone survived does. "It was a valley painted red with the blood of the dead and wounded, and a field engulfed with the stench of death and the cries of the dying."[1] Although a mass grave for so many, Latrun is truly a birthplace. It is here that a force of armored cars and recently released refugees from British detention camps in Cyprus declared the existence of the 7th Armored Brigade. It was at Latrun that it all began; it was at Latrun that it almost ended.

To the men who commanded the underground Jewish Army in Palestine in 1936, the notion of a future army of Israel one day deploying tanks or even armored cars was nothing more than schnapps-induced fantasy. In 1936 the *Haganah,* or Defense, Jewish Palestine's underground army, had enough trouble stocking pistols and rifles, let alone dreaming about fighting vehicles. It was the time of the riots—massive Arab-Jewish violence in Palestine—and the British Army found itself ill-equipped and outnumbered in its failed attempt to quell both Jewish and Arab gangs. One neutralizing factor brought into the equation was the fleet of light tanks and armored cars. Although insignificant specks of armor compared to the hulking beasts of steel that race across today's battlefields, these vehicles were daunting and deterring monsters—especially when thrown against irregular forces armed with nothing heavier than Turkish Mauser pistols and Molotov cocktails. Although the Jewish command of the *Haganah* despised the British for introducing armor to the riots as they were, many times, used against Jewish forces, there were *Haganah* officers who began to think how their future army would use armor in battle. "What if we had . . . ?" *Haganah* officers would think. "Where would we get them from?"

One officer who found himself enamored by the potential of tanks and armored cars was Yitzhak Sadeh. Known in the preindependence vernacular as the "Old Man," even before he was an old man, Yitzhak Sadeh was as close to a jolly eccentric as would be found in the *Haganah.* A wrestler from his days in the Crimea, he was a strong-hearted character full of life, energy, and, in the words of one officer at the IDF's Historical Branch, "A man who took shit from nobody!"[2] He was the perfect individual to help build the fledgling Jewish underground army in Palestine and rose through its ranks following his *Aliyah* (ascension) to Palestine in 1923. Sadeh, thinking of tactics in terms of his beloved wrestling, believed in the innovative and underhanded—hit the enemy hard, hit him when he least expects it, and utilize your small numbers to their ultimate advantage. Most importantly, Sadeh believed that the best defense was a good offense.

Haganah commanders felt empowered by Sadeh's exuberance and forthright confidence and, as a test, permitted him to apply his beliefs in practical terms. In 1936, at the outbreak of the bloody 1936–39 riots that gripped all of Palestine, Sadeh formed the *Nodedot,* a mobile patrol force of rifle-wielding foot soldiers, to defend the isolated and besieged settlements around Jerusalem. Instead of responding to Arab attacks, as the settlers had done from behind their sand-bagged gun emplacements, Sadeh taught his men to defend themselves by destroying their enemy before the enemy could launch any serious attack. Ambushes, nighttime "hits," and other commando-type operations were mounted daily by Sadeh's squads on the large Arab villages that the guerrillas used as staging areas. The effects of Sadeh's preemptive retaliation was incredible. Attacks against the Jewish settlements decreased by ninety percent, Jewish casualties decreased, and a qualitative edge had been given to the Jews' quantitative deficiencies.

The *Haganah* quickly expanded Sadeh's theories into additional mobile strike units; even the British, most notably the legendary Captain Orde Wingate, also took special notice of the *Haganah*'s penchant for special operations genius. *Haganah* commanders realized the unconventional riots of 1936–39 were a preamble to the inevitable conventional struggle for Palestine, and small bands of scouts armed with Mausers and Ottoman-era hand grenades would not be able to defeat an army. If only Sadeh's tactical doctrines could be translated into conventional means, *Haganah* commanders thought, conventional armies could be defeated. By the time war broke out in Europe, however, the *Haganah* was very far away from even the most unconventional of conventional means.

Even on irregular terms, the *Haganah* was poorly armed, poorly trained, and poorly led. Many officers were nothing more than political loyalists who were trustworthy enough to keep pistols at home and, as a result, trusted enough to lead forays against villages harboring Arab guerrillas. On dark and precarious nights, the *Haganah* was a capable force and a daunting deterrent to Arab terror. On a conventional scale, however, they were lacking in just about every facet of military structure that even the most basic of army formations could require. The Second World War changed the course of the *Haganah's* ability to serve as the basis for a future Israeli Army.

When the Second World War began, the *Haganah* urged the British authorities to train and arm the Jewish young men of Palestine for the fight against Hitler, but the British balked at the notion of equipping and training its prewar adversaries; empires, after all, needed to be preserved despite the struggle against Nazi Germany. A great many Jewish men volunteered, however. They joined the British Army, the Royal Navy, even the Royal Air Force;[3] several served in tank regiments. The *Haganah* did possess three elite companies of fighters. Known as the *Pal'mach* (Hebrew acronym for Strike Companies), they were trained by the British to be Fifth-Columnist guerrilla forces in the event that the Germans broke through British lines in Egypt and captured Palestine. One platoon was made up of Arabic-speaking commandos and intelligence officers who could operate in the Vichy-controlled confines of Lebanon and Syria; there was a German Platoon of native German-speaking Jews, refugees from Germany and Austria, who were tasked with infiltrating German lines in the Western Desert and German POW camps; and even a Balkan Platoon made up of immigrants from that region who were parachutist-trained and dropped into Europe to assist the SOE and the OSS.[4] In Palestine, the man responsible for gearing up the *Pal'-mach* for the inevitable struggle against the British and, later, Arab forces was Yitzhak Sadeh.

The Israel Defense Forces, as the obvious progression and continuation from the prestatehood *Haganah*, did not come about the way most "conventional" armies are created. Following the end of the Second World War, when many fruits of the British Empire fell off the tree to sprout their own independent entities, they used the indigenous regiments and divisions that had existed in the British military to form the base cadre for their own newly independent fighting armies. The Indians were able to create an army overnight using former regiments that had existed in the British Army; the same held true for the emerging Pakistani and South African armed forces, and the Moroccan, Syrian, and Lebanese armed forces took an already established cue from the departing French. In all these cases, the departing power had supplied the infrastructure, the equipment (including, most importantly, armaments, ammunition, and facilities), and the tradition of conventional fighting forces. The future Israeli army had no such luxury. The British did not leave the *Haganah*'s conventional units, already in place, with guns, tanks, and a fighting chance. The *Haganah*'s sole mobilized strike force, the *Pal'mach*, was an underground force of small units equipped with nothing heavier than a basement-produced flamethrower and a stolen British PIAT antitank bazooka. The fact that, by the fall of 1947, the *Haganah* was still an underground force, subject to arrest and deportation to British detention facilities on Cyprus, made nation-building through army-building a most dangerous, covert, and laborious task. Besides the *Pal'mach*, the *Haganah* did not have a mobilized force that could be dispatched to meet a conventional threat; its part-time soldiers, poorly trained in firing a Sten or a Lee Enfield .303 rifle, were a far cry from what would be needed once Israeli independence was declared and the inevitable Arab invasion crossed the newly declared frontiers of a partitioned land. Even the optimists in the *Haganah* High Command, men who relied on luck, guile, and some divine intervention, realized that the military picture was bleak.

As a result of this deteriorating and seemingly desperate situation, on November 7, 1947, a full three weeks before the United Nations would vote to partition Palestine into two separate states, one Jewish and the other Arab, the *Haganah* High Command finally acquiesced to the demands of their commanders in the field and conventionalized the force.[5] In essence, the war for Israeli independence was already underway, and the *Haganah* needed to mobilize and "conventionalize" their forces. The High Command divided up the *Haganah*'s field forces into five brigades, four of which were reserve:

- The Northern Brigade (*"Levanoni"*): Five battalions of infantry responsible for the Haifa area, and all points of northern Israel.
- The Mediterranean Brigade (*"Alexandroni"*): Three battalions of infantrymen responsible for the coastal plain from Zichron Ya'akov located just due south of Haifa along the Mediterranean coast up to the northern Tel Aviv suburb of Ramat Gan.
- The Southern Brigade (*"Giva'ati"*): Five battalions of infantrymen responsible for Tel Aviv and south including many of the kibbutzim near Ashdod and Ashquelon, and southeast toward the Negev and Beersheba.
- The Jerusalem Brigade (*"Etzioni"*): Two battalions of infantrymen.
- The *Pal'mach* Brigade: Four battalions of fully mobilized infantrymen spread throughout Palestine, under the direct control of the *Haganah* High Command. It should be noted that the 4th Battalion was the *Pal'mach*'s, and the *Haganah*'s elite force. It included special scout and intelligence units, the *Pal'yam* (the "Sea Section") and its fledgling Sea Section naval special warfare force, and the *Pal'avir,* the small force that would serve as the seeds for the future Israeli Air Force.[6]

The move was a necessary step to bolster the yet-to-be-declared independent Jewish State's ability to defend itself from the inevitable. There were nearly 40,000 men under arms in the *Haganah*'s newly mobilized Order of Battle; more would be desperately needed. There were no tanks, a few jeeps that could be modified as weapon carriers, only a handful of light civilian planes existed in the *Pal'avir*'s order of battle, and fewer that could be mobilized (stolen!) for light strike (hurling a grenade from the passenger's compartment) or reconnaissance.

Militarily speaking, the situation was grim and desperate.

The Arabs, on the other hand, did not face the restrictions of British harassment (British military forces tended to stay away from Arab areas following the United Nations decision to partition the land), nor did they suffer from lack of manpower or quality armaments. Their principal concern was time. The Arabs needed to wait until the last British soldier was out of Palestine and the Union Jack lowered from the last mast before unleashing their major conventional offensive. For the guerilla forces, it was a different story. The various Palestinian guerila bands did not look kindly on the partition of the land they viewed in its entirety as their own, and they commenced their attacks against Jewish targets, primarily strategic assaults against the Jewish areas of Jerusalem *immediately* following the United Nations decision. These guerrilla attacks by the forces emanating from Syria in the north, and guerila forces under the command of Hassan Salameh, father of famed terrorist Ali Hassan Salameh (better known to the world by his affectionate name of "The Red Prince"), in the Jerusalem area, were extremely bloody, vicious, and effective. These forces were guerrilla bands, however, and were undisciplined, poorly led, and motivated by sheer hatred. They were not professional soldiers but were lavishly equipped with small arms and grenades. It was the conventional Arab armies that were to liberate Palestine and push the Jews into the sea,[7] and they were a formidable force. In November 1947 the Arab military machine consisted of:

- Egypt: (Army) 35,000 men in two division and two independent brigades, including tanks, armored cars, and half-tracks and towed artillery. (Air Force) 4,000 men and 200 pilots with eight combat squadrons.
- Syria: (Army) 11,800 men, including forces in their desert force, and an additional 3,500 in the Gendarme. Force includes dozens of French-built Renault tanks, towed artillery, and mortar crews. (Air Force) 50 training aircraft easily modified for a combat support role.
- Iraq: (Army) 25,000 men in two divisions (one for mountain warfare), and one for mechanized and mobile division. These forces included over 20 tanks, almost 200 armored cars and half-tracks, and several battalions of towed artillery. (Air Force)

Four squadrons consisting of some 80 aircraft, including British Spitfires.

- Transjordan: (Army) 18,000 soldiers in the legendary Arab Legion commanded by John "Pasha" Glubb, as well as 6,000 conscripted Bedouins in the Desert Corps (camel riders), and a reported 15,000 cavalrymen. They were the elite of the Arab nations, commanded by British officers from battalion level upward. Although their armored forces were limited, mainly armored cars with small caliber main cannons, they were the only true professional military force in the Middle East at the time other than the departing British Army.
- Saudi Arabia: (Army) 25,000 soldiers and 12,000 reservists in the tribal militias.[8]

On Saturday night, November 29, 1947, the United Nations General Assembly voted to partition Palestine into separate Jewish and Arab states, with the holy city of Jerusalem safeguarded as an international city. The Jewish population of Palestine, known as the *Yishuv,* was grateful—a state, no matter how small, was better than the gas chambers and the ovens. The Palestinians and the Arab states would have none of it. From that historic day, until the end of the British mandate, set for May 14, 1948, full-scale civil war erupted in Palestine. As civil wars go, this one was as vicious and brutal as the rest, but it was a civil war meant to linger, to set the stage until the full-scale showdown was mounted once the last British soldier left Palestine forever. Inside the hallways of the still underground *Haganah* High Command, desperate efforts were underway to obtain conventional heavy arms (as were efforts to obtain small arms, such as thousands of Czech K-98 7.92mm Mauser Rifles) to meet the impending face-off on the battlefield. Agents of a secretive force called *"Rechesh"* ("Acquisition") were dispatched to every corner of the globe in search of jeeps, trucks, tanks, half-tracks, planes, boats, bullets, uniforms; even military manuals. *Rechesh* agents searched the former battlefields of Europe in search of surplus and destroyed material that might be repaired back in Israel. In Italy, Germany, France, and Belgium, *Rechesh* operatives bought—and "permanently borrowed"—damaged vehicles from U.S. Army junkyards. U.S. Army GIs were amused by these men in overcoats and fedoras going through scrap heaps and motor pools looking for whatever was salvageable. Some GIs even helped out, pointing out locations where lots of equipment was laying to waste on former fields of battle and turning a blind eye when these mysterious men identified themselves as working on behalf of the Jewish people.[9] *Rechesh* agents were also quite visible in the United States, searching catalogs and government auctions for the tools of war that the greatest fighting machine ever assembled in world history had brought back from Europe and the Pacific, and now found little use for. Dummy companies in New York and Los Angeles were opened, and a unique pipeline for smuggling weapon systems and aircraft from the United States via Panama and a whole host of third parties was under way.

Rechesh officials reported that their missions were successful, but they couldn't bring back enough material to supply the future Israeli Army. As a result, the *Haganah* High Command issued special and urgent directives that the fledgling basement arms industry in Palestine begin furious work on the production and acquisition of armored vehicles—primarily for busting through the growing siege of Jewish West Jerusalem, as well as being used as improvised armored personnel carriers for *Pal'mach* and *Haganah* field units. Any vehicle that could be claimed for national service was acquired—from city buses to lorries and ambulances. These vehicles were taken to *Haganah* work areas and fitted with sheets of steel plating to become the legendary "Sandwich Cars"; by April 1948 over 100 such vehicles were operating along the narrow road connecting Tel Aviv and Jerusalem.[10]

On February 24, 1948, the *Haganah* High Command summoned Yitzhak Sadeh to its headquarters on Tel Aviv's Rothschild Boulevard and informed him that he was to assume command of the forerunner of Israeli's Armored Corps when it sanctioned the creation of the "Armored Car Service."[11] Yitzhak Sadeh was a natural choice for the job. Although he had absolutely no experience—let alone instruction—in mechanized warfare, leading armored cars through the treacherous mountain passes was just the type of warfare that Sadeh excelled in. The armored car columns fought in small groups and broke through defenses and roadblocks overcoming superior numbers entrenched in fortified firing positions and relieving beleaguered and besieged settlements. An armored car crew member had to be a brave soul. The armor plating on the indigenous vehicles, never exceeding 8.5mm, produced in backyard shops, was barely able to stop a .303 round. The fastest speed the trucks reached was a sizzling 20 miles-per-hour (less when in low gear), and they had a tendency to catch fire. The Ford and Chevrolet trucks pressed into service were never designed to trudge up a winding road on the way to Jerusalem and, loaded to capacity, be in the cross-hairs of a few dozen Lee-Enfield rifles. Most of the drivers and gunners were volunteers from the *Pal'mach*, and they needed to be soldiers of a unique character. Service in the armored car units was a harsh and short-lived military career and one that many of the drivers likened to being B-17 bomber crews flying over Europe, though most of the convoy crews never made it to their "twentieth" mission. Crews that were trapped could not be relieved; few were ever taken prisoner, as the Arab guerrilla bands operating in the hills mutilated wounded personnel.

Even though Sadeh's armored cars were a pitiful stepping-stone for what would eventually become the most powerful Armored Corps in the Middle East, they displayed the typical Israeli knack for innovation and modification. Several of these rectangular-shaped contraptions were fitted with 52mm and 81mm mortars, others were fixed with improvised turrets sporting crudely mounted PIAT bazookas.

As the march toward war continued and intensified in the bloody internal conflagration in Palestine, the *Haganah* High Command took another step toward the creation of what would be known as the Israel Defense Forces when it called up all eighteen-year-olds and mobilized all reservists to create six functional territorial brigades. The brigades attempted, with the limited resources available to the fledgling state coffers, to coordinate the available manpower with weapons, equipment, and cohesive units that could *somehow* throw back a half-million-man invasion on five fronts. In

March 1948 the "proposed" IDF consisted of the following territorial brigades:

- The 1st *Golani* Infantry Brigade, with its five battalions of infantrymen, was to operate primarily in the north.
- The 2nd *Carmeli* Infantry Brigade, with its three battalions of infantrymen, was to deploy around the Haifa region in the country's north.
- The 3rd *Alexandroni* Infantry Brigade, with its four battalions of foot soldiers, was to function around the central plains region.
- The 4th *Kiryati* Infantry Brigade, with its two battalions of infantrymen, was tasked with the Tel Aviv environs.
- The 5th *Giva'ati* Infantry Brigade, with its four battalions, was responsible for the south and the Negev Desert.[12]
- The 6th *Etzioni* Brigade, with its three battalions of infantrymen, operated in the Jerusalem area, primarily around the Gush Etzion bloc.[13]

The *Pal'mach* was also divided into three territorial brigades. The *Harel* Brigade operated around Jerusalem, the *Negev* Brigade was deployed to the south, and the *Yiftah* Brigade operated in the north.

What the *Haganah* could bring to bear against the conventional armies of Lebanon, Syria, Transjordan, Iraq, and Egypt was pitifully insufficient. The Jews of Palestine were outnumbered 100-to-1, and the heaviest equipment in the Israeli arsenal were the armored cars. Something had to be done and soon, and the General Staff of the about-to-be-announced Israel Defense Forces looked for a mechanized solution. Another directive issued by the *Haganah* was that the *very* fledgling arms industry called *"Ta'as"* (or *Ta'asiya Tzava'it*) begin production of indigenous armored vehicles; in fact, the orders indicated that these bastardized vehicles be considered Israeli's first tanks. The armored fighting vehicles, basically cannibalized trucks and buses, were to be completely surrounded by armored plating with a turret built atop the roof—a .50 caliber machine gun would be mounted in the turret, and a Bren or Hotchkiss light machine gun mounted in a position near the driver. Many inside the *Ta'as* and *Haganah* hierarchy thought that this was an impossible order to fill, but by May 1948, three companies of these vehicles were in service with the 7th Armored Brigade.[14] Other vehicles modified by *Ta'as* were former U.S. Army M-3 half-tracks, brought over in the *Rechesh* program, armed with mortars, recoilless rifles, and especially flame-throwers. These vehicles were augmented by a lone Sherman tank, abandoned by the British at a loading area in the Haifa harbor.

It was a beginning.

As May 1948 brought about the final stage of the British withdrawal from Palestine, the level of violence decreased in the proverbial calm before the storm. Jewish military commanders knew that the moment the Union Jack was lowered by the last British launch to push out of the port of Haifa, the combined Arab invasion would begin. The six infantry and three *Pal'mach* brigades would need backup. On May 14, 1948, hours before columns of Egyptian tanks and mechanized infantrymen would be pushing toward Tel Aviv, the order was issued that a seventh brigade, a mechanized force, be summoned into action. The 7th Armored Brigade was officially on paper.

The brigade's commander was, perhaps, the only man in Israel capable of assuming command of Israel's first conventional armored fighting force. Shlomoh Shamir was born in Germany in 1912 and emigrated to Palestine in 1929 as a Zionist Youth representative. If there was any ground to be broken in the ranks of the *Haganah,* Shamir was usually in the front of the line with his rifle in hand. One of the founders of the *Haganah,* Shamir was among the first band of ten who entered the Hula Valley to supervise and safeguard the settlers' effort to drain the impassable swamps. A *Haganah* explosives instructor, Shamir was also the commander of all *Haganah* retaliatory strikes against Arab villages during the 1936–39 riots that gripped all of the British mandate. When Great Britain went to war against his native Germany, Shamir was among the first *Haganah* officers to shed his underground vow to secrecy and enlist in the British Army. A natural officer (and gentleman), Shamir was among the first graduates from a British Army officer's course for Jewish volunteers; he subsequently reached the rank of "major" and was directed, by modern Israel's patriarch David Ben-Gurion, to serve as commanding officer for all Jewish soldiers serving in the British Army.[15] In placing him in command of the 7th Brigade, Ben-Gurion was directing Shamir to break what had turned into the very crux of Israeli survival during those first few days of the war.

The Arab stranglehold on Jewish Jerusalem threatened the lives of nearly 100,000 inhabitants and was considered the single most pressing order of business the first few days of war. Relieving Jerusalem, slicing through the Arab control of the twisting mountain roadway linking Tel Aviv with Jerusalem, was a task that the IDF at the time was simply too outmatched and undergunned to accomplish. Pasha Glubb's Arab Legion was pounding the Jewish half of the city around the clock, the Transjordanian artillery companies obliterated much of the newer half of the city with their accurate volleys of 25-pounder fire. Arab Legion snipers, considered lethal marksman, positioned themselves atop the stone parapets of the Old City of Jerusalem and were able to pick off their prey with little difficulty. The Jewish defenders of the city, a mixed assortment of *Haganah* stalwarts, *Pal'machniks,* and Yeshiva students clutching newly issued Sten submachine guns, were able to hold their own, but only barely. The city was being squeezed from all sides, and the death toll was rising to catastrophic levels. Jerusalem, the City of David and City of Peace, was reduced to a Byzantine version of the rubble and destruction of Stalingrad.

As Pasha Glubb's army pounded Jerusalem, the guerrilla army of Faisal al-Husseini controlled the hills bordering the only road linking Jerusalem to Tel Aviv. The armored convoys that had once had such a difficult task breaking through to the city center with supplies of food and medicine, now found it impossible to get through. Most experts guessed that Jerusalem would fall in a matter of days.

The 7th Brigade was formed, in the words of Shlomoh Shamir, as a reserve force to be dispatched to wherever a serious trouble spot might arise, though Ben-Gurion ordered its creation specifically for a push against Jerusalem.[16] For the construction of the brigade, however, Shamir was told to raise a brigade of fighting men inside a week. He had no junior officers to rely upon, nor did he have any NCOs (those men were all at the front in different locations throughout the five fronts); he had little communications, and a meager supply of weapons and ammunition; there weren't even enough uniforms for what on paper would be a brigade-size force of soldiers. More challenging to the list of miracles that Shamir was ordered to perform, this brigade was to be an armored brigade; one battalion of tanks and vehicles, and two battalions of infantrymen.

Experienced in the art of professional soldiering, an experienced combat officer, and, most importantly, knowledgeable in the art of military logistics, Shlomoh Shamir was an invaluable icon of military knowledge. He was greatly respected and admired. He faced a daunting challenge, as raising a brigade of mechanized troopers from thin air was a miracle he just couldn't perform. While troopers that he knew well from their service in the Jewish Brigade of the *Haganah* were snatched from other units to form the 73rd Battalion (later renamed the 79th), the one that would be equipped with half-tracks and other vehicles, the majority of the brigade's soldiers had no military experience whatsoever; in fact, many weren't even in country. Tens of thousands of Jewish refugees were on ships heading to Palestine from newly torn-down British detention facilities on Cyprus; they had survived the Holocaust and were yearning for a chance to restart their lives. Most of them wanted nothing to do with another fight—their fight had been against Hitler and with that war over, they wanted to place it all behind them. The refugees for the most part were barely recovering from their awesome ordeal, and their physical and psychological wounds had yet to heal. Nevertheless, most were capable of putting on a uniform and holding a rifle. They were perfect 7th Brigade material. Upon landing in Tel Aviv, they were issued IDF identification numbers and dog tags and placed on buses to take them to Tel Levitsky, northeast of Tel Aviv, where the brigade was allocated a small patch of a fenced-in clearing to set up shop. Many of the newly conscripted men had wives and children who had preceded their arrival in Palestine; virtually all were from Germany,

Czechoslovakia, Poland, France, and Bulgaria. They wanted nothing more than to clutch their families and forget the hardships, but each man was handed a Czech-built Mauser rifle, issued a pair of poorly fitting fatigues, and taught how to shoot, slice an enemy soldier with a bayonet, and hurl a Molotov cocktail. They became the 71st and 72nd Battalion—the Tower of Babel Battalions.

For his echelon of junior officers, Shamir sought out comrades in arms that he served with in Italy while with the Jewish Brigade's elite 2nd Battalion. For his operations officer, he selected a truly remarkable man—Lieutenant-Colonel Chaim Herzog. Born in Belfast, Northern Ireland, in 1918, Herzog was the son of the Grand Rabbi of Ireland and equally learned in his own right—a yeshiva graduate, as well as a graduate of Cambridge, Herzog emigrated to Palestine in 1935 and immediately joined the ranks of the *Haganah*. He was truly among the first Jews in Palestine to volunteer into the ranks of the British Army at the outbreak of the Second World War, though unlike other Jews, he wasn't relegated to rear echelon units until the creation of the Jewish Brigade in 1944. A true officer and a gentleman, Herzog served as an intelligence officer in an infantry regiment and participated in the liberation of northwestern Europe. Shamir selected Herzog, soft-spoken and calm in the face of fire, to serve as the brigade's operations officer.[17]

Shamir picked an equally capable officer to lead the brigade's armored battalion, the 79th, in Major Chaim Laskov. Born in Russia in 1919, Laskov's family emigrated to Palestine in 1925, though their fortunes in their adopted homeland were anything but fruitful; in 1930 Laskov's father was brutally murdered by an Arab gang. A young recruit to the ranks of the *Haganah,* Laskov excelled as a soldier, an operative, and a commander. A member of Captain Orde Wingate's Special Night Squads (SNS), Laskov enlisted in the British Army in 1940, and eventually served in the Jewish Brigade's 2nd Battalion with the rank of major. Laskov was a true Anglophile, especially relating to anything connected to the British tradition of soldiering, and many hard-core nationalists in the *Haganah* did not trust him (or any admirer of the British military) and resented his professional swagger. He was a decorated field officer and a gifted organizer; he was chief instructional officer in the *Haganah* until the outbreak of the full-scale conflagration. In May 1948 he was appointed Shamir's de facto deputy and placed in charge of the 79th Battalion.

The 79th Battalion was the premier element of the brigade, and equipped with half-tracks and Bren-Gun carriers obtained through the dubious means by which the IDF obtained most of its equipment during the first days of statehood. The orders to create the 7th Brigade were cut on May 18, 1948, and Shamir was told that he had one week to organize, train, and dispatch his troops to battle. Israeli Prime Minister David Ben-Gurion, relying on faulty intelligence, believed that the key to breaking through the siege of Jerusalem was capturing what was listed on his map as "Hill 314": Latrun.[18] On May 18, Arab Legion troops swept across the approaches to Jerusalem from Ramallah to the north, southwest to the Ayalon Valley and Latrun, a hilltop village and police station safeguarded inside a Taggart fortress, almost completely cutting off the brunt of the IDF near Tel Aviv and from the Etzion bloc of beleaguered settlements near Jerusalem. Latrun sat on a fork in the main road that could lead to Jerusalem to the south, Ramallah to the north, and Tel Aviv and the heavily populated Jewish coastal plain. Most importantly, Arab control of Latrun literally cut the main Tel Aviv–Jerusalem Highway in half. In Ben-Gurion's eyes, Latrun was the key to cutting off the choke hold over Jerusalem.

Yigal Yadin, the IDF Operations Chief, opposed an all-out assault on Latrun, but Ben-Gurion could not see the tactical red flags in assaulting a fortified elevated target by a brigade that had yet to celebrate its one-week anniversary. Ben-Gurion, however, was receiving reports of the plight of Jewish Jerusalem—the starving babies, soldiers dying from their infected wounds, old people eating sawdust—all of which reminded Ben-Gurion of accounts he had heard from the Warsaw and Lodz ghettos and they broke his heart. Latrun had to be taken. Ben-Gurion named the assault "Operation Bin-Nun," after Joshua who had ordered the sun to stand still in the valley centuries ago. Ben-Gurion needed a miracle of biblical proportions.

Shamir and his staff assembled the brigade at Tel Levitzky and with little fanfare had them board buses and trucks and ferried to Na'an and Hulda. Because of its inexperience and untested manpower, the main effort of the attack fell with the *Alexandroni* Brigade's 32nd Battalion. A young lieutenant named Ariel Sharon was a platoon commander. The 32nd Battalion was entrusted with pushing up the hill and capturing the village of Latrun, and the police station and fortress. The 7th Brigade would cover the right flank and attempt to push up the right flank and go toward the main Jerusalem road. H-Hour was set for the early morning hours of May 23. According to Ben-Gurion's intelligence reports, Latrun was held by irregulars who were lightly armed. The police station and Taggart Fortress were, in fact, held by the elite 4th Battalion commanded by Lieutenant-Colonel Habis el-Majali, an extremely innovative officer who would one day become the Chief-of-Staff of the Arab Legion.[19] The Legion's 2nd Battalion moved into the area and occupied the surrounding hills and villages.

The attack commenced at 0400 hours—eight hours behind schedule. The attack was supposed to begin at 2000 hours under the cover of darkness so that by the time the sun appeared over the Ayalon Valley, the *Alexandroni* Brigade infantrymen would be positioned around the fortress. Under the cover of darkness, Shamir's brigade was to slice across the roadway and position itself as a strategic reserve to the *Alexandroni* assault. At 0400 it was too late for a full-scale assault up a hill; the sun began to rise as the *Alexandroni* troopers were moving through the impassable brush and thorny fields. By the time the first units reached the Jerusalem–Tel Aviv–Latrun junction, Legion gunners were offered a duck shoot illuminated by the rising sun.[20] Completely exposed and too close to their target to stage a safe withdrawal, the Israelis found themselves trapped. Using the parapets of the Taggart Fortress as cover, Legion snipers were able to pick off the advancing Israelis at will, while the Israelis, their eyes facing the brutal rising sun, were rendered completely helpless. The 7th Brigade troopers found themselves under murderous fire near the villages of Beit Jiz and Beit Sussin and it was a challenge they were incapable of answering. Confused, scared, and incapable of understanding the Hebrew orders being barked in their direction, most of the soldiers scattered in panic, caught in the crosshairs and shot in the back.

Operation Bin-Nun was launched on a day that is known in the region as a *Sha'arav*—a period of merciless heat. It must have reached one hundred degrees that spring morning, and the new immigrants, not in top physical condition to begin with and unaccustomed to the Middle Eastern climate, began to wither in the brutal and oppressive bake. Exacerbating the one-sided battles, the one piece of equipment that most of the brigade's personnel were not issued was a canteen. Soldiers dehydrated under the Byzantine sun in less than an hour. Soldiers went mad, sobbing wildly for water while forgetting about bullet and shrapnel wounds that were slowly taking their lives away. The soldiers attempted to crawl to a secure position and wait out the storm of fire, but the thorny underbrush ripped through their khaki uniforms and through their skins. A swarm of *Barkashim*, pesky small desert gnats, raced into the battlefield at the sweet smell of blood. They began pecking at the dead and the wounded in a horrible scene. Men, dying of thirst and now under attack by the Arab Legion and insects, simply stood up and attempted to flee the madness. Most were cut down by accurate volleys of Arab Legion 25-pounder fire.

The withdrawal commenced at midday and lasted nearly twelve hours. The brigade left hundreds dead on the slopes of Latrun. The road to Jerusalem was far from being relieved.

Ben-Gurion ordered another attempt to retake Latrun, and Operation Bin-Nun 2 commenced on the night of May 30, 1948, with the 7th Brigade in the vanguard. The plan called for the *Giva'ati* Brigade to move across the Jerusalem road and relieve the pressure on the vital artery by mounting an attack on Yalu, while Chaim Laskov's 79th Battalion would move in on the police station and village of Latrun and, after securing the Trappist Monastery in the valley below, assault the Taggart Fortress dominating the roadway. The attack commenced at night, though the *Giva'ati* Brigade's advance was broken by panic and Arab Legion small arms fire. Laskov led his half-tracks and vehicles up the winding roads. Without the *Giva'ati* diversion, Laskov's attack was doomed. His units managed to reach to within the walls of the fortress and take the defenders by surprise—they couldn't believe that the Israelis were mounting an armored assault, as they couldn't believe that the IDF actually had half-tracks! The attack, it appeared, was proceeding better than planned and ahead of schedule. When Laskov's tanks reached the fortress walls, however, the fight became a close-quarter melee. The Arab Legion defenders, who by now retreated to the rooftop firing pits, began throwing grenades and rifle fire down on the exposed half-tracks. A half-track carrying the battalion's sappers, who were supposed to blast through the wall, was hit and their explosives damaged. As a result, a company commander sent in a flame-thrower team to set the position alight. The barracks began to burn, but the light from the fire was so bright that it exposed the half-tracks as fully illuminated targets. Half-tracks began taking direct hits, casualties mounted, and, without the *Giva'ati* infantry support, the attack lost its ever-important momentum. Laskov ordered the survivors to withdraw back into the darkness.

There was a third attempt to capture Latrun, this time led by an American officer, Colonel Micky Marcus, known by the nom de guerre of David Stone. A Jew, and "volunteer advisor," Colonel Marcus was not a field officer but had incredible organizational skills and his ability to harness large numbers of men and material was something that the IDF senior staff was incapable of doing. Colonel Marcus was everything that the Israelis were not—energetically optimistic, outgoing, extroverted, and athletic. His gift was reviewing strengths and weaknesses and making the necessary connections in an organization's order of battle. He reached the 7th Brigade following the collapse of Operation Bin-Nun 2 with a letter of authorization from David Ben-Gurion, and a litany of suggestions and comments—not all of which the Israeli officers were eager to listen to. Ben-Gurion, however, made him temporary commander of the entire Jerusalem front by having him lead the 7th Brigade, the *Pal'mach's Harel* Brigade, as well as the Etzioni Infantry Brigade. Before Marcus could assemble the manpower and machinery needed for a concentrated Israeli push on the road to Jerusalem, he was tragically killed by a *Pal'mach* sentry near Abu

Ghosh. Marcus, not knowing a word of Hebrew, had gone into the woods to relieve himself and upon return could not return the password when ordered to do so. He was cut down by a burst from a Sten gun and killed instantly. Moshe Dayan, who had befriended Marcus, was one of the officers to accompany his body back to the United States for burial at West Point.[21]

Following the death of Colonel Marcus, the 7th Brigade continued to move south and east in an attempt to breech Jordanian defenses and move closer to Jerusalem (no matter how roundabout the means) while Colonel Yitzhak Rabin's *Harel* Brigade moved toward the coast in a valiant attempt to break through the stranglehold. Patrols from the two brigades linked up near Beit Sussin and Shlomoh Shamir recommended that the siege of Jerusalem be broken by circumventing the main roadway altogether; building a detour to link the roadway leading out of the city controlled by the Israelis with their forces currently deployed in the Ayalon Valley. The road that was soon built was called the "Burma Road," an honored recall of the mountain pass that linked India and China during the Second World War. To build it and plow through the unforgiving mountains, Ben-Gurion summoned virtually every piece of earth-moving equipment in Israel. When bulldozers were unavailable, men and women just off the refugee ships were handed a hat to protect them from the brutal sun, an ax, a pick, and a bottle of water. Trucks carrying meat, flour, water, and other essentials were brought to the farthest advance on the road and then transported, courtesy of mules and human porters, the few hundred meters to where *Harel* troops and vehicles from Jerusalem were eagerly awaiting their rush shipment to the cutoff city. It was a monumental effort of engineering and perseverance and a feat achieved in record time. The Burma Road had to be completed by June 11, the proposed date of the first United Nations–imposed cease-fire. Under heavy guard, the human wave of labor worked a small miracle. By June 10, 1948, the first lorry transport ferried supplies straight from Tel Aviv, along the Burma Road, to Jerusalem; on board were half a dozen American war correspondents.[22] In Israel, the Burma Road became known as the "7th Road," a road carved and secured by the 7th Brigade.

There was a third attempt, this time by the *Pal'mach,* to seize Latrun on June 9, but it, too, ended in failure. The 7th Brigade battle at Latrun remains one of the most controversial chapters in Israeli military history—certainly one of the most tragic. Accounts differ as to an accurate casualty report, but estimates range from 200 dead in the first battle to 2,000;[23] it is feared that many of the new immigrants were not properly documented and tagged. The fact that new immigrants, living shadows from the Holocaust, were used as targets in an ill-conceived and destined-to-fail operation, will forever haunt the Israeli Defense Forces; the fact that intelligence had been so off would also haunt IDF officers for years to come. But there is another point of view concerning Latrun and the 7th Brigade's first battle. By focusing so much attention on Latrun, the IDF was able to draw valuable Arab Legion resources *away* from Jerusalem and, in essence, open a new front allowing the besieged defenders inside the embattlement area to consolidate positions and retake strategic ground lost. Even Pasha Glubb, in his autobiography, wrote of how the attack on Latrun prevented him from sending battalions to Lod and Ramle and increasing his stranglehold on a far stretch of territory surrounding Jerusalem. "The battle for Latrun failed, but Jerusalem and Israel were saved," claims General (Res.) Shlomoh Shamir nearly 50 years after those crucial days of crisis. "There are very few units in the annals of military history that have the chance to participate in two battles on which the fate of their nations depend. The Seventh Brigade participated in such a battle at Latrun, and would do the same 25 years later in the Valley of Tears."[24]

Latrun remained in Jordanian hands until the Six Day War, when a reservist unit took all of thirty minutes to capture the fortress. In today's world of the Israeli Armored Corps, Latrun serves as a calling card of NEVER AGAIN much in the same way as Pearl Harbor serves as a memorial to America's resolve never again to be caught by surprise. Israel's armored forces will never again wage war unprepared and ill-equipped. In Latrun, during swearing-in ceremonies, the conscripts—soon-to-be tank soldiers—swear this statement of never again on the blood-soaked soil where the first soldiers of the 7th Brigade died in battle.

Although the second Operation Bin-Nun was the first true armored assault in IDF history, it should be pointed out that the 7th Brigade was not the IDF's *first* pure tank unit. The 8th Armored Brigade, created on May 23, 1948, and commanded by Yitzhak Sadeh was at first planned as an infantry brigade, but soon became a "second" armored unit when the 7th Brigade found itself being decimated at Latrun. The 82nd Battalion became the unit that received all the tanks, mainly Shermans, that the IDF had acquired, as well as most of its armored cars. There was also Moshe Dayan's famed 89th Commando Battalion that deployed from half-tracks and captured—and discarded—British Bren-carrier tracked vehicles.

Following the Latrun debacle, Shlomoh Shamir was offered the post of IDF Chief of Staff by Israeli Prime Minister David Ben-Gurion, though the proud and determined officer kindly turned down the offer, instead becoming the commanding officer of Israel's central front (known as "Front A"). In 1949 he was appointed the commander of the newly created IDF Navy, the *Heyl Ha'Yam*, and, remarkably, would also serve as commander of the Israel Air Force a few years later.

In early July 1948 the 7th Brigade underwent a complete and badly needed overhaul. It was no longer a strategic reserve force in the General Staff's order of battle and no longer human fodder to eat up Jordanian ordnance. It would now be a truly mechanized unit, an armored personnel carrier and tank formation, that would become the IDF's sole conscript armored unit. Shlomoh Shamir's command of the brigade had been a valiant one, but the carnage at Latrun and the tragedy of having recent survivors from the death camps suit up on a bus, go through the very rudimentary minimum of basic training, grab a Czech-Mauser and a bayonet, and charge a hill defended by the most professional garrison in the Middle East at the time had proved to be an impossible challenge to overcome.

As the IDF became a real army, and not an underground entity that had to hide its weapons from the British, arms sales of tactical significance were made. M-3 half-tracks from the junk piles of Europe were purchased and rushed to Israel on creaky, barely ocean-going vessels, as were additional M-3 Sherman tanks. Bren-gun carriers, stolen from British Army stores in Italy and France, were smuggled back to Israel as well. Also being imported at the time from overseas stock were human commodities that could help train, mobilize, and lead these newly created conventional units being formed at a hurried pace. In Hebrew, they were known as *Anshei Ha'Ma'cha'l*, the acronym for "Foreign Volunteers," and they were as valuable to Israel's ability to persevere in those desperate months as was any divine assistance by the Almighty in the land of the Bible. Most of the volunteers, decorated World War II veterans from the United States (like Colonel Marcus), France, Great Britain, Canada, and South Africa, were Jewish and feeling a sense of religious guilt for not having been able to do enough to help the victims of the Holocaust. Others, remarkably, were Gentiles who, bored with the postwar doldrums, sought adventure and a noble cause. They brought with them expertise, experience, flair, and confidence—four commodities that the fledgling IDF was desperately short of. After all, they would tell their Hebrew-speaking brothers-in-arms when asked why they came to this war, if they could survive Hitler and the Japanese, they could certainly survive the Egyptian expeditionary force.

One volunteer from Canada was a soft-spoken artillery officer named Ben Dunkelman. He was originally assigned to the IDF Artillery Corps as a heavy mortar instructor, and his experience in mechanized warfare with the Queen's Own Rifles of Canada Regiment made him a natural for some sort of command position. Ben-Gurion summoned him to his war room near the Tel Aviv shore and informed the volunteer that he had "just volunteered" to assume command of the decimated 7th Brigade. The General Staff promised the new brigade commander at least "two weeks off to train" and then they'd be dispatched north toward the war against the guerrillas and the Syrians in Galilee.

On paper, Dunkelman, known by his Hebraized name of Binyamin Ben-David, received three battalions of troops. In the real world, he had one capable battalion, and two remnants of walking wounded. The 79th Battalion, the mechanized force, had survived Latrun fairly intact; well equipped with new Czech small arms and heavy armored vehicles, it was also the sole battalion that achieved *positive* battle experience at Latrun. The 71st and 72nd battalions, made up mostly of new immigrants straight off the boats from Cyprus, were in terrible shape. They were thin, unfit, tired, and not willing to die after having been retrieved from the ashes of Auschwitz. Recalling the rants and tirades of drill sergeants in Canada, Dunkelman knew that idle time and staying put at the brigade's headquarters near Ramat Gan could only damage morale—possibly to a point of no return. Training and feeding his troops as they moved in convoys of trucks, Dunkelman slowly moved the brigade north, toward the Galilee highlands, where the 7th Armored Brigade would spearhead a large-scale Israeli counterattack on July 7, 1948—whether the brigade was ready or not.

The Arabs in the Galilee region were led by the Arab Liberation Army of notorious guerrilla leader Fawzi al-Kaukaji, a feared warrior gifted with Saladin's charisma and guile. Kaukaji's army held the high ground through Galilee and possessed a grand numeric and strategic advantage. The only trump card that Dunkelman had was an Auster Mk 3 piston-engine plane made available to him for aerial reconnaissance. The thin-skinned prop-engine plane, sporting a large blue Star of David on its wings and fuselage, was flown on a dozen or so sorties by Dunkelman so that he could gauge the challenges his men would face on the road north through Galilee, and to ensure that no unpleasant surprises, like the large-scale Arab Legion garrison at Latrun, would be waiting in ambush for the brigade once again.

The primary objective given to Colonel Dunkelman for the campaign in the north, known as "Operation Palm Tree," was to secure the Acre-Haifa roadway, and the routes of transportation in the area. One key to this pocket of territory was a hill known as Tel-Qisan, an elevation that overlooked virtually all the main roadways connecting the two cities, as well as the interior approaches toward the village of Shfar'am at the western approach to Haifa and then on to Nazareth and the "Galilee Finger" pushing north toward Syria and Lebanon. Much to Dunkelman's delight, the Arab gun emplacements and fortified firing pits were only in place to the west, overlooking the Israeli lines. If the Israeli task force could come in from the east, from behind, then Dunkelman believed that the position could be taken with little resistance. The 71st Battalion, led by Major Yehuda Verber, was tasked with capturing Tel-Qisan.

On the night of July 7, the battalion set out from its forward staging area for the long march to battle—vehicles were deemed as counterproductive, as the rumble of the engines would have alarmed Kaukaji's fighters. Verber led the advance at the front of the two column march in the middle of a moonlit night. His men, speaking a dozen languages among themselves, walked hurriedly and determinedly up the incline clutching their Czech-produced Mauser rifles. As they reached the crest, the lines closed ranks and safeties were removed from their brand-new Czech rifles. But, to everyone's delight, the position was captured without any serious resistance. Kaukaji's vaunted army surrendered quickly, and the battalion seized the ultrastrategic position without a casualty.

The victory electrified the battalion and the brigade. A victory was just what the good doctor had ordered and morale, which had still been in the subterranean areas following Latrun, now shot to sky-high levels. With Acre secured and Arab communication lines cut off to the west, it was time to erase the horror of Latrun and move on the offensive. The next objective was Shfar'am, a mixed Muslim and Druze village of 4,000 inhabitants on the road to Nazareth and Afula. Shfar'am was a strategic town, built like most Arab villages on the slope of a hill, and one that needed to be seized. Dunkelman, however, opted to increase the brigade's chances of seizing the location with the minimum of bloodshed. He conducted secret negotiations with the leaders of the village's Druze community and promised to leave their homes and families unmolested in exchange for an agreement of nonaggression. The Druze, at odds with their Sunni Muslim neighbors for centuries, were quick to comply. The capture of Shfar'am was attended to with the minimum of resistance, courtesy of the 79th Battalion's half-tracks and armored cars, and support by the 71st Battalion.

Stage B of Operation Palm Tree called for the brigade to capture Nazareth and its surrounding hills and villages. With the local Druze tribes staying out of the fight, the road to the city was open. The assault on Nazareth began on July

15 under a blackened sky. Kaukaji's army was waiting for the 7th Brigade this time, determined to put up a fight. Much to the surprise—and shock—of the 79th Battalion's half-track and armored car crews moving about in the impassable night, Kaukaji's forces were equipped with armored cars of their own—M-8 Greyhounds obtained from Pasha Glubb's Arab Legion only weeks earlier. Painted in an eerie camouflage scheme of sand and brown and adorned with Arabic promises to "Slaughter the Jews," Kaukaji's armor was a formidable obstacle on the road to Nazareth. The Arab crews, however, had little training in armored warfare. They did not know how to prepare an armored ambush and were inept in the accurate firing of their main armament weapons. The 79th half-track crews, on the other hand, were equally ill-trained in armored warfare, but they knew how to fire their PIAT bazookas and 37mm antitank guns. Kaukaji's armor was destroyed in less than an hour and, at 2040 on July 16, Colonel Dunkelman radioed the northern front commander with the good news that "Nazareth is in our hands!"[25]

It was the first armor-versus-armor battle for the IDF—and the 7th Brigade—of the 1948 fighting. It would not be the last.

While Yitzhak Sadeh's 8th Brigade, equipped with a mixture of British Cromwell tanks (obtained with the help of a generous Scotsman who decided not to depart Palestine), some captured French-built Hotchkiss tanks (in the 82nd Battalion), and an odd assortment of homemade and World War II surplus vehicles that could barely run and barely hold back bullets, was battling the Egyptians in the south, the 7th Brigade continued its push north. In "Operation Hiram," commencing October 28, 1948, the 7th Brigade pushed north through the crucible of Galilee toward the frontier town of Sassa, heading north all the way into southern Lebanon. Colonel Dunkelman split the brigade into two primary forces for the last major offensive north against Kaukaji's Arab Liberation Army, and the French-trained and equipped Lebanese military. Force A consisted of the 79th Battalion, commanded by Major Baruch Friedman-Erez, a company of Circassian[26] rifleman and scouts, and a force of mechanized infantrymen. The 79th Battalion "boasted" nineteen homemade armored cars (Ford and

Chevrolet vehicles surrounded by improvised 8mm-thick armored plating and a turret sporting a German-produced World War II-era MG34 machine guns), two British Marmon-Harrington armored cars; and two Daimler armored cars. The battalion's mechanized company boasted twelve M-3 half-tracks, some equipped with 20mm antiaircraft cannons. Following the 79th Battalion's movements were the 71st and 72nd battalions, providing infantry support for the territory overrun. Kaukaji's forces and the Lebanese Army were a barrier already beaten. Many of the liberation army's guerrillas fled at the sight of the half-tracks moving through the high ground, while the Lebanese soldiers put up a determined, though passable, defense. Several Lebanese units, armed with 37mm antitank guns, did delay the Israeli advance though the 7th Brigade moved north into Lebanon proper up to the Litani River.

According to the cease-fire and armistice arrangements, signed on the island of Rhodes, the IDF retreated from Lebanese territory in January 1949.

When Operation Hiram began, the tide of the war had changed for Israel. The dark and desperate days of May 1948 where the nation's very survival remained in question were over. The Jewish State had survived its first and most dire test. It had beaten back an invading Arab army ten times its size and had fought back and gone on the offensive. By early 1949, the IDF controlled all of Galilee, all of the Negev, and had troops on the Red Sea along the Gulf of Aqaba at a small outpost that would soon be known as Eilat. Only the campaign to unite the city of Jerusalem ended in failure. The road from Tel Aviv to Jerusalem, the one fought over so viciously from Latrun to the Bab el-Wad to the Kastel, remained eviscerated and elongated.

Nearly one percent of the entire Jewish population of the newly born state of Israel, over 6,000 soldiers and civilians, had been killed in the War of Independence. It was a brutal and unforgiving struggle, and it achieved survival—only future wars would straighten out the frontiers and help bring the adversaries to the peace table.

Following the war in 1949, the IDF demobilized and became a national defense force with universal conscription—

all eighteen-year-old males were called upon to serve three years; non-Orthodox eighteen-year-old females were required to serve two years. The transformation from an underground movement to a conventional military force began during the war, though the relative 8th Brigade was consolidated into the 7th Armored Brigade as the IDF's sole armored force. At first, the 82nd Battalion was transferred to the "Negev Brigade" for the mopping up operations in Sinai, but it was later transferred to the ranks of the 7th Brigade. For the newly established Jewish State, it was a period of nation-building and army-building, a period to turn a few dozen Shermans and armored cars into a cohesive fighting force. It was a daunting challenge.

In January 1949 the IDF commenced its first tank course for conscripts to learn the basics (very basics!) of the M3 Sherman tank. The course was less a military classroom than a symposium where, at times, pupils were as familiar with the curriculum as the instructors; if you could read a manual and had a strong voice, you were a candidate for tank instructor. When the War of Independence ended, however, foreign volunteers and returning veterans who had fought in the Second World War were enlisted for the uphill struggle of teaching new soldiers the A-to-Zs of the tank. It would be a long and lengthy process.

Many of the *Pal'mach* officers who stayed behind in the IDF as career soldiers had a lot of trouble with the tank as a weapon of war. These were men who literally won a war with their ability to march dozens of kilometers at a frenzied pace and their skill with taking down an enemy with one rifle shot. These men, now officers in *Heyl Ha'Shirion* (Armored Corps), grudgingly accepted the conventional IDF and their roles as tank commanders. The *Pal'mach*niks referred to their Sherman tanks as "Sardine Cans";[27] conscript crews referred to them as death traps. Even the IDF had a conceptual problem in deploying the companies that made up the brigade as a tank force. In 1951, for example, Southern Command dispatched the 7th Brigade on a retaliatory strike against Bedouin guerrillas and marauders in the Gaza Strip who had taken a steep toll in Jewish lives along the southern border in hit-and-run ambushes launched following the armistice signing. Although the brigade possessed two companies of tanks at the time, Southern Command sent in "B Company" of the 79th Battalion across the Egyptian frontier. Although the raid, known as "Operation Culti-vate," was considered a success, the 79th Battalion personnel were deployed as mobile infantrymen, not as an armored force. The raid was not an armored engagement and not the type of work that the IDF's sole force of trained tank sol-diers should have been called upon to execute.

The true turning point for the 7th Armored Brigade oc-curred in 1954 when France and Israel cemented a covert military alliance. The Israeli-Franco military connection commenced when the first Israeli officers ventured to France in 1952[28] to visit French training facilities and command schools. At the time, following 1948, the IDF had no conven-tional military doctrine of its own, and based its strategies on applied guerrilla techniques, and commandeered training manuals obtained from American, British, and even Wehr-macht sources. By 1954, however, France, battling Arab na-tionalists in Algeria, had found a receptive non-Arab political ally in the Jewish State, while the Israelis were grateful for any foreign contacts—especially with a NATO nation. In 1954, under incredible secrecy, the Armored Corps sent several weapons and ordnance experts to France, at the Bourges Arsenal, to work alongside French teams to design a new turret mounting for the Sherman tank and the 75mm French-produced gun it would sport. Although by today's standards of arms acquisitions and weapons sales, the Israeli venture with the French to acquire a modified turret housing seems benignly innocent, at the time it was considered a state secret of the highest order. Israel's mili-tary alliance was in a fledgling state—both nations needed this relationship, and both nations knew that the slightest leak could have disastrous effects.

In the summer of 1955, the first trial firing of this new gun was conducted at the French range at Bourges.[29] A small army of French military officers and technicians was on hand that hot muggy day, as were several Israeli officers and Min-istry of Defense representatives, and Lieutenant-Colonel Avraham Adan (Bren), the newly appointed commander of the tank battalion that would absorb the Sherman tanks equipped with the new French guns. The Shermans, designated the M-50, were shipped to Israel and incorporated into the brigade's order of battle in early 1956. At the same time, the first AMX-13 light tanks from France also reached the 7th Brigade. Fast, sleek, though thinly armored, the AMX-13s provided mobility and speed. They were not the type of tank to lead an armored spearhead, but vehicles that could support a lightning fast strike.

At the same time as the French influence was making an impact on the professional aspect of the IDF's day-to-day means of doing business, 7th Brigade commander Colonel Yitzhak Pundak opted to raise the brigade's level of professional deployment to that of a real tank brigade *in a real army!* Colonel Pundak had visited French armor units and was embarrassed by what he saw on parade grounds and training fields near Paris, and what he would view on a daily basis in Israel with *his* men. He vowed to build an elite brigade where skills and motivation would be of unquestionable caliber, not a brigade whose crews carried Molotov cocktails instead of hand grenades, and whose Sherman tanks would be used for tank-versus-tank warfare as opposed to a 32-ton truck used for obstacle clearance and occasional static artillery. He submitted urgent requests for large-scale purchases of surplus Sherman tanks that could be found anywhere from Italy along the Po River to the jungles of the Philippines, and ordered the tank companies within the brigade to start training as conventional tank battalions. The tank, Pundak argued to his superiors, was an offensive weapon of war, not a rusty piece of metal on hand for holding actions. Tank warfare manuals were purchased from open sources and staff war colleges in the United States, Great Britain, and France, and senior armor officers in the IDF were forced to study them, write full-length Hebrew-language evaluations, and then distribute them among the troops. The conscript tank crews were then forced to study the written philosophical aspects of tank warfare before being allowed to execute the practical "75mm" aspects. The Polish-born Pundak had been an infantry officer for the majority of his military career and had been a soldier used to the "attack." A veteran *Haganah* officer and desert warrior, Pundak came from a breed of Israeli fighting men who viewed defensive actions as a sign of weakness. Offense was the key to military victory and the tank, even in small numbers and with limited crews, was an all-powerful tool of war.

Because there were more soldiers in the brigade than tanks to place them in, Pundak initiated a revolutionary and novel approach to make sure that each soldier in the brigade was capable of being a qualified crewman. He divided the brigade into crews to ensure that there were at least three standby crews for every tank in the brigade's order of battle. The crews trained day and night, in all terrain and climactic conditions, to experience what it would be like to go to war inside a 32-ton contraption sporting a cannon and tons of high-explosive ordnance. The crews were split into three main forces—"A Team" consisted of the conscripts, and the "B Team" and "C Team" consisted of those soldiers nearing the end of the conscripted three years of service. At the end of an exhaustive course of training and study, one rivaling that of the paratroops in intensity and length, the tank crews had gone from a motley force of morale-lacking conscripts to a proud and capable unit. The "A Team" specialized in breaking through fortified defenses, close-quarter tank-versus-tank battles, and high-speed assaults with supporting infantry (as opposed to how it was done in 1948 with the tanks moved in as backup to the foot soldiers). Exercises for Pundak's experiment were usually held in the Negev Desert, near the old Turkish defenses of Beersheba, and it was there, under the brutal desert sun, that he observed his plan gel into an impressive display of firepower and maneuverability. It was the first time in the infant state's history that live ammunition had been allocated to an armor unit for training purposes, as hundreds of shells were launched at stationary targets meant to stand in for Egyptian armor forces in the desert. Seeing what a live round could do to a piece of metal mesmerized many of the tank crews who, until this juncture, had only heard about tank battles in a classroom setting. It motivated them, and when special privileges were issued for those crews who struck their target on the first pull of the trigger, marksmanship in the brigade, at ranges never exceeding 800 meters, became superb.

Squad leaders courses were soon run by the Armored Corps, as were officers courses and even company command seminars. The brigade was moving forward but Israel, in

1954 and 1955, was in the first throes of infancy and the army, designed to defend the nation's frontiers, was far too busy in the impossible task of nation building.

In 1955 Major Uri Rom, a career armor officer, was the deputy commander of the 9th Battalion, the 7th Brigade's mechanized infantry unit. "In those days," recalled Rom, "Israel's armored doctrine was that tanks support the infantry."[30] The tank was still something of a curious effect, rather than a centerpiece of offensive and defensive strategies. The General Staff still did not know what to do with the vehicles, nor did they realize the full value of an armored strike. And with the exception of a handful of officers who could read English, French, or German and studied the tank's role in the key battles of the Second World War, they didn't realize that Israel would have to develop its armored forces if it had any prayer of winning the next and subsequent wars. "But," as a senior tank officer would later recall, "the Armored Corps didn't even invest in the men it sent to the Seventh Brigade." While many of the officers were *Sabras,* the term for a desert cactus that has since come to personify the native-born Israeli (hard and prickly on the outside, yet soft and sweet inside), most of the brigade's soldiers were new immigrants to the Jewish State. They could barely speak Hebrew, they could barely afford to buy even a pack of smokes; some had never eaten with a fork and knife before.[31] The commanders spoke Hebrew and a few words of Arabic, German, and Yiddish, and the tank drivers and gunners spoke every language imaginable. "Imagine a class where the A to Zs of the Sherman tank was taught, the instructor reading off a Hebrew-language manual and soldiers looking at Romanian-Hebrew dictionaries, Polish-Hebrew dictionaries, Greek-Hebrew dictionaries, even Urdu-Hebrew dictionaries," claimed a tank officer of the time. "It was cultural chaos with a black beret, and an environment that made it impossible to teach the conscript 'how' to be a driver, a gunner, or a loader. How could a soldier concentrate on his military studies when he couldn't speak the language, knew nothing of the country, and cared more for sending money home to his hungry family at a relocation center in a swamp than the nuts and bolts of the Sherman 75mm gun."[32]

Such was the 7th Brigade in 1956—by IDF standards it

was considered the premier conventional combat brigade. NCOs at the time, fearful of the state of affairs inside the brigade, often joked that what the unit needed was a "Prussian Officer" at the helm. They got it in Colonel Uri Ben-Ari, appointed the commanding officer of the 7th Brigade on October 28, 1955. Born in Germany in 1925, Ben-Ari emigrated to Israel in 1939, months before the outbreak of the Second World War, and received an elitist kibbutz upbringing. An up-and-coming officer in the *Haganah,* he volunteered into the *Pal'mach* and was appointed a company commander in 1946. In 1948 he served as a battalion commander in the *Pal'mach's Harel* Brigade, Colonel Yitzhak Rabin's elite and beleaguered fighting force that struggled to liberate besieged Jerusalem from the Arab Legion. Uri Ben-Ari was a disciplinarian, but an egalitarian leader in true IDF character. He was capable and charismatic, and the IDF sent him where those traits would be the most useful—the Armored Corps. In 1951 he was appointed the deputy commander of the 7th Armored Brigade—a post he held for several years.[33]

Colonel Ben-Ari would have to wait only one year from the time the colonel's rank was pinned to his epaulets until he led the brigade into battle. The political situation was moving toward conflagration faster than the generals could prepare their armies. The situation along Israel's frontiers with Syria, Jordan, and Egypt had for years been deteriorating. Palestinian guerrilla attacks against Israeli border settlements had resulted in hundreds of dead and wounded.

Arab nationalism, sparked by the war in Algeria and the 1952 Egyptian revolution, had used the destruction of Israel as its catchword. The 1955 arms deal between Czechoslovakia and Egypt, in essence turning the Arab-Israeli conflict into a proxy of the cold war, also ensured inevitable bloodshed. Egyptian President Gamal Abdel Nasser, as charismatic an Arab leader as had been seen in the region since Saladin, had slowly commenced a stranglehold over the Jewish State. Although he denied any connection to the Fedayeen, the Palestinian guerrillas operating out of Gaza, Egyptian Military Intelligence ran the entire terrorist offensive. Nasser also ordered the Straits of Tiran, the only entrance to the Gulf of Aqaba and the port of Eilat, closed to

Israeli shipping. Israeli ships, bringing fuel from Iran and goods from the Far East, now had to circumvent Africa in order to reach Israel's Mediterranean posts of Ashdod and Haifa. That act, under international law, was reason enough for Israel to go to war. The alliance with France guaranteed that war would break out before 1957; Nasser's nationalization of the Suez Canal ensured full-fledged British and French participation, as well.

On October 21, 1956, Israeli Prime Minister David Ben-Gurion, Director General of the Ministry of Defense Shimon Peres, and IDF Chief of Staff Lieutenant-General Moshe Dayan flew to Sèvres, France, to meet with French Premier Guy Mollet, and British Foreign Minister Selwyn Lloyd to finalize the three-nation assault on Egypt. The three-party collusion called for the IDF to seize Sinai and race toward the Suez Canal. British and French forces would "intervene," looking after their interests near the waterway. The Sinai peninsula was a formidable obstacle 130 miles wide at its largest stretch, and 240 miles long, a landscape of mountain passes interspersed with pure and unforgiving desert. Egyptian forces in the Sinai Desert were defensive in nature, but formidable nonetheless: the Palestinian 8th Infantry Division situated in the Gaza-Rafah area; the 3rd Infantry Division centered in the El Arish and Abu Agheila area; the 1st Armored Brigade based in Bir Gifgafa; and an independent infantry brigade stationed near the ultrastrategic Mitla Pass. Egyptian armor units in Sinai consisted of nearly 500 tanks, including Shermans, T-34s, Joseph Stalin ISIIIs, and AMX-13s.

When the IDF, together with their French and British allies, launched their assault on Sinai on October 29, 1956, the IDF possessed *three* tank brigades—Colonel Uri Ben-Ari's 7th Armored Brigade, the reserve 27th Brigade commanded by Colonel Chaim Bar-Lev, a future 7th Brigade commander and IDF Chief of Staff, and the 37th Brigade commanded by Lieutenant-Colonel Shmuel Gilkna. The 7th Armored Brigade's order of battle in 1956 consisted of the 82nd Battalion, a force of Shermans and modified Super-Shermans, commanded by Lieutenant Abraham Adan (Bren); the 9th Battalion, a combination mechanized and tank unit sporting French-built AMX-13s, commanded by

Lieutenant-Colonel Y. "Beigele" Bigelman; and Lieutenant-Colonel Uri Rom's 52nd Battalion (that had, previously, been a mechanized force in the *Giva'ati* Brigade).

The Israeli battle plan was straightforward, though based on a lightning fast assault incorporating fast-moving units linking up with one another in strategic pushes. While a large portion of the IDF was moved opposite the Jordanian frontier (the scene of major Fedayeen raids from the West Bank) as a diversionary effort, ten brigades were assembled in the Negev Desert for the push into Sinai. The Israeli battle plan, choreographed in large part by OC Southern Command Major-General Assaf Simchoni, was an evolution of three stages first meant to fool the Egyptians altogether, and then divert their attention away from the actual IDF advance. In the General Staff codebook, the assault into Sinai was code-named *Kadesh*. Phase One commenced at 1700 hours on October 29, when Lieutenant-Colonel Rafel "Raful" Eitan's 890th Paratroop Battalion parachuted at the eastern end of the Mitla Pass near the Parker Memorial in order to seize the strategic passage and make sure that Egyptian troops from the mainland didn't reach beleaguered forces in Sinai once news of the invasion reached Cairo.

The 7th Armored Brigade consisted of Phase Two—seizing Abu Agheila and the crossroads of Egyptian defensive capabilities in Sinai. Responsible for taking Abu Agheila out of the equation was Colonel Yehuda Wallach's Ugdah 38, a task force consisting of the 4th (Reserve) Infantry Brigade, the 10th Infantry Brigade, and Colonel Ben-Ari's 7th Armored Brigade. Abu Agheila was a juncture that controlled the roads to El Arish to the north and Jebel Libni to the south, and was considered a crucial objective if Sinai was to be taken and Egyptian counterattack capabilities crushed. Its defensive composition consisted of three successive fortified ridges protecting the roadways that were defended by deep trenches, bunkers, and fixed firing positions, a gauntlet of barbed-wire obstacles, minefields, and camouflaged antitank cannon emplacements. Initially, according to Major-General Simchoni's battle plan, Abu Agheila was to be seized solely by the infantry components of Colonel Wallach's task force, but in order to exploit the speed and surprise of the Israeli invasion the 7th was sent into the fray as well.

Lieutenant-Colonel Adan's 82nd Battalion bore the principal responsibility of punching the armored hole through the Egyptian defenses, but after a probing action his Shermans came under intense—and accurate—anti-tank fire from dug-in Archer tank destroyers (self-propelled 17-pounder 76mm high-velocity guns produced in Great Britain). The Armored Corps' doctrine at the time, in orders issued by Armored Corps CO Major-General Chaim Laskov, called for Israeli tanks to open up fire on enemy targets at ranges of 1,200 meters to 2,000 meters in static operations, and at ranges of 400 meters to 800 meters when on the attack.[34] The Archer emplacements were not visible at 1,200 meters, and the Israeli tanks would surely be hit if they came as close as 800 meters, so Lieutenant-Colonel Adan dispatched his reconnaissance company to reconnoiter the area and find a soft spot in the Egyptian defenses out of reach of the fixed gun positions and minefields. The reconnaissance force, deployed on heavily armed jeeps equipped with the most powerful field glasses in the brigade's inventory, raced along the desert dunes, hugging the natural inclines in order to stay out of sight. After a five-hour search, they located a small opening, known on the maps as the Daika Pass. Situated in a wadi, the 12-mile-long defile was passable only to tracked vehicles, but negotiating its treacherous sinking sands meant that a force could reach the main highway leading from the Suez Canal to Abu Agheila and, subsequently, cut off the core of Egypt's Sinai defenses from the mainland.

Lieutenant-Colonel Adan was faced with a terrible dilemma when the reports of the Daika Pass's discovery reached him. Because it was passable only to tanks and half-tracks, the battalion would have to mount its attack far from its supplies of fuel and ammunition that were carried by truck. It was a gamble that needed to be taken. Adan made his move through the Daika defile toward Abu Agheila. The combination of Israeli air superiority and Egyptian tactical rigidity placed a supreme advantage in the 7th Brigade's favor and the Egyptian positions were overrun within an hour. Israeli air strikes, mainly by P-51 Mustangs flying low-altitude tank-hunting sorties, had softened up Egyptian defenses and resolve considerably. With the village of Abu

Agheila in IDF hands and Ben-Ari's AMX-13 force moving quite unopposed toward the Suez Canal, the main obstacle to the Abu Agheila defensive ring was a heavily fortified position known as the Reufa Dam. Built by the British to collect rainwater for the Bedouins, Reufa Dam was now used by the Egyptians as a fortified position. On the night of October 31, the attack commenced under a bright sinking orange sun and a choking cloud of dust. The Egyptian defenders, realizing that they were surrounded and cut off, fought for dear life. They threw everything they had against the advancing Shermans and scored considerable hits against the lightly armored World War II–era fighting vehicles. Lieutenant-Colonel Adan was surprised by the Egyptian resolve, and by their efforts. Every single tank in the battalion's task force was hit by enemy fire; many were seriously damaged, some destroyed altogether. A close-quarter melee broke out. Exhausted and running desperately low on ammunition, many of Adan's tanks decided to mount an Israeli kamikaze charge of sorts—they ran over Egyptian defenses when possible, as opposed to wasting the dwindling supplies of antitank rounds and .30 caliber machine gun ammunition. The scene was of absolute destruction. Egyptian vehicles and bunkers and hapless soldiers were crushed flat underneath the advancing Shermans. The dam had been taken, but there were approximately a dozen dead and scores more wounded in the battalion's ranks. It had been a hellish fight.

As Lieutenant-Colonel Adan's forces regrouped, repaired their vehicles and their shattered bodies, the Egyptians mounted a last-ditch counterattack from the east. Closing in from Umm Katef, it was a last ditch effort and one that ended badly.

For the next week, the 7th Brigade swept across the sands of the Sinai Peninsula in its march toward the Suez Canal. Forced to confront the Anglo-French invasion of the canal area, Egypt was unable to position suitable reinforcements to its Sinai garrison and the peninsula fell with little serious opposition. In fact, many historians concur, Nasser opted to abandon Sinai altogether. As his AMX-13 tank raced across the sweeping desert landscape, Ben-Ari received reports that the tattered Egyptian 1st Armored Brigade, a T-34/85 force, already decimated by relentless IAF sorties, was moving toward the canal in an attempt to flee the fighting. Without authorization, Ben-Ari took it upon himself to chase the beaten enemy. It was a risky move to extend the brigade far beyond resupply and support. Nevertheless, Ben-Ari found himself ten miles short of Isma'iliya and the Suez Canal. In essence, Israel had already won the war.

On November 5, 1956, Israeli units reached the Strait of Tiran and ended the blockade that had led Ben-Gurion down the path of war. The Anglo-French invasion, "Operation Musketeer," went well militarily but ended in a disastrous political crisis with the Soviet Union threatening Paris and London with missiles, and the U.S. President, Dwight D. Eisenhower, lambasting his allies for their unilateral, colonial-minded, military action. The 7th Brigade performed well during the 1956 Sinai Campaign and had proven itself to be a reliable tank unit that could spearhead any future Israeli military operations. The 82nd Battalion distinguished itself beyond all other tank units, earning citations and accolades for its courageous push through the Abu Agheila gauntlet. One unit, the 82nd Battalion's "A Company," was responsible for destroying six 25-pounder guns, seven 75mm antitank guns, and ten Archer self-propelled antitank guns in a single dedicated push.[35] Two 7th Brigade officers were decorated for valor during the seven-day campaign—Major Moshe Bar-Kochba, a burly Polish-born armor genius, and a young and temperamental officer named Captain Shmuel Gonen, the "A Company" commander. Gonen, a man who would feature prominently in the 7th Brigade's future, was severely wounded in his arm during the battle of Abu Agheila. Refusing to be evacuated to a battalion aid station, he continued to command the company even though he was in excruciating pain and in urgent need of a doctor. Only following the battle, a full 24 hours after sustaining his wounds, did he permit himself to be evacuated. After cursing the doctors and refusing orders to be sidelined, he commandeered a vehicle and returned to the company to resume his command.[36]

Colonel Uri Ben-Ari was replaced as 7th Brigade commander in December 1956 by Colonel Olek Nachshon.[37] The Shermans and AMX-13s remained in the 7th Brigade's order of battle until 1960, when the British Ministry of Defense reluctantly agreed to sell the IDF the Centurion Mk V Main Battle Tank. At the time, the Centurion was considered among the best tanks in the world. It was the first post–Second World War heavy tank to reach the precarious Middle East, though it first reached the hands of the Royal Jordanian Armored Corps, and the Elite 40th Armored Brigade. Designed with the lessons of the Second World War in mind, the Centurion was a capable, sturdy, and lethal tank on the battlefield. With its 105mm main gun, it was a long-range menace to any tank or armored vehicle that faced it on the field of battle. With Centurions in Jordanian camouflage colors overlooking the Jewish half of Jerusalem, and stationed along the strategic highway connecting Tel Aviv and the Israeli capital, the Jordanians were provided with a tactical edge of enormous importance. The Centurion in the IDF's scheme of dull grayish sand was an equalizer.

On July 9, 1961, Colonel Avraham Adan (Bren) was appointed the new *Ma'Hat,* the Hebrew acronym for *Mefaked Hativa* or Brigade Commander. The Israeli-born Colonel Adan was a warrior in the true sense of the world—a volunteer into the *Pal'mach* at the age of seventeen, he was a company commander in the Negev Brigade's 8th Battalion in the 1948 War and he fought in the harsh campaign to eradicate the Egyptian presence from the Negev Desert. The battles of the 8th Battalion, now the source of legend in Israeli military folklore, was desert warfare in its purest and wildest form. Jeepborne infantrymen raced through the sands of the Negev firing their vehicle-mounted German World War II–era MG-34 light machine guns at any target across the dunes. Late-night raids took place in the centers of major Egyptian bivouacs. Long stretches of territory were transversed on a few Jerry cans of gas and enough water as a body's discipline will allow it to ration under the blaring desert sun. From Beersheba to the liberation of Eilat in 1949, Captain Adan and his company of jeepborne operators raced through the very heart of Egypt's expeditionary force in Palestine and crushed it. In 1949 Adan joined the Armored Corps and became a tank officer. He created the "first" true IDF tank unit deploying abandoned and commandeered World War II surplus littering the battlefields of Europe. He was known as a courageous officer, and an innovative one. Although leaving the IDF for several years, he returned to active service in 1956, shortly before the Sinai Campaign, to command the 82nd Battalion. After the war, when the commander of the armored forces was Brigadier-General Chaim Bar-Lev, Adan was appointed the corps' chief operations officer. When Bar-Lev briefly left the armored forces in 1961 to study in the United States, he made sure that the premier tank brigade had the armored corps' premier officer.

Fate would have the 7th Brigade's future remain in Sinai for the next few years. A brigade that had been born out of the destructive forces that led to Israel's independence and that had been so decimated on the road to Jerusalem at Latrun had found, under its current composition, a niche in the desert. Its attack on Abu Agheila in 1956 signaled it as not only the IDF's sole conscript tank brigade, but a truly capable one, as well.

In 1967, again, the brigade would be tested in the desert. A test that would prove much costlier and more daring than anything it had achieved previously.

2

The Years of "Gorodish" and Glory: The "7th" in the 1967 Six Day War (the Before, the During, and the After)

December 15, 1966—Southern Israel: Sitting upright in his turret, the commander of an 82nd Battalion Centurion Mk V main battle tank awaited the order to fire. It was just before dawn on a cool winter's morning in the Negev Desert at an IDF training facility south of Beersheba. The five Centurions of the first platoon were waiting in line for their shot at the firing range when the first rank took its first shot. Peering through his field glasses, the young sergeant shouted the coordinates to his gunner and awaited the ballistic recoil of a 105mm gun firing its mighty shell. The target this morning was a World War II–era, Russian-built JSIII tank, a hulking beast of steel with its inches of armor plating, painted white with a large circle of black in the center of the turret. The first round fired by the lead tank landed wide, about five meters, exploding in an orange fireball just ahead of the hull. The second shot landed short, spraying the JSIII with a coat of sand and shrapnel. Yet before the lieutenant supervising the firing range could give the green light for the third shot to be fired, a jeep was seen racing toward the firing line at a furious pace. It was Gonen's jeep and that meant trouble. Pulling up in front of the tank, the figure emerged in a neatly pressed fatigue uniform clutching a series of maps and field glasses. "You call that shooting?" Gonen barked at the sergeant, now reduced to a trembling pillar of khaki and sweat. "I will ruin your service, your career, your life. You call yourself a tank soldier in *my* brigade? You call yourself a man? I'll cancel all leaves for the battalion if you fuck up the next shot." The sergeant disappeared into his turret and requested some help. He reviewed his coordinates out loud and then issued the order—*Esh*—"Fire!" The blast was deafening and the swoosh of the 105mm projectile racing through the dry desert air was heard throughout the valley. So was the impact of the shell hitting the JSIII's chassis. Before the young sergeant could turn his head to the left to hopefully get an approving nod from the commanding officer, all that could be seen was a trail of dust following the departing jeep.

It was the 7th Brigade's renaissance—the days of Gorodish. According to Major-General Avigdor "Yanush" Ben-Gal, "It was like a time from Dickens. For the brigade it was both the best of times and the worst of times."[1] A period of unrivaled work and preparations, and one of the world's greatest military victories. It was the 1960s.

Shmuel "Gorodish" Gonen was given the command of the 7th Armored Brigade on June 1, 1966. Born in Vilna, Lithuania, in 1930, Gonen (his original family name was Gorodish and it would stick with him as a nickname) made *Aliyah* to Palestine at the age of three with his parents. In Palestine, the young Gonen was brought up in the ultra-Orthodox neighborhood of Me'ah She'arim—an isolated island of pious living in what was becoming a secular driven Jewish State. Although an excellent yeshiva student, Gonen rebelled against his Orthodox upbringing by being the first-in-line volunteer to the ranks of the *Haganah*. Gonen was all of fourteen years old when he was handed his Sten gun and stationed around the volatile Jerusalem area in 1944. Wounded five times in battle in 1948, Gonen developed a reputation as a no-nonsense officer who was willing to sacrifice himself, and a soldier who expected nothing but the same from the men in his command. Following his recovery from the massive shrapnel wounds that scarred his body following the 1948 War, Gonen returned to uniform, joining the IDF as an armor officer in the 7th Armored Brigade. Unlike many of the officers, all native-born Sabras, Gonen was not a slim and sleek product of the kibbutz environment. Short and somewhat unassuming, Gonen made up for his lack of physical presence by confidence and competitiveness. He made many enemies along the way but managed to get noticed by the people who needed to see his skills and determination. Driven by that determination he knew that his capabilities were far beyond most of his contemporaries. It was this zeal that propelled him, like a 105mm round, through the chain of command and up the mined obstacle course of advancement in the IDF. During the 1956 Sinai Campaign, Captain Gonen commanded the first tank company to reach the waters of the Suez Canal, and he was awarded an *I'tur Ha'Oz* medal for courage for his bravery and command under fire. He was also seriously wounded in the battle and suffered a vicious shrapnel injury that many have said he never completely recovered from.

Gonen's predecessor at the helm of the 7th Brigade was, perhaps, his antithesis—Colonel Shlomoh Lahat, a man referred to for most of his life as "Cheetch." Lahat was a natural-born politician and commanded the brigade as if he were lobbying for office. The brigade was maintained as a top-notch fighting unit for the eighteen months that Lahat commanded the brigade from January 1965 to June 1966, but the men functioned out of a sense of duty and discipline imposed by junior officers and NCOs. Under Lahat, a man who would retire from the IDF as a major-general and eventually become a national icon as mayor of Tel Aviv, the brigade was a finely tuned instrument of high morale, and a force ready for war. When Gonen was made full colonel and appointed brigade commander on June 1, 1966, the brigade's strings were tuned nearly to their breaking point.

As a commander, the officers and NCOs knew that Gonen was as courageous as they come. "He was not the type of commander who led from a CP (command post)," recalled former Justice Minister Dan Meridor, a young sergeant in 1966. "He was brave."[2] He was also a fanatical stickler for discipline—far beyond what the Israel Defense Forces had been used to and, perhaps, some had suggested, far beyond what the Prussian Army might have demanded 100 years ago! Gonen's command centered on discipline. Training and the rudimentary war-footing environment that a brigade needs to experience in order to be ready for war became secondary. His theory was that you lead through personal example and achieve discipline by fear and intimidation. The brigade was everything and Gorodish was the brigade. It was as close to a dictatorship as Israel would ever see and it was personified in a fighting force of eighteen-year-old conscripts. His personality and method of command was a volatile mixture that displayed tremendous peaks and valleys on the behavioral scale but it was, as one former green recruit who would reach the rank of brigadier-general would comment, "an effective means for exorcising any remnants of civilian character from the young soldier's body."

Gorodish knew that his soldiers—and, indeed, many of his officers—greatly feared him, and he relished his ability to intimidate and motivate through threat and tirade. He was one of the first Israeli military officers with an agenda and an ego, and he had plans that far outstretched the boundaries of the IDF and his khaki fatigues. He was also among the first IDF officers to understand the value and merit of media exposure and often saw to it that newspapers and army periodicals wrote about the brigade and, most importantly, him. Journalists, never before invited to military installations, were frequent guests at the unit's main base in the Negev Desert and were often dazzled by parades and live-fire demonstrations. Gorodish viewed himself as an Israeli "Patton." The press was impressed by this uncharacteristic Israeli spit-and-polish and the men in the field, going through the motions of the dog-and-pony act, were terrified to miss a step or a beat or—God forbid—a target and subsequently endure the wrath of an embarrassed and nonimpressed brigade commander.

In newspapers such as *Yediot Aharonot* or *Bamachane,* the army newspaper, the 7th Brigade was a media dynamo. Indeed, for the 7th Armored Brigade, the mid-1960s were the best of times. For the brigade as a fighting unit, it was a period when many of the green recruits who would turn out to be the Armored Corps' most famous soldiers were eighteen-year-old conscripts fresh into their three-year conscripted service in the IDF not knowing the difference between a Patton and a python. It was a period when the 7th Brigade went from a brigade equipped with World War II rejects and French light tanks to MBTs used by the big boys—the Americans and the British. Because the true might and ability of the IAF was still untested and unknown, the Armored Corps—and the 7th Brigade—was considered the IDF's mightiest arm. When a foreign dignitary visited the Jewish State, he was ushered around the usual sites, such as the Holocaust Museum at Yad Vashem in Jerusalem and the Knesset. The VIP would also be driven south to the Negev Desert and the home of the 7th Armored Brigade. Nicknamed by many "the Hollywood Brigade," Colonel Gonen initiated a period of celebrity status behind the brigade that he commanded with an iron grip and an almost fanatic—some even suggested sadistic—degree of discipline.

Gorodish did not view his behavior or authoritarian style as anything less than necessary. "I received the brigade before the war," Colonel Gonen told the army newspaper *Bamachane* in 1968. "I felt that I had better train the brigade for war, I prepared the brigade *for* war, and *I* turned the brigade into a division of steel." For the soldier inside the tanks, Gonen's philosophies of command, or the justification of the brigade's degree of publicity, had little bearing on life in the field. The eighteen-year-old soldiers, fresh out of high school, knew only one thing: You needed nerves of steel, steel stronger than a Centurion's armor plating, to survive service in the unit. Soldiers often joked as to what was a crueler way to die—getting hit by a tirade by Gonen or by an Egyptian 100mm round? The answer, of course, was the tirade by Gonen—it made you miserable years before you died, as opposed to the instant demise caused by getting hit by enemy ordnance. Colonel Gonen made men cry, made them shit in their pants, and made them regret the fact that they were ever born. If he hated you, you were marked forever, and if he liked you he could turn on you at a moment's notice. Soldiers whose boots were not polished properly (a rarity in the IDF), or whose pants were not properly creased (an even greater rarity in the IDF) could sometimes end up in the stockade or, worse, not be allowed to visit their families by having their weekend passes revoked—in the IDF, a punishment of enormous harshness. Gonen was the sole figure of command in the brigade and what he said, ordered, and directed had to be carried out. *Every* aspect of life in the brigade hinged on discipline and, Gonen believed, if a soldier could be relied upon to shine his boots, then he could be counted on to place a 105mm or 90mm round square in the center of an Egyptian T-55.

The IDF model had for years been leadership through example—the "Follow me" ethic of command. Gonen's brand of *Pikud* (leadership) was intimidation and threats. He would lead at the helm, but, some soldiers would say, from that vantage point he couldn't check to see whose faces were shaved and whose boots were polished. Soldiers in the brigade had no choice but to grin and bear it and hope to survive; it was, however, reported, that at the time of Gonen's command of the brigade, the numbers of conscripts volunteering for anything *other* than the Armored Corps reached record levels. Some junior officers, like a young captain named Avigdor "Yanush" Ben-Gal, a man who would make the brigade his life, would have none of it and transferred out of the unit rather than be around Gonen at all. Others used it as a learning experience. Captain Elyashiv Shimshi, a company commanding officer in the 82nd Battalion in early 1967, reflected, "He was an incredibly difficult and harsh man, but he was cool and sometimes impervious to his surroundings while under fire. A true anomaly that was hard to figure out."[3]

As a nation, Israel was still in its infancy, traversing through the struggles of preserving her frontiers and nation-building. From the time the last of Colonel Uri Ben-Ari's Shermans evacuated the now demilitarized Sinai Desert in 1957, hundreds of thousands of additional immigrants had settled into the new State of Israel and the IDF had changed from a nation of European immigrants and refugees to a melting pot of faces, languages, and cultures covering over one hundred nations. The IDF had become an egalitarian nation-builder, providing each soldier—whether his roots were seventh-generation Jerusalem or a newly arrived wide-eyed conscript from Tripoli—with a common experience.

New immigrants eager to prove their patriotism and self-worth worked feverishly to succeed in the army. For the IDF, there never was—and probably never will be again—a more dedicated talent pool at its disposal.

Both his detractors and supporters admit that one of Gorodish major achievements was truly integrating an element of the IDF to all ethnic and social classes—"he hated you no matter what your background," some would say. Although the image of Israel as an egalitarian paradise was touted as fact by the policy makers in Jerusalem to anyone who would listen, there was a definite class system in existence in Israel, and it was based on a tier of racial discrimination, elitism, and wealth. In no forum was this expressed more candidly and more viciously than in the IDF. The socialist kibbutzim, the true social soul and conscience of the Zionist movement, had for years produced the true Israeli fighter—young, lean, muscular, and a faithful follower of self-sacrifice. Eighteen-year-olds from the kibbutzim, the true elite of Israeli society, were politically left-of-center and tended to all volunteer for pilot's training. For those who weren't aviator material, there were always the various commando units, the *Sayerot* (recon forces) to volunteer into. Most eighteen-year-old kibbutzniks entering their three years of mandatory military service, in fact, were desperate to make the grade and serve in an elite fighting formation. Many suffered—often times self-inflicted—disgrace if they returned home on leave without a red beret, jump wings, and some behind-enemy-lines war stories. An Armored Corps black beret and tank badge was not considered a status symbol—to a kibbutznik it was a badge of shame. The infantry, artillery, and tanks were for the most part the domain of the new immigrant and the physically not perfect, the city dweller and the "average" soldier. Conscripts didn't volunteer into the Armored Corps, they were hoarded onto a bus at the IDF's Absorption Base and sent to basic training—like it or not. Even though these soldiers were not pilot material and would not have survived reconnaissance commando training, one man in the IDF believed them to be elite—that man was Gorodish.

A good portion of these soldiers putting on their black berets for the first time were new immigrants from what is known as the Arabic Diaspora—Jews from North Africa, Syria, Iraq, and Yemen. The elitists on the kibbutzim and the Ashkenazi Jews from Europe who made up the Israeli ruling class viewed many of these kids as too similar to the Arabs to be true Israelis, and as a result they were discriminated against in "regular" society and in the military. Some units, especially a small and highly covert squad, such as the top-secret General Staff Reconnaissance Unit *Sayeret Mat'kal,* found a special home for these immigrants. The brainchild of one Major Avraham Arnan, a veteran intelligence officer, *Sayeret Mat'kal* openly recruited urban kids, especially those young Israelis whose parents came from the Arabic Diaspora. Although discriminated against in the European-dominated, Labor-led Israel of the late 1950s and early 1960s, and usually excluded by the air force and the other elite reconnaissance commando units, these kids that the state labeled as disadvantaged understood the Arab mentality, knew Arabic, and, most importantly, had a chip on their shoulder that translated into a competitive edge that the other Sabras, or native born Israelis, would have to emulate.[4]

Most importantly, many high-ranking officers viewed these new immigrants, many incredibly gifted soldiers and highly heroic individuals, as unworthy for officers' course. One such 7th Brigade victim of this discrimination was a young NCO named Avigdor Kahalani. Born in 1943 to parents from Aden, Yemen, Kahalani grew up in the southern town of Ness-Ziona, along the Mediterranean coast, and was conscripted into the IDF at the age of eighteen in 1962. Although he wanted to be a pilot, a defect in his right ear shot down his flight future, and although he tried to volunteer into the ranks of the red berets of the paratroopers, his flat feet made the airborne doctors wary of his abilities to traverse long distances on foot. Although trained in school as a mechanic, Kahalani wanted anything *other* than to end up in the Ordnance Corps and spend his three years of military service drenched in grease and hydraulic fluid. He wanted action and he wanted to be challenged. He found himself—quite against his will—in the Armored Corps in the 7th Armored Brigade.

Although he wrote his father that "tanks are not for me,"[5]

Kahalani excelled in basic training and in the basic tank course, eventually heading to tank commanders' course in 1963. At his graduation and the awarding of "excellent pupil," the rank of sergeant was pinned to his sleeve by the Armored Corps commander, Major-General David "Dado" Elazar; Colonel Avraham Adan (Bren), the school commander; and Major Tuvia Raviv, the course commanding officer. In the 82nd Battalion, considered the IDF's premier tank force, Kahalani became known as one of the finest tank commanders in the company and the battalion. In the unit, he met up with First-Lieutenant Elyashiv Shimshi, also a Yemeni-Jew, who was also blazing a trail in the brigade as a rising star. Kahalani's commanders were impressed by him and knew that he possessed not only the courage to command, but the charisma to lead men into battle, as well. In 1963 he was sent to *Ba'Ha'D 1* (Hebrew acronym for *Basis Ha'Dracha*, or Training Base), the IDF's West Point, for his six months of physical and academic honing up that would turn a sergeant into a second lieutenant and tank officer.

But *Ba'Ha'D 1* was a bastion of the ruling elite of the Jewish State, and not a happy home for Kahalani. A month into the course, Kahalani was summoned to a board of officers and asked a series of odd questions ranging from what should a platoon commander do if dispatched across the border and ordered to set up an ambush, to who was the King of Yemen? It was clear to Kahalani that the purpose of this gathering was to humiliate him and bounce him out of the course; "unsuitable to academic material" was the official reason. Yet the IDF likes to keep personal tabs on those who show promise and to make sure that they don't fall through the cracks, and Armored Corps commander Major-General Elazar kept tabs on Kahalani. Upon hearing that the officer candidate was returned to his brigade, he summoned Kahalani to his office for a meeting. Upon hearing the truth, Elazar was outraged. "Be strong and don't let them break you!" Kahalani didn't know what could be done—without passing *Ba'Ha'D 1,* he wouldn't be a commissioned officer (known in the vernacular as a platoon commander) in the IDF and without being an officer he could not begin tank officers' course, which, in the natural course of events, followed *Ba'Ha'D 1.*

Elazar's intervention paid off. Kahalani was sent directly to tank officers' course even without his platoon commander's badge. At tank officers' school, Kahalani excelled both in his academic requirements and in the days that turned into nights that turned into days that was field training. He graduated from the course and remains only the second officer in the history of the IDF to be an officer without having passed *Ba'Ha'D 1*.[6]

Kahalani returned to the 7th Brigade in charge of a tank platoon in the 82nd Battalion.

Beyond the national significance of its immigrant base and the eager faces of the men—and women—entering the IDF, the most important aspect of the period was the IDF's arms acquisitions. Although nothing could make the Israeli soldier "look" professional, shipments from France and the United Kingdom were slowly turning the Israeli military into a regional player with significant capabilities. In the air, the IAF was replacing its piston-engine P–54 Mustangs with jets—primarily the best subsonic fighters and bombers from France, like the Fouga Magister and Ouragon. These aircraft were soon updated with supersonic warbirds of incredible potential (especially in IAF hands) like the Mystere and the Mirage IIIC. The Armored Corps was a hodgepodge of aging Shermans constantly being updated to make them only marginally obsolete, along with French-built AMX–13 light tanks that were lightly armored, lightly gunned, and no match for most Second World War–era MBTs. The Centurion, from Great Britain, was the deciding factor—the great equalizer that brought the IDF to a seemingly modest state of parity with the T-54/55's being fielded by the Egyptian and Syrian militaries, and the Centurions and Pattons that the Royal Jordanian Armored Corps had stationed all along the elongated frontier with the Jewish State.

The British and French, the great colonial powers in the region, still exerted considerable influence on the players in the areas they once controlled. In 1962, however, the Middle East became a true superpower battleground. United States President John F. Kennedy authorized the sale of American-made HAWK surface-to-air missile batteries to the IAF; weapons sales from Washington had been something of a taboo issue for some time, but President Kennedy saw the strategic need for military assistance. President Johnson, in 1964, reinforced this notion when he authorized the transfer of M-48A2C Patton tanks from U.S. Army stores in Germany to Israel. Officers in the Israeli Ministry of Defense had worked feverishly to secure the Pattons—officers in the Armored Corps, primarily the 7th Brigade, were ecstatic.

In early 1964, a small and secretive group of 7th Brigade officers, under the command of deputy brigade commander Lieutenant-Colonel Shmuel Gonen were dispatched to Germany to learn the Patton from A to Z and supervise its transfer from northern Germany to the port of Haifa. This mission was classified "Super Top Secret" and the Israeli contingent (consisting of nearly a dozen officers) was told to speak English among one another while in Europe and go under the guise of being students; "There was no doubt we were soldiers," Kahalani would later reflect, "all one had to do was look at our haircuts and our rigid style."[7]

In Germany, the group of Israelis were issued with Bundeswehr uniforms and taught the art of the Patton tank by the Germany military (in order to provide the United States government with a seed of deniability) and introduced to a tank that, in their eyes, was everything American—big, powerful, and easy to drive. The Centurion was a good tank, these officers knew, but it had its shortcomings. It wasn't the easiest tank in the world to drive or maneuver, and it often jammed and had clutch problems; British engineering was not viewed as user-friendly. The importance of the clandestine visit to Germany was to acquaint the future commanders of a new battalion within the 7th Brigade with the basics of the M-48A2C. Additional instruction and training of the conscripts and NCOs who would staff this battalion would all be carried out on Israeli shores.

The battalion was the 79th, and its first commander was Lieutenant-Colonel Ya'akov "Jackie" Even; the deputy commander was Major Natke Nir. For nearly a year, from early 1965 until just about the time that Colonel Gonen assumed command of the ridge, the 79th Battalion was one of the most secretive units in all the IDF. It trained in absolute seclusion from other units and was restricted to the remote and very isolated Camp Natan near Beersheba. When tanks were not in the field firing their .90mm main armaments cannons, they would be parked under palm trees or under camouflage sheets to shield them from the prying eyes of Soviet satellites or Soviet and/or Egyptian aerial reconnaissance. For a while the secret held true, and even seasoned soldiers in the 82nd were kept in the dark about the "hush-hush" activities in the desert. It wasn't until Radio Cairo's chief propaganda series, "Radio Thunder," congratulated the IDF and the 7th Armored Brigade upon its new American toy that it became known. Much to Gonen's delight, a stiff sense of competition developed between the two battalions—each one eager to prove that it was the premier force within the brigade. Within each battalion, each company of 14 tanks and its technical and ordnance crews competed with the other companies for the title of battalion, brigade, and even divisional best. It was Centurion versus Patton, 105mm versus 90mm, 82nd versus 79th! Gonen's level of intimidation had created a vacuum of morale that was shored up by the interunit competition. If they focused on being the best, then, as brigade commander, Gonen had achieved virtually all his objectives. His only test would be during war.

Colonel Gonen had also inherited command of a tank brigade that had been under a two-year revolution—the "Talik" Revolution. Until 1964, there was no philosophy behind armored warfare in the IDF—tanks in the field would acquire a target, get within range, and destroy it before it had a chance to destroy the tank. Reaching a target, getting to within range, became half the battle and the art of tank gunnery marksmanship had been sorely overlooked. On November 3, 1964, two days after Brigadier-General Yisrael "Talik" Tal became Major-General Tal and commander of the Armored Corps, there was an exchange of gunfire along Israel's frontier with Syria, near Tel Dan at the Syrian outpost of Nuheilleh. The battle had lasted nearly an entire day and consisted of tanks on both sides of the frontier shooting at one anther. As insightful and hands-on an officer as the Armored Corps—and the IDF—would ever have, Tal rushed to the northern frontier to view the battle scene and interview the unit commander, the commanding officer of the 82nd Battalion, Lieutenant-Colonel Benny Omri. Eager for a count of Syrian BTRs and T-34s hit, Tal eagerly asked

Omri, "How many tanks had been destroyed?" Omri, somewhat embarrassed, replied, "None, sir!" "Well, how many rounds did the battalion fire?" Even more embarrassed, Omri responded, "Eighty-nine." Tal was furious and ready to explode. He vowed an inquiry.[8]

That inquiry yielded the findings that human error and an inherent flaw in how Israeli tank gunners were taught to function led to so many rounds of ammunition being fired without one actually hitting and destroying its target. Gunners had been taught to fire in groups, from something similar to a mobile artillery platform, and to hit what was well into range. At border skirmishes, like at Tel Dan, such artillery platforms had a tendency to escalate the ante of violence, incorporate larger units, and even risk the potential for starting a full-scale war. General Tal, quite familiar with the ability of the Centurion's long-range 105mm main gun, realized that the black berets were doing it all wrong. If that weapon would be utilized properly, for long-range operations, a tank crew could take out an intended target with *one* well-placed shot. Beforehand, IDF tank crews had allowed themselves to aim at targets with "approximate ranges and coordinates," according to one IDF tank officer. "During the 1967, you aimed, set the variables, and said a prayer that the round hit the crosshairs. Most of the time it didn't, but we considered it part and parcel of what a tank could and could not do. After all, we were taught in basic training, the 105mm gun is not a hunting rifle!"[9] Crews, Tal discovered when examining the embarrassing events at Tel Dan, had been taught to use their vehicle's main armament cannon as a hit-or-miss artillery piece. Tal would not tolerate that mind-set anymore. The age of the *Tzalaf,* or sniper, in the tanks of the Armored Corps was born.

Previously, Armored Corps doctrine formally stipulated that any shell landing within a 40-meter radius of its target was considered as scoring a direct hit; the theory was that the blast and ricochets were *bound* to result in damage. Gunners used to fire their rounds, watch a shell land, and then proceed to the next order of business. Tal, speaking to tank gunners at the squad and platoon levels, issued strict directives that gunners follow their targets continuously—after they think it has been hit, even after a ball of red flame emerged from the commander's turret.[10] "Also," according to a retired Armored Corps officer, "tank gunners were ordered stop the 'macho bullshit' of what was then considered face-to-face combat in *Heyl Ha'Shirion!*"[11] Instead of engaging targets at ranges varying from 500 meters to 1,200 meters away, Talik ordered that the minimum range of engagement be 1,500 meters with 2,000 meters being the optimum range to fully utilize the Centurion's long-range 105mm gun. Beyond the frugal requirements that went into Talik's new directives, there was the practicality of being able to score long-range kills on a vastly superior enemy that would be trained along Soviet lines to attack in uncoordinated swarms. Talik would be damned if, in the next war that was bound to erupt in the region (that IDF planners thought would erupt in 1969), another unit like Lieutenant-Colonel Omri's would fire 89 rounds at an enemy target and destroy absolutely nothing.

Being a *Tzalaf,* a calibrated 105mm marksman, was something of a necessity that 7th Brigade crewmen took to like magic. Intensive gunnery training turned the gunners into true snipers that, in turn, turned tank crews into four-man teams of confidence and arrogance. They knew that a T-55 at 2,000 meters range was almost as good as dead on the first shot, certainly on the second try, and the fear of actually engaging the enemy in combat was diluted with the knowledge that they were as professional and capable as could be found. In exercises in the Negev Desert in the fall of 1966, 7th Brigade marksmanship scores proved remarkable—most targets hit on the first try. Gonen, impressed, was determined not to let on. The brigade trained harder, pushed further, and raced its men close to the envelope of endurance and tolerance. Perhaps never in the history of the Israel Defense Forces had there been a military formation readier for the trials of full-scale warfare than were the black berets of Gonen's 7th Armored Brigade.

War would not come to the Middle East in 1969 as *A'man (Agaf Mode'in* or Intelligence Branch) predicted, but rather in 1967 and it promised to be a bloody conflict that would test the very plight of Israeli survival. The IDF, as well as Egypt, Syria, and Jordan, had been gearing up for this conflict for nearly eleven years and the hammer hit the anvil in

April 1967. On April 7, near Tel Dan, the Syrian garrison atop the Golan Heights launched a massive artillery bombardment on Kibbutz Tel Katzir; 130mm shells ripped through nurseries, homes, and factories. Outraged by the bloody attack, Chief of Staff Lieutenant-General Yitzhak Rabin ordered the air force into action to take out the Syrian gun emplacements that had harassed Israeli agricultural settlements in Galilee once and for all. A flight of Super Mysteres was sent to take the guns out, and they, in turn, were intercepted by a flight of Syrian Air Force MiG-21s, which, in turn, was ambushed by a flight of French-built Mirage IIIC jets sporting the Star of David. The Syrian guns were removed and six MiGs erupted into balls of flame over the Golan Heights.

Radicals in Damascus and Cairo argued for Israel's complete annihilation. Following the embarrassing incident government radio in Damascus and Cairo openly called for a second Holocaust and for the Jews to be pushed into the sea. Although the skirmish took place between Israel and Syria, all eyes turned to Cairo. Since Egyptian President Gamal Abdel Nasser promoted himself as the leader of the Arab World, the Middle East, from the fertile crescent to the North African nations, would follow his lead. On May 15, 1967, Nasser placed the nearly million-man Egyptian Army on full alert. On May 18, 1967, Nasser ordered that the 5,000 United Nations peacekeepers that had kept the Sinai Peninsula demilitarized since 1957 evacuate their positions. Egyptian armored divisions quickly moved across the canal into the desert wasteland of Sinai and set up camp directly opposite strategic roadways leading into southern Israel, the coastal strip, and into the Negev Desert. On May 30, 1967, Jordan's King Hussein visited Cairo to sign a mutual defense pact with Egypt, combining the armed forces of the two countries and placing the elite British-trained Jordanian military under overall Egyptian command.

As the Egyptian propaganda machine spoke openly of massacres, rapes, and a sea of red Jewish blood, the IDF, too, took emergency steps on the road to war. An emergency cabinet, including the political opposition, was established, and Prime Minister Levi Eshkol named the charismatic former Chief of Staff and 1956 War hero Moshe Dayan as his defense minister. The conscript army was placed on full alert and dispatched to front line positions from the Lebanese border to the Gaza Strip. Reservists were ordered back to their units, and children and housewives began digging ditches and defensive barriers along the plush cafe- and tree-lined boulevards of Tel Aviv.

In May it was apparent to all in Israel that war would break out soon. The dogfight over the Golan Heights, while an insignificant footnote to history by itself, was one of those events in the furor-driven politics of the region that could not be dismissed. In May 1967 after ordering the United Nations to withdraw its Emergency Force from Sinai, President Nasser reinforced his troops in the Peninsula to six divisions, moved about 40 fighters on to the Sinai airfields, concluded defense arrangements with Jordan, Syria, and Iraq, and closed the Straits of Tiran to Israeli shipping. When three Egyptian divisions were concentrated on the Israeli frontier, the Israeli Defense Forces (IDF) were mobilized. Whereas Egypt could menace the Negev with her Regular Army indefinitely, Israel could not remain mobilized long without damage to her economy. Concerned that an Arab military combination might move against her on three sides, the Israeli government decided on a preemptive war. As Egypt possessed the largest armed forces among her Arab neighbors and presented the most serious and immediate threat, Israel decided to deal with it first. If the other Arab states remained quiet, no action would be taken against them. If not, Jordan would be attacked next to relieve the pressure on Jerusalem and the rest of Israel. Syria, which threatened no vital point immediately, would be dealt with last. To forestall a concentrated attack and to beat the "diplomatic clock" in the Security Council, speed was essential.

Israel's war aims were clear—destroy the enemy before it could reach a numeric advantage and set forth a wave of motion and momentum across Israeli defenses. The key to Israel's strategy was air power and the destruction of the Arab air forces. Once that was achieved, the ground forces could destroy as much of the enemy as a superpower-controlled United Nations Security Council would permit.

The generals of the *Mate Ha'Klali,* or General Staff, knew that Israel could, indeed, win an all-out war with all her Arab neighbors, but it would hinge on three factors: (1) Israel would have to strike first and decisively; (2) Arab air power would have to be destroyed in its entirety; and, (3) the largest Arab army, Egypt's, would have to be handled first. Directing the brunt of the IDF's small manpower and resources in a fight against the Egyptians in Sinai was risky. Jordanian soldiers were positioned only a stone's throw away from the Israeli capital in Jerusalem, and Syrian forces had a bird's-eye view of much of northern Israel from their series of fortifications atop the Golan Heights. Yet the Egyptian Army was the most daunting foe, and for the other strategic problems along Israel's central and northern tiers to be handled, the Egyptian military in Sinai had to be pummeled to the point where they presented a threat to no one.

In terms of an all-out air strike that would cripple the Arab forces, there had been a massive Israeli intelligence-gathering effort before the war, courtesy of such famous, though ill-fated, spies as Eli Cohen in Syria and Wolfgang Lotz in Egypt. The Israeli military knew virtually every intimate detail about Syrian and Egyptian air bases, including where pilots had their breakfast, when they went to sleep, and even who their mistresses were.

The air strike—on tactical levels an attack similar to the Japanese strike on Pearl Harbor on December 7, 1941—was considered the crucible to an Israeli victory, and the IDF General Staff had supreme confidence in its pilots, aircraft, and intelligence-gathering efforts. A ground war and bloodbath in the trenches presented far more possibilities for Murphy's Law to take over. Indeed, the Egyptian presence in Sinai was a mighty one.

Initially, the Egyptians had only two infantry divisions on the Sinai border, the 20th Palestinian in the Gaza Strip and 7th Infantry Division on a front 140 miles long between the sea at Rafah and Kuntilla. The 7th was shuffled sideways to the coast to allow the 2nd to take over its right in the Agheila–Umm Katif area. The 3rd and 6th were deployed in depth behind the 7th and 2nd respectively and the 4th Armored Division was kept well back in the Bir Gifgafa area as a strategic reserve. One of the brigades was detached to the Quraya Pas area for an offensive in the Negev to link up with the Jordanians at Beersheba. The Egyptians were deployed for defense in great depth with the option of a small-scale offensive. Their divisions were too far apart for mutual support and their logistic system was in disarray.

Eshkol's Israeli Cabinet, stiffened by the appointment of General Moshe Dayan as defense minister during the crisis, took the decision to initiate a surprise attack on the evening of June 3, the day Iraq joined Nasser's Arab Pact. Any possibility of strategic surprise had evaporated during the three weeks of tension. The next day, the unclassified items on the previous night's cabinet agenda were published together with a disarming press statement by Moshe Dayan that diplomacy "must now be given a chance." Israeli Military Intelligence engaged in an immediate and highly successful disinformation campaign to lull the Arabs into a state of false security. Israeli military sources saw to it that news wire photographers were able to film reservists relaxing on Israeli beaches, reading newspapers underneath camouflage netting, and showering in the nude at forward field showers. All efforts were made to show the IDF as an army not poised for the attack. The Arab propaganda machine, fueled by its own lies and fantasies, used the reports of Israeli troops relaxing as a sign of cowardice. "[They] are too frightened to fight back—We will push the Jews into the bloodred sea in a matter of hours," claimed Radio Cairo. The disinformation campaign was enough to give the Israelis tactical surprise on the following day.

Air superiority was the key to success in the war as a whole. A combination of brilliant planning, surprise, and execution knocked out the Egyptian Air force on its airfields in two hours and fifty minutes on the morning of June 5. When Jordan and Syria entered the war later in the day their air forces were dealt with in two strikes lasting just twenty-five minutes each. From the army's point of view freedom from enemy air attack conferred immense advantages but, initially, it would have to rely on limited air support from the slow Fouga Magister trainers until the high-performance Mirages, Mysteres, and Ouragons could be released from the airfield strikes.

The plan for the Sinai campaign was the work of the Chief of the General Staff, Yitzhak Rabin, and OC Southern Command, Yeshayahu Gavish. The aim was the destruction of the Egyptian Army in Sinai. Sharm-esh-Sheikh, controlling the Straits of Tiran and the east bank of the Suez Canal, would then fall into Israel's lap. The plan was to be executed in three phases. First, two *Ugdot* (reinforced divisions) were to break through the Egyptian crust defenses at Rafah and Abu Agheila to open the two main routes into Sinai while a deception operation distracted enemy attention toward Kuntilla. A third Ugdah was to infiltrate an armored brigade along the Wadi Hareidin, a supposedly impassable route some ten-to-fifteen miles south of the coastal road, which had been secretly reconnoitered, to prevent reinforcements being sent against Tal's Ugdah on the coast and to win the armored battle that would ensue when the Egyptian 4th Armored Division counterattacked. The Ugdah's second brigade remained in reserve. In the second phase the three main passes through the Western Hills (Khatmia, Giddi, and Mitla) would be seized behind the Egyptians so that their forces could be destroyed in the third phase.

Egyptian President Nasser had good reason to be confident about his chance to overwhelm Israeli defenses along the southern frontier. Positioned throughout the Sinai peninsula, Nasser had 100,000 men divided into seven divisions, including two armored divisions, that possessed nearly 1,000 tanks, 850 artillery batteries—all supported by 400 combat aircraft. Egyptian defenses in Sinai were threefold. The first line of Egyptian forces, close to the Israeli border, consisted of fortifications around Rafah, Umm Katif, Ketzaymeh, and the Gaza Strip; most of the defenses were infantry-manned with 100 tanks and little heavier firepower than artillery in its positions. The second line of defense, the armor gauntlet, consisted of lines stretching from El Arish to Jebel Libni, Bir Hasnah all the way to Nahal. The final Egyptian defensive line, a fire-zone of last resort, lay in the depths from Bir Gifgafa to Bir Themada—with the Egyptian 4th Armored Division as its main muscle. Egyptian forces in Sinai consisted of the 20th Palestinian Infantry Division stationed in Gaza and the 7th Infantry Division positioned in Rafah, El Arish, and Bir Lahfan. The Egyptian 2nd Infantry Division was positioned around Abu Agheila, the 3rd Infantry Division was its backup, and the 6th Infantry Division in the southern tier of the second line of the defense.

In the ten years that passed between the 1956 Sinai Campaign and the Six Day War, the Egyptians invested a lot of effort into transforming the northwest of Sinai into a large and fortified military setup, organized to protect itself, on one hand, and, on the other, ready to serve as an attack base on Israel. The roads that existed before the 1956 War were all repaired, and new ones were built. In the area of the border with Israel, mainly along the road from Gaza through Rafah to El Arish, and from El Arish through Abu Agheila, the Egyptians established fortified structures that included defense points, fortified army bases, and an airport in El Arish. The Gaza Strip and the Rafah area were transformed during these years to a large defense point, dug into the sand, and equipped with armor, artillery, and a network of trenches for infantrymen.

Later, as a result of the Egyptian involvement in the War in Yemen, the Egyptian infantry developed into a light, though highly mobile force of tank killers—especially the paratroop units and the commando entities. The enlargement of the Egyptian Army brought upon a divisional setup, and there was a division based in Sinai on a regular basis. Between the years of 1965–67, the Egyptian Armor Corps obtained T-55 tanks, and the end of the war in Yemen enabled intensive development of the Armored Corps and a cadre of junior officers and NCOs. The Egyptian military was based on the Soviet model—hordes of infantry supported by lines of tanks—and Nasser's forces sported a massive armored punch. The armor element consisted of two main forces. The first, commanded by General Shazli, was a special armored force of T-54s and T-55s brought up to a staging area near El Quseima that was, when the green light was given, to slice into southern Israel at Mitzpe Ramon and then knife a wedge southeast toward Eilat. The second main Egyptian armored force in Sinai was the 4th Armored Division, considered the country's best, that was spread out on a defensive line from Bir Gifgafa to Bir Themada. Deployment of the Egyptian military force was in the Rafah-El Arish section.

That area of northern Sinai was the key to the entire peninsula. The Rafah scuttle and the Gaza Strip have always been a passageway to and from Israel. This area has water sources and is located on the edge of the desert on the way from Egypt to the north. This area was used as a base by every army ever to come from the south in order to conquer Israel. In the main road there were a class A road, the railroad tracks, and two crossroads that connected the shore road in Sinai with the central road Isma'iliya–Bir Gifgafa–Abu Agheila–Nitzana. Militarily speaking this was one of the most essential areas in Sinai. The Rafah scuttle is a direct geographical continuation of the Gaza Strip. It is shaped like a triangle, with the base in Rafah, and is about 15 kilometers, narrowing down to a few dozen meters in the area west to Sheik Zawid. In the north, south, and west of the scuttle are sand dunes, untraversable by vehicles and very difficult for tanks. On the other hand, the soil of the scuttle is firm, covered with a thin layer of sand, and has a few sand hills which are impossible to go around. The area is covered with greenery and is largely cultivated by the Bedouins. It has trees, castor-oil plants, and huts, making camouflage and the hiding of units possible and practical.

The Rafah–El Arish area was a divisional defense section under the command of the 7th Infantry Division. The Egyptian force consisted of six infantry brigades (including Palestinian brigades), and about 100 tanks in two formations: the front formation in the area of Rafah scuttle to Sheikh Zawid, and a deep formation in the area of the Jiradi–El Arish–Bir Lahfan. The Egyptian defense military positions were dug out and built according to the Soviet doctrine—continuous linear arrays, consisting of three long canals, one after the other. There were connecting canals between them, into which—in accordance with the land conditions—they combined positions for heavy machine guns, antitank canons, and tanks in well-hidden trenches. The front digging was protected with minefields that reached all the way to its end. The Rafah area was maintained by two infantry brigades, spread along the destroyed road of Nitzana–Rafah, starting at a point north of Rafah junction, reaching twelve kilometers south, blocking the entire zone. The arrangement was loaded with thousands of Egyptian soldiers, half-tracks and jeeps, antitank cannons, field artillery, and mobile anti-aircraft guns.

Israel's defensive plans for the south were always offensive in nature—should Egypt attack, IDF planners had argued, the lack of Israeli strategic depth would be such that only a miracle could save cities such as Ashqelon and Ashdod and the agricultural settlements between the Gaza Strip, Beersheba, and even Tel Aviv itself. OC Southern Command, Major-General Yeshayahu Gavish, had understood that a lightning strike against overwhelming odds was an edge that the IDF needed to maintain if any campaign against the massive Egyptian Army in Sinai were to end favorably to Israeli forces. Gavish's battle strategy consisted of the capture of the entire Sinai Peninsula, adhering to the following set of objectives and timetables:

Phase One (H-Hour + 12)

A. *Capture of Rafah and the coastal line, including the Jiradi defile.*
B. *Capture the positions around Abu Agheila and send a force of tanks into central Sinai.*
C. *Penetration of an armored force along the route of Wadi Hareidin and Bir Lahfan.*
D. *Capture of the Gaza Strip.*
E. *Silencing of enemy forces around Kuntila and El Quseima.*

Phase Two (H-Hour + 24)

A. *Capture of El Arish and the push south toward Bir Lahfan and Jebel Libni.*
B. *Capture of Abu Agheila.*
C. *Continuance of harassment operations against Egyptian forces in Kuntila and El Quseima.*

Phase Three (H-Hour + 36)

A. *Destruction of all Egyptian forces around Kuntila and El Quseima and the southern rear areas.*

B. *Destruction of all Egyptian forces in the Abu Agheila, Bir Lahfan, Jebel Libni pocket.*

Phase Four
A. *Destruction of all Egyptian forces in the rest of Sinai and the capture of the peninsula.*[12]

To achieve these objectives, Major-General Gavish possessed three Ugdot, or consolidated divisions, that would split the Sinai among them and destroy the mightiest military machine in the Arab world. One division, Ugdah 31, commanded by Major-General Avraham Yaffe, consisted mainly of reservist infantrymen and the 200th Armored Brigade, and was responsible for pushing along the Bir Lahfan defenses. An Ugdah under the command of Major-General Ariel "Arik" Sharon would move in on Abu Agheila and then slice into the central Sinai for the push to the canal. The major effort, however, would be along the coast, from Gaza to Khan Yunis to Rafah and then on to El Arish, capital of Sinai, and forward toward the canal. That daunting task fell to what became known as *Ugdat Ha'Plada*, the Steel Division, commanded by OC Armor Corps Major-General Yisrael "Talik" Tal. General Tal's division was based around one primary unit—Colonel Gonen's 7th Armored Brigade.[13]

Throughout the long nights of late May, until the first few days of June inched toward that fateful 7:45 A.M. commencement of hostilities, Colonel Gonen and his deputy, Lieutenant-Colonel Baruch "Pinko" Harel, reviewed maps and intelligence reports, as well as the latest intelligence files on Soviet armor and topographical studies. The officers had both been in Sinai before, 11 years earlier, and knew its treacherous sands could be a death trap for advancing armor—even more so if that armor was forced to roll along narrow roadways amid the urban sprawl of the Gaza Strip. Both men knew that the brigade had prepared for war every day since Gonen had assumed command of the force a year earlier, and both officers knew the capabilities of the men in their command. The brigade, those early June mornings, was a mixed force consisting of British-produced Centurions,

American-made M-48A2C Pattons, and M3 half-tracks. The 82nd Battalion, a force of Centurions, was commanded by Lieutenant-Colonel Gabi Amir and consisted of Major Shamai Kaplan's "H Company," Major Elyashiv Shimshi's "Z Company," Major Amir Yaffe's "K Company," Captain Aharon Tal's "T Company," and a mechanized infantry company commanded by First-Lieutenant Yossi Melamed.

The 79th Battalion, the force of Pattons, was commanded by Major Ehud El'ad and consisted of Captain Avigdor Kahalani's "B Company," Major Ben-Tzion Carmeli's "G Company," Captain Yom-Tov Tamir's "S Company," Captain Gilad Aviram's "T Company," and the mechanized infantry company commanded by Captain Moshe Kahane.

Gonen's mechanized force was the 9th Mechanized Infantry Battalion commanded by Lieutenant-Colonel Mordechai "Maksi" Avigad and consisted of half-tracks and jeeps used to mop up and support the tanks advance through enemy terrain. The 9th Mechanized Infantry Battalion's order of battle was made up of Captain Yossi Peled's "T Company," Captain Yoav Vespi's "C Company," Captain Uzi Lantzer's "L Company," and the 643rd Reconnaissance Company commanded by an up-and-coming star in the Armored Corps, Captain Orri Orr.

Major-General Tal's *Ugdat Ha'Plada* had one primary objective according to Southern Command's plan of attack— to carve its way through the coastal sector of the peninsula, along a wedge from Khan Yunis to the entrance to Rafah, capture Sheikh Zawid, Jiradi, and El Arish, and then link up with the 200th Armored Brigade from Major-General Yaffe's Ugdah and jointly launch an offensive toward Abu Agheila, Jebel Libni, and Bir Hasnha. Colonel Eitan's 35th Paratroop Brigade, with the assistance of the 46th Armored Battalion (a force of Pattons) would seize the abandoned United Nations facilities south of Rafah junction (as well as the southern portion of the junction). The 60th Armored Brigade, a mixed brigade of Shermans and AMX-13s commanded by Colonel Menachem "Man" Aviram, would secure much of the paratroop's movements and assist in the capture of El Arish.

The 7th Brigade was tasked with the Ugdah's most challenging assignment—Colonel Gonen's forces were to move toward Khan Yunis, seize the northern portion of Rafah junction, move to Sheikh Zawid, HQ for the Egyptian 7th Division, capture the Jiradi defile, and reach El Arish. Resistance was expected to be heavy, and Colonel Gonen, reviewing intelligence maps with the same religious conviction he once used to study the scriptures as a child in yeshiva, decided that the safest route of advance was on the same roads the Egyptian forces used to link their various bases and posts throughout Sinai. These roads would not be mined, thus eliminating a hindrance to sweeping armored movement, but they would be heavily defended. Although the Egyptians possessed several hundred artillery batteries stationed right along the planned Israeli attack route, Colonel Gonen believed that these guns would not prove a major obstacle. The zone of advance that the brigade's tanks would follow was smack in the center of major population centers and concentrated areas of Egyptian foot soldiers. In case Egyptian artillery *did* seriously challenge the Israeli onslaught, Gonen had "ordered" a special flight of Fouga close-air support gunships and French-built subsonic tank-killers to be ready to fly in and selectively and accurately eliminate any hard targets. The Fouga pilots, as brave and fly-by-the-seat-of-their-pants as could be found in the IAF, had trained to fly in their armored tubs barely above the treetops and to blast at any enemy targets found on the ground. These pilots were hardened and trained to fly against hails of antiaircraft artillery and small arms. They were cocky and confident and were told that once war erupts, they wouldn't see an Egyptian fighter in the skies. Most of the pilots didn't worry about MiGs or Sukhois—they wrote letters home and studied IFF charts determined not to mistake a Centurion for a T-55.

June 5, 1967, was one of those days anyone in uniform would never forget. A surreal atmosphere of calm and sunshine engulfed most of the IDF forward positions. Under advertisement posters for beer and tea *("Nesher beer is good for the tank!")*, the men of the 7th Armored Brigade readied their tanks and equipment for war. The forward staging area near the Egyptian frontier at the Gaza Strip was a piss-hole surrounded by vehicles and fear, recalled one brigade soldier, but war was inevitable and necessary. Morale was high.

For the commanders, morale was not a question—just the professional execution of their assignments. Keeping morale—and the mission—in the mind of Gonen was Talik's role, and it was a task he fulfilled with extraordinary skills.

"Now that the plans are all clear to you all, and the steps we need to take are clearly listed on these maps, I want to tell you a few additional words that when the battle begins, *nothing will go down as it's written down here on the schematic!*" Talik professed to the Ugdah's commanding officers, who were chain smoking cigarettes and drinking bottles of soda and orange juice. "The lines and routes will be completely different," Talik continued, "but this shouldn't strike anyone as odd because the battle never goes as scheduled according to lines and red marks on a map." After talking about various stages of morale and personal loyalty that both commander and soldier go through during the course of a battle, Talik ended his olive-drab pep talk with a rousing and sobering bit of reality. "This battle will be a struggle of life and death. Each one of you will move forward without thinking about the consequences. There will be no moving back, no stopping, just pushing ahead forward!"[14]

Colonel Gonen, visibly nervous and anxious, was reported to have called a meeting of his junior officers and NCOs and repeated General Tal's speech almost verbatim. For once, the veil of iron-willed discipline and bravado that he had displayed to his subordinates from day one as brigade commander was showing signs of collapse.

From where the 7th Brigade had assembled, along the Green Line and the United Nations demarcation lines at Nir Yitzhak, Khan Yunis was only six kilometers away, and Rafah junction only sixteen kilometers away from the first objective. Gonen's battle plan called for the 79th Battalion, along with a reconnaissance contingent, to break through the minefields in no-man's-land near Nir-Oz, and then follow the artillery road's path to Beni-Suheilla through Khan Yunis toward Rafah. The 82nd Battalion, the Centurions, would follow behind the 79th Battalion's advance, and then swing around to try and reach Rafah from the south. The reconnaissance force would follow the 82nd Battalion into battle and the 9th Battalion would remain behind as "backup." The second stage of the plan had the 82nd Battalion (minus two companies that would remain behind as a brigade cover force) moving along the Khan Yunis–Rafah road, while the 79th Battalion would capture Rafah. The 9th Battalion would move in from its base behind the demarcation line and seize the Egyptian fortifications at Umm-el-Kaleb, advance past the rail station at Rafah, and link up with the 79th Battalion. The last stage of Gonen's plan for the final 48 hours of fighting was to have the reconnaissance company lead the way toward the Jiradi defile.

Resistance, Gonen had estimated, would be heavy. The Egyptians had been priming for a fight against the Israelis, morale was at a fever's pitch, and Nasser had treated his military well. Khan Yunis and Rafah had to be breached—there were no two ways about it. Tal's aim was to break through this formidable "crust" as quickly as possible and at all costs, so that his armor, and that of Yiska Shadmi's Brigade moving down the Wadi Hareidin, could deploy clear of the defenses in time to beat off the Egyptian 4th Armored Division's expected counterattack in the open. The attack had to succeed at the first attempt. There would be no opportunity to regroup and mount a second attack after a battle of attrition, as at El Alamein. The obvious place to attack was the "Opening of Rafah," a narrowing tract of good going between the sand dunes on the coast and the sand sea to the south at the hinge between the Egyptian border and the Gaza Strip. The Egyptians had blocked the approach with barbed wire concertina, various obstacles, and thousands of antipersonnel and antitank mines. Tal knew that the Egyptians had not registered their camps and towns in the Gaza Strip and reasoned that they would not have mined the coast road and railway supplying them. His plan was to concentrate behind a low ridge along the cultivation four miles south of the Gaza Strip. The 7th Armored Brigade would break into Khan Yunis, brushing aside the Palestinians occupying the town, and, using the road and railway as axes of advance, would take Rafah junction from the north and drive on to El Arish. Raful's 35th Paratroop Brigade would cross the frontier south of the hinge to pinch out Rafah junction from the south. The 60th Armored Brigade would drive along a track through the sand sea five miles south of the coast road to link up with a drop by the 80th

Parachute Brigade on El Arish airfield. Tal had enough artillery to engage the Egyptian defenses with covering fire but not enough for counter-bombardment. To silence the Egyptian guns he would have to rely initially on the Fouga Magisters.

At 0845 on June 5, 1967, the historic words of *Sadin Adom*, "Red Sheet," were heard over several thousand sets of Motorola military radios throughout the Jewish State—war had been authorized and had begun. The IAF had already knocked out the Egyptian Air Force, turning the most daunting Arab air power into a smoldering hunk of twisted metal, and the Jordanian, Syrian, and Iraqi air forces would soon follow. Israeli frogmen had already infiltrated Alexandria harbor (and had already been captured), and the war was a remarkable one hour old when Colonel Gonen, standing upright in his tank, ordered the brigade to move forward into Sinai. The brigade's reconnaissance company led the way across the border in single file to minimize the mine threat and proceeded slowly, expecting heavy enemy resistance. At first, though, the Egyptians, surprised by the unfolding events, responded with nothing heavier than heavy machine gun and mortar fire. As the reconnaissance force "plowed" a way for the 79th Battalion into the outskirts of Khan Yunis, Gonen discovered that the town was occupied by a brigade instead of a battalion. Colonel Gonen decided on a two-pronged attack. The 79th Battalion was sent around to the right and half of the 82nd Battalion straight on. The other half remained in reserve under the brigade's deputy commander. The mechanized battalion had been sent to occupy Karem Shalom in case the Egyptians launched a counterattack on the hinge.

Egyptian fire from Beni-Suheilla and then into Khan Yunis escalated each meter the Israelis traversed. At first, the 7.62mm rounds began peppering the jeeps and half-tracks of Captain Yossi Elgamis's reconnaissance company; then, however, dedicated antitank fire was brought to bear on the advancing Israeli troopers. An M3 half-track, the company's artillery directional vehicle, was struck by a 100mm round and set ablaze. Less than an hour into "Red Sheet" and already there were fatalities. The sight of the smoldering vehicles and bodies was a sobering sight to the advancing tanks moving toward Khan Yunis, but this was no time to take stock of one's fears or anxieties. The reconnaissance unit's advance was the brigade's forward thrust, and Gonen had issued strict orders for Captain Elgamis to slice through the preliminary Egyptian defenses.

One antitank fortification was proving troublesome—a series of bunkers controlled by a tower—it was directing accurate antitank fire at the advancing column of jeeps, half-tracks, and Centurions. Captain Elgamis ordered the half-tracks to move forward, across a series of antitank ditches toward Beni-Suheilla and Khan Yunis; all the time, his men were unloading incessant bursts of .30 and .50 machine-gun fire from their vehicle mounted weapons. The battle became close-quartered. Palestinian volunteers, many carrying bazookas, emerged from the dust-filled chaos to fire their weapons at point-blank range; the Israelis responded by driving their vehicles directly atop the trenches and peppering them with machine-gun fire. A spray of dust and blood emerged from the death trap, but some Palestinian soldiers succeeded in launching their weapons at their intended targets. A round went through Captain Elgamis's head and he was killed instantly. Battalion doctors attempted open-heart massage on the reconnaissance unit commander, but it was all in vain. "G Company" commander, Major Ben-Tzion Carmeli, led a force of Pattons directly behind the reconnaissance operators, but two of his M-48A2Cs detonated antitank mines and they began to burn amid the close-quarter melee. Additional vehicles were taking fire, and several exploded upon impact. The march to Khan Yunis would not be uncontested.

Colonel Gonen, realizing Egyptian defenses were stronger than intelligence had reported, ordered a two-battalion attack on Khan Yunis—already throwing out Talik's map and battle plan. Lieutenant-Colonel Gabi Amir's 82nd Battalion would bypass Khan Yunis from the south, while the 79th Battalion moved in from the north. The task of seizing Khan Yunis fell with Lieutenant-Colonel Baruch "Pinko" Harel, authorized to keep two companies from the 79th as reserve along with 18 Centurions and, at his immediate authorization, the 9th Battalion was to move forward and stand at the ready.

At the entrance to Khan Yunis stood the Umm el-Kaleb fortifications—a series of bunkers and pits supported by the standard Soviet-style interlocking trenches. This time, however, Egyptian resistance was not as determined. The sight of the Centurions firing their 105mm guns at the pillboxes and bunkers caused a panic. Emplacements were abandoned, soldiers emerged with their hands up and white flags soon adorned sand-bagged positions. Lieutenant-Colonel Harel then ordered his vehicles to move toward the Khan Yunis railway station, located at the eastern approach to the town; once again, resistance was becoming a nonissue. With IAF jets flying overhead in an overwhelming show of ground support and the massive Centurions moving through the narrow streets, the Palestinian defenders of Khan Yunis wanted nothing to do with this fight. Scores of soldiers, wearing sloppy, light, sand-colored uniforms, raised their hands in surrender. With no infantry available (the 9th Battalion had yet to reach the city limits), Lieutenant-Colonel Harel was forced to do the unthinkable. He collected the guns from most of the surrendering Palestinians, said a hearty *Shuqran* (thank you), and told them to go on home. Many returned to the battlefield hours later with different weapons, others went home and locked their doors, grudgingly accepting their fate.

For the 82nd Battalion, however, moving to Rafah junction, the advance would not go uncontested. The Egyptians allowed the reconnaissance company, serving as vanguard for the battalion advance, to come within 100 yards of Rafah junction before ambushing it to reveal a second brigade where only a battalion had been expected. Gonen, again facing unexpected opposition, changed plans again and ordered another two-pronged attack, the Centurions along the road, the Pattons to the west of it. Lieutenant-Colonel Gabi Amir, left with little choice, split his battalion in half, sending two companies under his second-in-command, Major Eliezer Globus, along the edge of the dunes to the north to swing in from the west while he attacked frontally with the remainder of his forces. Gabi Amir was known throughout the brigade as a cautious and highly capable officer. Popular with his men, a sort of antidote to the autocratic style of Gonen, he instilled confidence through example and leadership through charisma—something Gonen's style lacked. According to one former officer in Gabi Amir's battalion, who still demanded anonymity nearly thirty years after the fact, "The men knew that Gonen was a smart and courageous officer, but they were terrified of him. Gabi was a smart and courageous officer, but the men in the battalion respected and *liked* him!"[15] Lieutenant-Colonel Amir would need all his resources. They were facing a numerically superior force and the confrontation was moving toward close ranks and close-quarter ranges. Not the type of fight for the faint of heart.

The Egyptians counterattacked against the main thrust of Amir's line of Centurions—an assault of 100mm firepower from the southwest with a T-54 tank battalion. It drove straight into the jaws of the Israeli pincer movement and was repulsed with the loss of nine tanks. With the defeat of their armor the Egyptian infantry entered the fray, but the foot soldiers, armed with little heavier than a few scattered bazookas, were no contest for the Pattons moving in from the south and the Centurions advancing due south past the rail lines. An Israeli estimate placed at least 100 Egyptian dead in the few minutes of man-versus-tank fighting.

Khan Yunis was now completely in the hands of the 7th Armored Brigade. Rafah junction lay ahead.

The battle for Khan Yunis and Beni-Suheilla involved two of the brigade's tank battalions in a fight that the brigade did not want against entrenched infantrymen supported by artillery and antitank ordnance. The fighting lasted several hours and was hampered by the difficult terrain, narrow built-up areas, and a communications difficulty that the Israelis were finding to be a disabling phenomenon—tank commanders relying too heavily on visual signals over radio synchronization. By noon, under a glaring Gaza sun, Gonen's command vehicles were close behind the Centurions of the 82nd Battalion and eager to mark off an obstacle that Gonen knew would be a bloody one to crack. The Egyptians, intelligence reported, had fortified the strategic crossroads and realized that its capture meant that the Israelis would possess a vital road link to the coastal lock of the peninsula.

Standing in their way was the Egyptian 16th Armored brigade and its complement of T-34 tanks.

The battle commenced at noon with the battalion's 643rd Reconnaissance Company leading the M-48A2Cs of the 79th Battalion into the fight. A probing force of two M-48A2Cs, three M-3s, and four jeeps slowly moved toward the junction when, 100 meters away from the crossroads, a murderous volley of antitank fire erupted all around them. The reconnaissance company commander, Captain Orri Orr, radioed to Gonen that the junction was *heavily* defended, but then a ricochet sliced through the captain's radio and communication between the unit and Gonen was disrupted.

The Egyptians had managed to set alight several M-3s and damage a few of the jeeps, but the Pattons had succeeded in scoring direct hits with their 90mm main armament guns, and destroyed two T-34s at a close range of 200 meters. Unable to withdraw and unable to use the banks of the road for maneuvering room (they were heavily mined), Captain Orr opted to take the hero's way out—destroy the Egyptian ambush at point-blank range. He rallied his men, organized the tanks, half-tracks, and jeeps, and ordered them to race at full speed directly into the center of the Egyptian fire. "I thought," recalled Orr nearly thirty years later, "that the easiest way to destroy the gauntlet was by getting inside it."[16] The battle looked like a wild scene from the Western Desert—the unit's jeeps raced along the roadway firing their mounted .30 caliber machine guns in mad bursts of fire. With all the Israeli vehicles firing in a mad and desperate attempt to reach the Egyptian trenches and purify them, several jeeps touched off antitank mines and exploded; several soldiers were flung out of their vehicles and seriously hurt. Egyptian infantrymen began lobbing mortar shells where the wounded lay.

Captain Orr was relentless in his command of the purification of the first line of Egyptian defenses at the junction; leading with sheer guts, he turned disaster into a victory. As the trenches were secured, Captain Orr ordered his survivors back onto the main roadway. His half-track touched off a mine and blew up; the wounded were placed on a weapons carrier, and Orr ordered his men to jump on board a Patton for the ride back to lines. Nine men had died, nine had been seriously wounded.

While Captain Orr battled the Egyptian trenches and pill-boxes at the entrance to the junction, Lieutenant-Colonel Harel, two companies of Centurions from the 82nd Battalion, and the brigade reconnaissance unit reached the Rafah water tower, approximately four kilometers from the bloodletting and were ordered in to back up the beleaguered *Sayeret*. Four Centurions entered the fray and they were met by murderous fire from nearly a dozen T-34s. The fourth tank, commanded by First-Lieutenant David Peletz, was struck dead center between the turret and the chassis and erupted into a fireball. Peletz, commanding the tank in the IDF manner of being upright in his turret, was flung from the tank and propelled to the ground; his overalls on fire, he suffered debilitating burns though he managed to rub out the flames by turning himself around in the surrounding sand. Severely wounded and in pain, Lieutenant Peletz returned to his tank to extricate his three crewmen. The loader, Avraham Ma'atok, was killed instantly, though the driver and gunner were still alive—albeit in critical condition. Under Egyptian cannon and machine-gun fire, Lieutenant Peletz managed to rescue his two surviving crewmen and pull them to safety from the burning tank. An M-3 from the battalion aid station picked them up and raced them back to the rear evacuation center, but the half-track was struck by a T-34 round and Lieutenant Peletz and his crew were killed.

By monitoring the brigade frequency and listening to the roar of gunfire and the cries of the wounded, Gonen realized that a pitched battle had developed, one capable of sidelining the brigade's advance, and that his presence was desperately required closer to the fighting. His M-3 and Centurion moved into the conflagration, slowly advancing through a gauntlet of minefields and artillery rounds. The 16th Armored Brigade had prepared its defenses well—T-34s were in fortified pits with a clear field of fire before them; antitank guns littered a series of emplacements; and infantry formations, with heavy machine guns, were poised and ready to defeat any advance by mechanized units. The most daunting challenge of the set-up was the Egyptian talent for camouflage. The Egyptians had learned from the first rounds fired in the war that when five antitank guns are fired simultaneously, not only did they provide a severe obstacle of fire and destruction to advancing enemy armor, but the large blast virtually made it impossible for Israeli crews to point-point an emplacement's exact location.

This time, even in disagreement with Talik's promise, the attack went as planned and as briefed on the attack maps. Standing atop an M-3, face already blackened by the soot and grime of war, Gonen ordered his tanks to group and attack. The 79th Battalion attacked from the north and in their first fusillade of 105mm fire managed to destroy T-34s somewhat exposed to the west. "Good shooting," a pleased brigade commander was reported to have complimented the crews their sniping skills. "Hits at one thousand meters are always good ones."[17] The Pattons, at this time, were moving in from the south, also scoring considerable success against the entrenched Egyptian defenses. It was clear from the onset of the battle, especially for Major Haim Erez, deputy commander of Major Ehud El'ad's 79th Battalion, leading the Patton advance, that the Egyptians were not going to deploy their armor inventively and engage the Israelis in a mobile counterattack. Instead, it was more evident that they were adhering to the Soviet doctrine of defensive fortification spread out over a fixed plain. The Pattons moved forward in a three-pronged attack—one force under the command of Major El'ad, one force under the command of Major Erez, and the other force, of Centurions, under the command of Major Shamai Kaplan. The M-48A2Cs moved in from the north while Gonen's task force of Centurions battled the Egyptians from the south.

Major Kaplan sliced through the junction and "set afire" two T-34s. The fire that the 105mm rounds slicing through the T-34's armor skin caused reached a circumference of 30 feet around and 90 feet high. The high-rise balls of flames became an artillery landmark and soon IDF batteries—and flights of Fougas—used it as an enveloping guide by which they dedicated their batteries and air-to-ground ordnance. With the Pattons moving in from the north and the Centurions coming around from the south, Gonen had, in essence, squeezed the Egyptian defensive pocket of any chance it had to extricate itself and regroup—it was now faced with the dilemma of a fight for its life or cut its losses and run. The Egyptians stood and fought, but they were beaten. The 16th Infantry Brigade was obliterated by the pincer movement of Israeli armor and their supporting sweepers of mechanized infantrymen; the T-34s of the brigade's armor battalion, too, had been badly beaten. Their defeat opened the path for Tal's division to move toward Sheikh Zawid, the staging area for the mighty Egyptian 7th Armored Division and its forces of T-54 and T-55 tanks.

The battle for the junction had been a costly one for the brigade, however, and the historical impact of the Israeli sweeping victory in the conflict was lost in the sheer horror of actual combat. With the war less than six hours old, the brigade had, in one major engagement, 26 dead and 20 seriously wounded. Nine Centurions had been destroyed in the fighting, along with five M-48A2Cs.[18]

With the northern portion of Rafah junction in IDF hands, Gonen moved ahead with the 79th and 82nd Battalion—committing his reserve to two Centurion companies and the reconnaissance company under his deputy commander westward to El Arish. A company of Pattons under the command of 79th Battalion commander El'ad moved past Sheikh Zawid in the sandy shoulders of the roadway, while two kilometers behind it, the 82nd Battalion followed along the rail line toward El Arish. The Egyptians were not allowing the brigade to advance without putting up a fight, but the "sniping" doctrine that Tal had set forth in 1965 was proving a lifesaver. Egyptian tank gunners were used to firing their 85mm guns from ranges starting at 1,000 meters—a habit that suited the Patton and Centurion gunners just fine. By the time the Egyptian tank commander was ordering his men to stand by, a 105mm or 90mm round fired by an Israeli gunner turned the Soviet-built tank into a flaming coffin. A force of tanks under the command of 82nd Battalion commander Lieutenant-Colonel Gabi Amir, moving west, destroyed nine T-34s before the Egyptians had even a chance to deploy for battle.

By 1400 hours, six hours into the war, Captain Aharon Tal's company was 40 kilometers behind the Green Line, the old frontier separating Egypt and Israel, and only 20 kilometers east of El Arish. Captain Tal's force of Centurions came across the tattered remnants of an Egyptian T-34 unit that, only a few minutes earlier, had been the target of a Fouga strike. The battle was lopsided and one-sided. The Centurions, in a span of less than three minutes, destroyed ten Egyptian T-34s. The sight was so unnerving to Egyptian infantrymen and crew members that they began removing their undershirts and light sand shirts, waving them high over their heads atop their rifles and submachine guns, and surrendering. It was a humbling sight and reinforced the fragility of the human element of the battle. Observing the collapse of an Egyptian line of defense, Gonen leapt off his tank, commandeered a jeep, and raced to each one of his units, instructing them not to harm Egyptian soldiers raising their hands in surrender.

At 1405 hours, when the first Egyptians began surrendering en masse, six hours had passed since the brigade crossed the frontier into Egypt. Already there were 43 dead and 41 wounded in the brigade's ranks, and 18 tanks had been destroyed. The battle for the Rafah junction ended— officially—at 1830 hours. The battle and the push for El Arish succeeded in cutting off Gaza and its surroundings to the Egyptian 7th Division and placed the IDF in a full sweeping move to take the ultrastrategic northwestern coastal area of the peninsula. At the Jiradi defile, where the road winds down a short steep sand dune into a wadi, the Egyptian battalion group was asleep and the Centurions drove on to El Arish without casualties. The reconnaissance company, following in its wake, was not so lucky. It lost two more vehicles and was forced to remain on the near bank. At El Arish the Centurions met the rest of the Egyptian reserve brigade, knocked out three T-34s, and retired into a palm grove to await the arrival of reinforcements.

Colonel Gonen went on the brigade radio frequency and announced the next course of events for the end of the 7th: "Until now everything has been okay ... We are continuing to the Jiradi defile. Eighty-second Battalion will move in the rear, the Seventy-ninth along the left flank, and the reconnaissance company will lead the way."[19]

Colonel Gonen was about to continue his address when

his deputy communications officer tugged at his perspiration-soaked olive fatigue blouse and said that Talik wanted a word with him. Gonen raised Tal on the radio and learned that Colonel Rafel "Raful" Eitan's 35th Paratroop Brigade was in trouble and in need of help. At 1405 hours Raful radioed Tal with a startling claim, "We got stuck against a large concentration of enemy forces. We are fighting tooth and nail, and we need help."[20] Raful left the microphone open, holding its transmitting button down with one hand and firing his Uzi 9mm submachine gun with the other. Throughout the three-minute transmission, in which the sounds of gunfire and explosions was a daunting reminder to Tal, Raful's voice remained steady and cold as ice. Major-General Tal thought Raful to be one of the most courageous officers he had ever known; there was no one better on a dark night behind enemy lines. He wouldn't ask for assistance unless it was absolutely necessary, and it was. Tal ordered Gonen to extricate the paratroopers from the gauntlet of fire; the paratroopers had stumbled across a reinforced formation of Egyptian infantrymen supported by several JSIII heavy tanks. Raful and company could take care of the infantrymen, but the JSIII was a hulking heavily armored beast from the Second World War adorned with inches of steel protection—400mm worth! "Roger," Gonen replied to Tal's order. He ordered the 82nd Battalion to remain with him and return to Rafah to help out the paratroopers.[21]

Aiding the paratroopers delayed Tal's relentless advance. Tal halted the advance on El Arish temporarily to divert the 82nd Battalion, as well as the 9th Battalion, which was still holding the hinge at Kerem Shalom, and the 60th Armored Brigade's 141st Mechanized Infantry Battalion from the southern axis. During the time it took to extricate these units the Fouga Magisters had dealt with the JSIIIs and Eitan had fought his way north to Rafah junction. The diverted units were returned to their brigades, except for Gonen's mechanized battalion, which was set to work with a company of Pattons to clear the Egyptian brigade north of Rafah junction while the 35th Paratroop Brigade mopped up the area to the south. The 60th Armored Brigade was making slow progress through the soft sand to the south when news arrived that the parachute brigade he was to relieve at El Arish airfield had been diverted to Jerusalem. Jordan had entered the war and was shelling the entire Jewish half of Jerusalem, as well as launching 155mm artillery barrages against the suburbs of Tel Aviv.

War with Jordan became a news flash of trepidation to most of the conscripts in the brigade. Many came from the hub of Israel's population, Jerusalem and the coastal plain, and the entire region was threatened now by undoubtedly the most professional military in the Middle East. The soldiers in the brigade were no longer fighting alone, as soldiers, a war against an enemy 1,000 meters away in the desert abyss. It was likely that their mothers were hunkered down in air-raid shelters, their fathers were probably in emergency reservist formations, and their homes were blacked out expecting artillery strikes. The home front suddenly mattered—it suddenly became as important as what was happening through the crosshairs of their 105mm and 90mm main guns. There was a danger that the men could become sidetracked. Momentum was as important to a unit's progression as the tools in its arsenal, and both Gonen and Talik did not want to lessen the progression of the advance.

Realizing that Raful was still under a fierce Egyptian onslaught, Gonen took the majority of the 79th Battalion with him *back* to Rafah, while he sent his second-in-command, "Pinko," on to the Jiradi defile with the Centurions of Gabi Amir's 82nd Battalion. The "Jiradi," as the narrow pass was known, was an ultraimportant strategic approach to the capital of the peninsula, El Arish, and any formation with vehicles heading toward El Arish had to navigate its precarious thirteen-kilometer-long route into the town. The Egyptians understood the value of the Jiradi defile and had split the pass into three separate sectors, each one divided into a fortified series of trenches, pillboxes, and antitank gun emplacements. The Trenches were separated from one another at two-kilometer intervals, with the last one, considered the strongest, positioned six kilometers in front of El Arish. The entire pass was defended by hundreds of machine-gun and antitank cannon emplacements, supported by two tank battalions and a condensed infantry brigade. It was considered one of two true obstacles in defeating Egypt—the other was the Suez Canal.

At 1630 hours, Raful radioed, "Rafah is in our hands," to a grateful and relieved Major-General Tal; Gonen's help had been crucial.[22] At that same time, Lieutenant-Colonel "Pinko" Harel and his task force of seventeen Centurions and two Pattons reached the entrance of the Jiradi defile. Pinko was under very strict orders not to engage in a serious head-on confrontation—if resistance was light, he was to proceed as ordered to El Arish; if resistance was strong, he was to pull back, regroup, and await reinforcements. Major Shamai Kaplan, the commander of the battalion's "H Company," led the entry. Major Kaplan had been serious wounded in the day's fighting, yet remained inside his Centurion even though both his hands were bandaged, and he reported feeling weak as a result of losing so much blood. "H Company," along with Pinko's command group of M–3 half-tracks, entered the pass along with two Pattons riding shotgun for the reconnaissance team.

As the task force moved in, slowly and cautiously, Pinko ordered that the tanks fire high-explosive and antipersonnel rounds into the trenches that surround the heavily mined shoulders of the roadway. Scanning the menacing narrow pass, Pinko was shocked at what he saw: rows of dug-in Egyptian T-55s on both sides of the roadway with their guns pointed at the oncoming Israeli column; heavily camouflaged antitank gun emplacements covered by camouflage netting; heavy mortar positions, fixed on pinpoints on the roadway, nestled in the surrounding sand dunes; and heavy machine gun emplacements and rifle pits interlocked by concrete-lined trenches and communications lines.

The Egyptians were under strict orders *not* to fire at the first echelon of armor that the Israelis would throw at them. Indeed, the first row of Centurions under Kaplan's and Pinko's command was allowed to enter the pass unmolested by Egyptian fire even if the Israeli tanks entered the defile with guns ablaze. The Egyptians hid in their camouflaged positions, and the Israelis believed that the Jiradi had been abandoned—as a result, the T-54/55s that were dug in were not destroyed by the advancing Centurions since they were considered "abandoned trophies of war."[23]

When the vanguard of "H Company" Centurions reached the end of the defile, the Egyptians targeted the battalion's reconnaissance team that was sandwiched in the middle of the advance. The volley of fire was murderous and incessant. The first antitank round struck one of the two Pattons safeguarding the reconnaissance team's jeeps and half-tracks. The second round slammed straight through a reconnaissance jeep, slicing it in a cascade of metal fragments, fire, and obliterated flesh and blood. The third Egyptian round also hit its target dead center—it was the reconnaissance unit's ammunition and command M-3 half-track, and it detonated in a mushrooming fireball. With the reconnaissance team decimated, the Egyptian gunners turned their flaming barrels on the column of Centurions in Captain Aharon Tal's company. One antitank round penetrated the turret of Captain Tal's tank, killing the loader, while another round hit the connection between the turret and the chassis. The Centurion began to burn like a Roman candle and the .50 caliber ammunition for the commander's turret-mounted machine gun was set alight and detonated, wounding Tal in his hands and back. Miraculously, Captain Tal managed to extricate his surviving crew members while continuing to use hand signals and anguished cries of command to organize his remaining tanks in a retreat away from the crossfire.

The battle for the Jiradi had begun and the Egyptians had the upper hand. A portion of the 82nd Battalion had gone through the pass and was on the outskirts of El Arish, the reconnaissance team lay smoldering in the center of the defile, and the remainder of the battalion was perched at the Jiradi's entrance.

At 1545 hours, General Tal's Divisional Chief of Staff Colonel Herzl Shapir, himself a commander of the 7th Armored Brigade (from 1963 to 1964) ordered Gonen out of Rafah and back to the brigade. Major-General Tal established his headquarters at Rafah junction and ordered Gonen to resume the advance on El Arish with the 79th Battalion, leaving the two remaining Centurion companies in divisional reserve. Joining the reconnaissance company at the Jiradi defile, Gonen found a well-prepared position. The wadi was mined and covered by machine guns, antitank guns, and tanks. The palm grove to the north was too thick for armor and the ground to the south was soft sand on open ground dangerously exposed to enemy artillery spotters.

When the 79th Battalion arrived at the defile at 1700 hours, there was a tremendous sense of urgency to crack this nut—and now! The portion of Lieutenant-Colonel Harel's task force and the 82nd Battalion that had made it through the pass was cut off and isolated. They had been fighting nonstop for nearly 12 hours and were running desperately low on fuel and ammunition. Should the Egyptians in El Arish mount any serious counterattack, Pinko's armor could do little else than try and run the Egyptians over. Tal ordered Gonen to go into the Jiradi again, but gave emphatic instructions that should the 79th Battalion face stiff resistance, he was to withdraw, regroup, and mount a coordinated nighttime attack with the 60th Armored Brigade. The 60th Armored Brigade was to take the defile from the south, but the sand was too soft and the attempt had to be abandoned.

Standing atop his M-3, a concerned Gonen ordered Major Ehud El'ad to personally lead a frontal attack straight down the road and a flank attack over the open sand to the south. The frontal attack was repulsed and the flank attack bogged down in soft sand; many of the M-48A2Cs, already having traversed an enormous stretch of territory on difficult terrain, were encountering mechanical difficulties exacerbated by the fine and damaging sands. Under heavy Egyptian artillery and antitank fire, Gonen leapt from his vehicle, without so much as wearing his helmet and, impervious to the flying shrapnel around him, reviewed the plan of attack with battalion commander El'ad. It was decided that the battalion would move to the left of the pass and come around and attack from the south. The unit chosen for this breakthrough was Captain Avigdor Kahalani's "B Company." As one of the brigade's finest and most capable officers, both Gonen and El'ad had confidence that if anyone in the 7th could pull it off, it was Kahalani.

"All stations Kahalani, this *is* Kahalani. Forward to El Arish!"[24] Kahalani's battlecry over the battalion network inspired the needed confidence in the tired and now frightened soldiers to give it a little extra. Egyptian fire by now was murderous. Just as Gonen had hoped not to lose the precious commodity of momentum, now the Egyptian defenders had gained the luxury of focus and dead-on fire. Shells, mortar rounds, and tank fire were landing all around, kicking up a white cloud of sand and smoke around Kahalani's charge. Visibility was virtually nonexistent. Approximately 150 meters from the roadway, en route to his semipincer of the first line of defense, Kahalani ordered his tank to stop so that he could gauge the enemy targets and concentrate on the dug-in armor and antitank gun pits. Kahalani's Patton never had a chance to fire. An Egyptian antitank round cut through the company commander's tank and set it afire. He managed to extricate himself from the smoldering chariot of steel and, although badly burned, managed to reach his battalion commander's tank on the move and report the events of a few moments ago. "Kahalani, what's happening?" an inquisitive El'ad asked his company commander seeing that his friend was in terrible pain and his clothes still smoldering. Barely able to move and suffering the horror of having one's flesh roast, Kahalani stared at the turret cupola and replied, "The fire was stronger than me!"[25]

Kahalani was evacuated on a jeep and brought back to Israel for emergency life-saving care and well over a dozen operations.

By this time, the Pattons of the 79th were locked in a life-and-death struggle with the Egyptian gauntlet in the Jiradi defile. There were accounts of incredible courage recorded during this fierce battle, and of incredible sacrifice. One Patton, commanded by Sergeant Dov Yam, had his arm blown off when an Egyptian antitank round ricocheted off the turret where he was standing upright, the shrapnel slicing off his limb. With his tank on fire, Sergeant Yam, bleeding profusely, organized the evacuation of his crew. As he awaited transport to the battalion aid station, he came across Colonel Gonen, grabbed his brigade commander, and said, "I hope I did all that I could have done?"[26]

Perhaps no soldier in the battalion did more than its commander, Major El'ad. Fighting ferociously, with one hand on his microphone and the other on the trigger housing of his .50 caliber machine gun, he led his tank through a zigzagging maze of possible assault routes. Searching for targets and looking for that one weakness in the Egyptian defenses, El'ad was relentless in his command through the impassable enemy fire. Under hails of Egyptian fire, he led from an exposed turret making sure that his tanks and men were safely behind him. An Egyptian shell landed directly atop the turret of El'ad's tank, and the 79th Battalion commander was killed instantly. El'ad's second-in-command, Major Haim Erez, himself a most capable and respected armor officer, assumed command of the battalion. From a commander's point of view, Major Erez could not have taken over at a more challenging time: the battalion commander was dead, and two company commanders seriously wounded, as were the battalion operations. Men were battered, bleeding, and frightened, and their equipment was trapped in the Jiradi's deceptively soft and lethal sand traps.

There was, however, a force that Gonen had yet to deploy. "G Company," a force of Pattons from the 46th Armored Battalion, the unit that had functioned as Colonel "Raful" Eitan's 35th Paratroop Brigade armored fist and reserve. First-Lieutenant Shalom Angel joined the 79th Battalion in the fight for the pass at this critical juncture. Before Major Erez was able to lead a cohesive charge away from the sand trap and make it back to the roadway, he left 18 Pattons behind. It was a tremendous blow for the battalion and for the brigade. In terms of manpower and equipment, the 7th Brigade had entered a critical phase of the war.

As the only reserve force left unmarked by the fighting, First-Lieutenant Angel was determined to make a mark on the desperate fighting for the Jiradi defile. With his tanks now in the vanguard and the survivors of the 79th Battalion behind him, First-Lieutenant Angel gunned up his tank's 810 horses and raced into the pass at the M-48's top-speed of forty-five kilometers per hour. It was 1830 hours. The company entered the pass with its 90mm cannon and .50 caliber machine guns ablaze, with each tank keeping a significant distance one from the other. This way, if the Egyptian fire was too thick, the tanks wouldn't get bottlenecked. Although this was tactically sound, it forced each tank approaching the lines of Egyptian defenses to endure a few minutes of what survivors have categorized as nothing less than hell. One tank speeding on a roadway became the target of hundreds of weapons ranging from heavy caliber anti-tank cannons to infantrymen firing their Port Said 9mm submachine guns at the tank commanders. Because the Egyptians were entrenched and dug-in, every Patton that passed through made it toward El Arish to link up with Lieutenant-Colonel Harel and the 82nd Battalion's Centurions. It was a desperate gamble, but a necessary one. It was costly. From the eighteen tanks in First-Lieutenant Angel's company, only seven got through.

The last Patton that came through reached the forward 7th Brigade staging area at the entrance to El Arish at 1930 hours. The situation was serious—critical, in fact. It was getting dark and Tal's division was spread over a still-contested battleground 30 miles in length; virtually one-and-a-half tank battalions of the 7th Brigade were at El Arish, while Gonen and the remains of the reconnaissance company were on the east bank of the Jiradi. The brigade's two remaining Centurion companies were in divisional reserve and the mechanized battalion group was clearing the area north of Rafah. The 35th Paratroop Brigade was still clearing the area south of Rafah junction and the 60th Armored Brigade was stuck in the sand to the south. Both Tal and Gonen were becoming incredibly anxious. Should the Egyptian 4th Armored Division arrive in time for a counterattack the next morning, the push toward El Arish and the canal could turn into nothing more than a desperate holding action over meaningless real estate already paid for in blood.

Tal ordered the 60th Armored Brigade to make one more effort to reach the Jiradi but by 1930 his tanks were stuck in the sand, were short of fuel, and had lost touch with their infantry in the dark. This attempt was also abandoned.

Scanning through his field glasses, optical points that were virtually glued to his eyes, Gonen panned the Jiradi gauntlet and saw dug-in positions that would be hard to hit from the air but harder still to hit from the ground An amber light of dusk had engulfed the sands of Sinai and the eeriness of nighttime operations in the desert were illuminated by the even more eerie glow of tanks and men burning in the un-contested no-man's-land of the battlefield.

Still, fuel and ammunition had to be supplied to the two battalions at the entrance to El Arish and Gonen, and the brigade's remaining echelons tried once again to enter the pass. Egyptian fire, as always, was dead-on in its impact on the first vehicles to dare enter the defile's treacherous and narrow opening. In a perfect world, Gonen knew, he could simply order the vehicles that had made it through to out-flank the Jiradi and attack it from both sides, but tanks that were running on fumes and left with only three or four rounds of ordnance could not be expected to perform mira-cles. Gonen's only remaining option was to use the 9th Mechanized Infantry Battalion, which was still on divisional assignment clearing through the alleyways of Rafah, to mount an infantry assault on the Jiradi at night. The third time the charm, Gonen thought. He had to be right. Tal agreed. The divisional attack had lost momentum; the Ug-dah's only uncommitted reserves were the two Centurion companies. A lesser man might have given up or at least waited for daylight, but the whole campaign depended on a rapid breakthrough and Tal was as determined as ever to maintain the aim. He decided to take a risk at Rafah junc-tion where Gonen's mechanized battalion and a Patton com-pany were clearing the area to secure it for the Divisional Administrative Area. He sent the battalion group to Gonen and added a Centurion company to it.

The problem that Tal faced was how to rally the mecha-nized battalion group, spread over seven square kilometers, in the dark. Fortunately its commanding officer was another remarkable man. Lieutenant-Colonel Mordechai "Maksi" Avigad was quiet and unassuming but resourceful and enter-prising. He radioed his company commanders, telling them to return to their half-tracks and jeeps and drive to the main road. Motoring along the road he picked up each company in turn and led the complete unit to Tal at Rafah junction. Although not one used to displaying emotion openly, espe-cially in the field, Tal could not contain himself and the delighted general kissed the commanding officer on both cheeks![27] Every artillery piece on the division's order of bat-tle was placed at the commanding officer's disposal, includ-ing a whole store of flares and projectors. The Centurion company was sent on ahead to join Gonen at the Jiradi who then deployed it to gain a foothold in the defile and prevent the Egyptians from moving reinforcements from one side of the road to the other.

Pinko, meanwhile, had the awesome task of preparing the two battalions (remaining shreds of battalions) in a defensive holding pattern until they could be relieved and resupplied. Not only did he have to spread out his small and damaged force all around El Arish and its ultrastrategic roadways leading toward the canal and the main staging area for several Egyptian divisions, but he also had to worry about a counterattack from the rear, from the Jiradi. Each tank was ordered to report its situation concerning fuel left, ammunition remaining, and the medical condition of its crews. Virtually every tank in Pinko's task force had been damaged in one way or another during the day's fighting—especially the Pattons that survived the charge through the Jiradi. Many of the crewmen had been badly hurt and had loosely bandaged gunshot, shrapnel, and burn wounds that required urgent medical attention at a field hospital. Now, this motley assembled force had a task of not only preventing the Egyptian garrison at El Arish from breaking out, but also preventing any concentrated counterattack.

Communications, or lack thereof, was a major obstacle for Gonen. Tal's operations officer and Gorodish's brother, Major Yoel Gonen, worked feverishly to connect all the units in the field with the divisional command post, but it was an impossible mission to accomplish. Units were cut off, antennas blown off their radios and vehicles, and units were commanded by lieutenants and sergeants because the majors and captains that once led these companies and platoons were dead or wounded. Colonel Gonen, for example, did not know that much of the 79th Battalion had, indeed, made it through the Jiradi and had linked up with the 82nd Battalion near El Arish. Gonen, in fact, still did not know that Major El'ad had been killed in action.

To reinforce the chances for the night assault, Tal ordered the 60th Armored Brigade to move in from the south and attempt, at night, to slice a strategic wedge inside the Jiradi and hammer its defenses. The 60th Brigade commander, Colonel Menachem "Man" Aviram, sent in his 141st Mechanized Infantry Battalion and the 19th Armored Battalion—a force of French-built AMX-13 light tanks—but the assault bogged down, once again in the soft and unflinching sands. It was now left to the 9th Battalion to make or break the situation. It was 2100 hours. The brigade had been fighting nonstop for nearly 13 hours and the day's final and most important battle was about to be fought. It was time for the 9th Battalion to show what it was made of as the division looked on anxiously. Two battalions of the 7th Brigade were cut off behind enemy lines; the 35th Paratroop Brigade had just completed its 12 hours of hell and bloodshed in Rafah and its surroundings and needed at least an additional 12 hours to regroup before it could be dispatched to the Jiradi; and the 60th Brigade was stuck in the sand and completely out of gas and ammunition.

When the 9th Battalion raced from its mopping-up operations around Rafah to the Jiradi defile, it passed through a roadway littered with destroyed Egyptian tanks (the victims of Fouga assaults and Israeli tank gunners sniping skills), destroyed Iraeli tanks, columns of Egyptian POWs, and hundreds of Israeli walking wounded. It was absolute chaos as only the State of Israel going to war could be. Some reservists joining their units at the last moment opted to bring their own civilian vehicles to the front instead of relying on more conventional transports, and the roadway was one giant traffic jam of military vehicles, tanks, ambulances, and other miscellaneous wheeled contraptions that, only weeks earlier, had been used by Israeli men to take their families to the park on picnics. Military Police units—soldier cops that should have been directing traffic—were themselves swamped with the enormous challenge of processing and securing the hordes of Egyptian military personnel surrendering and the Palestinians in Rafah and Gaza that now came under Israeli control.

The chaos on the roadway was so intense that it took Lieutenant-Colonel Avigad's battalion nearly three hours to reach the entrance of the Jiradi. Gonen ordered a company of infantrymen to enter the pass on the roadway, and to then leap off their half-tracks to engage the Egyptians in their lines at close-quarter range. "Let's show the Egyptians that the Jiradi doesn't only belong to them, but it's ours, as well," Gonen told the mechanized troops in a pep talk before they headed into the pass.[28] The troops were determined not to let Gonen down.

Before ordering the 9th Battalion inside the pass, Gonen assembled the remaining tanks in his command: a Patton company and several Centurions. At Jiradi Station, at a small shack that was the only landmark recognizable in the dark, he halted the battalion, placing the Pattons and one mechanized company as a roadblock facing west. The tanks, set up with cover of surrounding hills, began to engage the Egyptians in a long-range artillery duel. This was ample cover for the mechanized infantry to enter the fray. Batteries of fixed artillery illuminated the skies with flares, and the men of the battalions leapt off their World War II–era half-tracks and engaged the Egyptians in the close-quarter hell of trench warfare. The Egyptians, having scored considerable success at long range with their heavy guns, now found themselves faced with having to use their AK-47 and SKS 7.62mm assault rifles, and having to fight with their fists and guile. The compact Israeli-produced Uzi 9mm submachine guns that the infantrymen carried proved ideal for the narrow confines of the bunkers and trenches. The bloodletting was absolute, and of enormous magnitude. Trenches already filled with empty shelling casings and bullet cartridges now filled with blood and the dead. Infantrymen from the 9th Battalion swarmed the dug-in tank positions, and with the toss of a fragmentation grenade, destroyed vehicles that only hours earlier had turned a good many Centurions and Pattons into flaming landmarks on a road to nowhere. Unlike the previous attempts to cross the Jiradi, Gonen was not content with simply permitting his units to race through the pass and continue onward. This time, at least, he was adamant about clearing the 13 kilometers of trenches and bunkers of its garrison. The 9th Battalion remained in Jiradi— not leaving until the last of the Egyptian defenders had been killed or captured. Contrary to Lieutenant-Colonel Harel's initial thought of taking the Egyptian equipment back to Israel as a trophy, very few pieces of Egyptian equipment ever made it out of the pass in one piece.

The final battle for the Jiradi defile lasted all of four hours—four hours of incessant fighting. As the battalion was busy mopping up the defile's network of defenses, Gonen led his trucks, half-tracks, and jeeps through the pass. In an emotional scene, one mixed with exhaustion and relief, Gonen was reunited with Pinko and Lieutenant-Colonel Gabi Amir. Momentum was the key, and Gonen ordered the brigade's newfound fuel and ammunition supply as the basis for a new push. Moments after the battalion and brigade officers shook hands at the entrance to El Arish, the brigade was once again on the move. Gonen ordered El Arish airport seized and it was taken with little opposition. The airport, mainly used by Egyptian generals and staff officers was situated nine kilometers south of the city, on the El Arish–Bir Lahfan roadway. Major Haim Erez led the Patton charge, and he encountered several Egyptian T-55s and batteries of antiaircraft guns that were now pointing their 40mm barrels at a ninety degree angle toward the advancing Israeli armor. At 0600 hours, Erez radioed Gonen that the airport was in Israeli hands.

Major-General Tal reached El Arish shortly after the city's capture. Gonen's face illustrated the anguish and exhaustion of a man who had led a brigade through the channels of destruction and emerged with the majority of his troops and vehicles intact and more determined than ever to reach their ultimate objectives. His eyes were puffy and red, his cheeks and chin engulfed by stubble, and his entire body covered in the grime of dust, smoke, and oil. Upon reaching the city, Tal grabbed Gonen by the shoulder, paused, and said, "It was a heroic battle. In the history of armored warfare there are very few examples as striking as yours [the brigade's]!"[29] There was still much fighting ahead, however.

The next morning, the 7th Armored Brigade concentrated at El Arish, where it turned south to fight its way through the last Egyptian defenses at Bir Lahfan. The position was fortified in depth and the approaches were constricted by a wadi and sand dunes. When the brigade attacked this time the tank crews made use of their long-range marksmanship and such maneuvering as the ground permitted. It took the whole morning of June 6 to chip away the position, but by midday the brigade had broken through to link up with Colonel Yiska Shadmi's 200th Armored Brigade (from Major-General Yaffe's division) moving down the Wadi Hareidin to cut the El Arish–Jebel Libni road south of Bir Lahfan. Together, the two brigades defeated a counterattack by elements of the Egyptian 4th Armored Brigade. The "advance at all cost" phase was over. Tal and Gonen had achieved their objectives and the ever-elusive commodity of momentum.

Tal had achieved his aim by sheer perseverance—one brigade had become hopelessly bogged down in the soft sand on the southern flank; the planned parachute drop at El Arish was canceled; a second brigade, with insufficient time to convert paratroops to mechanized infantrymen and train with tanks, had fought resolutely but had been hard-pressed to clear the area south of Rafah junction; and the third brigade had driven through a defended town, cleared the area north of the junction and pushed some tanks through to El Arish. The Egyptian defenses had turned out to be far stronger than anticipated. Twice the Egyptians had cut the axis at the Jiradi defile. With single-minded determination more tanks had been sent through to El Arish, despite the risks, and a desperate operation to clear the defile had succeeded in the dark. The brigade had concentrated at El Arish for a further breakthrough battle at Bir Lahfan. When the last defenses of the frontier "crust" had been breached the brigade took part in the repulse of the Egyptian armored reserve. Mistakes there were plenty, especially in all arms cooperation, but as an example of the successful and determined pursuit of an aim, Tal's leadership and the 7th Armored Brigade's performance have few equals.

Over the course of the next three days, the 7th Brigade joined the other forces of Tal's Steel Division in the race toward the Suez Canal. On Wednesday, June 7, the 7th Armored Brigade engaged a massive Egyptian armor presence at El Hama and Bir El Hama, obliterating dozens of Egyptian T-34s, SU-100s, and T-54/55s. Battling the Egyptians in the open desert proved just how capable the tank gunnery skills of the Centurion and Patton crews were. At ranges of 1,500 meters and beyond, tanks from the 82nd and 79th destroyed hundreds of Egyptian tanks and endured very few casualties. The Egyptian forces deep in Sinai had already been the target of the IAF, victims of their senior commanding officers abandoning them in the field, and with the Israelis able to hit them from daunting ranges, the fight was all but over. Those who could abandon their vehicles in the sands made a dash for the canal, and hoped for survival. An equal number opted to wave white flags in the hopes that their improvised banners of surrender would be seen through the cross-hairs of the 90mm and 105mm guns. Those who stayed and fought endured a quick and brutal fate.

Later in the afternoon of June 7, the 7th Brigade moved on through Wadi el-Malez, Bir Salim, and seized the military bases west of the giant military complex at Bir Gifgafa. The next day, for nearly 12 hours, the 7th Armored Brigade battled the Egyptian garrison at Bir Gifgafa in, perhaps, the last great tank-versus-tank battle of the 1967 War. It was the Egyptian Army's last stand in the peninsula. Without air support, momentum, and the tank sniping skills that Major-General Tal had instilled in the Armored Corps' crews, the Egyptians didn't stand a chance. The carnage was absolute and one-sided. Before Egyptian T-55 gunners managed to acquire their targets, a Centurion or Patton had succeeded in hitting it. Once hit and on fire, the smoldering shell of an Egyptian tank became a larger target and was hit again.

All that stood in the way of the Suez Canal and Colonel Gonen was the desert and a few stragglers operating in company-size pockets. With the brigade on the move toward the waterline and the main roadway linking the peninsula to Isma'iliya, victory now seemed a matter of time. On the late afternoon of June 8, Major Shamai Kaplan, commander of the 82nd Battalion's "H" Company, found himself 25 kilometers south of Bir Gifgafa close to the canal area. For nearly 72 hours, Major Kaplan had endured a remarkable charge as commander and soldier. Called affectionately the "King of the Centurion," Major Kaplan's tank had "personally" destroyed thirty Egyptian tanks—eight at Rafah Junction, twelve at Bir El Hama against the Egyptian 14th Brigade, and ten at Bir Gifgafa.[30] Already a decorated officer, he had received a commendation in 1966 for a cross-border foray and was considered one of the shining stars in the brigade and the Armored Corps. Always smiling, always reassuring, Kaplan was as known for his incredible ability to motivate men, as he was for his coarse black beard and charming grin. Although wounded during the first day of fighting, he managed to hold his own even though he passed out on one occasion from the excruciating pain. Bleeding and having breached the envelope of endurance, he refused orders from his battalion and brigade commanders to evacuate his vehicle and go to the battalion aid station.

Major Kaplan's mission the afternoon of June 8 was to rescue a platoon of AMX-13 tanks on the road to Isma'iliya that had stumbled across an ambush by a company of Egyptian T-55s. Major Kaplan realized that the thinly armored AMX-13s were no match for the 100mm main guns of the T-55, and he raced to the battle area with his Centurions at full speed. The Centurions reached the ambush and quickly destroyed several T-55s; they had seen the smoke billowing out of the remnants of the AMX-13 tanks and used them as landmarks when ranging and firing at the Egyptian tanks. Destroying the ambush wasn't good enough for an armor officer worth his salt. At the IDF Armor School, every tank commander learns the following phrase: *"It is forbidden to break contact with the enemy—you must hit him as long as you can see him."*[31] Major Kaplan could still see several Egyptian tanks that had been part of the ambush fleeing toward the canal, and he pursued them. Major Kaplan ordered his driver to park on a bank by the main road so that he would be in optimum position to snipe at the fleeing Egyptian armor. This time, however, it was Major Kaplan's tank that was sniped at. When the vanguard of the brigade made its path toward Isma'iliya hours later, they found Major Kaplan's tank smoldering at the side of the road. The company commander and the crew of the Centurion had been killed.

After his death, historians and intelligence officers learned that Kaplan had stumbled across an entire brigade of Egyptian T-55s.

At 0100 hours on June 9, 1967, the first units of the brigade's reconnaissance forced reached the waters of the Suez Canal directly across from Isma'iliya. In one of the most famous pictures of the war, a young lieutenant named Yossi Ben-Hanan left his tank and jumped into the sweet refreshing waters of the canal clutching the AK-47 he had seized from a dead Egyptian soldier. It became an international symbol of the Israeli victory, as it appeared on the cover of *LIFE* magazine,[32] and embodied the exuberance of defeating one of the world's largest armies in a matter of 89 hours. Later in the afternoon, the 7th Armored Brigade linked up with the 35th Paratroop Brigade at the Firdan Bridge overlooking the canal. Major-General Tal's Steel Division had reached the canal in record time.

"It was a miraculous time," recalled Brigadier-General (Res.) Elyashiv Shimshi, commander of "Z Company" in the 82nd Battalion. "We had done so much against such odds and above all heard of the capture and reunification of Jerusalem while on the move in our Centurions."[33] There was still the campaign against the Jordanians in the West Bank, and the Israeli push to take the Golan Heights from Syria. They were six remarkable days in the modern history of an ancient region.

Near the canal, the 7th Armored Brigade assembled at a forward encampment to celebrate its victory as a now clean-shaven Colonel Gonen stood atop a podium and addressed his men courtesy of a microphone and improvised sound system. The brigade had scored an incredibly victory, Gonen impressed upon his troops, but the sacrifice of the fallen should not be forgotten. Although the war lasted six days for the State of Israel, Colonel Gonen's forces battled for only 96 hours. To most of the men in the brigade, the first day was the one that mattered—the one where the most blood was spilled and the most lives lost and shattered. Of the 70 7th Brigade soldiers who were killed in the 1967 War, 61 died that first day; from the 131 wounded soldiers in the brigade, 92 were injured that first 24 hours. Of the 29 7th Armored Brigade tanks hit during the war, 27 were hit by enemy fire that first day.

Few brigades in the history of modern warfare had achieved as much, in such a short period of time, as had the 7th Armored Brigade. Few brigades have issued as many decorations for valor as did the 7th Brigade in 1967, even in an army that rarely acknowledges heroism in the field. There were two recipients of the *I'tur Ha'Gvura* yellow medal for valor, Israel's highest decoration for courage under fire: five *I'tur Ha'Oz* red medals for courage, Israel's second-highest decoration for heroism; and twenty-nine recipients of the *I'tur Ha'Mofet*, blue medal for exemplary service. Dozens more received Chief of Staff, Southern Command, and Divisional citations, as well. Many awards for valor were issued posthumously.

Peace, of course, did not follow the 1967 Israeli victory. In September 1967 the Egyptians initiated what became known as the War of Attrition, a scaled-back though never-ending level of hostilities that continued for 1,000 days. The brigade, still under the stellar leadership of Colonel Gonen, served in the southern front along the Suez Canal, along the northern frontier against Lebanese and Syrian targets, and against the Jordanian Army and the Palestinian guerrillas inside the West Bank and across the Jordan River. Joint-security operations against Palestinian guerrillas had become increasingly bloody and incessant missions for the IDF—even tank units. By early 1968, the Palestinian terrorist faction, Fatah, had turned Jordan into one large training and operational base from which to launch attacks against Israel. The IDF responded on countless occasions both in pursuit of these terrorists and in retaliatory strikes meant to punish the guerilla warlords after an attack had been perpetrated inside Israel or along the frontier. One cross-border retaliatory operation, in particular, against Palestinian guerrillas in Jordan would become the 7th Armored Brigade's most controversial and costly action ever.

After the Six Day War, the Jordanian army recovered from its losses and was reorganized. Its order of battle included two infantry divisions, one armored division, one mechanized division, two commando battalions, one Royal Guard battalion, and the general security force, which was responsible for the police, the border police, and the security services. The army had at its disposal about 350 tanks (250 Centurions, 100 M-47 and M-48A2C Pattons), approximately 230 artillery pieces, approximately 130 armored cars fitted with 7.62mm cannons, about 140 "Ferret II" armored cars, about 400 armored personnel carriers (280 M-113 and 120 "Saracen"), and about 200 M-42 antiaircraft tanks (double-barreled 40mm cannons mounted on Walker-Bulldog carriers). The Royal Jordanian Air Force had not been restored to its previous strength, and most of its aircraft was stationed in Iraq.

The reinforced First Division was deployed in the Kara-meh area. The division consisted of three infantry brigades, one mechanized brigade, three field artillery battalions, one mechanized artillery battalion, one heavy artillery battalion, one engineering battalion and one antiaircraft battalion. The division was equipped with 105 Patton M-48 and M-47 tanks, 88 artillery pieces (54 25-pounders, 18 105mm mobile M-52s, 8 155mm Long Toms, 8 203mm pieces), 18 107mm mortars, 24 M-42 antiaircraft tanks, and 24 M-55 four-barreled 12.7mm heavy antiaircraft machine guns. The division was commanded by Major-General Mashhor Hadisah.[34.]

As a result of the lessons learned by the Jordanian army from its defeat in the Six Day War, the First Division was endowed with all the basic defense principles. The division was deployed on three major axes linking the Jordan Valley with Amman; with protective formations in the Jordan Valley and its major deployment at the points of entry into the mountainous area. On the Damia-Ma'adi-Tsvillah axis, an infantry division reinforced by a tank company, a field artillery battalion, an engineering battalion attached to the main divisional deployment in the Ma'adi perimeter and company deployment at El-Matsri, and deployment of an infantry company and a tank company in a defensive formation for the Damia base.

In addition, a number of units were held in reserve on the mountain crests, and could be deployed in any of the axes according to the commander's decision. This force included the 60th Armored Brigade, divided into three battalions. Each battalion included two tank companies, one mechanized infantry company, an M-52 mobile artillery battery, and an engineering platoon. The three battalions were positioned with one at Tsvillah to counterattack along the Ma'adi axis, one at Wadi Sir to counterattack along the Shunat-Nimrin axis, and one at Naor to counterattack along the Kuferian axis. The division's heavy artillery was deployed over the entire area, one battery at Yira and another at Tsivihi, and was defended by the divisional aircraft battalion.

The Jordanian battle plan, in case of any large-scale Israeli action, provided for the division to operate as follows: Defensive units were to identify the enemy's major breakthrough effort, determine its strength, and slow down the enemy attack as much as possible before finally withdrawing to the divisional perimeter in the mountains. It was in this area that the major battle was to take place, and the defensive formations were to be reinforced from the rear echelons or the division's reserves, according to need, with the ultimate goal of a joint counterattack to annihilate the invader and recapture the Jordan Valley.

The town of Karameh lies four kilometers east of the Jordan River and five kilometers north of the road that connects the Allenby Bridge with Shunat-Nimrin, and has about 20,000 inhabitants. Several thousand refugees settled there after the Six Day War, but most of them fled deeper into Jordan in 1967 and at the beginning of 1968, when the town turned into the principal base of the terrorist organizations. At the time of the operation, there were no more than a few hundred refugees in the town. Primarily, it was used by Yasir Arafat's Fatah as an operational and training facility, and Israeli intelligence reports estimated that there were anywhere between 900 and 2,000 fighters there; most of the fighters had been transferred not long before from El Hama in Syria to Karameh. There was also an important base of the Popular Front for the Liberation of Palestine in Karameh, as well as the remainder of the 141st Egyptian Commando Battalion, which was transferred after the Six Day War, first to Syria and then to Jordan.

The terrorist organizations, in particular Fatah, were in complete control of Karameh. The town was used as a command post, briefing, and training area, as well as a supply base and staging area for operations across the Jordan River. In Karameh at the time were the headquarters of two terror organizations, a warehouse, a training base, a prison, and a communications center. The Palestinian (not Jordanian) flag flew over the center of town. The Palestinians were equipped primarily with light weapons, including 7.62mm Kalashnikov rifles, 7.62 machine guns, a large quantity of RPG-2 and RPG-7 antitank weapons, a number of 84mm recoilless guns, and a number of 82mm and 120mm mortars, which were meant for shelling Israeli settlements west of the Jordan River.

On March 18, the IDF started calling up reserves for a retaliatory operation against Fatah positions in Karameh. The planning and preparation took place at the highest levels. The task force, which was drawn from various units attached to the Central Command, was brought to the Jordan Valley. IDF elements involved in the operation included three brigades under the control of Central Command (two infantry and one armor), and three artillery battalions. Central Command's operational orders, which were approved by the General Staff, read as follows: "The Central Command will take control of the Fatah bases in the Karameh area, will demonstrate its presence in the area and will withdraw when ordered." The statement clearly defined the scope of the operation with its reference to Karameh, but the expression "will demonstrate its presence in the area" was open to a wide range of interpretations. The tactical procedure decided on was to isolate the operational rear on three sides by deploying an armored brigade south of the town, an armored battalion to the north, and a heliborne paratroop reconnaissance company to the east. The town was then to be conquered and mopped up by a paratroop brigade, supported by air, artillery, and engineering units. The 80th Brigade, commanded by Colonel Rafel "Raful" Eitan, had the mission of isolating the operations area from the north by seizing the Damia post and blocking the El Matsri junction from the north and east, defending the corresponding section of the valley, and ensuring the arrival of an engineering force that would erect a bridge over the Jordan River. To carry out the first part of the mission, the brigade set up a reinforced battalion-size armored formation based on the 268th Battalion of the 60th Armored Brigade under the command of Lieutenant-Colonel Tuvia Raviv. The formation included a company of thirteen M-51 Sherman tanks, a platoon of three Centurion tanks, an AML-90 armored car company with nine vehicles, three paratroop companies on armored vehicles, two engineering platoons on armored vehicles, and three teams of SS-11 antitank rocket launchers with twelve launchers.[35]

The armored element fell with the men and tanks of Colonel Gonen's 7th Armored Brigade. The brigade was given the mission of isolating the battle zone from the south by seizing the Allenby Bridge post and blocking the junction between the Jordan Valley Road and the Shunat-Nimrin and Kuferian axes, as well as blocking any advance of Jordanian forces westward on those two axes. To carry out this mission the brigade assembled two reduced battalion-size armored teams, which consisted primarily of the battalion commanded by Lieutenant-Colonel Abraham Rotem and the force commanded by Lieutenant-Colonel Aharon Peled. Rotem's battalion included eleven tanks and another engineering section transported on a half-track, while Peled's force included eleven tanks, an engineering section transported on a half-track, and the Artillery Corps' liaison officer's half-track. There was also the brigade's mobile forward command post, which included Gonen's tank and six tanks kept in reserve under Captain Solomonov, which were to support Rotem's battalion on the Shunat-Nimrin axis.

Another force consisted of a reduced tank company with four vehicles under the command of Captain Stoler. Its mission was to seal off the operational area from the north (in the direction of Karameh). Finally, three armored platoons were positioned on the west bank of the Jordan. One platoon faced the Beit Ha'arava Bridge outpost, one faced the Muatas Bridge, and one covered the road to the Allenby Bridge outpost.

For Operation Inferno, Colonel Gonen had brought forty 7th Armored Brigade tanks and vehicles to the mix.

The paratroop brigade under the command of Colonel Danny Matt was assigned the mission of annihilating the Karameh terrorist base, destroying Fatah's installations, blowing up buildings from which firing took place or where weapons were stored, mopping up the town, flushing out the Palestinian terrorists and, of course, capturing them. For this task, the brigade assigned three paratroop battalions on half-tracks (one of them reduced to company size), along with an engineering company and the brigade's reconnaissance unit (originally under the direct control of the Central Command), which were to be transported by helicopter (eight S-58 and two Super-Frelon helicopters). This force was also to seal off the battle zone from the east, blocking any attempt to escape from Karameh. The brigade was organized as follows: one battalion commanded by Lieutenant-Colonel Dan Shomron, which was composed of half-tracks, one additional battalion with twenty-three half-tracks, a "condensed" paratroop battalion on seven half-tracks (formerly part of the brigade's reserves); one reduced tank battalion commanded by Lieutenant-Colonel Avraham Bar-Am with seven tanks, and about 800 soldiers.

The overall commander of the operation, OC Central Command Major-General Rechavem "Ghandi" Zeevi, was known as a no-nonsense paratroop officer and authorized a rigid timetable for the execution of what was known in the coded, secretive vernacular of IDF operations as "Operation Inferno." The timetable consisted of the following objectives:

(a) 0530: the 7th Brigade was to cross the Allenby Bridge and proceed on its mission.
(b) 0545: paratroopers were to be dropped east of Karameh.
(c) 0600: a light plane was to drop leaflets on Karameh, calling on the Palestinian terrorists to surrender. A paratroop brigade was to follow the 7th Brigade across the Allenby Bridge and proceed on its mission. The 80th Brigade was to cross the Damia bridge and proceed on with its mission.[36]

At 0533 on March 21, 1968, the first tanks of the 7th Brigade started rolling over the Allenby Bridge. The armored advance surprised the Jordanian outpost, and the company that occupied the bridge did not have time to set off the demolition charges; in fact, they fired only several rounds of small-arms ammunition at the advancing tanks and then fled in haste. The leading tanks destroyed most of the weapons in the bridge post: six recoilless guns, heavy machine guns, and 81mm mortars. The surviving Jordanian soldiers fled toward Shunat-Nimrin. The brigade advanced with Lieutenant-Colonel Rotem's battalion in the vanguard, followed by the brigade's mobile command post, and then the reserve, Stoler's unit of four tanks. Peled's unit, along with an additional force, was to advance on Karameh as quickly as possible. As the Allenby Bridge was captured intact, and its garrison subdued in a matter of minutes, the bridge became the main axis of movement over the Jordan in both directions.[37]

This force was the fifth element of the brigade to cross the

Jordan, and after a brief conversation between Lieutenant-Colonel Peled and Colonel Gonen, it moved to carry out its mission, blocking the exit to the Naor-Kuferian axis, which overlooked the valley. While moving toward the road linking the Allenby Bridge to Shunat-Nimrin, the force went off the road one kilometer east, with the intention of crossing the cultivated area diagonally toward a point southeast of Kuferian. But as it reached a point one kilometer south of the road, the commander noticed that he was in the middle of flooded banana plantations. He feared that his vehicles would sink into the soft ground and changed the direction of his advance, turning east on a road that ran between cultivated plots. It is notable that, before the operation, the force did not receive a briefing about the condition of the terrain, and the commander did not anticipate these difficulties. As it reached the road, the force came under fire from the northwest positions at Kuferian and, in the ensuing exchange, destroyed several Jordanian tanks and jeep-mounted recoilless guns. An hour later, the force reached Tel Adma and came under tank fire from Jordanian Centurions—tank crews that impressed the Israelis with their tactical skill, courage, and, most of all, long-range gunnery skills. One of the tanks took three direct hits, went up in flames, and burned for several hours. Subsequently, in an effort to close off the eastern axis of the advance, one tank platoon was left facing the road that descends from Kuferian, and the rest of the force, seven tanks in all, took up positions on both sides of the El Mazr junction, with one platoon facing east and another one facing west toward Beit Ha'aravah.[38]

At 0711 hours, the force reached El Mazr and remained exposed to heavy fire from Kuferian until 1600 hours, when it was ordered to withdraw. For nearly nine hours, the troops were 1,000 to 1,500 meters from the enemy's tanks, recoilless guns, mortars, and heavy machine guns, and were continuously exposed both to flat-trajectory fire and to over-the-horizon pounding by artillery units, whose guns had been carefully targeted in advance.

The Jordanians were most concerned by the Israeli advance—they didn't realize that Karameh was the ultimate objective and thought that the Israelis had launched a 1967-like surprise attack to gain control of the shortest direct road to Amman, and so did their utmost to block its advance. They used all their available firepower against it, and also mounted a dedicated and highly capable counterattack with an armored battalion from the 60th Armored Brigade, supported by a tank and recoilless gun company from the local infantry brigade. The Jordanian counterattack, which began at 1300, was brought to a halt with the destruction of seven or eight tanks and a number of recoilless guns. The Jordanians kept up their pressure until Israeli forces were ordered to withdraw. When the IDF began to leave the area, the commander noted that two half-tracks of the artillery liaison unit and the engineering corps, which had left the road, were unable to extricate themselves. A tank that tried to haul one of them out got itself bogged down. After a number of attempts, the incapacitated vehicles were finally brought back to the road and the force began rolling toward the bridge. Until 1900, when the last tank crossed the Allenby Bridge, the force came under constant artillery pounding.[39]

The blocking action by the Israeli tank contingent, nearly a battalion-sized formation, made no contribution to the fight for Karameh, since protection from the south was in any event provided by the 82nd Battalion's operations around Shunat-Nimrin. It did, however, convince the Jordanians that the road to Amman was seriously threatened, prompting them to fight for it with incredible resolve and courage and not deploy additional resources to Karameh to bolster the Palestinian garrison.

Lieutenant-Colonel Rotem's battalion started crossing the Jordan at 0535, covered by one tank platoon from the Israeli bridge outpost known as "Saipan." The battalion surprised the Jordanian defenders. Most of the Jordanian garrison's weapons, recoilless guns, mortars, and heavy machine guns were destroyed, and its tanks withdrew to the north, in the direction of Mandasa. This battle took place during the move from the side road to the main road. As soon as the tanks crossed the river, an engineering section took control of the bridge, neutralized the explosive charges attached to it, and secured it until the end of the operation. The battalion continued its advance, with the commander's tank following the two lead tanks. According to plan, the tanks were to stop at Tel Nimrin and take up positions on both sides and to engage the enemy to the east. But the officer in the lead failed to identify the hill, which was relatively low and hidden by the village's buildings and vegetation, and moved east instead, followed by the other two tanks, including the commander's. The hill was apparently a landmark for the Jordanian tanks, which opened fire on the Israeli armor as soon as it was within range. The commander's tank, as well as another one, along with two half-tracks carrying the forward command post and the artillery liaison officer, were hit and remained exposed to Jordanian crossfire without the possibility of being extricated. Jordanian fire was fierce, accurate, and relentless. The 7th Brigade's remaining tanks took up positions behind the hill, and under the orders of the battalion's second-in-command, Major Elyashiv Shimshi, provided covering fire for the commander's tank, which was finally able to extricate itself to the rear. "Jordanian fire was brutal, accurate, and dedicated. We found ourselves under a murderous barrage from moment one when we crossed the bridge and it didn't let up until we left back across the narrow waterway. As we were engaging the Jordanian tanks and antitank guns, Gorodish appeared on the scene to evaluate Jordanian resolve. I was shocked to see this colonel, unaffected by the explosions erupting around him and the automatic fire landing at his feet, directing the battle. Take cover, I told him, but he shrugged me off and continued to stand there and expose himself. I thought he was crazy but that was Gorodish. He was that kind of commander."[40]

From 0615 to 1600, the tanks of Rotem's battalion, which had been reinforced with the brigade's six reserve tanks under Solomonov, remained within the destruction zone of the Jordanian position, despite repeated attempts to extricate the disabled vehicles and their crews. Meanwhile, the battalion's medical half-track overturned while moving toward the disabled tanks. Its driver was hit by Jordanian fire and lost control of the vehicle, but the battalion field doctor, together with a number of other soldiers, managed to reach the tanks and evacuate the wounded.

During those ten hours, other tanks were hit, mostly by accurate artillery fire that the Jordanian spotters were directing on the exposed armored vehicles. Jordanian forces in the area assumed that the IDF intended to advance toward

Wadi Sir and Amman, and this position was reinforced with a battalion-size formation from the Jordanian 60th Armored Brigade, which counterattacked Rotem's battalion, seized vantage points, and engaged in exchanges of fire with the battalion throughout the day.

The 80th Brigade was assigned two main missions: to conquer the Damia post and to cut off the valley road south of the El Matsri junction. The purpose of the second mission was to prevent the escape of enemy forces from Karameh, and to keep Jordanian reinforcements from the Ma'adi post from reaching the battle zone. The brigade employed four major forces: the first was an armored company-size unit that was made up of a platoon of M-51 Sherman tanks, a platoon of paratroopers on half-tracks, and an engineering section on a half-track. This force was led by a company commander from the 268th battalion. At 0550 when permission to advance was granted, the force, together with the rest of the brigade, supported by a platoon of Centurion tanks, an SS-11 battery, and the brigade's artillery, quickly took control of the brigade, took up flanking positions at Tel Damia, and opened fire on the enemy, while sappers neutralized the explosive charges and, together with the paratroopers, secured the bridge. The operation was executed quickly and achieved total surprise, as the supporting troops and artillery knocked out two tanks, as well as most of the sources of fire within the enemy position.

As soon as the bridge had been secured, the second force, commanded by Lieutenant-Colonel Raviv, crossed it. The force consisted of a reduced tank company with five M-51 Sherman tanks, though one had to be abandoned because of a technical breakdown in the entry area; a reduced armored corps company made up of nine AML-90s; a reduced paratroop company on half-tracks; and an engineering platoon. The plan called for the force to advance southward after crossing the bridge, to circumvent the Damia post from the south through an area that was thought to be suitable for an armored advance through the Wadi A-Ratsifi riverbed, and to take up positions south of the El Matsri junction, with the purpose of blocking the bailey road. As the unit left the road at Zor and followed the Jordan riverbed, the vehicles began to sink into the ground. The battalion commander's tank sank after reaching the Wadi A-Ratsifi riverbed and made two attempts to proceed. At this point, Gonen noted that the flanking maneuver was not proceeding according to plan, and ordered the third force, led by the battalion's deputy commander, to conquer the position. The third force was a reinforced company-size armored group, which consisted of a paratroop company on half-tracks and a reduced tank company with five M-51 Shermans. The force moved in quickly, two tanks and the paratroop company attacked the outpost in an effort to clean it out from behind, while the other three tanks advanced to the edge of the Havar Hills, from where they engaged the remaining tanks from the Jordanian company, which had arrived from Ma'adi and had taken up positions overlooking the El Matsri junction.

When it was clear to Gonen that the outpost had been taken and the road was open, he ordered the second force to retrace its path and return to the road and follow it up to the El Matsri junction and block the valley road at that point.

At 0715 it became clear to Gonen that the paratroop brigade was already in Karameh and had taken control of the valley road leading north, which made the conquest of the El Matsri junction unnecessary, especially since it was possible to direct tank fire at the valley road from the Havar Hills at a range of 2,000–2,500 meters. Therefore, he ordered the paratroop company of the second force to return to the western bank of the Jordan. At that point, Lieutenant-Colonel Raviv was left in command of three tanks from his original force, as two were stuck at Wadi A-Ratsifi; two tanks from the deputy commander's force (after three tanks were put out of action by the Jordanians just after reaching the crest of the Havar Hills); six armored cars (of which three, including the company commander's car, got bogged down in the muddy impassable terrain); and the paratroop company that continued to mop up the position, and which was not under his command.

The battalion commander decided that under these circumstances, the conquest of El Matsri was still necessary to extricate the various vehicles that were unable to move or were disabled by enemy fire (another tank had been hit in the meantime). He decided to carry out this mission with the armored cars alone, while the four tanks were to provide covering fire. The battalion commander himself accompanied the armored cars in his half-track. Meanwhile two armored cars sank in the mud, leaving only four fit for action. He raced toward the El Matsri junction and started moving among the buildings. Almost as soon as they arrived, however, an armored car and the commander's half-track were hit and set on fire by antitank fire. Two other armored cars tried to withdraw, but one was hit, overturned, and went up in flames. The second managed to escape. In the meantime, the battalion commander, who had jumped out of his burning vehicle, managed to make his way on foot to one of the two armored cars that had remained at the junction. He informed Gonen what had happened and asked for an emergency extrication. From the point the Jordanian antitank rounds sliced through the Israeli vehicles, at 0800, until 2200, the effort to salvage the tanks, the armored cars, and the 80th Brigade's half-tracks went on continuously, by means of a company of Centurion tanks brought up from the south. At the same time, a bridge was erected near Damia to enable the Centurions to cross, but the bridge was completed at a relatively late stage and was used only by the tank company returning from Karameh after the rescue operation.

The force that fought the advanced Jordanian positions in this area (a tank company under Lieutenant-Colonel Raviv's command) lost two soldiers and eleven were wounded. Despite the lengthy salvage operation, a tank, an armored car, and a half-track had to be abandoned. Of the entire force entrusted with the 80th Brigade's main mission—cutting off the valley road—only one armored car and four half-tracks actually reached the road, and only one armored car managed to return without being hit.

Lieutenant-Colonel Avraham Bar-Am's force of seven tanks, which kept close to the end of 7th Brigade convoy, brought up the strategic rear of the Israeli task force. The main force of the unit followed about ten minutes' driving time behind. It consisted of a paratroop battalion with four supporting tanks, followed by a Na'ha'l battalion supported by a platoon of AML-90 armored cars. The rear guard consisted of a reduced paratroop battalion. According to Gonen's plan, the convoy was to move steadily after the brigade, without stopping before reaching its objectives in

Karameh. Bar-Am's battalion, which led the convoy behind the 7th Armored Brigade, moved north after passing the Allenby outpost and advanced along the eastern edge of the Havar Hills to the paved road from Mandasa to Karameh. At that point, one tank slipped and sank into the shoulder of the road. Another tank had gotten lost after crossing the bridge and joined the Rotem battalion. Led by a force of five tanks, the battalion burst into Karameh from the south, firing in all directions, drove past the town, and took up positions three kilometers to the north—all this without suffering any casualties. In effect, the battalion carried out the mission assigned to the entire 80th Brigade.

At 0656, the main force of the brigade reached the town. The paratroop battalion entered the town from the east and Na'ha'l battalion from the west. The battalions advanced on parallel streets from the south and moved toward their objectives in an attempt to seize the terrorists' installations and seal off the entry and exit points from the town. Together with the reconnaissance unit, which had reached the town earlier from the east, the brigade began clearing out all the terrorist targets it could identify. The installations were manned by several hundred Palestinian terrorists equipped with automatic and antitank weapons, mortars, and explosives. The fighting continued until 1100, when it was decided to disengage even though the town had not been completely cleared of Palestinian terrorists. The Israelis quickly blew up some of the buildings still standing and quickly headed west.

In the Operation Inferno, the 7th Brigade lost 13 men and 25 were wounded in the course of the operations south of Karameh. Of the 33 tanks that crossed the Jordan River from west to east that winter's morning, 27 were hit. Some were abandoned by the retreating Israeli forces and later inspected personally by King Hussein following the battle and taken to the sprawling Jordanian Military Museum in Amman. Palestinian terrorist organizations sustained 156 dead and nearly 400 wounded, while the Jordanian army suffered 13 dead. Palestinian terrorists, numbering 141, were captured and brought back to Israel, 175 houses were blown up, and a great deal of booty was seized, including large quantities of automatic weapons, explosives, 81mm and

60mm mortars, recoilless guns, and even an intact Jordanian tank, a Patton M-48A2C. The armored force that was to block access from the north moved to the area assigned to the 80th Brigade, joined it, assisted it in the evacuation of damaged vehicles, ultimately crossed the Jordan on the temporary bridge erected south of Damia, and returned to Israeli lines.

While on paper Operation Inferno was a military success, it was too costly a strike for a retaliatory mission. The main lesson to be drawn from the results of the Karameh operation—the many casualties; the fact armored vehicles had to be abandoned in the field, sometimes with their dead crews inside; and the massive intervention of the Jordanian army—is that quick, one-time operations making use of massive force cannot succeed in stamping out the terrorist threat. The loss of flexibility and speed dictated by the use of large-scale military forces enables the guerrilla fighters to slip away. Even when some of them remain behind to make a stand, those who escape without making contact can return after the battle and regain control of the disputed area. When the propaganda benefits derived by the Palestinian terrorists from the Karameh operation were taken into account, with the resulting increase in terror activity against Israel, the political damage at the United Nations and in the world at large, and the corresponding increase in support for the Palestinian cause, it can only be concluded that any notion of eliminating guerrilla organizations with one blow constitutes a most dangerous, if widely held, fallacy. Experience shows that the damage that can result from such an operation far outstrips any possible benefits.

The Battle of Karameh was the largest engagement for the 7th Armored Brigade during the 1967–70 "1000 Days" War of Attrition—a bloody and unforgiving slugfest that saw over 1,000 Israeli servicemen killed and scores more wounded. It was also a harbinger for worse to come and a testing ground for what would transpire atop the Golan Heights and the Sinai Desert three years later. A first taste came on July 7, 1970, when an Israeli tank patrol along the Suez Canal came under a coordinated Sagger missile attack. It was the first time that Israeli armored forces would encounter the portable, wire-guided, tank-killing Sagger.[41] It would not be the last.

The Gorodish-era ended on June 15, 1969, when Colonel Gonen was promoted to the rank of brigadier-general and given a divisional command. His replacement, Colonel Ya'akov "Jackie" Even[42] was a competent and capable officer, but he was a lackluster replacement for a man who had been so controversial, sparked so much emotion and opinion, and who had elevated a single brigade into an international icon. Never before had an Israeli brigade commander caused men in the field, decorated combat veterans, to tremble in his wake and never before had an Israeli brigade commander made the cover of *LIFE* magazine. It was, indeed, the best of times and the worst of times for the 7th Brigade. It was a period of innocence and exuberance, uncontested national zeal and affirmation of the mighty ability of the tank on the battlefield.

For the brigade, and the nation it served, it would all collapse on one October afternoon in 1973.

Footnote: Twenty-four years after the end of the Six Day War and the most dramatic and important week in the Middle East's 2,000-year-old history, a poignant footnote to the conflict was written when Major-General Shmuel "Gorodish" Gonen, sixty-one-years-old, died of heart failure while preparing to fly from Rome to the Central African Republic where he had business dealings for a growing diamond business. General Gonen's death was, perhaps, the only footnote that the saga of the brigade in the 1967 War could evoke— the tragic end of a man propelled to the very pinnacle of power and glory and eventually torpedoed to humiliation and self-induced exile. It was, in many ways, a self-induced journey up and down the panoramic tour of personal accomplishments and defeats. Gorodish was a man who had lived most of his life with an asterisk next to his name. Singled out by his own public relations machinery as the man responsible for Israel's Sinai victory in 1967, he was also singled out by the investigating Agranat Committee (and some day Defense Minister Moshe Dayan[43] and Prime Minister Golda Meir) for being partly responsible for the lack of Israeli preparedness against the Egyptians during the first few days of the 1973 Yom Kippur War, where he served as OC Southern Command. In many ways, Gorodish represented the brash, abrasive, and superconfident Israeli that raced through Sinai that June morning in 1967 and forever changed the face of a nation and a region. He could not— and did not—survive being the self-doubting, ego-exploded, insecure Israeli that would forge itself into the Israeli psychosis following the surprise of October 1973. He felt he became a scapegoat for the 1973 failure and left the country in self-imposed exile. Gonen resigned from the IDF in 1976 and worked in the diamond mining industry in the Central African Republic. He only returned to Israel three times during his 15 years of self-imposed exile—two times to clear his name when interviewed by the IDF's Historical Branch working on an official history of the 1973 War and, finally, on October 4, 1991, when his body was brought back to Israel for burial; he had suffered a fatal heart attack during a business meeting in Italy.

For a man who evoked so much argument and emotion, Gonen's funeral at the Kiyrat Shaul cemetery near Tel Aviv was meant to be an honor guard salute to a fallen hero. Six generals served as pallbearers, including Major-General Amram Mitzna, Major-General Ilan Biran, Major-General Matan Vilnai, Major-General Yitzhak Mordechai, Major-General Yossi Ben-Hanan, and Major-General Danny Yatom. A small army of family members, politicians, and former comrades-in-arms followed the coffin in a full military service meant to salute a fierce and courageous warrior. Some, like Yossi Ben-Hanan and Mitzna, had served under Gonen during the 1967 War; others, like Mordechai, had served under him during the 1973 War.

No matter what Gonen was as a man and as a commanding officer, what he represented to a nation and a brigade of soldiers in time of war was a stoic symbol of leadership and courage. When the 1967 Six Day War began, the 7th Armored Brigade was Israel's sole conscript armored force—a combination of already obsolete tanks piloted by eighteen-year-old conscripts. When the war, for the brigade, ended four days later on the banks of the Suez Canal, the unit became the most decorated in Israeli military history. Perhaps it is that legacy that should be remembered of Shmuel "Gorodish" Gonen when his 29 years of service to the IDF is recalled. He was the man who led the country's finest brigade at its finest hour!

3

An Epic Tale of Courage:
The 7th Armored Brigade
in the 1973 Yom Kippur War

*Leave the wounded behind! Whoever makes it back
makes it back!*
>   —**Israeli Defense Minister Moshe Dayan,**
>   **October 7, 1973**

September 1, 1972:
Qastina, Southern Israel

Wearing his characteristic oversize Class A uniform in its
truly characteristic unkempt form, Lieutenant-Colonel Avigdor
"Yanush" Ben-Gal walked into the headquarters of the Armored Corps in the sprawling southern base of Qastina and
received the news that the scuttlebutt was true—he had been
promoted to the rank of *Aluf Mishne,* or full colonel, and given
the command of the 7th Armored Brigade. The wily colonel
had accepted his posting with grace and typical "Yanush" flair.
He placed his hand across his head pulling back his long hair
and contemplated all that needed to be done. There was a lot
of work ahead for Yanush. The Gonen-family era had ended.

Yanush had not fallen victim to the mythical command of
Shmuel Gonen as tank soldier trailblazer while commanding
the 7th Armored Brigade. In fact, Ben-Gal's dislike of

The shelled remnants of the Taggart fortress at Latrun, scene of some of the bloodiest fighting of the 1948 War of Independence. Today it is the Armored Corps' Museum. *(© Samuel M. Katz)*

One of the 7th Brigade's nemeses of the 1956 War: an Egyptian "bastard" tank—a Sherman chassis with an AMX-13 turret. *(© Samuel M. Katz)*

The first post–Second World War tank to sport the 7th Brigade flag—the French-built AMX-13 light tank. *(© Samuel M. Katz)*

Stoic portrait of a 7th Brigade tank commander—June 1967. *(IDF Archives)*

A young 7th Brigade officer as photographed a short time before the October 6, 1973, surprise Syrian attack. *(IDF Archives)*

A 7th Brigade Centurion hit by a direct 100mm round lies abandoned at the western approach to the Valley of Tears, October 7, 1973. *(IDF Archives)*

A 77th Battalion Centurion moves cautiously through a still-unsecured roadway en route to trying to stem the tide of the Syrian advance, October 8, 1973. Note destroyed Syrian T-55 behind a Hebrew sign stating: "Danger: A Firing Zone, Fire in this Area!" *(IDF Archives)*

During a momentary lull in the fighting, a 7th Brigade Centurion crew enjoys a brief rest and meal atop the Golan Heights. *(IDF Archives)*

Syrian T-55 destroyed by a direct hit from one of the 77th Battalion 105mm main armament guns that directed lethal fire into the Valley of Tears. Note "Bosster" hill in the background. *(IDF Archives)*

'th Battalion commander Lieutenant-Colonel Avigdor Kahalani, Golan Heights, October 1973. *(IDF Archives)*

The carnage at Nafekh——a Syrian tank and soldier that never breached the IDF defenses. *(IDF Archives)*

Tank ditches that stemmed the tide but couldn't stop the flow of Syrian armor. T-55s lay in ruin, hit by 7th Brigade "snipers." *(IDF Archives)*

The road to Damascus littered with the remnants of both 1 Israeli and the Syrian militaries. *(IDF Archives)*

A 7th Brigade trooper takes a Syrian tank commander prisoner at the "Purple Line," October 16, 1973. *(IDF Archives)*

One of the 7th Brigade's saviors in 1973—679th Armored Brigade commander (right) Colonel Orri Orr, as seen on the Golan Heights, October 1973. *(IDF Archives)*

Syrian T-62 stands as a monument at the 77th Battalion's monument in the Valley of Tears. *(© Samuel M. Katz)*

The almighty Merkava—the 7th Brigade's chariot of steel: Golan Heights, 1981. *(IDF Spokesman Photographic Unit)*

June 8, 1982: 7th Brigade Merkava's move into Lebanon, east, toward Syrian lines. *(IDF Spokesman Photographic Unit)*

Syrian armor lay in ruin in the Beka'a Valley during the close-quarter tank-fighting of the 1982 Lebanon War—targets of 7th Brigade snipers. *(IDF Spokesman Photographic Unit)*

A 7th Brigade tank crew displays its skill in changing a tread in a matter of minutes—during a demonstration for the top brass atop the Golan Heights. *(IDF Spokesman Photographic Unit)*

The Armored Corps' wall of remembrance at the Latrun memorial and museum. *(© Samuel M. Katz)*

The Merkava Mk III: the latest version of the mighty "Chariot" and—7th Brigade commanders hope—the next brigade workhorse. *(IDF Spokesman Photographic Unit)*

Gonen and his autocratic behavior caused him to demand a transfer from the brigade months prior to the outbreak of the 1967 Six Day War. "He was a maniacal dictator," Ben-Gal would comment in retrospect. "I was determined to be a dictator, but not maniacal." But in accepting command of the 7th Armored Brigade, Yanush realized his survival as a commander and his unit's operational existence were still linked inexplicably with Major-General Gonen, who had also been promoted, to the all-powerful rank of OC Southern Command. The Egyptian front had been quiet since the U.S. Secretary of State William Rodgers initiative, but war with Egypt was still "MAJOR SCENARIO NUMBER ONE" at the IDF General Staff. Syria, a serious foe, was not considered as lethal a threat as Egypt's million-man army. The threat from the south, of an Egyptian crossing succeeding in pushing all the way to Tel Aviv, was viewed far more seriously than a Syrian move from the north meant to split the country in two. Chief of Staff Bar-Lev, an ex-armored officer, had pushed for an aggressive general to be in the south; his tenure with Major-General (Res.) Ariel "Arik" Sharon, a man who in the Hebrew lexicon defined aggressive, had proven most successful. Gonen was brash, aggressive, and a rising star among the increasingly politicized and media-hungry generals in uniform. Bar-Lev's replacement, Lieutenant-General David "Dado" Elazar, also a tank officer, knew Gonen and wanted his man in the south. The south was where the 7th Brigade would also find itself— as part of a division meant to beat back any Egyptian attempt to cross the canal and then to facilitate a counterattack. Once again Shmuel Gonen was in command of the 7th, though Colonel Ben-Gal would have to do all in his power to exorcise him from the brigade's mentality, personality, and means of doing work.

Colonel "Yanush" Ben-Gal inherited a brigade on the cutting edge of Israel's defense strategy. The 7th was the best, the most capable, and most experienced armored unit in the IDF's order of battle. Its service in the 1967 and Attrition wars confirmed the myth to be fact. While the Armored Corps had ballooned in size and mandate with the creation of many other brigades incorporating new tanks and new doctrines, the 7th was still considered the old reliable. Should war break out, either in the north or south, the *Heyl Ha'Shirion*'s armored ring around the country, a wall of defense of fire and steel, would be the 7th Brigade.

Tall and lanky with a wild flow of hair, Yanush was the opposite of the Gonen family legacy left on the brigade. Quiet and unassuming, he chose to lead by example and respect rather than rants and raves and threats. Soldiers needed to be rallied, not broken, Yanush believed. They need to know that their overall commander is on their side, a comrade; but he isn't their friend or enemy—he is a figure of leadership. Leadership in those first days of the "Yanush" era over the 7th Brigade meant preparations for war. For the IDF, 1972 was the best of times. A time when full-scale war with the Arabs was a distant, almost incomprehensible, thought. The War of Attrition had ended and it was the beginning of the war against Black September when many in the Israel defense establishment believed that the Arab's inability to defeat Israel on the battlefield meant that they had now brought the conflict far from the IDF's wrath, onto the streets of Europe. While it was the zenith of Israeli special operations, especially in counterterrorist strikes, conventional units entered into a twilight zone of training for war when none was expected. After all, "How could the Arabs even consider entering into a conflict with the IDF after 1967!"

Yanush belonged to a vocal minority in the IDF who did not believe for a second that the threat of a conventional conflagration had ended. Yanush, in fact, was so certain that war would break out[1] that he urged his senior commanders to continuously place several units on full alert, posed to launch a counterstrike along the front. These men, primarily brigade commanders of conscript units, had fought the Arabs before and knew that they would be fighting them again in the near future. Most of these chagrined and realistic-minded officers were sure that the Egyptians would be the ones to open hostilities and launch a major offensive along the canal in the hopes of seizing a chunk of the Sinai. Ben-Gal differed from his colleagues, as he thought that the major part of the fighting, this time, would be in the northern front, along the Syrian border, and that the conflict would escalate quickly into a three-frontier conflict encompassing the Syrians, the Egyptians, and even the Jordanians (such a widespread war, of course, would also encompass elements from throughout the Arab world—from Iraqui, Saudi, and Lebanese units rushing to the eastern front to aid the Syrians; and Libyan, Algerian, and Moroccan units fighting alongside the Egyptians). Whether the fighting was destined to take place on the Golan or in Sinai, the brigade commanders readied their units for war which, for the 7th Brigade, was somewhat of a problem.

Unlike armor units that had been positioned along the northern frontier during the War of Attrition that had participated in the fighting—albeit small-scale counterinsurgency operations and incursions into Lebanon—virtually ninety percent of the brigade's personnel had never fired off a shot in anger. While many battalion and company officers had seen combat, most of the conscripts had entered their mandatory military service after the 1967 victory. In fact, these green eighteen-year-olds, weaned on stories of absolute victory and the almighty power of the almighty IDF, were as cocky and confident as they come. Many of these soldiers, some fresh out of basic training in 1972, viewed the serious low-jowl expression on Yanush's face as ridiculous. Many were confident that they would not see combat during their stint with the brigade. They were a cohesive and well-trained brigade, but one that couldn't comprehend that the Arabs were capable or willing to risk another war against the IDF. Morale, however, was high. The days of Gonen frightening his men to perform were over.

From day one as 7th Brigade commander, Yanush prepared a chart in his office in southern Israel that he titled, "DAYS TO GO TO WAR: REQUIRED PREPARATIONS." Every month the chart would be renewed and revitalized and Yanush knew that one day, in the middle of his monthly schedule for honing his men for combat, an attack would commence somewhere and the brigade would find itself fighting a desperate holding action or swift assault. Even though the brigade's permanent area of responsibility was the south of Israel, Ben-Gal frequented the Golan Heights on fact-finding missions and demanded that his senior command staff, from battalion level down to company commanders, acquaint themselves with every inch of the volcanic plateau towering high above the Sea of Galilee. "Know this area like you know your backyard," Yanush would tell his men. "You'll be fighting for your lives here in the near future." So sure was Yanush of his prophecy that he urged and eventually convinced OC Northern Command, Major-General Yitzhak Hofi, to authorize an exchange program where brigade tank crews could join northern units during operational assignments so that they, too, could familiarize themselves with the topography, the surroundings, and the reality of fighting in the north, so close to the northern settlements. Fighting atop a limited stretch of terrain, 30-square miles of volcanic rock and ash, boulders, and sparse foliage, was a far cry from the vast desert wasteland of the Sinai. There would be little room for classic maneuvering atop the Golan, little room for textbook tank warfare. Any tank battle on the Heights would be a slugfest, a street brawl with the vanquished destroyed and the victor badly bruised.

Yanush's 7th Armored Brigade that sizzling summer of 1973 consisted of two tank battalions, the 82nd and 77th, and one mechanized infantry battalion, the 75th. The 82nd Battalion was commanded by Lieutenant-Colonel Haim Barak, a veteran tank officer who had made a name for himself during the 1967 fighting as a no-nonsense tank soldier from the Gonen mold whose three *D* philosophy of command (*discipline, discipline, discipline*) demanded the three *A*'s from his men (*accuracy, adherence to the target, and absolute dedication to the mission*). The 82nd had recently upgraded itself from the M48/M60 Patton to the Centurian MBT. The 77th Battalion, known by its Hebrew numeric acronym of *Oz*, or "Courage," was commanded by Lieutenant-Colonel Avigdor Kahalani, already a living legend within IDF Armored Corps circles, a walking testament to returning from a life-threatening injury and already one of the most decorated and commended soldiers ever to serve in the IDF. The 77th, too, was a Centurion unit, and the battalion deputy commander, Major Eitan Kauli, was considered one of the rising stars of the Armored Corps, as was another officer in the unit, Major Avraham "Ami" Pelnat. The 75th Battalion, the infantry edge to the tanks, was commanded by Lieutenant-Colonel Yossi Eldar, another spit-

and-polish disciplinarian who was considered an above-average tactician with more than above-average courage. He was, according to Kahalani, "the type of man you'd like to have with you on a dark night behind enemy lines."[2] The 75th was a mixed bag of aging M3 half-tracks, relics from the Second World War that the IDF was finding painfully obsolete, and the newer M113 APCs recently received from the United States. The brigade's reconnaissance platoon, the *Plugat Siyur*, was commanded by Captain Uri Karshani, a tough paratroop-qualified officer who realized the importance of mobility and firepower when deploying with a tank unit, especially in defeating infantry ambushes.

Throughout the latter portion of 1972, and throughout 1973, Colonel Ben-Gal put the brigade through the ringer—mainly in offensive doctrine exercises. Preparing for possible action against the Egyptians along the Suez Canal, he organized water-obstacle exercises, full-scale maneuvers, for the entire brigade. He engineered these large-scale obstacle-crossing maneuvers to prepare the brigade for crossing the antitank ditches that cut through the Syrian frontier atop the Golan Heights. Most importantly, Yanush ensured that his tank crews were expert shots. No matter what front the unit would be deployed to, Colonel Ben-Gal realized that the brigade would be an outnumbered entity. Quality against quantity, especially in tank-versus-tank warfare, meant that you killed more of the enemy than they could kill of you. Targets had to be hit on first or second shots, and new targets acquired immediately and aggressively. Such skills were not inherent in the psyche or physical abilities of Israeli soldiers. They were hammered home in the classroom and in the field, in the developing relationship between a commander and his gunner, and in the realization that while a subpar performance in an exercise would probably spark the wrath of an officer, against the Syrians it meant being burnt like a piece of kebob inside a steel death trap.

The brigade was spread out through the southern portion of Israel and Sinai in keeping with its operational assignments. It kept to its regular training regimen during the summer of 1973 and successfully completed maneuvers and exercises. The 82nd Battalion had just completed brigade exercises with the 35th Paratroop Brigade, the IDF's conscript airborne force, and the 77th was completing a smaller scale exercise, including *Tza'ma'p* maneuvers with many of its platoons. As the blazing summer of 1973 moved into autumn, the brigade was busy planning its role in celebrating the twenty-fifth anniversary of the unit to be held at Latrun, as well as the country's 25th birthday.

Tensions grew. A march to war, one well-calculated by the Arabs, had begun. The Egyptians had planned to go to war in the spring of 1973 but had been dissuaded from doing so by the Soviets, who still pulled the strings. But the dogfight over Lebanon and its escalating hostilies was an obvious harbinger of worse to come. It was also a useful smoke screen for the true essence of the Egyptian and Syrian plans. With tensions on the rise and threats of war emanating from both Damascus and Cairo, men and materiel could be moved toward the front without sparking too much extraordinary interest. Now both Egypt and Syria had been secretly preparing for war, coordinating their time of attack and preparing it all with Soviet assistance.

All that was needed was a spark.

On September 13, 1973, a patrol of IAF F-4Es, RF-4Es, and Mirage IIICs were ambushed by a flight of Syrian Air Force MiG-21s while on a reconnaissance sortie near the port of Latakia. In the ensuing dogfight, the IAF jets downed 13 Syrian aircraft without suffering a single loss. Expecting Syrian retaliation or at least a mobilization ordered from Damascus, the Israelis bolstered their own defenses. *Rosh Ha'Shana* (Jewish New Year) leaves were canceled, and combat engineers worked around the clock building two new bridges across the Jordan River, while also improving the antitank ditch that ran along the Syrian frontier (known as the "Purple Line") and earthen ramparts that were to serve as tank firing positions in case the Syrians ever decided to launch an attack across the 1967 Cease Fire Line. On September 13, 1973, Yanush's "DAYS TO GO TO WAR: REQUIRED PREPARATIONS" chart received its justification.

For Lieutenant-Colonel Avigdor Kahalani, commander of the 77th Battalion, the fall meant that it was time to put a new roof on the house before the late autumn rains. Signs pointed to war but the impending rain meant it was time to mend the roof and fix the heating system. "I hope there's time to get around to everything," Kahalani recalls telling himself. "I don't think there'll be much time off from the brigade this season."

The IDF was—and is—an army where everybody knows everybody else, and for officers in the brigade, the talk of war that September was far more than gossip meant to pass interludes between maneuvers and maintenance. Low-level intelligence officers in Southern Command, young and capable men fresh out of Intel School who were not tainted by bureaucracy and personalities, could see the signs of an Egyptian buildup growing day by day and even hour by hour. Their reports were filtered through the chain of command where, as the seeds of the disaster of 1973 were planted, they were lost, ignored, or dismissed as inexperienced. *A'man,* the Hebrew acronym for *Agaf Mode'in,* or Intelligence Branch, was one of the most capable intelligence-gathering services in the Middle East and certainly the world, but it, too, was subject to the disease of bureaucracy and complacent career path. Many officers found the desk work a comfortable profession and lost their sense of actual threat and combat that they once possessed as conscript foot soldiers. Such was the case in the South Command's Military Intelligence Egypt Desk, where senior officers routinely failed to analyze and disseminate the daily updates from spotters along the canal and from agents inside Egypt; aerial reconnaissance photos were also pretty much ignored even though IAF pilots were shocked by the Egyptian preparations for war and the Israeli lackadaisical response. The subject of the Israeli military intelligence failure concerning monitoring the movement of Egyptian and Syrian troops, as well as analyzing the unfolding events in Cairo and Damascus, has been the subject of much myth and proclamation, much study and examination. For the men in the field, the soldiers who would absorb that first devastating blow of the Egyptian or Syrian blitz, how military intelligence and the Israeli leadership bungled its data and assets, was inconsequential. The results of the debacle, including an emergency summit in late September between Prime Minister Golda Meir and Jordan's King Hussein (a man many Israeli military officers called "the intelligence officer of the Middle East") where the monarch warned the Israeli that a joint Arab attack was imminent,[3] guaranteed a desperate first few hours on the battlefield.

Colonel Yanush Ben-Gal was a man who by his very nature as a "soldier's soldier" disliked what is referred to in the IDF vernacular as the *Jobnik,* the paper pusher behind the desk who is more office worker than soldier and combatant. Yanush understood that conscripts who were *Jobniks* were soldiers that for a variety of personal, physical, and home-related reasons were behind a desk. Junior officers working in Intelligence Branch were usually young enough to have missed the Six Day War yet old enough to have fought in the War of Attrition. They were not jaded by the victorious exuberance that infected the IDF, nor were they battlefield virgins. Many were skilled and capable. Such understanding was not afforded staff officers, however. Yanush read the junior officer reports and didn't like what he saw.

Yanush's days grew increasingly longer and longer. His primary thought was full-scale war with Egypt and he studied the intelligence library on Egypt with great eagerness. Did they have any new tanks? Any new bits of equipment and ammunition? What were their night-vision capabilities like? What infantry-held, antitank weaponry did they possess? Were any Mi-8 choppers transformed into tank-hunting gunships? Yanush had been through the books before, as had all his officers, but time was running out. The "DAYS TO GO TO WAR" chart was growing close. All the battalions were visited with greater frequency and the men ordered to tow the line with greater discipline and stress. According to one conscript in the 82nd Battalion, "There was a tension in the air around Qastina that could not be identified, but one that everyone felt."

The IDF Northern Command ordered the 77th Battalion to the Golan front on New Year's eve. The soldiers were processed out of Southern Command, flown to the IAF airfield at Rosh Pina, and then issued with new equipment and Centurion tanks from an emergency warehouse at a forward staging base. Kahalani's battalion was meant to serve as a reserve and backup unit to Colonel Ben-Shoham's 188th Barak Brigade—the conscript unit on station across the

Syrian lines. Kahalani was to assist in Ben-Shoham's counter attack repelling Syrian forces back behind the frontier. If only everything had been that simple.

Throughout the slow buildup among officers who had the foresight to predict war in the south, IDF Operations officers failed to fully realize the actual threat in the north. The Syrian Army was a 650,000-man force of conscripts and professional soldiers considered by some IDF intelligence to be better than the Egyptians, and far more brutal. Like the Egyptians, the Syrians were equipped solely by the Soviets and their armored forces consisted of T-62s, T-55/54s, and the gamut of BTR armored personnel carriers. Fighting in the north was different than battlefield scenarios in the south. There wasn't a vast frontier from which to guess where an Egyptian crossing might take place. The Golan was 13 miles wide at its widest point and the frontier with Syria was 36 miles long. Unlike the Suez Canal that separated the warring factions in the south, man-made obstacles of a different nature kept the Syrian Army out of the Golan—defenses that consisted of antitank ditches, minefields, and defensive-firing ramps. The antitank ditch was built two kilometers inside Israeli-controlled territory—the Syrians could cross the Purple Line, Israeli defensive strategy preached, but once they reached the ditch, they would enter a tank killing zone of unprecedented destruction. In hindsight, the ditch was a great success with one great flaw— it worked against an enemy that stopped coming and ran out of crews and vehicles.

The Syrian battle plan called for the capture of the entire Golan Heights before pushing into central and northern Israel and they hoped to reach the Jordan River bridges by the end of the first 12 hours of fighting. As a result, the primary focus of the Syrian advance would be the southern Golan Heights and the shortest route to the Jordan River bridges. By October 2, 1973, the Syrians had amassed across the Purple Line three infantry divisions (the 5th, 7th, and 9th), along with mechanized and special forces elements, and two armored divisions (the 1st and the 3rd). The Syrian attack force for their "flash bang" bid to overwhelm the Israelis included 1,500 tanks (T-62s, T-55/54s, and 40 PT-76 amphibious tanks). The Syrians had 155 heavy artillery and mortar batteries and dozens of surface-to-air missile batteries, the lethal SA-2, SA-3, and SA-6s, and dozens of mobile antiaircraft guns, such as the lethal ZSU-23-4 and ZSU-57-2s. A lethal missile and gun umbrella, a counterweight to the IAF, had been set in place from the Purple Line to downtown Damascus.

On October 4, the Israelis noticed that the Syrians had abandoned their secondary defensive lines and that units stationed in Katna and Kiswe had moved toward the Purple Line in emergency deployments. IDF Northern Command, commanded by Major-General Yitzhak Hofi, could draw but one conclusion—the Syrians were intending to attack.

Defending the Golan Heights were the men—and women—of the 36th Armored Division,[4] a combined *Ugda* incorporating the 188th "Barak" Armored Brigade and the 1st Golani Infantry Brigade. The 188th was Northern Command's regular brigade, and, in case of war, was responsible for drawing a defensive line from the divisional HQ at Nafakh[5] all the way south toward the Jordanian frontier. The 188th was commanded by Colonel Yitzhak Ben-Shoham, who, after a stint as commander of the IDF Staff and Command College, received the brigade in May 1973. Born in Turkey, Ben-Shoham was a charismatic leader who had been described as a natural among the men in his command. Augmenting the Israeli defensive lines throughout the length of the frontier were seventeen *Mutzavim* (Positions), fortified trip wires that were defended by squads of infantrymen and positioned to the west of the forward defenses and ditch; Position 107, interestingly enough, was the sole position situated east of the ditch between the barrier and the frontier. The antitank ditch was designed to slow down a Syrian armor advance and channel the oncoming armor into predetermined killing zones. Covering these tank hunting grounds were 2.5-meter-high elevated earth ramparts (specially designed for the Centurion MBT's nine-degree gun depression) from which tanks in hull-down positions could bring accurate fire to bear on the encroaching armor below.

On Friday, October 5, on the eve of Yom Kippur, IDF HQ declared *Konenut Gimel* ("Alert C") the highest state of alert for the standing conscript army. The details laying last-minute mines went about their business and orders were cut for the entire 7th Brigade to join up with the 77th Battalion atop the heights. Yanush preceded his men and equipment, though he accompanied his officers on terrain familiarization tours. Both Yanush and Ben-Shoham, together with Raful and other senior officers spent the night preparing defensive plans and strategies. War was expected to break out any moment. Yanush had prepared his brigade for a fight in the desert—this was to be a completely different ball game.

Camp Sa'ar, Central Golan, October 6, 1973, 1000 hours

The mood inside the brigade's field HQ at "Camp Sa'ar" was beyond tense four hours before the attack. The talk now was of the great unknown of war. Career officers who looked confident in their Nomex coveralls were liteally walking anxiety cases. Would they see their families again? What kind of war would this be? Men like Kahalani and Eldar were able to maintain the level of confidence and posture mainly for their men; "You lead by example and gain respect by example," Kahalani would say. They had been through the wringer before but many of the soldiers, the eighteen-year-old conscripts, were visibly shaken by the thought of war. Many of the religious soldiers were deep in prayer in the base synagogue, uttering the prayers of the Day of Atonement in their coveralls and field caps, their Uzi 9mm submachine guns by their muddied boots. Many of the secular soldiers, irreligious individuals who in times of peace would be sleeping this day off or sneaking in a meal, were also deep in prayer.

All battalion commanders attended the meeting at Camp Sa'ar along with their deputies and intelligence officers. The room, a concrete square protected from the elements by a corrugated tin roof, was full of smoke and nervous leg twitching. Yanush stood by a four-foot-high map of the Golan Heights and read through Northern Command's latest intelligence reports. A few last-minute tactical items were discussed, but on the whole the meeting was meant to reiterate a sense of confidence among the battalion commanders and to discuss the allocation of the brigade throughout the Golan Heights' northern sector. That Yom Kippur morning, the 7th Armored Brigade's order of battle consisted of 105 Centurion MBTs and several dozen M3 half-tracks spread out along an axis from Nafakh junction of the Oil Line to West junction.

Yanush's briefing to all battalion and company commanders lasted nearly 30 minutes. The meeting ended warmly, though distanced. According to the latest intelligence reports straight off the *A'man* wires, war was scheduled to erupt at 1800 hours, and there were still eight hours to go. As the officers raise their tired bones out of their chairs, Yanush informed them that the final briefing would be at 1400 hours. The officers wished their fellow battalion and company comrades a "Good Luck" and *"Le'Hitra'ot"* (Hebrew for "See You Later"), smiled, and took their jeeps back to their units. The 82nd Battalion was based at Sindiana, the 71st Battalion was based at West junction, the 75th Battalion at an army staging area, and the 77th at Nafakh junction. Each battalion and company commander used the last hours of quiet to tour their areas, reconnoiter the frontier and tank defenses, and be seen by the ranks as being in charge. Everyone knew that once the shooting started the commander's voice would be a fixture over battalion and company radio frequencies, but seeing "the man" instilled confidence and settled stomachs.

Eighteen hundred hours seemed a logical hour to attack. A bright orange sun would be settling to the west and showing the heights with a soothing glow. Israeli tanks in their ramps would be silhouetted against the dipping sun for at least an hour providing the first wave of Syrian armor with a very clear, and very tempting row of targets. "Even bad Syrian tank crews would have no problem seeing the Israeli tanks in that lighting," recalled one tank officer. "It would have been a crap shoot." At 1350 hours, most of the men of the 7th Armored Brigade were in their vehicles or around them—some ate combat portions after IDF rabbis approved eating on Yom Kippur, others wrote letters home, others cleaned their weapons and maintained their vehicles. All smoked. There were still four hours to go. In the distance, however, the beating sounds of helicopter rotor blades were heard in the north, in the direction of Mount Hermon. All eyes turned toward the "Old Man," the Arabic nickname for the most valued intelligence-gathering position in the Israeli inventory. "Mother," uttered one 77th Battalion gunner. "Shit," screamed his tank's driver. It has begun. The muffled sounds of explosions coming from Mount Hermon were soon even more muffled by the sounds of IAF jets flying in the background and frantic cries of confusion over division radio. At 1400 hours on the dot, nothing but explosions and screams were heard atop the Golan Heights. The Syrian blitz was massive. First came low-flying Sukhoi Su-7 attack jets firing their 30mm cannons and 37mm rockets, then dropping their load of two 500 kilogram and two 750 kilogram bombs. Their aircraft runs were effective. A minute into the blitz several tanks were damaged, a few half-tracks destroyed, and countless targets in the rear set ablaze; their billowing black smoke clouds began to cover the warmth of the setting sun in the east. After the Syrian jets came Syrian artillery. The barrage was incredible and incessant. Over 200 artillery batteries on the Syrian side of the frontier unleashed a volley of high-explosive death and destruction. It was, according to one Israeli infantryman in a forward position, the most fantastic display of power that he could have ever imagined.

The attack caught most units by surprise—the shock was absolute. Second-Lieutenant Benny Habit was a young mechanized infantry platoon commander in the 75th Battalion when the Syrian attack commenced. He had just completed platoon exercises and was expecting new soldiers when the unit was rushed north to the Golan. After meeting with other brigade officers, Second-Lieutenant Habit returned to his units and was in the middle of handing out tins of white paints and brushes to his men in order to paint white aerial identification stripes on the unit's vehicles. The men were busy painting their vehicles and wondering about what the next few hours would have in store for them when suddenly, without warning, a swarm of Syrian Air Force Sukhoi Su-7 fighter-bombers flew overhead showering the Israeli troopers with cannon and rocket fire.

The Syrian barrage and assault were equally as ferocious along the entire stretch of the Purple Line. To the tank soldiers in both the 7th and Barak Brigades, they couldn't tell which was worse—the artillery assault that was ripping across the earth in which they were dug into, or the small green and brown dots moving toward the frontier in neat and increasing velocity rows. The advancing Syrian armor wasn't daunting, it was all-encompassing. The Syrians threw almost 400 tanks at the Israeli lines that initial blitz, moving in at two points—a smaller effort in the north, with the brunt of their armor vanguard mauling the front lines in the southern half of the Heights. Throughout the brigade and division frequencies, monitors could hear tank commanders ordering their loaders to place a round in the breech and for the gunner to await the order of *"Esh!"*

When the first Syrian shells landed, the 7th Brigade brought to the battlefield two full tank battalions: the 77th and the 82nd; the 75th battalion was made up of elements of the brigade's reconnaissance company and a company of mechanized infantrymen still in the middle of basic training. The brigade's reconnaissance unit, the *Sayeret Hativatit,* was tasked with brigade operations along the front and behind the rear to secure supply lines from attack by Syrian commandos, and the mechanized troopers weren't even risked along the front lines. The entire battalion consisted, basically, of the command element of Lieutenant-Colonel Yossi Eldar, though at the last minute the 71st Battalion, commanded by Lieutenant-Colonel Meshulam Retes, was attached to Eldar's command, and students in the midst of professions training at Armored School, along with their instructors. Retes did not know the Golan Heights and had only been in the area with his family on a weekend outing a year or so earlier. After the Golan Heights was divided between the 7th Brigade and the 188th, two additional units made their way to Yanush's command: units from the 188th Brigade's "Sa'ar Battalion" under the command of Lieutenant-Colonel Yair Nafshi, and several platoons of infantrymen from the 1st Golani Brigade who were to man the *Mutzavim* along the Purple Line. In turn, Yanush handed over the 82nd Battalion under the command of Lieutenant-Colonel Haim Barak to Colonel Ben-Shoham and the 188th. Barak, a new and inexperienced battalion commander, did not know the Golan Heights at all. Yanush retained one unit from Barak's Battalion as a brigade reserve unit: Third Company under the command of Captain Meir "Tiger" Zamir.

Opposite the Israeli positions was the largest army the Syrians had ever succeeded in fielding. The initial Syrian line of attack consisted of the 5th, 7th, and 9th Infantry Divisions supported by 900 tanks; the secondary line of attack consisted of 500 tanks divided into two armored divisions. Only 100 tanks were left in reserve and they were positioned at strategic defensive firing pits in Damascus; President Assad had gambled the national defense in this bold attack on Yom Kippur Day. Throughout the Syrian lines, 155 artillery batteries had been positioned to shell Israeli positions, and 32 antiaircraft emplacements, mobile SAMs, and 23mm and 57mm guns were also placed in strategic lots behind the advancing armor to provide the much-needed aerial umbrella. The roadway from Damascus to the Purple Line was a massive parking lot of infantrymen and their supply vehicles.

There were some troubling signs indicating Israeli unpreparedness. Two tank brigades defended the Heights, but there was little coordination between the two and there was still no formal allocation of forces into operational districts only four hours before the Syrian onslaught. In fact, only at the very outbreak of fighting, when both Yanush's and 188th commander Ben-Shoham's command centers were under attack, did the two men divide the Golan Heights tank units among themselves. The 7th Brigade formally received the northern tier of the Heights as well as Lieutenant-Colonel Yair Nafshi's "Sa'ar" Battalion of mechanized infantrymen. The 188th Brigade was formally charged with protecting the southern portion of the Heights and it received control of the 7th's 82nd Battalion.

When the attack commenced, the 77th Battalion moved along the Nafakh-Ein Zivan-Quneitra line and positioned itself between Booster and Position 110. They were a blocking force right in the center of a major venue for a Syrian advance and Kahalani was exactly where Yanush wanted him. The 71st Battalion moved along the West Achamadiya junction–Buqata line and positioned itself "with guns drawn" between Positions 104 and 105. Lieutenant-Colonel Eldar's 75th Battalion, that had been reinforced with one of Kahalani's companies, moved along the West Line and Achamadiya junction, and positioned itself in the area of Hermonit. Yanush allowed Lieutenant-Colonel Nafshi and his three companies of armor and infantrymen to remain in his original position along the Purple Line around Positions 105, 107, and 109.

There was nothing fancy to Yanush's strategy and battle plan for the northern portion of the Golan Heights—it was all pure textbook. Strategy was an important aspect of armored warfare but more often than not it proved to be a matter for the war-gamers and strategy players at Command School. Defensive action relied on a brigade's tools: the quality of its vehicles, the number of vehicles available, and the iron will of its men. The Centurion was a good tank—not a great tank. Numbers were a problem, but Yanush knew that his men were second to none. The first line of defense was Lieutenant-Colonel Nafshi's three companies of tanks. They had been stationed atop the Heights for far longer than the 7th Brigade's battalions and they knew the terrain like the back of their hand. Their mission was to destroy the vanguard Syrian armor breaching the antitank ditch and to call in artillery strikes against advancing Syrian formations. Yanush also wanted Nafshi's units to act as a stopgap reconnaissance force and to provide intelligence (as well as a harassing presence) against the never-ending columns of Syrian tanks moving west. The three battalions of the 7th Brigade were to provide the main defensive obstacle to Syrian aims—the 71st, 75th, and 77th Battalions were to destroy any Syrian armor advancing through the first line obstacles and fortifications and prevent any breach of the last line of defense before Galilee. One company from the 75th Battalion was held in reserve south of Quneitra to respond to any audacious Syrian moves behind Israeli lines, as well as to be an on-call force of last resort for any battalion on the verge of annihilation. Yanush's primary objective was to hold the line and prevent the Syrians from gaining access to the Quneitra-Masada Line—a route that would have served as a conduit for a massive breakthrough into northern Israel. The 7th Brigade wouldn't have to hold out forever—seventy-two hours maximum was the common perception—

just until the reserve units were mobilized, equipped, and in-place to relieve and support. Seventy hours was the time allotment during maneuvers and in General Staff symposiums. Seventy-two hours didn't take into consideration a surprise attack and a war on two fronts, however.

Looking through their field glasses and target acquisition systems, the Israeli tank commanders and gunners peered through the smoke and debris to see the first wave of Syrian armor. The first vehicles across the mangled barbed wire fortification were Russian-made MT-55s and MTU-20 brigade-layers and Czech-produced MT-55s—and they were the only vehicles that the gunners engaged at long range. It was crucial to keep them from establishing a launch over the antitank ditch—crucial to keeping the Syrian onslaught at bay. Even if it stalled them for an hour.

The Syrian advance proceeded in such a way that the first 7th Brigade unit to encounter the enemy was the Centurions of Lieutenant-Colonel Yoss Eldar's 75th Battalion. The Syrians, although dedicating most of their assets in the direction of the 188th Barak Brigade, were also pushing quite heavily in the direction of the Valley of Tears: a flat plateau named *Wadi Bakha* in Arabic and *Emeq Ha'Becha* in Hebrew, which connected the two hills of Tel Hermonit, the volcanic hill near El Rom, and a lower hill approximately three miles to the south nicknamed "The Booster." The initial Syrian advance, a rolling procession of T-62 MBTs was a full-scale combat litmus test of sorts—they were probing and testing Israeli resolve and Israeli accuracy. Eldar's tanks proved capable. When the T-62s MBTs reached a range of 1,000 meters out, the Centurions opened fire with their L7 105mm cannons. In the first engagement, the Syrians lost ten tanks and five were damaged. The Israelis suffered no casualties. As Eldar ordered his vehicles to move about and reconfigure their firing positions, he noticed the Syrians pulling back out of range and waiting for the onset of darkness. That was a troubling sign. It meant that Syrian tanks were equipped with infrared night-fighting equipment. The 7th Brigade wasn't. It was going to be a long night.

As darkness fell and the battle commenced again, Lieutenant-Colonel Eldar leapt off his Brigade OC APC and played Bedouin—he placed his ear toward the chewed-up path and attempted to listen to the oncoming Syrian armor—if you can't see them, then you might be able to hear them and destroy them. Many of his tankers thought it a bit odd and unsettling to see their commanding officer "go native" on them, but gut reaction, instinct, and a good ear are sometimes as valuable as the latest Soviet-produced night-fighting gear. Eldar wanted his men to light up just one tank—it didn't matter which one. The blazing armored vehicle would then provide a range reference and just enough illumination to place the advancing armor in shadow and silhouette. But as late as 2000 hours the battlefield was still quiet—too quiet. The tank crews sat poised for immediate firing, but nothing was coming at them. Nervous by not having the Syrians follow his expectations, Lieutenant-Colonel Eldar radioed in for artillery to fire flares over the antitank ditch. By midnight, when the Syrian commander ordered his tanks west, the Israeli gunners finally obtained their chance to set off armored torches in the distance. One tank, whose commander was standing upright atop the turret, was trying to gauge the position of the oncoming tanks and fired off several armored-piercing rounds at what they thought were targets. The blast of the 105mm gun firing was followed by a white-hot trail into the darkened distance. A shell that missed its mark was heard. The one that hit its tank, a company commander's T-62, erupted into an orange ball of fire that refused to extinguish. The torch had been lit and targets were available. The tank battle had begun. Peering through his field glasses, Eldar noticed that five Syrian tanks had *already* crossed the antitank ditch and were only 500 meters from the defensive ramps. They were immediately locked on and destroyed.

Just as the fourth Syrian tank burst into flames and its crew attempted to escape, they, too, were on fire and screaming as they rolled onto the ground in a failed attempt to extinguish their burning overalls and charred flesh. The battalion OC APC was hit by artillery fire: a 115mm round landed inches from the tread of the M113 and ripped a section of the tracks and wheels into twisted and flaming metal. Three officers were wounded in the "hit," including Eldar who found his shoulder peppered with shrapnel. Bleeding quite badly, he summoned 77th Battalion commander Kahalani on the brigade radio and asked for help. The Syrian onslaught was encroaching and their guns were becoming more accurate. A battalion aid station was set up with the serious cases brought back to Safed for care and the walking wounded patched together and sent back to their tanks. The choking stench of cordite had already engulfed the usually crystal-clean Golan air. Fires could be seen burning on both the Syrian and Israeli ends of the border, and tracer fire turned the blackened sky into a muted fireworks display.

Eldar's wounds turned the show in the Golan's north over to Kahalani and the 77th Battalion. Of all the units in the brigade, the 77th Battalion was best suited for the task at hand simply because they had been atop the Heights the longest and knew the area better than tank commanders in the other brigade battalions. According to Major-General (Res.) Orri Orr, a brilliant tank officer who would have a tremendous role in pushing the Syrians off the Heights all the way to the outskirts of Damascus, "Knowledge of the terrain is more important than knowing how to breathe in tank warfare. In order to be able to kill the enemy the tank commander must know every nook and cranny of the terrain on which he is fighting. Where is a good ditch for concealment? Where is there soft earth that could entrap my tank at high speeds? Which rocks are likely to move and slide and cause the tank to tumble down an embankment?" Kahalani's men, and indeed virtually all the tank soldiers of the brigade were quite intimate with the sands in Sinai, but not at all familiar with the volcanic ash plateau of the Heights. Maps meant little when fighting for one's life. Instinct drives the mind and instinct told commanders that grids "X" and "Y" on the map were not good for ambush positions, and coordinates "4" and "5" favored the infantry in engagements against mechanized forces. This unfamiliarity with the terrain was, of course, compounded by the Syrian penchant for advancing at night under cover of darkness. "In war," recalls Brigadier-General (Res.) Elyashiv Shimshi,[6] "soldiers should be like police officers—they should know every corner of the patch of territory they have been tasked to secure." In Sinai, had the brigade remained in its predetermined defensive zones,[7] they would have been able to fight blindfolded and move throughout the territory unhindered by darkness. Atop the Golan, the situation was somewhat different. Tank commanders had to spend as much time and effort finding their way and negotiating the environment as they did in dodging Syrian antitank rounds and enemy RPG flurries. Through his field glasses, Kahalani could see that the Syrians had positioned nearly 90 tanks on "their" side of the antitank ditch, directly opposite the no-man's-land of the Valley of Tears. They made several attempts to cross the barrier, but found crossing the ditch on bridging equipment under constant fire to be a difficult, if not impossible exercise. Kahalani ordered artillery units to open fire on the ditches or at least to fire some flares over the battlefield, but each request was answered with a negative response. Already, only 12 hours into the battle, artillery batteries had run out of ammunition.

There were already remarkable stories of courage and the unique, "chance" and the bizarre, that unfold during the chaos of the fog of war. In one instance, in the middle of the first night, soldiers from Captain Eli Geva's First Company encountered elements of the technical platoon alone in the field attempting to repair their damaged APCs. As the tanks approached, the relieved soldiers, who were working on the vehicles together, heard the roaring sounds of tank engines closing in fast. But just as quickly as they appeared the sounds vanished into the distance. The soldiers prepared a defensive perimeter while the APCs were repaired. After being relieved of guard duty, one soldier in the company, Herzl Zla'it, grabbed his parka and made an impromptu bed for himself atop an APC. As he drifted into dreamland for that ever-so-important 15 minutes of sleep soldiers seem to catch whenever they can, he heard shouting in Hebrew, "Shoot them, shoot them!" A second later, a stern voice was heard in Arabic. It was a Syrian soldier, AK-47 assault rifle in hand, who was demanding that the Israelis drop their guns and surrender with hands in the air. A Syrian T-55 also arrived at the bivouac and aimed its 100mm main cannon straight for the command APC under repair at a point-blank range of five meters. Several of the Israeli soldiers began to cry; all were hysterical.

A native Arabic speaker, Herzl shocked the Syrian soldier

when he told him to wait a minute and calm down. The Syrian soldier, dumbfounded by the ongoing negotiations in the field, actually lowered his rifle and stared openmouthed at the Israeli soldier. It was a lapse in concentration that Herzl was waiting for. Determined not to become a POW, especially in Syrian hands, he removed the safety from his Uzi 9mm submachine gun and removed two fragmentation grenades from his canvas waist pouch. In a move that in retrospect reminded many of a bad Hong Kong martial arts film, Herzl jumped off the APC, opened fire on the Syrian soldier, and threw a grenade at the Syrian tank. The Syrian tank commander had left his turret hatch open, and the M26 fragmentation grenade bounced into the turret, detonating three seconds later. A muted explosion was heard and a cloud of black and acrid smoke was seen coming from the tank. The driver, still alive, managed to pull the gears into reverse and return to friendly lines. Unimpressed by saving his comrades and destroying a tank, Herzl grabbed more grenades and raced after the tank. "You're crazy, come back," his crewmates yelled, "there are Syrian commandos out there."[8]

The hustle and bustle at Camp Sa'ar was frantic in the early morning hours after midnight. Operation rooms, intelligence rooms, and command rooms were all ablaze with activity: officers sent by company and battalion chiefs back to HQ for urgent manpower and supply requests, intelligence officers on the radio with IDF HQ in Tel Aviv finding out any new information that would hold the units in the field, and Yanush and company attempting to direct a war that was slowly turning out to be a fight of desperate survival. "The scene was a claustrophobic scene of chaos," recalls a division intelligence officer.[9] "With the first shell a tremendous group of individuals headed toward the base's intelligence bunker to conduct the minute-by-minute handling of the defensive action. There were command reps there, along with division officers, as well as deputies of Yanush, Ben-Shoham, and anyone and everybody who had something to do with fighting the Syrians. The Intelligence Bunker was small, dimly lit, and poorly ventilated. The air conditioner conked out and it stank to high heaven in its small confines."

In a back corner of the base, men in olive fatigues and long and flowing beards, army rabbis, were preparing the dead for burial the next day. Throughout the front the situation had been bad, and the fate of the 188th Barak Brigade in the south was still somewhat of a mystery to Yanush. Divisional commander Brigadier-General Eitan, described after the war as a soothing pillar of confidence and courage amid a storm of death, was attempting to defend his zone while waiting for the reserve. He had met with Yanush and 1st Golani Infantry Brigade commander Colonel Amir Drori, as well; Colonel Ben-Shoham, literally fighting for his life, was not available for staff meetings. Artillery batteries, those left operational following the Syrian blitz and aerial strafing runs, were running out of ammunition. Air support was there but minimal—the IDF and the IAF were too small an entity to wage full-scale war on two fronts. IAF strikes were dedicated and some of the low-level runs truly successful, but the Syrians—as would the Egyptians in the south—had followed Soviet military doctrine to the letter and had slowly inched their advance along, covered by a vast and impervious network of mobile surface-to-air missile batteries. Syrian MiG pilots dared not engage the IAF, but each IAF sortie was met by the swooshing symphony of SA-2, SA-3, and SA-6 surface-to-air ordnance homing in on radar and heat sources. Infantrymen, positioned in every corner of the Syrian advance, were also armed with the lethal antidote to low-flying aircraft and helicopters: the SA-7 Strella. The *Hayalim Ha'Pshutim,* or "simple soldiers," as ground soldiers are often referred to in IDF slang when compared to special forces personnel and pilots, once thought the IAF's flyers to be invincible. They could do no wrong, encounter no foe that could defeat them at Mach 2 excellence, and provide the most accurate of ground support from the most dashing speeds and dizzying altitudes. But atop the Heights that first few hours, tank soldiers saw a sight that they could not have even fathomed before the war. IAF fighter-bombers, A-4 Skyhawks, and F-4E Phantoms were being blown out of the sky in record numbers. As darkness fell, many 7th Brigade tank commanders on the ground even mistook exploding Israeli aircraft for artillery flares that they had requested. Tank soldiers realized that they were somewhat alone in this fight, and so did Yanush. It had been a busy first 12 hours.

At 0200 hours on the morning of October 7, Yanush received reports that part of his battlefield chess game strategy was paying off. The last tier of the 7th Brigade's defensive posture, the defense of the Rafid-Quneitra line, was in the charge of one Captain Meir Zamir, commander of Third Company, 82nd Battalion. From the time the first Syrian shells landed until the early morning hours of October 7, Zamir's company was part of Major Eitan Kauli's roaming force of armor deployed on a highly mobile axis between Position 100 and Quneitra. They were, in essence, a tank-hunting element of the brigade tasked with engaging probing actions by Syrian armor far ahead of the main advance; they had chased a platoon of Syrian armor from the fields of Kibbutz Ein Zivan at 2300 hours, for example, but the Syrians fled before an engagement could commence. Captain Zamir's code name over the brigade network was "Tiger," and as a result his force of seven Centurions operated under the code name of "Force Tiger"; a mysterious and menacing nom de guerre meant to instill confidence in its ranks as well as lead Syrian intelligence-gathering posts eavesdropping in on Israeli transmissions to think that they were up against a far larger force than originally believed. Yanush's fear was that the Syrians would attempt to outflank the brigade and take advantage of the gap left between the areas under 7th/188th division to make a pincer movement south and then northwest to encircle the brigade and finish it off. The Rafid-Quneitra line was a vital link in the Golan Heights overall defenses. Should the Syrians succeed in breaking through, they would not only have been able to decimate the shoot against the brigade's supply lines (and supply stores), but also link up in other Syrian units moving in from the south to moving in on the Bnot Ya'akov Bridge and isolate Israeli forces on the Golan with those moving in reinforcements from the south. "Force Tiger" had a daunting task ahead of it—the Syrians had sent a force of 45 T-55s toward the brigade's last line of defense.

Captain Zamir was known throughout the brigade as a cocky and most capable officer. When faced with insurmountable odds, commanders can make a stand and fight it out in a desperate flurry of bravado and guts, or employ the powers of guile and attempt to get into the enemy's mind. Zamir chose the latter option. He divided his vast legion of seven tanks into rows of primary, secondary, and third-level forces and positioned his units force on opposite ends of the Syrian's advance. They would use the terrain and darkness as cover and attack the advancing Syrian tanks after they had entered the killing zone—the lead and rear vehicles would be hit first, bottlenecking the rest of the armor into a position where they were helpless, disoriented, and ripe for the killing. Had this been peacetime and Zamir had offered his plan as a staff college paper, he would have certainly received a high grade. At 0100 hours. Yanush contacted Major Kauli and ordered him to deploy Force Tiger in an ambush ten kilometers south of Quneitra on the western slope of Tel el-Hariya. Captain Zamir was told, "Tiger, forty-five Syrian tanks are moving toward you from south to north. We have to stop them. If we succeed, we'll make history."[10]

The tanks, elements of the 43rd Armored Mechanized Brigade, moved into Force Tiger's killing zone in a confident and proper advance. They weren't even cautious in how they moved and their formation resembled a parade on the streets of Damascus rather than a careful and slow-poking advance through terrain that could have been infested with antitank mines, infantrymen armed with antitank weaponry, and enemy tanks. Being ambushed at ranges of 20 meters, the territory of face-to-face ballistic bravado, was risky. A few mistakes and the ambushed force would be in perfect position to kill the ambushing force at what is known as "no-mistake ranges," as well. Yet hitting a target at close-range boxed it inside the killing zone—making it unable to take evasive action and maneuvers. Zamir understood the risks, but also realized that being outnumbered over six-to-one, he would have to gamble.

Along with Captain Zamir's tank were two additional tanks (one under the command of First-Lieutenant Uri Segal and the other "piloted" by a sergeant); two other tanks situated near Position 110, under the command of deputy company commander Second-Lieutenant Abromovitz, would act as the trip wire of the ambush and warn Zamir when the

Syrians approached, then enter the fight from the rear, trapping the Syrians in a killing zone.

At approximately 0240 hours on October 7, Second-Lieutenant Abromovitz radioed Zamir and informed him that the party was about to begin—40 guests in all. Both forces took positions and silently awaited that perfect moment to open fire. The first salvo was unleashed when the Syrians were only 30 meters away and within seconds 5 T-55s were on fire. The ambush had worked perfectly. The Israeli barrage had so surprised the Syrians that they began to move helplessly in a mad choreography of fear and confusion. Tanks bumped into one another; at least one Syrian tank was hit by a fellow T-55 who was firing madly in all directions. The neat paradelike advance was now a chicken with its head cut off. Five minutes into the melee, Lieutenant Segal turned on his tank's large Xenon projector light and blanketed the Syrians in a floodlit hell. The Syrians, too frightened to engage the Israelis, attempted to return toward their own lines but Second-Lieutenant Abromovitz's tanks came to block their retreat. It took 45 minutes for the ambush to end—45 minutes for 20 T-55s and 20 crews to be obliterated.

With First-Lieutenant Segal's projector lights, Zamir could count the destruction, though he realized that 20 tanks had escaped the bloodletting and were heading north. There was no point in pursuing them in the darkness, as many in the company urged, but rather Zamir opted to reach a hiding spot near Tel el-Hariya and ambush them at dawn's first light. When the sun emerged over the Syrian mountains four hours later, Captain Zamir, now reinforced by elements from Lieutenant-Colonel Nafshi's 74th Battalion, was once again in ambush. This time the ranges were several hundred meters but the results the same. In 11 minutes, an additional 20 Syrian T-55s had been turned into armored coffins ablaze on a volcanic ash plateau. Not a single Israeli tank had been hit and not a single Israeli soldier received even a scratch.

Exhausted, and already in combat for 18 straight hours. Zamir dragged on a cigarette and reached Yanush to inform him of the night's eventful conclusion. The usually restrained Yanush, an officer who rarely expressed emotion or joy in front of his men, had spent the better part of 19 hours hearing nothing but bad news and setbacks. Zamir's report was cause to celebrate and break tradition. Yanush exploded in a burst of joy. "Tiger, I love you," cried Yanush over the brigade network. Force Tiger had, indeed, made history.

That first 24 hours went well for the 7th. They had been tested but not for real. Unfortunately, the same could not be said for the 188th Barak Brigade. They were fighting for their lives in a desperate struggle of point-blank armored warfare that has never been replicated in modern warfare. The 188th Brigade's saga is forever linked with the fate of Yanush's 7th Brigade, and their story must be told.

At 1421 hours on October 6, a major Syrian advance was reported in the area of Position 111. The lead force of defenders from Lieutenant-Colonel Oded Erez's 53rd Battalion attempted gallantly to hold the line and stem the flow, but the Syrians continued to advance in massive numbers. Faced with little choice but to retreat from his first line of defense, Ben-Shoham pulled back and sent his second battalion, a force held for reserve, into the fray. The 188th Brigade's gunners had proven courageous and skilled, and they destroyed nearly 100 Syrian tanks in the first few hours of the fight, but the Syrians were throwing an entire armored division against a few scattered battalions and skill and courage were not impervious to overwhelming numbers. Ben-Shoham left his HQ at Nafakh and attempted, as best as he could, to block major gaps in the Israeli defenses with repositioning platoons and companies from various forces. Leaving one company of armor with him, Ben-Shoham tried valiantly to protect the al-Jukhadar, El Al Tapline Route access, but the fighting was so fierce that Syrian snipers were now targeting Israeli tank commanders standing upright in their turrets. Not only were tanks of the 188th Brigade engaging the Syrians with 105mm tank fire, but crewmen from both the Israeli and Syrian sides engaged one another with small arms and grenades. It was, in the words of one 53rd Battalion survivor, "utter madness." The commander of the Syrian 9th Infantry Division, Colonel Hassan Tourkmani, realized the Israelis were weak and exploited his advantage by rushing additional units into the fray. By 2100 hours the Syrians had over 200 tanks racing about the 188th Brigade's lines, pushing to Nafakh in the north and the Jordan River in the south. They had surrounded the 188th Brigade in the process. Ben-Shoham, at the time, had but 15 tanks remaining.

Ben-Shoham attempted to reorganize his force along the Gamla Rise near the settlement of Ramat Magshimim, but at the same time, Captain Tzvi "Tzvika" Greengold led a force of four damaged tanks to counterattack against the Syrians along the Tapline. Known on the battalion network as "Force Tzvika," Captain Greengold led a remarkable charge against advancing Syrian armor at odds of fifty-to-one. Soon, the three tanks accompanying Force Tzvika were hit and one captain commenced a lone fight against an entire brigade: a monumental act of heroism and determination. Force Tzvika destroyed nearly thirty tanks that night. He fought without respite and relief until he hooked in with the first reservist arriving on the scene.

The Syrians pushed to Nafakh, where Raful and his staff manned defenses with bazookas in hand, but the main push headed toward the Jordan River bridges. The 188th Brigade tanks that had run out of ammunition moved to ram Syrian vehicles rather than run and surrender. It was a stoic and epic defense, but the brigade was doomed. Without reinforcements and outnumbered at times by 100-to-1 odds, they were overrun. Colonel Ben-Shoham was killed, as were most of his officers. The brigade suffered sixty-six percent casualties. Only the arrival of Colonel Orri Orr's 679th Armored Brigade at Nafakh and reservists reaching the Bnot Ya'akov Bridge saved the southern half of the front and Galilee from being overrun.

Back in the northern sector, no sooner was Captain Zamir enjoying the fruits of his second ambush when Lieutenant-Colonel Kahalani found himself facing yet another Syrian attempt to cross the antitank ditch and breach the defensive lines around the Valley of Tears between Hermonit and Booster. This was a more determined effort than the previous afternoon and evening, and the number of Syrian T-62s and T-55s proved a daunting spectacle. Syrian infantrymen, moving about like ants in their green fatigues and netted helmets followed closely behind the armor. They were eager to make it across the ditch and then establish harassing antitank ambushes behind the Israeli defenses. Already, reports of Syrian antitank commando teams, moving throughout the Israeli rear had caused considerable concern. These soldiers were far better trained than the regular infantrymen in Assad's army, and, armed with RPG-7s and Saggers, were highly capable of destroying significant numbers of armor and killing hundreds of men. Dressed in leopard camouflage fatigues, the commandos had a fierce reputation for brutality and a penchant for close-quarter killing. All carried daggers and trained, as proof of their mettle, to bite the heads off snakes. Tank soldiers didn't like fighting infantrymen—especially commandos.

Kahalani's battalion held the topographically advantageous high ground while the Syrians were blessed with an overwhelming numerical advantage. High ground wasn't enough, however. By the dawn of Day Two, Kahalani had lost several vehicles and, more importantly, a company commander and nine platoon and tank commanders, and one crewman had been killed. Already, at Day Two, the fruits of the IDF's Armored School were paying off and taking their toll. By standing upright in their turrets and directing the battle from an eyes-on and hands-on approach, the battalion (and all the brigades fighting on both the Golan and Sinai) were able to minimize their numerical inferiority and maximize their numbers to the ultimate end. But being exposed on a battlefield where .50 caliber machine gun rounds are considered BBs is a dangerous and short-lived manner of conducting one's business. Losing officers and tank commanders could have demoralized and shut down the battalion, but these soldiers weren't performing on exercise—this was their lives in the balance. Privates began acting like lieutenants, sergeants took the helm of platoons and companies.

The Syrian advance was systematic and unflinching. If a T-62 or BTR was hit, another one followed in its place. The Israelis were firing at the optimum ranges of 1,000 meters and 1,500 meters, and their training in the south was now proving most successful. Many Syrian vehicles were hit on the first round—others on the second or finally the third, but yet they continued to advance. In one or two instances, the Syrians managed to establish a bridgehead over the antitank ditch using their MTU-55 bridge layers; destroyed tanks perched inside the ditch were providing impromptu means of crossing as well. Several Syrian tanks reached to within 100 meters of Kahalani's positions, but they were destroyed before they could get any farther. By the end of the second day of fighting, a slow day in the north, Kahalani's ramps were defended by only seven operating Centurion MBTs, although elements of the 74th Battalion provided backup, primarily around Position 107. The principal Syrian push came toward Position 109, toward Hermonit, and toward Position 105. The Syrians attacked in the same manner as they did on Day One—two intensive pushes during the day and one consolidated effort under the cover of darkness. The Israelis engaged them at ranges of 500–1,000 meters. The courage of the tank soldiers aside, the true hero of the fighting so far was turning out to be the Centurion's 105mm main gun.

There were also remarkable moments of courage being waged all across the Heights.

On Monday, October 8, the 77th Battalion received word that they were to assume control over the territory between their defensive line between Hermonit and Booster and the antitank ditch. The order wasn't truly understood, since it meant that the battalion would have to weaken its already thinned defensive line and enter the valley toward the ditch and minefields. Some tanks were sent into the mix by Kahalani, but Syrian artillery spotters saw everything, and hundreds of shells rained down on the descending tanks. These tanks now found themselves trapped in a valley surrounded by artillery-induced craters and the smoldering skeletons of Syrian armor. Syrian tanks thought that they had found an ambush of their own and dispatched armor to meet the Israelis head-on. A battle erupted and the Syrian vehicles were destroyed in less than ten minutes; Syrian artillery proved quite accurate, however, and several of Kahalani's tanks were hit. Seeing no point at this exercise in futility, he ordered them back to the ramps.

The battalion had been fighting for nearly two full days and had run out of fuel and ammunition. Left virtually in charge of the strategic bottleneck to the northern Heights Kahalani and the straggling units in his command were forced to pull back to an emergency resupply center and hoard enough material and ammunition to sustain the tanks and APCs for at least the next 24 hours of fighting. In the afternoon, as the exhausted tank soldiers lugged crates of HESH (High-Explosive Squashed-Head) and AP shells into their tanks and supply vehicles, Kahalani was informed that the Syrians had made a cohesive push toward Position 109, consisting of a dozen tanks, and that they were making headway. Kahalani ordered the supply detail to fire up their engines and they raced back toward the lines opposite the Valley of Tears—all the time wary of Syrian special forces that had infiltrated into the area and were taking a toll ambushing Israeli vehicles and personnel. In a change from the norm of the war so far, Kahalani ordered his gunners to engage the advancing Syrian armor at long ranges, 2,500 meters, and most of the Syrian tanks were destroyed with direct hits; others, damaged, were abandoned by their crews who hurriedly made it back to their divisional lines. Kahalani remained at his firing ramps most of the night until they were moved toward Quneitra to block what was perceived to be a major Syrian offensive. By the time most of the battalion was in position around the approach to the capital of the Golan, the Syrians were in the midst of their most coordinated and dedicated bombardment of the war. Wave after wave of Sukhoi and MiG aircraft strafed Israeli positions around Quneitra. The artillery barrage was deafening and highly accurate; some reports listed shells landing every three seconds. Yet no tanks were encountered by Kahalani's vanguard defensive force and the town not captured.

Tuesday, October 9, the fourth day of the fighting, was perhaps the first turning point in a war defined by turning points, Arab reaction, and Israeli recovery; the day was certainly the turning point in the defense of the Golan Heights and as a result a turning point in the course of the entire war. By 0400 hours, defenses in the southern Golan had collapsed completely. Syrian tanks had reached the divisional IDF HQ at Nafakh and had moved toward the Bnot Ya'akov Bridge. The loss of the bridge would have facilitated Syrian access to the very heart of Galilee and brought back the specter of the 1948 War with full-scale fighting being waged so close to major Israeli population centers. Syrian tanks in Galilee, in Tiberias, Safed, Qiryat Shmonah,

Ma'alot, or even Haifa was a thought that threatened the very survival of the Jewish State. Brigadier-General Eitan's division, primarily the 7th Brigade, had been left pretty much unscathed by the fighting as most of the action was in the southern section where the Barak Brigade had met its demise. They had faced an initial Syrian attack on a line of hills two-and-a-half miles from the Purple Line and the anti-tank ditch separating the Golan Heights from Syria. But now, with the south secure, it was time to consolidate the gains and guarantee the reclamation of Syrian territory by launching an attack against the northern half of the Heights.

For an armor officer worth his salt, there was only one place where the Syrians could have attempted a major breakthrough across the northern half of the Heights, and the Syrian Army had hundreds of tank officers that were more than capable. Brigadier-General Omar Abrash's 7th Infantry Division, with support of Brigadier-General Mustafa Sharba's 3rd Armored Division concentrated their push against the 7th Brigade's lines between Tel Hermonit, the volcanic hill near El Rom, and a lower hill approximately three miles to the south nicknamed "The Booster." The Valley was a flat and placid area ideal for tank transport and battle. According to Colonel Y,[11] at the time of this book's writing the commander of the 7th, "It was the kind of terrain that was great for driving tanks and great for blowing them to bits."

As the sun emerged over the Tel Hara Mountains to the east, Kahalani had positioned a reconnaissance screen of jeeps and armored personnel carriers from the brigade's reconnaissance platoon and a dozen of his own battalion's tanks in the valley's defense. Several Centurions were in place atop the defensive firing ramps and were in ideal firing position to literally pick off any encroaching target. The weak point with the defense of the Valley of Tears was the beauty of its geography. While the firing positions, embankments, obstacles, and other defenses completely dominated any Syrian approach from the east, it silhouetted the defenders against the skyline in the gunsights of Syrian tanks approaching from the southern half and the low ground.

Kahalani's battalion CP was at El Rom where he completely dominated the Hermonit area. Half of the battalion, under Major Eitan Kauli's command, was positioned in the very saddle of the valley of Tears. His tanks were on a heightened state of alert and ordered to do three simple things: "Kill the enemy, be frugal with the ammo, and survive!" Kauli's company was what is known in the tank game as the sacrificial lamb—exposed on all sides, and meant to act as a plug, a finger in the dike. Morale was high but exhaustion was testing the very power of adrenaline and fear. Most of the tank soldiers hadn't slept in three days. For all, this was their first baptism of fire. "It was like losing your virginity with a nymphomaniac instead of your timid high school sweetheart. It was madness for men so green to face a wall of fire and blood that horrific."[12]

Many inside IDF Northern Command knew that this day would be the turning point. The Syrians had achieved half their objectives, but the courageous self-sacrifice of the 188th Barak Brigade had bought just enough time for the reservists to be mobilized and brought to the front in order to establish a static line of defense. The Syrians were no longer simply advancing in the south unhindered or meeting insignificant resistance—reservists, the backbone of the Israeli military, were now in the mix and fighting well. OC Northern Command Major-General Yitzhak Hofi, Division Commander Brigadier-General "Raful" Eitan, and Yanush knew that the Syrians needed to exploit the Valley of Tear's defenses and do it soon. If they succeeded, then they would have opened a gap permitting them to move west and south and, in essence, assume control over much of northern Israel. Should they fail in one monumental effort, then the tide of war would have changed in the north. The 7th Brigade would have held until relieved and the Syrians never again afforded the opportunity to break through.

Reinforcements would come from central Israel and from the central Himalayas.

Early in the morning of October 9, Raful and Yanush both looked at the latest IAF reconnaissance photographs of the Syrian lines and were none too happy with what they saw. Overall, more than 100 Syrian tanks, primarily brand-new T-62s from the elite Republican Guards, were all poised for the push through the northern gap above Quneitra—straight toward the Valley of Tears and the 77th Battalion. The forces that would be attacking included some of the best tanks in the Syrian arsenal, hundreds of infantrymen ferried in dozens of BTRs and BMPs, and the possible deployment of Syrian antitank commands brought in under cover of darkness by chopper.

The 7th Brigade at the opening of the Syrian attack consisted of the pocket of defenders seemingly under the control of the 77th Battalion and Lieutenant-Colonel Kahalani. Yanush handled the campaign from Nafakh and as a result was the source of considerable criticism for not adhering to the "Follow Me" ethic of command. As the 77th Battalion was the only force defending the entire Heights that dark and fateful Wednesday morning, every vehicle, crew member, and shell in its order of battle was of monumental importance. The brigade was also augmented by elements of the 75th battalion, who were mainly operating a resupply run to the isolated Position 107 (Position 107, considered to be the strongest of the *Moazim* next to the Mount Hermon position—which was since overrun—was actually east of the anti-tank ditch completely surrounded by Syrian armor) and Captain Meir Zamir's six Centurions of the 82nd Battalion.

Unlike what Hollywood would like audiences to believe in war movies, there was no silence before the storm that Wednesday morning as one of modern military history's most epic and close-quarter tank battles was about to be fought. For the Israeli tankers it had been a long and difficult night. Crews operated at fifty percent capacity as two crewmen slept and two stayed on watch; mostly, tank commanders manned the vigil and their crews grabbed a few z's, munched on unappetizing combat rations, and checked and rechecked their vehicles, guns, and engines; many even took a few spare moments to clean their Uzi 9mm submachine guns as a point-blank fight was expected. Darkness had provided a brief respite, but there was no silence. The unbearably loud swooshing of IAF jets flying too low and too often for the tankers' good, and the sounds of explosions and fire in the distance engulfed the eerie night. Senior officers in the brigade, like Yanush, Kahalani, Nafshi, and Eldar knew that the gunfire in the distance was a good sign—the remnants of the 188th Brigade and the reservists support were still resisting.

The Syrian attack, the assault of the vaunted Republic Guard, commenced on schedule at 0900 hours with two T-62 battalions moving west. The Israeli gunners opened up at maximum range in order to stem the flow as best as possible, but this was proving to be a difficult task. The Syrians advanced in the Moscow-choreographed march of a tight formation following the philosophy of mass assault over strategic territorial grabs. They moved bunched closely together in order to maximize their fire potential and also confuse tanks as per individual targeting. Indeed, the Syrian tactic was sound. The Israeli tank positions, spread out throughout the line, had a hard time identifying single tanks amid the smoke, clouds of dust, and a lack of clear silhouettes. The gunners were ordered not to waste ammunition and fire only when the silhouette of a T-62 was clearly between the crosshairs of the Centurion's L7 105mm main armament gun. To coordinate the impact of their rounds, many of the brigade's tank officers stood in their turrets or even atop their vehicles—completely exposed. This permitted the commanders to direct their gunners to actual targets, but it also meant that Syrian gunners could see small figures in olive green in the center of their gunsights as well. Dozens of tank commanders were killed by this *Heyl Ha'Shirion* practice; their mutilated bodies serving as a grim and terrifying reminder to their men of the horror of armored warfare. Other tank commanders were seriously wounded and forced out of action. Companies, platoons, squads, and individual tanks once commanded by officers, captains, and lieutenants were now led by sergeants and even privates. Men taught only to operate the 105mm guns were now serving as commanders without the benefit of *Kurs Ma'Kim* (Squad Commanders Course) and *Kurs Ktzinei Shirion* (Armored Officers School) and without learning their skills under the calmness and control of exercises and a CO's yelling bark.

The remnants of Kahalani's battalion (along with remnants of the 75th and 82nd battalions) were positioned along their axis in a U-shaped ringed defense. The 77th Battalion consisted of a single company, commanded by Kahalani personally, around Merom Ha'Golan protecting the "Yakir" lateral road and Quneitra; the 71st Battalion remained in position in the northern sector of the brigade's zone; and the 75th Battalion had retreated to 400 meters behind the defensive ramps. Kahalani was concerned by the fact that the ramps had been abandoned and the defensive edge removed from the brigade—quality over quantity was, indeed, a virtue, but it wasn't enough to base a defensive statement on. In the first stages of the battle for the Valley of Tears, Kahalani led a force of seven Centurions, all battered after having been in duty for 72 straight hours, into the valley. He wanted to see if he could reinforce the positions left open by the retreat of the battered 75th Battalion 300–400 meters behind the ramparts after the relentless Syrian barrage had thrown them off their perch. Syrian armor had, by now, slowly infiltrated significant numbers of tanks—estimated by Kahalani to be over 150 already in the mix. Without the ramps in Israeli hands, Kahalani's tanks couldn't see the oncoming enemy until they were close, and close-quarter combat was not a prudent form of tank warfare when ammunition was a dwindling commodity. Already the odds were nearly ten-to-one and Kahalani realized that he was facing one more obstacle in holding the line: The various units operating in the field were not connected on the battalion frequency. Tanks from the 75th couldn't communicate with Kahalani's 77th or Lieutenant-Colonel Retes' 71st. "It was like a lot of chickens running around with their heads cut-off," recalls Kahalani, "and it was no way to fight a war."[13] More importantly for the task at hand, it was impossible to coordinate the recapture of the ramps. From Camp Sa'ar Yanush could hear that the remnants of the brigade were in dire straits, and he ordered his strategic reserve, the 71st Battalion, to bolster's Kahalani's chances. The battalion, however, had been reduced to a strength of only eight tanks. Lieutenant-Colonel Retes' deputy, Major Gideon Wiler, had been killed the night before and most of the damaged tanks were not among the "rolling wounded." They were mauled by Syrian cannon fire and incapable of returning to the front. Retes received Yanush's order and proceeded with his "task force" from a westerly approach, but en route to the fight Retes' tank was hit by a 115mm armor-piercing round and it erupted into a ball of flames; Lieutenant-Commander Retes and his crew were killed instantly. Two other 71st Battalion tanks were hit; other commanders, standing upright in their turrets in the midst of a barrage, were wounded. At that point, however, just as it appeared that the battalion would be destroyed, the notified communications officer managed to raise the surviving tanks and one-by-one guide them toward Kahalani's line.

Back at HQ, Yanush realized the situation was grim and the clock was ticking toward an ultimate and final engagement that it didn't look like the 7th Brigade would be capable of winning—or even surviving the melee—by fighting from the center of the fight. Yanush acquiesced to his most adamant instincts about not retreating and authorized Kahalani to withdraw to a defensive line approximately 400 meters to the rear where their firepower could be concentrated for maximum effect. Lieutenant-Colonel Yair Nafshi's 74th Battalion was pulled out of a ring near Position 107 toward easier ground to defend, and Captain Meir Zamir's mini task force of Centurions from the 82nd Battalion were ordered to assume positions alongside a ridge near Tel Git—on the approaches to the Damascus Highway north of Booster. Zamir, the saving grace of the first night of fighting, was not in position to perform another grandstanding display of ambushing genius in this battle. The three days of fighting had taken its toll on his men, as it had the entire brigade, and attrition of dead and dying soldiers was showing its debilitating effect on the unit's abilities to mount any type of defense. Only six Centurions were at Captain Zamir's disposal and they could boast only 16 rounds of 105mm ammunition between them.[14]

The unsung heroes of this battle to stave off the Syrian avalanche of armor were the artillery gunners of Brigadier-General Eitan's 36th Armored Infantry Division[15] who tirelessly peppered the hole in the ditch with accurate artillery fire. The barrage, waged until the last 155mm and 175mm rounds were launched, destroyed a fair number of Syrian tanks, but also slowed down the advance to allow the Israeli tankers, already displaying a superhuman effort, to breathe and fight.

As the battle began to increase in intensity and the Syrian

bridgehead across the antitank ditch expanded and more armor flew across under heavy Israeli tank fire, eight Syrian Mi-8 "Hip" transport choppers ferrying nearly 160 Syrian special forces and antitank commands were seen flying close-to-the-earth toward the Yakir roadway in order to cut off retreating units and reinforce reservists. Yanush realized that two things would happen in the next 12 hours: Either the remnants of the brigade would be destroyed and Israeli defenses overrun, or Kahalani would be able to hold out long enough to await relief. The scenario for a collapse of the line, similar to what had happened to Ben-Shoham, was horrific; the Syrians would be able to expand their pocket, mop up resistance, and push west and south. Kahalani, too, realized the grim reality of the task at hand. When Yanush radioed his battalion commander to ask for an equipment check on the air to see how many tanks were in the field, Kahalani responded, "Forty, correction, an additional tank has just joined me, forty-one!"[16] Kahalani knew that Syrian military intelligence and their Russian GRU advisors were listening in on every IDF frequency atop the heights. *"Shiga'on* (Terrific),"* responded Yanush, adding to the deception. "I am sending three more tanks. Good Luck."

As Kahalani moved into position, using the convenience of a stone wall for cover, he was immediately confronted by four Syrian tanks from the 70th Tank Brigade. The Syrian T-62s were only a few yards away and Kahalani and his gunner, David Klion, faced an awful dilemma. Which one do you engage first and will you have enough time to destroy all four tanks? "Stop," Kahalani ordered his driver yelling into the intercom in an uncharacteristic bark. His gunner was told to aim the gun at midlevel and fire. No range was needed. Any shot would do. The first T-62 went up in a ball of flames so huge that the heat was felt inside Kahalani's Centurion; another battalion tank followed him from behind the wall and helped Kahalani destroy the remaining three pieces of armor. The *immediate* threat dissolved—for the moment. Kahalani returned to his cupola for a scan through the rear for Major Ami Pelnat. Kahalani had to rally the battalion—what was left of it—to return to the 77th frequency in order to rally whatever vehicles and pieces of equipment were available into a coordinated push to remove the Syrians from the ramparts. Just over 300 yards now separated Kahalani and his ad hoc task force from the unit's old position atop the ramps. There were significant numbers of Syrian armor between them and their battlefield objective, but 300 yards was definitely a doable stretch of territory to cover.

Tanks were engaging whatever they saw, and the Centurions were proving capable foes. The L7 105mm gun had proven the true master of the battle, and the 77th Battalion gunners were earning their marks as *Tzalafim* or snipers— able to pick off an oncoming Syrian tank on the first shot. It was this marksmanship that would save the day for the battalion, the brigade, and the front. The gunners' ability to save ammunition was of enormous importance, but so was hitting the enemy before he could see you, range you, and hit you. In tank warfare, in those prehistoric pre–Gulf War days before computerized laser-range finding made spotting a target nothing more than going through the motions of an extensive video game, a missed round alerted the enemy as to your position. While you reloaded, he was scanning your particulars and locking on; if you were lucky, you could hit him before he had a chance to let off a round in your direction. If you were unlucky, you missed just as he had a round in the breech.

Choreographing an armored battle is an exercise in chaos, especially when embroiled in the fight as well, yet Kahalani managed to perform this task with remarkable finesse and skill even though he was a participant and not an observer and director. As his wall of armor, closing in on the ramps, advanced slowly though steadily, he dispatched several of his vehicles to the higher ground to the southeast where they could simply pick off the advancing Syrian thrust without presenting themselves as too tempting a target The difficulty was the fact that many of the tanks involved in the battle were fighting their own private little wars. Tank commanders from the 77th, the 71st, and the 75th were not coordinated on the battalion network and were simply firing at what they saw with the sole objective at hand being the killing of the enemy. "It was like a bumper car ride at the Lunar Park," recalled Shimon, a 75th Battalion driver, "everybody firing in different positions against their own special targets. It was chaos and totally uncoordinated." Coordination was never a prerequisite of victory, however. Numbers could decide a battle but so could good soldiers, and the 7th Brigade tank soldiers were damned good.

Yanush was monitoring the ongoing battle over the radio while attempting to rally reinforcements for the battle from the encroaching columns of reservists now poised to do battle. "How many Syrian tanks have been destroyed in the area?" he asked Kahalani in a quiet and confidence-building voice that tends to be a trademark among Israeli brigade commanders. "From sixty to seventy is a rough estimate," returned Kahalani, but the 77th Battalion commander was in trouble. He was trying—with little success—to rally the tanks in the valley into a cohesive single force for a final push to reach the ramps. A reconnaissance unit M113 had been abandoned by the ramps and its coordinating communications officer, meant to hook vehicles into the various networks, was not functioning. Kahalani asked Yanush to scan the frequencies and get the tanks on line. Yanush tried to reach the tanks in the communications room, but that was proving to be almost as difficult as holding the line. Many of the vehicles were "crawling wounded." They had been hit, had run over mines, or had been peppered with 12.7mm and 14.5mm heavy machine-gun fire and key instruments—like radios—were not functioning. In a tremendous act of courage, Kahalani was directing a tank battle and directing his own tank's movements and engagements by standing upright in his turret waving a flag and going through the entire dictionary of arm signals. Those tanks that saw this incredible display quickly followed the program, but it was impossible to get everyone's attention. The thunderous firing was deafening, and shells, mortar rounds, and Syrian tank fire was landing everywhere. Over the distance, Kahalani could see the mini task force of surviving 71st Battalion vehicles heading his way. The situation was changing—possibly for the better.

Back at HQ, an alert brigade communications officer realized why the communications problems were still plaguing so many of the tanks fighting it out with the Syrians—the older variant of Centurion MBT was equipped with a different communications set than the newer models used by the 77th Battalion. The communications officer suggested, calmly, that Kahalani change his frequencies in order to be on line with the various vehicles dispersed throughout the battlefield, but Kahalani refused to consider the insane request—realizing that it would create far more problems than it would solve.

Exacerbating the command, communication, and control difficulties plaguing the unit at this most volatile stage of the battle, Kahalani observed that Retes' tanks were pulling back—away from the fight. Kahalani did not realize that Meshulam Retes had been killed, as had his deputy. The survivors of a battalion were now led by sergeants and privates, and frantically, Kahalani attempted to flag down the vehicles while standing upright in his turret cupola while in the center of a massive enemy bombardment. At that point, two Syrian T-62s emerged from behind a smoke screen and began to engage Kahalani's tank—known as *Shoter* ("policeman") on the brigade network. Several 115mm rounds were fired, as were several rounds of 105mm fire from Kahalani's tank. It appeared as if Kahalani had finally been silenced by the Syrian onslaught and, indeed, an excited platoon commander got on the network and announced: *"Ha'Ma'Gad Ne'Herag ... Ha'Ma'Gad Ne'Herag!"* In a scene that couldn't have been replicated better by Hollywood, silence engulfed the radio following the announcement and the battlefield also went silent for a few brief seconds. "It was eerie and almost solemn," recalls one platoon member. "It was like a moment of silence for the dead." Kahalani, of course, had not been killed, though his tank was almost hit by a round that landed a few centimeters from his treads. "This is the battalion commander, this is the CO, and I am still alive. I am not killed off so easily!"

According to Major-General Orri Orr, known in IDF circles as among the more capable and charismatic leaders to ever wear the black beret, "Leadership is instinct, example, and the ability to build confidence and trust." Kahalani was such a leader, such a commander, and his ability to reinstate confidence in the battered remnants of a once mighty unit was an achievement as impressive and as important to the overall defense of the Valley of Tears and the northern tier of the divisional lines as was a regiment of armor. Charisma could not stop armor, however, nor could it block incoming RPG and 100mm and 115mm rounds.

Kahalani was attempting to stop the collapse of his wall of conglomerated armor while fighting a battle simultaneously, and the situation had suddenly deteriorated. He considered retreating to another tier of defensive spots behind, but then reviewed the importance of retreat on morale. Morale was already teetering on collapse. His men had been fighting for three full days with little rest and relief. Their comrades had been killed and horrifically maimed before their eyes, and their most noble display of courage and survival yielded nothing more than a stop gap for Syrian units that continued their advance unhindered. If the battalion retreated, then it would collapse. The Syrians would have perched themselves in numbers atop the ramps, they would have seized Booster and Hermonit, and they would have staked their flag to an ultrastrategic piece of the Heights before the might and freshness of the reservists could play a role in the course of the battle and the war. Kahalani ordered all vehicles capable of hearing him to raise a flag and follow in close pursuit, as he issued orders to advance. The Centurions moved about slowly and cautiously, but they were on the attack nonetheless.

At HQ Northern Command and at Nafakh, it appeared as if the Valley of Tears had been lost and the IAF liaison officer had authorized an air strike. As Kahalani peered through his field glasses toward the ramps, the loud roar of supersonic jet engines approached from the southwest. Two A-4 Skyhawks, the workhorse of the IAF's fighter bomber command, began to swoop in from an altitude of 10,000 feet and prepare their loads and cannons for a run against any and all vehicles found atop the plateau—after all they were all supposed to be Syrian. Not wanting a friendly fire incident to be the difference between a heroic last stand and foolish destruction, Kahalani went on a frantic search for the air controller capable of calling off the attack.

The Republican Guard's 2nd Battalion, the T-62 force that was now pushing at Kahalani, were all manned by soldiers handpicked to serve as the guard to President Assad's regime. They were intelligent, capable,.loyal, and above all well-trained. Their numbers were strong—over 50 tanks—and they hadn't been fighting for the past 72 hours without sleep or relief. Kahalani realized that the sole saving plan for the defense of the gap was to attack—to launch the combined entity under his command directly into the center of the Syrian advance. "This is the Battalion Commander," Kahalani reassured the 15 tanks he had managed to rally, "a large enemy force is located between the ramp and we will move forward to occupy the positions ahead of us!" The courage of the assault was followed by its temporary success. The Syrian tankers stopped in their tracks and their assault turned into a confused dance of insecurity. Some of the tanks began firing into their own lines, others simply believed Kahalani's charge to be the harbinger of a much larger assault and crews soon abandoned their tanks, racing madly into the plateau back across the ditch. Zil trucks, camouflaged and netted, were soon unloading their men after they stalled with nowhere to go. Kahalani moved ahead approximately 100 meters, but will was proving to be a dwindling commodity. Over a small ridge Kahalani's force found another 50 or so T-62s moving forward.

At this stage Yanush ordered in Lieutenant-Colonel Meshulam Carmel's largely unused and untested unit from the Armor School in order to bolster Kahalani's exposed northern flank. Leaving one platoon near Hermonit, Carmel's company strength force of Centurions raced to Kahalani's aid, but they soon encountered stern Syrian resistance. Lieutenant-Colonel Carmel was killed ten minutes into the fight, and four additional tanks destroyed by well-placed 115mm rounds. Kahalani absorbed the remnants of this force into his battalion net and continued his advance. It was stalled.

The forces supporting both of Kahalani's flanks, the tanks that were, in essence, covering the battle with 105mm fire, were running out of ammunition and asking—begging—for permission to withdraw. Yanush now feared the worst. He feared total collapse with Israel losing its first war. The brigade was exhausted, "fighting on fumes," as Kahalani would later recall, and the sheer vastness of their outnumbered state had set in. As Yanush radioed Raful to describe the desperate situation of his unit, "Captain Zamir radioed in to inform the brigade commander that his tanks were now completely out of ammunition; hand grenades were distributed to the crews, and they planned assaulting the Syrian tanks the way infantry units have been doing for years—hurling "frags" into the commander's turret opening and hoping for the best.

Kahalani now realized that he had to do something—otherwise the front would collapse. There was nothing behind Kahalani's wall but a fully exposed northern Israel; paratroopers, stationed behind the tanks, prepared their grenade stores for final suicidal stands of their own. Many of the brigade soldiers, kibbutzniks from Galilee, were literally fighting for their homes, but they were also battling the demoralizing effects of exhaustion, hunger, fear, pain, and anxiety. Although in possession of just seven tanks, Kahalani knew that attack was the only way to make this final stand. He went on the battalion network and actually challenged the survivors. "What are you, a bunch of chickens?" the battalion commander challenged the tank commanders.[17] "Witness the courage with which the enemy climbs the position before us. I don't understand what is happening to us, but when all is said and done they are Syrian soldiers. Are they better than us? Move forward behind me and in line. I'll be flying a flag."

The "I'll show you mine if you show me yours" method of command via bravado was never popular and Kahalani had always used understatement and gentle tones with his men. He didn't like threats and psychological techniques to convince his men to follow because he didn't think it worked in the long run, but in the present, atop the Valley of Tears, it worked fine. The tank commanders, all six of them, raised their hands defiantly up through their turret cupolas. "You are advancing fine," Kahalani continued to push them, "continue at this speed."

Kahalani's tanks survived the charge and made it to the ramps overlooking the antitank ditch. They wasted little time in relishing in their victory and began firing at the oncoming armor with the few rounds left in their tanks' depleted bins. When the tanks were down to their last rounds and the enemy vulnerable, a miracle happened.

Raful, known in the IDF as one of the country's most

courageous and levelheaded soldiers, had made a name for himself in the paratroopers as a man who could lead one against a million on a dark and dangerous night. Wounded in virtually every one of Israel's wars, he was a humble man who disliked speaking to groups or using his vocal skills beyond the bare necessities. He had been in one desperate fight for survival 25 years earlier in Jerusalem, in San Simon, and rarely became excitable on the field of battle. On the Golan, during the second fight for his life, he had raced from Northern Command HQ in Galilee to Nafakh conferring with OC Northern Command Major-General Yitzhak Hofi,[18] all the time wearing his Australian bush hat and his hand bandaged from a carpentry accident. Now, an illuminated and desperate Raful was pleading with Yanush. "Tell them to hold on just a few minutes longer. Help is on the way." Raful was right. He never lied to one of his men.

Lieutenant-Colonel Yossi Ben-Hanan, who, until two weeks before the war, was commander of the Barak Brigade's 53rd Battalion, was on his honeymoon when the war broke out in, of all places, Nepal high atop the Himalayas. By hook and by crook, he raced for Israel along with his newlywed bride, reaching the country two days later. Racing home only long enough to fetch his fatigues and his Uzi, Ben-Hanan raced north to Major-General Hofi's command post where he demanded tanks and an assignment. Ben-Hanan, the owner of a superb combat reputation was told to fetch the remnants of the Barak Brigade and place them in an ad hoc tank force that would be used in a counterattack. Dozens of crews were without tanks and dozens of tanks were in emergency IDF repair centers being repaired for a quick return to the front.

Along with Lieutenant-Colonel Oded Erez, commander of the 53rd in Ben-Hanan's absence, Ben-Hanan built a force of 13 Centurions and crews in less than 36 hours; their efforts were reinforced by the management skills of the battalion's deputy officer Major Shmuel Askarov, who had been seriously wounded on the first day of the fighting, but had checked himself out of the hospital in order to return to his unit. Now, around noon on a fateful morning, they had saved the day and the 7th Brigade.

Ben-Hanan's force of thirteen tanks approached from

north of the Booster salient. They joined four surviving tanks of Lieutenant-Colonel Yair Nafshi's 74th Battalion and the three tanks that could still move from Kahalani's 77th Battalion. Kahalani, whose tanks had but a handful of rounds left was suddenly in the vanguard of a mighty force of twenty tanks. The newly rejuvenated armor wall split into three with Kahalani retaining the central axis, Lieutenant-Colonel Ben-Hanan's tanks pushing from the north, and Major Askarov moving from the south. Beating back the Syrian assault was slow-going, but it was getting done. Ben-Hanan was wounded and left his tank long enough to get his wounds patched up at the aid station. Major Askarov was shot through the head by a T-62 driver whose vehicle had just been hit.

The Syrians had been badly beaten and the fact that their overwhelming numbers failed to crush such an insignificant numeric obstacle was a fatal blow to the morale of the Syrian soldiers and their commanders. The Republican Guard, vanquished, attempted to flee the battlefield at their vehicle's top speed of 50 kilometers per hour. Some tanks ran over fleeing soldiers, others collapsed into ditches, and some smashed into trucks and destroyed tanks. The battle ended only when the Israeli tanks, completely exhausted of all ammunition, reclaimed the ramps.

The destruction in the Valley of Tears had been so absolute, so incredible, that many of the Israeli tankers could not believe the grandness of the horror that lay smoldering before them in the volcanic crest below. When the last tanks retreated to behind the ditch and the tankers knew that victory had been achieved, they emerged from their vehicles stinking of cordite and perspiration, as well as the other amenities of life. The air that they tried to refresh themselves with was filthy with the stench of blood and smoke, burning metal, and blazing flesh. Looking through their field glasses, tank commanders could see dead Syrian soldiers littered about the battlefield like discarded beer cans on the beach. Many had been hurled out of their vehicles when an AP round had landed right in the slot connecting the turret to the chassis, propelling the turret off the tank like a macabre beheading. Corpses were lying on their vehicles, in trees and decapitated alongside the roadway; their uniforms had singed off their flesh and their blackened flesh had roasted under the heavy flames. An identical scene of unbridled carnage was mirrored on the Israeli side. Tanks, as far as the eye could see, also littered the Valley of Tears. Some appeared to be untouched from the outside, but must have either been abandoned or hit by a slicing shot of AP fire that left little visible damage to the exterior but chewed up the interior of the tank and its occupants like a branch being chewed wildly by a chipper. Other tanks and armored personnel carriers, however, lay motionless and twisted as if they had been made of plastic. "If I had known that 203mm of steel could be penetrated like a knife through cheese, I would have gone into the paratroopers," claimed Eli, a sergeant in the 71st who emerged from his Centurion the survivor of a 12-hour hell. Other tankers proved so overwhelmed by what they had been through that they acted as if nothing had happened. An Israeli TV crew, remarkably, had managed to drive through the craters and falling ordnance to reach the brigade only moments after the last shots of the battle were fired. As the black-and-white film ran, one tank commander emerged from his Centurion to greet the crew. His Nomex coveralls were drenched with sweat and grime, and his face completely covered by a thin black film of cordite. Without emotion or promotion, he told the cameras, "We simply sought a target and fired, repeating the process the entire day. I found eighty burning tanks in my sector."

For the "bosses," Kahalani, Eldar, Nafshi, and Yanush the meaning of what they had been through was clear. But the day hadn't been a total victory. At 0800 hours, Captain Uri Karshani, commander of the brigade's reconnaissance company, led a force of the *Sayeret* to rescue wounded personnel from Buqata and bring them to the battalion aid station near Achamadiya junction. As the jeepborne unit, the elite fighters of the brigade, headed back on the main road from Buqata, their vehicles came under murderous antitank attack from embankments and fortifications 50 yards away. It was a classic ambush and a deadly one. The Syrians, generously supplied with RPG-7s and Saggers, had positioned themselves behind boulder fences and trees, and from defensive bunkers that the Syrians had put in place prior to the 1967 War. The reconnaissance troopers had motored head-on into a crossfire where antitank ordnance destroyed the lead and rear vehicles and RPK machine-gun fire in place took care of the rest. Captain Karshani, an experienced and decorated officer, did what a reconnaissance officer was expected to do—he fought back and ordered a counterattack. In a scene reminiscent to Captain David Stirling's Long Range Desert Group in the Western Desert, the "surviving" *Sayeret* jeeps raced toward the Syrian positions with their mounted machine guns ablaze. With the jeeps assaulting at full throttle, half the company then began a pure infantry battle against the Syrian positions. This was the reconnaissance company's own Valley of Tears, though instead of battling it out with 105mm guns and main battle tanks, this close-quarter melee was fought with Uzis, AK-47s, grenades, fists, and boulders.

Captain Karshani and his lieutenants thought that they had encountered a full battalion of infantry the way the Syrians were fighting; the level of Syrian fire was awesome. They were, of course, two companies of commandos. Through guts and determination, they inched their way closer to the Syrian positions in order to lob grenades at them and then wipe them out with machine-gun fire. The tank soldiers, also trained as commandos, entered the Syrian bunkers and began an hour-long process of hand-to-hand combat where gun butts, rocks, and even teeth were used to kill. It was, in retrospect, among the most gruesome encounters of the entire front. Before the last Syrian soldier was either killed or captured, Captain Karshani, most of his officers, and operators, virtually the entire *Sayeret,* had been killed; a few dozen men lay seriously wounded. An entire battalion had been removed from the fight in one 65-minute battle.

Although a tragic footnote to the battle of the Valley of Tears, the ambush of the reconnaissance company and its ultimate destruction did destroy the principal effort by the Syrian Army's 1st Command Group to cut the Masada-Buqata-Quneitra line and, in essence, opened the route to the reservists who would be flooding into the area by early afternoon. In retrospect, the sacrifice of the *Sayeret* in the battle was almost as important to the overall defense of the Heights as was the courageous stand by Colonel Ben-Shoham's Barak Brigade two nights earlier.

Looking at the battle on October 9, 1973, for the Valley of Tears the brigade had achieved a victory of historic proportions, but casualties had been so heavy and the toll such a dear one. Nearly 50 men had been killed, and as many wounded. Dozens of tanks permanently destroyed, and much of the brigade's infrastructure of junior officers killed off. A generation of tank fighting leadership, command, and experience had been lost that gray and smoldering day.

Viewing the remains on the field, Yanush stood shocked and stoic atop an M113 gazing through his field glasses. Only an hour earlier, he had resigned himself to death fearing that an enemy breakthrough would wind up splitting the nation in two. His men, the brigade that he had trained for war from his first hour as a commander, had performed beyond heroic and beyond epic. As commander of the brigade, Yanush had achieved a remarkable level of readiness in his brigade—one not originally mandated to fight atop the Heights. He had prepared his team of officers well for the ordeal, taking them on daily ground reconnaissance tours and explaining to the exact letter of the law how he wanted the Heights defended. He didn't tell his battalion and company commanders that everything would be okay. Yanush instructed them that the Syrian attack would be ferocious and that they'd be in for the fight of their lives. In the valley below his staff jeep, Yanush counted over 250 steel coffins, all destroyed in a single morning of combat. They had not been destroyed by a division of comparable armor and not even by a brigade, but by the remnants of a brigade fighting in company strength. When the battle began, the 7th Brigade fielded 72 Centurions (from the 105 tanks it began the war with), and at the end of the battle, it was left with only seven vehicles still fully operational.

As Yanush gazed across the battlefield, between two ramps he saw an Israeli Centurion, completed charred by flames, with its 105mm cannon touching a Syrian T-62 tank, also charred black by flames. Seventy-six 7th Brigade soldiers had been killed in the battle. The fighting had, indeed, been savage.

For the men of the brigade, soldiers who still faced a great deal of combat ahead of them in the days to come, they had persevered through the darkest challenge of destruction and emerged miraculous in victory. From the moment they had entered conscripted service and were allotted spots in the brigade, they had begun to forge tight loyalties and comradeship that would give them the faith needed to trust their crewmates when Syrian tank rounds rained down on them. In the bravado—and relief—of eighteen-year-old soldiers who only six months ago were happy civilians but were now veterans of one of the most brutal battles in modern military history, the men who had survived the hell began acting like eighteen-year-olds. Some began painting *Ha'Tachana Ha'Ba Damesek* ("Next Stop Damascus") on their vehicles, and most ran to unit support stations where they could find writing paper to scribble a note home or even a telephone to call their mothers and girlfriends to say that they were alive.

The war, however, was far from over.

The failure of the Syrian Army to exploit their success against the 7th Brigade proved to be a turning point in the course of the fighting up north, as well as in the south. The Soviets had taught the Syrians that nothing defeated enemy morale more than killing large numbers of them. By failing to exploit their advantage of surprise and sheer overwhelming numbers. the Syrians were now vulnerable to counterattack and ultimately defeat. President Assad immediately ordered the investigation into the conduct and behavior of his troops under fire, and even had several officers courtmartialed and executed for failing to bring the Golan back into Syrian hands. President Assad also sent urgent messages to Egyptian President Sadat urging him to launch a major offensive in Sinai, even though the Egyptians, too, were busy consolidating stretches of territory that they had captured. The Egyptians would eventually acquiesce and eventually launch a major offensive on October 14 that would see the destruction of over 300 tanks of their own in the largest tank battle fought since Kursk. By October 14, the United States aerial bridge, the ceaseless supply of fresh weapons and ammunition, allowed Israel to carry on the fight with a vengeance. That battle, like the Valley of Tears, would change the course of the war in Israel's favor.

For the brigade, they would enjoy 48 hours off during

which they could sleep, eat, and work at a feverish pace to repair their damaged vehicles and return them to the battle-field. Dead comrades were remembered and wounded buddies thought of. The idea of ending the damn war filled everyone's mind. Raful and the reservist division commanders that had joined the fight all wanted to have their vanguard units leading the push into Syria. That honor went to the 7th Brigade without debate. Following a 24-hour recovery period for the brigade's commanders, the post–Valley of Tears brigade consisted of 100 tanks divided into the 77th, 75th, and Sa'ar Battalion (remnants of the *Barak, Machat,* and *Sa'ar* Battalions from the Barak Brigade). Kahalani and Ben-Hanan's force would act as point, followed by Lieutenant-Colonel Eldar's 75th Battalion and force of tanks from the Armored Corps School under the command of Major Amos Katz. The target of the counterattack was to repel the Syrian presence from territory to west of the Purple Line and then push on, north, toward the Syrian capital. The attack was scheduled for 1100 hours on October 11.

Before the counterattack commenced, Yanush summoned his surviving officers to his headquarters for the preassault briefing. Not one for emotion, Yanush had been humbled by the previous week of fighting and the desperate hours he had survived. With tears in his eyes, Yanush looked at his sunbordinates, his comrades, and friends, and said, "We are about to fight the Syrians and we are going to seek revenge against them for how they insulted this country, and for them decimating the One-eighty-eighth Brigade, our sister brigade. The fallen from that brigade, the commander, Colonel Ben-Shoham, may he rest in peace, and his deputy, David Yisraeli, will serve as a sign and an example for us to fulfill our mission to its ultimate end." Yanush, wearing the same Nomex coveralls he had worn from day one of the fighting, had addressed a group of men who appeared just as ragged as he. The officers smelled and hadn't shaven or showered since their arrival atop the Heights. They had been to the boundaries of hell and had rebounded and worked for their own reprieve. Now, in a crowded tent, Yanush had placed it all in perspective. It was about revenge and honor and survival. That moment was, in Yanush's words, "the biggest of my life!"

At 1058 on the morning of October 11, a few hundred artillery crews belonging to a patchwork of units assigned to Northern Command's assault placed their shells inside their gun breeches and awaited the signal for the *Hatkafat Neged*—the counterattack. The barrage, at H-Hour, was sweet revenge and the Israeli gunners had the Syrian emplacements squarely in their sights, and this time it was Syrian positions that were under attack and Syrian personnel scurrying for cover. The IAF, badly mauled in the first days of the war by the SAM umbrellas, had worked out tactics to counter the lethal effects of the Soviet-built missiles, and while the Skyhawks, Mirages, and Phantoms were still vulnerable to antiaircraft fire and still suffering casualties, they were now able to provide close air support to the tank and infantry formations moving on the offensive.

The breakout from across the Purple Line was a two-dimensional assault splitting the brigade in two. The northern push consisted of Kahalani's 77th Battalion and "Force Katz" consisting of Amos Katz and his company of Centurions. The northern task force broke through the minefields that had separated Israel and Syria prior to the outbreak of fighting, and pushed to the Hadar-Tarnaja junction from where it pushed north and then proceeded toward Tel-Ahmer and Mazrat Beit Jan along the main roadway. The advance was also supported by mechanized infantry units from the Goleni Brigade and from various conscript and reservist paratroop units who fanned the flanks of the advance in search of infantrymen armed with antitank weaponry. The advance was smooth and relatively easy compared to the hell of a few days earlier, but in the early morning hours of October 12, the Syrians mounted a counterattack. A sizable Syrian tank and mechanized force made a last-ditch effort to halt the Israeli armor before it could pick up speed and continue on toward the main Damascus arteries. In all, Kahalani's tanks were encountered by 30 T-62s, all equipped with night-fighting equipment. The attack was augmented by infantry units—all armed with RPGs and Saggers—and artillery support. The Syrians put up a determined attack, though the infantry assault meant to bottleneck the roadway and trap the Israeli tanks in a killing zone failed due largely to the efforts of the Israeli infantrymen. The

Syrian attack failed, and the burning chassis of 27 tanks were scattered throughout the roadways of Mazrat Beit Jan.

The southern push consisted of three principal units: "Force Ben-Ḥanan," the 75th Battalion, and Lieutenant-Colonel Nafshi's 74th Battalion. The force broke out across from Jubta el-Hashab and Tarnaja, and had to cross a particular dense section of the Purple Line minefield (a crossing that resulted in the destruction of two of Ben-Hanan's tanks) and their advance route was terrain not ideally suited for tank movement—hilly embankments, ditches, and rocky patches that most vehicles—and tanks—would never succeed in crossing. The advance, therefore, went slowly, though steadily, capturing the village of Horfa on the first day of the assault, and the strategic Maatz junction early the following morning. Syrian antitank fire was determined and several tanks were hit and damaged, though Syrian gunnery skills seemed to lose their accuracy at ranges in excess of 1,000 meters. A significant number of Moroccan tank units had joined the Syrian front at this time; they were part of a motley Pan-Arab force that had filtered to both the Syrian and Egyptian armies in small numbers, insignificant formations, and were not properly integrated into the overall Arab chain of commands. The Moroccans had little training, no experience, and virtually no motivation to die for the regime of President Assad, though Moroccan mountain troops, expert in the treacherous art of hill fighting, were also positioned atop the Syrian peak of Mount Hermon, as well as with Syrian special forces atop the captured Israeli peak.

The second day of the Israeli counterattack, the push into Syria, began at dawn when Kahalani's 77th Battalion advanced to take Mazrat Beit Jan, and seize the high ground commanding its approaches. Capturing the village guaranteed access to the main road leading to Kiswe which, in turn, secured a major assault route for the push on Damascus. From 1000 hours to 1400 hours the Syrians put up a determined resistance to the Israeli advance. Syrian commando teams, deadly accurate with their RPGs, succeeded in damaging several tanks and destroying a few APCs; from an overlooking ridge, the tanks under Amos Katz's command provided accurate cover and the commandos were neutralized. Syrian Air Force Sukhois also attempted to stave off Kahalani's entry into Mazrat Beit Jan, racing several strafing runs by the advancing tanks of the battalion. But the IAF flew close cover and the attackers raced back to their airfields in Damascus and Homs. At 1400 hours Kahalani's tanks entered the village while mechanized infantrymen cleared out the abandoned homes and storefronts. The built-up area fighting was a world apart from the tank-on-tank quick draw fought atop the Valley of Tears, and it was nice for the soldiers to be fighting on Syrian soil for a change.

To the south of this push, Ben-Hanan's push toward Tel Shams, overlooking the main Damascus highway, encountered difficulties. Yanush had ordered Lieutenant-Colonel Ben-Hanan to take Tel Shams but didn't confer or confirm the plan with Raful, who was busy coordinating the first attempt to retake Mount Hermon and consolidating the recent Israeli successes. Tel Shams was what is known in the vernacular as a "key"—an element that could gain entry to an ultimate objective: Damascus. Tel Shams sat astride a hill whose perch commanded the four-lane highway leading from the Golan Heights to the Syrian capital. If Tel Shams could be captured, then the IDF would have in its possession a springboard from which to launch an assault on Damascus. But an assault on Tel Shams required infantry units, and Ben-Hanan's task force consisted solely of tanks. Nevertheless, Lieutenant-Colonel Ben-Hanan reviewed the assault plan with Yanush and commenced the attack.

Leaving two companies to his exposed flanks as cover, Ben-Hanan led a twenty-tank charge up the main artery heading into the village. He entered the area through a roundabout path meant to outflank the Syrian tanks waiting in ambush along the main road. The ground was treacherous to cross on tank treads and the advance was slow. When finally in position to confront the Syrian armor, it at first appeared as if Ben-Hanan's plan was ingenious. His tanks immediately destroyed ten Syrian T-55s, but before the rest of the accompanying companies could be drawn into the fight, Syrian gunners emerged from behind boulder-concealed firing pits and unleashed a lethal barrage of anti-tank cannon fire, along with swooshing flurries of RPG and Sagger fire. The Syrian defense was fierce and extremely effective. Four of Ben-Hanan's tanks were immediately hit and set ablaze. Other vehicles retreated down the boulder-strewn slopes, but before he could coordinate an orderly withdrawal, an RPG sliced through Ben-Hanan's Centurion ripping the turret clean off the main body. Critically wounded, he lay motionless in the volcanic field until para-troopers, led by Major Yoni Netanyahu, the man who three years later would reach world fame as the commando leader of the Entebbe rescue killed during the raid, launched a daring rescue foray behind Syrian lines to extricate the dead and wounded Israeli tankers. For his courage under in-credible fire, Major Netanyahu would be awarded the *I'tur Ha'Mofet* (Exemplary Service Medal) for volunteering to lead a squad from his 18th Paratroop Battalion to retrieve the hurt and killed tankers.

The 7th Brigade never got to hoist the brigade flags over Tel Shams. That honor went to an Israeli paratrooper unit that captured the town during the night of October 13 in a fierce battle.

The push into Syria was sweet revenge for the brigade, but it wasn't without its price. In 48 hours of combat, from October 11 to October 13, the brigade lost 18 killed in ac-tion, nearly 50 wounded, and the destruction of 20 tanks. There was still much fighting ahead of the brigade. In the south, the reservist brigades had scored a major—though hard-fought—victory against the last Syrian presence in the southern Golan Heights, and in the territory directly east of Quneitra where they fought and beat back hundreds of Syrian tanks, as well as Jordanian Centurions from the elite 40th Armored Brigade and elements of an Iraqi armored division that decided to enter the war after it had already been lost.

The southern half of the Israeli counterattack, the push that led to the ousting of Syrian presence in the entire Golan Heights and reclamation of the territory seized during the first days of the war from the Barak Brigade, was a two-divisional push of reservists. One division, the 146th,[19] was commanded by Brigadier-General Moshe "Musa" Peled and consisted of the reserve 9th Armored Brigade, a Sherman unit commanded by Colonel Mordechai Ben-Porat; the re-serve 4th Armored Brigade; a combined Sherman and Centurion unit commanded by Colonel Ya'akov Hadar; and the reserve 205th commanded by Colonel Yossi Peled, a Centurion unit. The second division was the 240th[20] commanded by Major-General (Res.) Dan Laner and consisted of the reserve brigade under the command of Lieutenant-Colonel Ran Sarig, and the 679th Armored Brigade commanded by Colonel Orri Orr. Lieutenant-Colonel Orr's story of reaching the front and participating in the combat is typical of the reservist units who were summoned to the mobilization on the morning of October 6, 1973.

Colonel Orri Orr, an officer who had made a name for himself in the ranks of the 7th Brigade in 1967 had been issued command of the 679th Armored Brigade two months before the war started, after completing a one-year course in the USA, at Fort Knox. It was an advanced armor course, and the beginning of an exchange that would flourish following the war. Now a major-general in the reserves and a member of Israel's Knesset, Orri Orr's story is typical of the type of fighting the reservist units encountered as well as an insight into the life of a reservist force:

I was the youngest brigade commander, or the second youngest in the entire IDF, at the time I got the brigade. It was at the end of August '73. Two months before the war broke, October '73. It was a very young reserve brigade, of people who just got out of the army. It was an interesting brigade ... very young brigade, consisting of people still at the end of their conscripted service—some of them, some were in companies of Hesder, yeshiva boys, some were experienced tank men, that served three years as tank soldiers, some were Na'ha'l—infantry men who converted to armor. But it was a very young brigade, compared with all the other reserve brigades, just like conscript soldiers. It was a Centurion tank brigade, which was the main tank in the IDF at that time. Four days before the war broke, "Raful," our division commander, called us to the Golan Heights, and they told us "the situation is unclear. We don't know whether this is an exercise or war." We toured the borderline and watched with binoculars, when there was, indeed, uncertainty, what is really going to happen. However, each one of us returned to his brigade and did the necessary preparations before the mobilization of the unit. Checking the equipment, checking the vehicles, using the staff that we had.

Since it was a reserve brigade, the majority of the people—at least in my brigade—were students. We did not get an order to mobilize the men, there was no approval to mobilize the men, and there was a limited staff of conscripted people, attached to the unit—very limited. That staff was responsible to routinely care for the vehicles, in peacetime, before the war. So what we did was we canceled all vacations to the whole limited conscripted staff, we checked all the vehicles, and the people started patrolling the area.

But there was no order for mobilization, only we remained sitting in the brigade's emergency warehouses, not knowing exactly what's going on. We actually got the mobilization order on Yom Kippur Day at 9 A.M. Then there was an order to mobilize, and we started calling up the people. It means that already two to three days before the war we were already not at home. We stayed at the brigade, checking the mobilization net, checking the vehicles, as many things as we could check with the limited conscript staff. The commander of the conscript brigade, who was responsible for the line, at that time, during the conscript process, was a good friend of mine in the war, Ben-Shoham, and I knew him very well, I used to be his deputy once. As the alert started, and the mobilization began, I took my jeep, I put it near the office and opened all the communication devices, the communication nets, to see what was going on, without waiting for reports. And while mobilizing, I followed in the net with what they were making public. How the Syrian planes were attacking, and we immediately understood that over here there is a war beginning and not just another battle day, or something else.

Therefore, I had information, because I was immediately listening in on the communication networks, even before the event started. Both because a good friend of mine commanded the battalion which was on the Golan Heights, and of course, in order to get the proper intelligence during the men's mobilization. I would like to say that by me were people who had come from home, and within five to six hours were already entering the battle. And that was the biggest difficulty. We could widely discuss this, and many stories were and will be written about this. Since the people entered the battle, not according to their units, but by the order in which they came from home. According to the time they arrived. People trained and got used to their commanders, their platoons, their companies. What happened here is that men entered the fray because they arrived early, whoever got there first. We rebuilt the crews all over again because the reports I heard on the communications network were that the Syrians were soon going to come down from the Golan Heights. So, first vehicles got their crews very fast, and started climbing up, in the Golan Heights. They started to climb up in the Golan Heights, and that was the main difficulty. Every one would think: Psychologically, what is the significance to a person who goes to war with a commander he is less familiar with?

The friend he got used to during training is not to his right or left. They went to war in a framework he wasn't familiar with, and this, I think, was the main difficulty of the first days. Except from the fact that people entered the Golan Heights not in the areas that were planned for them ahead of time. Each brigade had its own area, its own sector. Over here, men entered sectors because the Syrians broke into them, with no connection, of course, to the places they knew better.

In the beginning I started sending each platoon that was ready into combat. I gave an order, and they started climbing up to the Golan Heights. Within a very short time, I realized that if I continued with this method, I would soon be left by myself, and have no brigade to command. And I had an argument with the division commander, and with the division commander's deputy. I said: "I'm now leaving with every tank group that gets ready, I'm going up with them." And

I did do that, and already on the first night of the Yom Kippur War I went. It was about 20 tanks or more that left with me, and we immediately climbed toward the Golan Heights. And we immediately got responsibility for the Quneitra area.

There were tanks we sent to battle with only half the amount of the ammunition. I remember one of the young platoon commanders telling me: "Brigade Commander, Brigade Commander, I don't have a full supply of ammunition," and I said to him, "Never mind, the Syrians don't know how much ammunition you've got. You have forty shells! Get up there because we are pressed for time right now, we'll complete your ammunition supply while fighting"—a thing we really did.

We faced an unsolved equation of people who had just come from the synagogue, came from home, on Yom Kippur. In the Golan Heights they were already shooting, the Syrians were pouring in, and I had to connect the individual with a vehicle and formation, to equip the tank, prepare him to war with the tank, and to get him up there, and this was the . . . this was THE problem of that first day of the war. While exchanging fire with Syrian tanks very close by, I suddenly got an extremely urgent message in the communications net, directly from the Command commander, not even from the division commander, marked urgent. That the Syrians are cutting the Heights in two, really, and advancing toward the Bnot Ya'akov Bridge. And their head, their leading body, is already present in the Nafakh area. We don't have a map here, I don't want to go into a description, I don't know, it is not our role here.

Right here, I divided the brigade into two. When I say brigade, one has to remember, it consisted of between 30 to 40 tanks out of my brigade. But I immediately divided the brigade into two forces, and—actually, whoever knows the Golan Heights map—we had to go back! The Syrians cut us from the rear, and were going to the rear of our brigade and the 7th Brigade.

So, I, together with the main force, moved along the borderline in a wide outflanking, in order to try and catch them as far back as possible. And a smaller force was riding in the shortest way to Nafakh, to try and block them in the Nafakh area. As we were going up the mountain chains, a fire was opened on us, approaching in the Nafakh direction. Then I saw, for the first time, in action, a T-62 brigade. It was then the most modern tank, they were sparkling, a brand-new brigade. It was of the Syrian Third Division, which broke in at this region. And I realized that what the OC North Command had said was indeed true. The lead tanks were already inside Nafakh—just a few minutes before I arrived. And over here, a battle developed, clearly in uneven force relations in the Syrians' favor, like I said before. Quantity-wise, and you know what—also quality-wise, our tank was inferior. But here, thanks to our tank crews who were only ten hours in the battlefield, and their professional level. And we began to hit the Syrians hard with tank and artillery fire.

This battle lasted nearly eight hours. The end of the battle was that we actually stopped that brigade, destroyed most of it, and more, the Syrians—and we narrowed the defense line, and the Syrians did not succeed to reach Nafakh again. Therefore, this idea, that I came to them from the rear, with a small force in the front, it confused the Syrians. By the time they maneuvered and opened and rearranged their forces, we were able to destroy a large part of their forces, and mainly force them to begin withdrawing back to the Syrian line. I would like to say here, and I am truly saying it in short, I found myself with almost no company commanders.

While entering the battle, within a few hours, it was clear that whenever their level would go down, it would always become high again. In the hits, in fire corrections, in their ability to improvise—that's the most important thing—the improvisation of ability, of the commander, and our team members. We spoke before about how we entered the war. Unprepared vehicles, lack of ammunition, lack of time, things were unfinished, but the improvisation abilities of the commanders' in the lower levels is what determined the war's results.

> *So if we say, because of our soldiers' professional level they hit a lot better than the Syrians, their level, their ability to improvise, and of course, their heart's courage and the command. These are points that were expressed in this difficult battle and they caused defeat to the Syrians—however, like I said—with a very heavy price. The firing, and the bombs that explode, and the ricochets, is all camouflage. The real war is not outside, but in your head. Because being a commander is a tremendous responsibility you have over the men you lead. And I saw in the Yom Kippur War, to what extent the men are obedient, how much the men wanted someone to tell them what to do, to have an address, who to look up to, and to have someone they can count on. And I saw, while in the war, what a huge responsibility I had as a brigade commander. Anything I said to the men, I can tell you this for sure, they would do. Because they trusted me with their eyes closed.[21]*

On October 13, 1973, Colonel Orri Orr's 679th Armored Brigade encountered the Iraqi 3rd Armored Division near Tel Antar—a force of nearly 200 tanks moving northwest into the battle. The Iraqis had never fought a tank battle before and were completely ill-prepared to meet an experienced enemy unit—especially one eager to settle a score. Colonel Orr allowed the Iraqis to move to within 275 meters of his positions and then issued orders for his Centurions to open fire. The battle was as one-sided as could be. The 679th Brigade shot the Iraqis to pieces, destroying nearly 100 tanks without suffering a single casualty. Later that night, the 9th Armored Brigade, a force fielding World War II–era Shermans, destroyed another 80 Iraqi tanks in another one-sided battle.

For the 7th Brigade, the remaining week of the war was spent consolidating positions already seized and shoring up defenses against expected Syrian counterattacks. On the night of October 13–14, the brigade pushed southeast and assumed control of the hills commanding the Kfar Nasaj routes, as well as Tel Fatmah and Tel Mar'i, Tel a-Rus and Tel-Sarja. They were now supported by battalions of the Golani Brigade and permitted to fan out and gain territory where the situation allowed. During this week, they repelled three serious Syrian counterattacks, all launched at night, including one major push on the night of October 16, when Kahalani's battalion was challenged by thirty T-62s—all of which were damaged or destroyed.

On October 21 and October 22, as the cease-fire approached, the 7th Brigade launched a two-tier armored push to move forward along the main highway to Damascus. The first attack moved in the direction of Dir 'Ads and the second to Tel Arid. By the end of the day's fighting, Israeli tanks were only 40 kilometers from the gates of the Syrian capital.

Officially, the war ended on October 24, 1973, with the Israeli recapture of the position atop Mount Hermon and the subsequent signing of the cease-fire arrangement. Nearly 100 of the brigade's soldiers, NCOs, and officers had been killed, and twice as many wounded. The war had been a terrible one and for the first time since 1948, the very survival of the Jewish State had been seriously challenged. In all, 3,500 Syrian soldiers were killed in the eighteen days of combat, nearly 10,000 wounded. The Syrians lost 1,150 tanks and armored fighting vehicles throughout the fighting, the Iraqis lost 200 and the Jordanians 50. Israel's total losses for the Golan fight were significant: 772 dead, 2,500 wounded, and 250 tanks damaged (150 of which were returned to active duty during the fight). Sixty-five Israelis were taken POW, some from the 7th Brigade, and some never returned. For the next six months, the brigade remained in their positions waging a war of attrition against Syrian commandos, east-bloc special forces, and Cuban tank regiments.

Following the war, as Yanush was promoted to brigadier-general, Colonel Orri Orr was named commander of the 7th Brigade in early 1974.

The 7th Brigade emerged from the fighting true heroes of the Jewish State. Just as the *Pal'mach* emerged from the 1948 fighting as national icons, just as the reservist paratroopers from the 66th (Res.) Brigade had embodied themselves as national—and in the case of the paratroopers who liberated Jerusalem in 1967—spiritual saviors, so, too, did the 7th Brigade emerge following the war's end. The words *Valley of Tears* demanded reverence and thought—appreciation for the sacrifice and for the terrifying images of what could have been the wall of courage and the fire and steel collapsed under the weight of the Syrian armor. In fact, the brigade and the 77th Battalion in particular would become the subject of, by Israeli standards, unprecedented fame and glory. Kahalani, while a colonel and commander of the 7th Armored Brigade, wrote his now epic book on the battle for the heights titled *Oz 77*. It was later translated into English and a dozen other languages as *The Heights of Courage*. His book was a marvelous oral history of the life of a tank unit tasked with staving off the inevitable under impossible odds and became an instant Israeli best-seller and must-reading at military academies and staff colleges from West Point to Sandhurst. Dozens of the 7th Brigade officers were awarded medals of valor for their courage, including Lieutenant-Colonel Kahalani, who received Israel's highest award for valor, the *I'tur Ha'Gvura* (Heroic Service Medal), for his command and courage under fire on October 9. *I'tur Ha'Oz* (Courageous Service Award),[22] Israel's second-highest medal of valor, recipients from the brigade include Major Shmuel Askarov for his escape from a hospital in order to return to the fight and organize a task force of 13 tanks in the holding action; Lieutenant-Colonel Yossi Ben-Hanan for the battle of Tel Shams; Captain Meir Zamir for his company's destruction of 60 tanks during the October 9 battle for the Valley of Tears; and Lieutenant-Colonel Yair Nafshi and Lieutenant-Colonel Meshulam Retes, both awarded the medal posthumously. The 7th Brigade recipients of the *I'tur Ha'Mofet* (the Exemplary Service Medal) included Lieutenant-Colonel Yossef Eldar, Captain Oded Yisraeli, and Captain Amnon Lavi. Dozens of other soldiers received medals as well as Chief of Staff, Divisional, and Command citations.[23] A statement as to the mettle of the men found in the brigade that fateful October is the fact that Kahalani's tank crew, conscripts at the time, eventually rose through the ranks to reach senior officer status: Yuval Ben-Ner is today a lieutenant-colonel in the reserves; the operations officer, Giddi Peled, is today a lieutenant-colonel in the reserves; and David Klion, the gunner, is today a lieutenant-colonel in the reserves.[24] Lieutenant-Colonel Eitan Kauli, a ranking officer in the 82nd Battalion was also awarded the *I'tur Ha'Mofet*, as was Major Avraham "Ami" Pelnat, Lieutenant-Colonel Kahalani's deputy, who at the time of this book's writing is IDF's Chief of Armor Officer.

Unfortunately, the defense of the Golan Heights has, in recent years, been the source of terrific controversy and in-fighting. In the true Israeli fashion of petty peeves and jealousy, many inside the IDF disliked the attention the brigade received as a result of the publicity and books, and others felt that the 7th Brigade—and its key players—needed to be knocked down a peg or two. As the 20th anniversary of the 1973 war neared and the celebrations and memorials were planned and promoted, the ever-vibrant, ever-in-search-of-controversy Israeli press began its quest for material to break down the war's myths. The war of words began in September 1993 with an article in the weekend supplement to the newspaper *Ma'ariv*. The article, by noted journalist Emanuel Rosen, was titled, *"Lama Hufkara Hativat Barak?"* ("Why Was the Barak Brigade Abandoned?") and included the following issues: "A New Study Exposes Amazing Discoveries Concerning Decision-Making at Northern Command and Reveals Many Questions!" "Why Didn't OC Northern Command Yitzhak Hofi Authorize the Implementation of the Defensive Plan?" "Why Did Command Operations Officer Uri Simchoni Send the 7th Brigade to the Northern Golan When the Main Thrust Was to the South?" "On What Basis Did Yanush Ben-Gal Conclude That the 7th Brigade Destroyed 800 Enemy Tanks During the War When the Syrian Force Facing the Brigade Only 380 tanks?" "Explosive Historical Material."[25] Other articles were equally as vicious and equally determined to strike a chord of disharmony among the veterans of the fight. One typical headline was "Yanush and Kahalani Took Our Glory."[26] As the debate about the peace process exploded in Israel following the September 13, 1993, deal between the PLO and the Jewish State, so did debate over the fate of the Golan Heights, and spectacular headlines, spoken by the men who fought the last battle there, sparked the national debate.

Postscript: Winter 1993 "Valley of Tears" with the 7th Brigade

As the 20th anniversary of the 1973 War approached, many in Israel began a solemn, if not painful, process of soul-searching attempting to understand, fathom, and place meaning on the events that unfolded on October 6, 1973, at 1350 hours as an October earthquake caused the foundations—and survival—of the Jewish State to buckle.

Years following the 1973 War, the 7th Brigade's role in defending the Golan Heights and northern Israel suddenly became the source of national controversy. Many in the Israeli press, eager for nerve-striking headlines, wanted to start a war of words between the survivors of the 7th Brigade and those fortunate enough to have persevered through the hell of the 188th epic struggle for survival. For those in the brigade, they would have none of the controversy. The IDF prides itself on its keen understanding and appreciation of its own history. Battles of early statehood's plight for survival are rarely mentioned, as it is the domain of the recent that they relish and fight for. Stretches of land with shell craters, twisted armored skeletons, and minefields are not just grids on a map to be studied at a War College, they are living cemeteries and memorials to courage, defiance, and the defense of one's country. For the men—and women—serving in the 7th Brigade atop the Golan Heights, they live among the memories of those who have fought and have fallen. All new soldiers of the brigade are taken to the unit's memorials and battlefields the moment they arrive up north after completing their basic armored training. Usually the soldiers are ferried to the Valley of Tears, by the destroyed remnants of a Syrian T-62, and given what in the IDF is known as the *Moreshet Krav*—or Battle Lineage. Usually the lecture is given by the brigade commander; it is always a moving speech.

On one cold Golan afternoon, when the frigid wind off Mount Hermon swept south toward Quneitra, several dozen young men and woman left the warmth of their quarters for the 15-minute bus ride to the Valley of Tears. "They look very green," commented the brigade intelligence officer as he engaged in small talk with the 77th Battalion deputy, "their parkas are still clean!" The officers' talk was bravado. A captain, he had yet to see combat either—full-scale combat that is. He had been conscripted into the IDF a year after the 1982 invasion of Lebanon and while never fighting a tank-versus-tank engagement, he was an experienced combat officer. Most of the brigade officers present for this lecture had never seen "real" action before, but they were the Armored Corps' best because they had been sent to the 7th Brigade. The same held true for the "green" men sitting on the moist volcanic ash that had proven to be a fertile patch for growing strong blades of grass. The officers smoked cigarettes and munched on candy bars, the soldiers simply looked nervous and dwarfed by their surroundings. Some were blowing on their hands, others were wearing Nomex pilot gloves issued to tank soldiers. All carried Glilon 5.56mm assault rifles with two 30-round clips.

The brigade commander's white Ford Escort arrived just as the sun settling to the west created a clear, though dramatic shadow over the valley below. He wore his black beret and Class A fatigues, but wore no jacket even though temperatures were closing in on freezing. As he positioned his Glilon assault rifle on its sling across his shoulder, he placed his hands in his trouser pockets revealing a pair of jump wings and a Lebanon War medal pinned above his tunic's left breast pocket. He didn't introduce himself, nor did he need to. The three leaves on his epaulets were all the introduction he'd need. He stared at the assembled soldiers, paused for a brief moment to absorb their youth and inexperience, and then began his talk.

The place where we're standing today, is the place where the 7th Armored Brigade, whose commander I am today, stopped the Syrian army in the Yom Kippur War. This battle or collision between the armored forces, brought out the force of the Israeli armor. The battle here, was at ranges between one hundred to two thousand meters, when they fought day and night, and the best one was the one to win. The tank itself proved that it is the only vehicle which can withstand a tank bombardment. And one can view this as the develop-

189

ment of the tank as the main feature in the IDF's land army, today. And the only one who could prevent the Syrians from reaching central Israel.

In the Syrian Army, a tank commander is usually a soldier who came from a very particular segment of the population, which has the ability to, later, lead the Syrian population to certain achievements. In the Israeli army, the tank commander is an ordinary soldier, who was sent to commander course, and could, later on turn into an officer.

This is a fundamental difference from the Syrian Army, where the commander starts his service and turns to a commander. The second difference is the means of fighting, meaning the tank, and the way it is operated. In the Syrian Army, the tank works within a framework, fights the framework, and activates its cannon—the main armor of the tank. In the IDF, the vehicle does work within a framework, however, a very strong emphasis is given to teamwork, as a fighting teamwork, almost autonomous within the framework of a platoon of company. We can find the Israeli tank crew, firing in certain ranges, all by itself, or with the help of another tank or tank(s).

In the Syrian Army, we'd find the tank firing within the framework of platoon, commanded by the platoon commander only. In addition, we put a lot of importance into the conditions and the comfort of a tank crew member, inside the tank. Inside the Western tank, the M-1, the Centurion, and the Merkava, it is the crew member on which most of the good conditions are focused. In order to work the tank in a high level of performance, and in addition, to get the best out of his personal ability. However, the Syrian tank is crowded and very difficult to operate. It is a tank with a limited ability for individual fighting and is built for working in large frameworks. In addition, when you fight for your home, and when you turn back you see the settlements of northern Israel, and your own house, it's easier for you to fight, as opposed to someone who fights for some distant agenda, and who has no direct threat *on his ordinary existence. Which for us is an everyday life thing.*

The fundamental difference in the feelings and notions of a soldier who fights for his home and another soldier who attacks whose home is far away and who is fighting a war in order to achieve some political objective he, many times, cannot understand nor has any stake in deciding.

A soldier who is recruited by the Armored Corps, is a person who works within the framework of a tank. Teamwork is highly important, when each person's contribution, in his single profession, eventually brings the tank to its highest level of performance. The tank is a fighting system, operated by a team, equaling an infantry platoon in its operation ability, and the same or more in its destroying ability. Harmony at work is the most important part.

Colonel Y., the commander of the brigade at the time, didn't end his speech by seeing if any of the soldiers had any questions, or if anybody wanted to add anything. The soldiers had yet to learn the topography, had yet to move a 60-ton tank through the defensive lines and ramparts and yet to observe the enemy from across the fortified no-man's land of the Purple Line.

The soldiers returned to base a bit smarter that evening, somewhat overwhelmed by being placed into the crosshairs of perhaps the world's second-most-vulnerable flash point, and humbled by the task at hand. The brigade commander's speech meant that the NCOs and officers would push them extra hard this frigid evening. They'd check and double-check their tanks and APCs, and probably be ferried to the Purple Line for a firsthand look at the trip wire. Just in case the inevitable unthinkable hopefully never happens on their watch.

4

The Snowball of Lebanon: An Unpopular War Against a New and Improved Enemy

This is no country for tanks, not even a Merkava. This is no place for me. Damn this hellhole they call Lebanon!
—A 7th Brigade NCO, Israel-Lebanon Border, 1983

Spring is a cherished time for those serving atop the Golan Heights. The harsh winds rolling from the southwest have yet to bring their hot, dry, and suffocating air to the volcanic plateau, and the days are still bearable enough to work and the nights are cool and refreshing. The purple thorny flowers that dot the Heights begin to bloom in the early spring and by May they are in full color and blossom atop the Heights amid the shell craters and minefields. The beauty of this time of the year was interrupted by the sounds of Teledyne Continental AVDS-1790-6A V-12 diesel engines powering tracks and steel across the volcanic plains. The tanks of the 7th Brigade, a fixture of the geography atop the Golan Heights, were preparing for war.

Full-scale war between Israel and Syria was not expected in the spring of 1982, but nothing was ever left to chance. After all, as late as September 1973, Israeli military intelligence had failed to pick up the impending signs of a Syrian attack. Spring, however, had historically been a time of tension and intermittent strife in the region, and Syria's impressive bid to reach strategic parity with Israel had not gone unnoticed in the halls of military intelligence and Mossad headquarters in Tel Aviv. In fact, top-secret intelligence reports distributed to the government of Prime Minister Menachem Begin listing Syrian arms acquisitions indicated but one thing—Syrian President Hafaz al-Assad was restructuring and bolstering his army for a possible strike to reclaim the Heights, or at least gain a foothold and hold it before the superpowers, led by the Soviet Union, could initiate a cease-fire. Israeli military planners realized that Syria did not need to retake the entire Golan in order to score a victory in the eyes of the Arab world. In fact, Syria did not even have to keep the territory it would initially raise its flag over again and *could still* obtain one of its primary objectives in any conflict against the Jewish state—its rightful place as leader of the Arab world. Egypt had fortified that distinction by signing the peace accord with Israel, and it had also secured isolation in a region where being alone and without allies is as precarious a means of existence as can be found. Spring was also a time that saw Israeli troops do the unthinkable—battle fellow Israelis, settlers, and zealots, who fortified themselves in the Sinai town of Yamit, in order to implement the final phase of the Camp David Accords with Egypt. Many in the smoke-filled halls of IDF HQ in Tel Aviv envisioned a scenario where Syria might make a move to retake the Heights and torpedo the Camp David Accords simultaneously just as the last Israeli military units were departing the sands of Sinai.[1]

The 1973 War had devastated the Israel Defense Forces and the Armored Corps far more than any other of the IDF's six combat branches. With so many of its commanding officers dead and wounded, and with so many tanks destroyed and damaged, top IDF commanders wondered whether the corps could recover from the "October Earthquake." Given the precarious situation on the frontiers, *Heyl Ha'Shirion* was not afforded the opportunity to regroup and quietly rebuild; it was still at war! There was no easy Israeli military victory in 1973. The shock of the surprise attack, with its initial setbacks, demoralized the IDF, as well as the

Israeli nation as a whole. Instead of returning home to jubilant crowds celebrating another sweeping victory, the men of the IDF found themselves still at the front and engaged in a vicious and continuing war of attrition. The tanks lost by Egypt and Syria during the war's 18 days of fighting had been immediately replaced by their Soviet allies in a massive arms resupply effort. Israel received quite generous emergency arms supplies from the United States as well, but with almost all of its combat personnel at the front, *Heyl Ha'Shirion*'s task of absorbing the new tanks and armored vehicles was an onerous one.

Heyl Ha'Shirion's training doctrine dictated that the high levels of professionalism demanded from its soldiers and NCOs be acquired through long training and instruction periods in which indoctrination, combat skills, and leadership are achieved over a strictly controlled timescale. Unfortunately, almost all of the trained tank soldiers (from support personnel to battalion commanders) were stationed at the front; and the necessary time available to train a whole new generation of tank soldiers was unavailable. Major-General Avraham Bren Adan (still acting GOC, Armored Corps) decided that a radical approach was needed if manpower and quality levels were to be increased to an acceptable combat footing. Bren realized that no matter how fervently new tank crews trained, something vital would still be lacking without the necessary leadership and time to develop their skills. He came up with a revolutionary concept that proved to be astoundingly successful—militarily and psychologically. Bren ordered every tank crew at the front to adopt a crew straight out of basic training. New tankers were rushed to the front after only the briefest of introductions into the Armored Corps and were able to train in a genuine combat environment. The veterans at the front were relieved of the menial, though necessary, tasks and overall morale improved. New crews had the opportunity to study technical and operational aspects of their service while actually practicing them. In effect, they became seasoned veterans after serving in the IDF for only a few months. By January 1974 Bren was able to boast proudly that not one operational tank in the IDF was without a fully trained crew!

After the 1973 War, the Armored Corps (like the IDF as

a whole) was forced to analyze its tactics and determine future strategies on the modern battlefield. The War had created a political uproar in Israel; a nation used to being initiator and victor now found herself the victim of surprise and unpreparedness. A commission headed by the Chief Justice of the Israeli Supreme Court, Dr. Shimon Agranat, was formed to determine exactly what had gone wrong in October 1973. The commission's findings, intended to appease a disturbed public, led instead to dramatic political and military resignations (including the resignation of Prime Minister Meir, Defense Minister Dayan, and Chief of Staff Elazar; the GOC, Southern Command, Major-General Gonen was found to have shown poor tactical judgment and was sacked). In addition, numerous strategic doctrines in the IDF were found to be obsolete in the missile-age battlefield, and a revolutionary change to IDF thinking and tactics was ordered. Between the 1967 and 1973 wars, the IDF had been fighting a defensive war of attrition that had caused it to lose track of technical and tactical developments. A seriously negligent atmosphere of overconfidence infected much of the thinking of top IDF commanders leading to a lack of initiative in the development of new strategies. The future battlefield, with a marked improvement in antitank and antiaircraft missile capabilities, saw the IDF seriously lacking in defensive and offensive responses to these new threats. The "pure tank" strategy employed by the IDF since the 1967 War was deemed totally ineffectual in a battlefield environment where infantry antitank forces posed such devastating obstacles. A combination of all the IDF's combat arms, acting in concert with one another in battle, was desperately needed. *Shiluv Kohot* (or "Combined Arms") was born. Infantry and paratroop forces were now combined into armored fighting units, with training and maneuvers oriented toward the fighting that could be expected on future battlefields.

The task of rebuilding and rehabilitating the Armored Corps was led by Major-General Moshe "Musa" Peled, who became the IDF Armored Corps' ninth commander on April 16, 1974. Musa faced enormous problems. Although the borders were now quiet, and a more relaxed defensive posture was possible, the Armored Corps still had to be rebuilt from scratch. But the lessons learned in 1973 were heeded, and most tanks and APCs were upgraded in armor protection to minimize crew casualties. The MBT upgrading took many shapes and forms, some quite basic, others ingenious. To increase protection against infantry antitank weapons, additional .30 and .50 caliber machine guns were placed on the tanks. To decrease damage from antitank weapons such as the RPG and Sagger, add-on armor plating was introduced to the Centurion and M-60. Known as "Blazer" reactive armor, these armor plates were meant to explode on impact, severely limiting the penetrative ability of armor-piercing projectiles. Although these additions increased vehicle weight and decreased mobility, it was felt that crew safety was paramount.

Alongside the modification of existing weaponry and vehicles, new items were procured. Modern American MBTs such as the M-60 and M-60A3 were received in large numbers, as were large supplies of mechanized self-propelled artillery, and infantry antitank weapons such as the LAW and Dragon antitank guided weapons. Drawing upon lessons learned in 1973, the IDF also received M113 APCs equipped with TOW antitank missiles, and the mechanized M163 Vulcan 20mm antiaircraft guns. Although these were support vehicles, their weaponry would have an impressive impact in future fighting.

It was still realized, however, that tanks and APCs with maximum armor protection counted for little without qualified and capable manpower. Following the large losses in life and material in 1973, very few new conscripts volunteered for the Armored Corps, and the burden placed on the reservists increased quite unreasonably and morale declined. To repair the manpower damage, Peled turned to the IDF's "woman power!" Females were drafted into the Armored Corps and trained to be instructors, first going through full armor proficiency courses themselves. Women soldiers have proved to be more intelligent, disciplined, and well-adjusted to their IDF service than their male counterparts, and they met the new challenges with great skill and success. In fact, women instructors motivated the men to achieve their goals faster, because making a bad impression on one's instructor now involved a certain loss of face.

In order to overcome the Armored Corps' public-image problem, Peled initiated a program to increase motivation and opinion of the Corps, from within and without. Junior and senior officers visited high schools throughout Israel to persuade future conscripts to opt for the black beret and armor badge. "War stories," illustrating the bravery of the 7th Armored Brigade, also helped increase interest, respect, and, more importantly, volunteers for the Armored Corps. Peled also boosted morale and performance within the Corps. In 1977 a major study undertaken by the IDF General Staff reinforced Major-General Peled's success rate. Of the conscripts joining the Armored Corps in August (one of the larger call-up periods in the IDF), more than eighty-five percent stated that they had volunteered to serve in *Heyl Ha'Shirion,* and ninety-seven percent of conscripts stated that the Armored Corps was among their three top choices—most choosing tanks wanted the 7th Brigade.

Not only did the Armored Corps need urgent rehabilitation and rebuilding, but so, too, did the various brigades, including the 7th. Some brigades, like the 188th, had to be rebuilt altogether—new officers, new NCOs, and new vehicles. The 7th Armored Brigade was fortunate in many ways. It had suffered enormous casualties but its key officers were not only alive but survivors of a terrible ordeal. Experience is worth all the education in the world, and the officers of the brigade had emerged from a battlefield university like no other in recent military history. The key players all became IDF superstars rising quickly through the chain of command en route to the General Staff. Colonel Orri Orr assumed command of the brigade in 1974, and he was soon followed by a promoted Avigdor Kahalani. The period from 1974 to 1981 was a difficult and rigorous period for the brigade. Peace, albeit a temporary status quo, had come to the Golan Heights, but Lebanon was heating up. On March 11, 1978, a Palestinian suicide-squad launched from southern Lebanon landed on Israel's Mediterranean coast halfway between Tel Aviv and Haifa and seized two busloads of holiday travelers. In the ensuing standoff with security forces near a vital Tel Aviv junction, 38 hostages were killed and 70 wounded in one of the worst terrorist outrages ever perpetrated inside the Jewish State.

On March 13, 1978, the IDF—and the Armored Corps in the vanguard—entered southern Lebanon to root out the PLO terrorist presence from Israel's northern vulnerable frontier. The miniwar, labeled "Operation Litani," was a limited strike by a limited number of Israeli forces. Although the 7th Brigade participated in the fighting, mainly in support of paratroop and Golani Brigade units, it was the reborn and reequipped 188th Brigade that saw most of the fighting.

At this time the Armored Corps, together with the Ordnance Corps and Israel Military Industries, was busy working on its most ambitious project to date, a Main Battle Tank (MBT) manufactured in Israel. The man behind the indigenous tank production program by the Ministry of Defense was Major-General Yisrael Tal. Born in 1924 in Be'er Tuvia, near Tiberias in Galilee, Tal volunteered into the British Army in 1942. He served in the 2nd Battalion of the Jewish Brigade and saw action in northern Italy against German forces. As much of the "Jewish" element of the British Army was returned to Palestine following V-E Day, Tal remained in Italy along with fellow *Haganah* personnel to participate in the massive *Rechesh* (Acquisition) program underway. It is here, many believe, where Tal's penchant for manufacturing and quality control was born. More than a master at the controls of the tools of war, he was considered a natural at evaluating equipment—no matter how old and decrepit that equipment, he could devise a way to reinstate it into top-grade serviceable condition. Oddly enough, "Talik," as Major-General Tal is known to both privates and generals, spent the early portion of his military career as an infantry officer—fighting first with the *Giva'ati* Infantry Brigade and then with the *Oded* Brigade toward the end of the 1948 fighting. Perhaps the turning point in this stern-faced officer's career was being sent to Czechoslovakia to supervise the shipment of weaponry, from small caliber rifles to larger machine guns and cannons and piston-engine fighters, such as the Avia S.199 (the indigenous copy of the German Me-109). It was here, as an addition to his experience in Italy, that Talik learned of the importance attached to the tools of war. He remained in the infantry until 1957, when he was appointed the deputy commander of the Armored Branch, and from 1960 to 1964 was personally involved in the 7th Brigade's day-to-day operations. He also commenced foreign contacts to solidify the IDF's acquisition of a modern armored fighting vehicle. For the brigade during Talik's tenure, it was the age of the Centurion—at that point the most modern piece of equipment to be found *anywhere* in the Middle East. It was Talik's insistence that led to the first stages of the Patton program.

Because Talik had been in uniform since preindependence days, he was acutely aware of the difficulties Israel faced in arms procurement and the dangers that this presented during times of war. Talik never wanted the IDF and *his* Armored Corps to be held hostage by a foreign arms supplier in time of dire national emergency. Even though the relationship with the United States had blossomed into a full-fledged alliance by 1974, Talik came from a generation of Israelis that trusted no foreign power. To them, every war was like 1948—a struggle for survival—and the Holocaust touched every aspect of their military thought. The decision to produce an indigenous Israeli main battle tank dates back to the 1956 War when for the first time in Israeli military history the tank proved to be the decisive weapon fielded in battle. The 1948 War was an infantry campaign with little armor and the subsequent counterguerrilla operations of the early 1950s involved special forces and irregular warfare. Israeli armor in 1956 consisted of aging World War II–era Shermans, French-built AMX-13 light tanks, and any other armored bits that could be found on the scrap heaps of Europe. Tank warfare, as the battles of the Second World War indicated, was the dominant form of land warfare and as a result likely to be the factor deciding any future major Arab-Israeli conflagration. In 1956, a primitive struggle by today's standards, Israel was already outgunned by Soviet-built tanks fielded by Egypt. Following the war, however, the Egyptians replaced their aging Soviet-built World War II–era tanks with T-54s—Israel needed to obtain modern and heavy tanks and fast. In 1960 the Israeli government and Great Britain reached an agreement on the purchase of nearly 50 Centurion MBTs; the tank, nicknamed *Shot* ("Whip"), was the first modern tank to be deployed by the Israelis and at the time it was the most modern piece of hardware in the Middle East. In early 1964, the Israeli government arranged for several of its officers to travel to Germany and undergo a secret training course in the A-to-Z operation of the American-made M48 Patton. A few years earlier, the Israel Defense Forces (IDF) received its first modern main battle tanks from Great Britain in the Centurion Mk 5. Both the Centurion and M-48 were virtually obsolete the moment they were painted in Israeli colors, but they were far more suitable for full-scale warfare than the M50 Shermans and AMX-13s tanks then in front line service with IDF tank units, and compatible with the T-34s and T-54/T-55s flying the Egyptian, Syrian, and Iraqi flags. By having Centurions and Pattons in its order of battle, the IDF also had reached tactical parity with Jordan, a strategic threat to the east, whose British-trained and highly disciplined and motivated army also operated both the Centurion and Patton. But the IDF in 1964, as small and primitive by today's standards as it was, was an army with some very serious problems and some very innovative ideas about how to solve them. Israeli generals, all veterans of the brutal 1948 War of Independence where armor played virtually no role as Israel possessed only a handful of tanks, realized that the next full-scale conflagration between Israel and her Arab neighbors would be a tank war. It would be a blood-fest of large-scale tank-versus-tank battles not seen on the battlefield since the Second World War. Full-scale tank warfare, many of these officers studied in their courses in the United States, Great Britain, and France, meant heavy casualties. Tanks got hit, tanks suffered mechanical failures, and vehicles and crews needed to be replaced. In a tank battle, many believed, an attrition rate above fifty percent for vehicles was not uncommon.

Israeli generals realized that in order for Israel to win a full-scare war, it would need a sizable fleet of tanks, top-quality MBTs, that were suited to Israel's specific geographic and tactical requirements. Many generals and Ministry of Defense officials dreamt of having Israel produce its own vehicles, its own combat dynamo that would not only be the best main battle tank to be found in the region, but also one that put Israeli laborers to work and removed the "arms sales umbilical cord" that made Israel reliant and dependent on Britain and France for its frontline weapons. These visionaries were restrained only by the boundaries of their imagination and by Israel's very limited financial resources.

Israel had possessed an indigenous arms-producing industry even before its independence; the *Haganah*, the preindependence underground, had built its own guns and ammunition. Producing 9mm ammunition was one thing, as was mass-producing a relatively simple weapon like the Uzi, but building and mass-producing a 60-ton tank, one with sophisticated range-finding gear and armor protection, was a daunting challenge. Major-General Yisrael "Talik" Tal, a tank officer whose philosophy of lightning attack was the thesis behind the 1967 Six Day War victory, was the man who lobbied for the production of an Israeli-built tank and the man who inherited the job of supervising the tank's design, development, and production. In the eyes of the Armored Corps, there was tremendous urgency in getting this indigenous program off the ground. Following the 1967 War, the French embargoed all arms sales to Israel—including Sa'ar missile boats and Mirage jets already paid for. The British, at the time Israel's leading tank supplier, had been under tremendous pressure by the Arab states to cease all Centurion sales to the IDF. Israeli and British tank officers had worked closely for several years not only to accelerate Centurion sales, but to engage in a codevelopment program for the British-produced Chieftain tank—an armored fighting vehicle viewed by the IDF as Israel's tank for the next quarter century. The British offered the IDF a deal for the joint cooperation venture. The British needed money in order to complete their own future modern tank's development, the Chieftain with a 120mm caliber main armament gun, and the Israelis needed tanks. Israel would purchase hundreds of old Centurions at a significant discount in exchange for being allowed to take part in the final stages of the Chieftain tank's development. Britain would sell Israel the Chieftains and help build an assembly line in Israel to manufacture an indigenous version of the tank, under license, in Israeli factories.

In October 1966, two Chieftain MBTs arrived in Israel under great secrecy for extensive trials with the IDF Armored Corps; British engineers, also operating in Israel under considerable secrecy, supervised the project. The cooperation with the British lasted less than two years. After the 1967 Six Day War, however, Great Britain canceled the project as a result of Arab political pressure. This led Israel to search elsewhere for her next generation of MBT. Israel refused to supply the British with its recommendations for Chieftain modifications—feedback that, it is reported, the British Ministry of Defense and the manufacturers of the Chieftain desperately wanted. Britain canceled the exchange at the same time that Egypt and Syria took delivery of their first Soviet-produced T-62 tanks—at the time, the top-of-the-line MBT in the Warsaw Pact order of battle. The British balk was a major blow to the Armored Corps. Not only had Great Britain violated a legal contract as a result of Arab political pressure, but they informed Major-General Tal and his development staff as to their final decision a year after they had acquiesced to the Arab demands so that Israeli feedback in the Chieftain's design could be analyzed and incorporated into the final variant. More damaging, the British Ministry of Defense had lobbied the United States Department of Defense *not* to sell the IDF any American tanks, so that the Israelis would still follow through with the now-doomed Chieftain project. The time was 1969 and Israel was embroiled in fighting a multifront War of Attrition against the conventional armies of Egypt, Jordan, and Syria, as well as Palestinian guerrillas. Israel still had no new tank of its own as boatload after boatload of Soviet cargo ships unloaded their cargoes of brand-new T-62s into the ports of Alexandria and Latakia.

Yet it was Talik's command of the "Steel Division" during the 1967 War, a force which included the 7th Armored Brigade, that brought him international accolades. Immediately following the war, the Ministry of Defense appointed him responsible for development of armored fighting vehicles inside the IDF. It came at a time when the British embargo led government ministers to realize that Israel could not allow her national security to rest with unreliable allies. In August 1970, after a budgetary battle with Defense Minister Moshe Dayan, a man who wanted nothing to do with the project, the Finance Minister gave a thumbs-up to the indigenous program. Talik's objectives in designing and developing the "Israeli tank" were threefold: to provide the IDF with its first ever state-of-the-art main battle tank (in its history, no country had ever agreed to sell the IDF a new tank); to guarantee that a foreign-led arms embargo never denied the IDF a continuous supply of tanks; and that the indigenous-designed main battle tank be built specifically to Israeli specifications, produced to meet the unique needs of the IDF (the new tank was not to be an off-the-shelf-type item built for mass-production export). By the time the project, known as *Tochnit Ha'Merkava* ("Chariot Program"), got off the ground in 1971, some of Israel's most capable engineers and tank officers had been hand-picked by Talik to participate in the program. The tank had to be revolutionary though frugal, cost-efficient though powerful, produced of homegrown materials and technology though able to meet and master the most modern Soviet-built tanks to be encountered in the Arab arsenals. The question was, then, not whether it was justifiable to develop and manufacture a tank in Israel, but whether it was within Israel's limited resources to carry out such an ambitious plan, both from the technological and industrial points of view. In addition, there was the question of whether it would be possible to carry out the goals at a reasonable price and without hurting the economy in Israel. Some argued that Israel should continue to acquire existing main battle tanks, such as the Centurion and Patton, and completely refit them with Israeli-produced electronics, hydraulics, mechanics, and other additions that Israel's lessons on the battlefield have taught would be useful. But after initial studies entertained these ideas, it was discovered that developing systems for existing tanks would not only be cost-foolish, but would still result in the IDF Armored Corps' fielding of an antiquated system with modern technology. It was a stopgap approach—not a plan for the future. Talik would have none of it. Israel needed to be armor independent. It would have to be.

Over 6,000 tanks participated in the 1973 War and over 2,500 Israeli soldiers were killed in the conflict—the great majority of them were tank soldiers whose epic stands amid the advancing multitudes of enemy armor, indeed, saved the nation from probable destruction. Yet Israel was not a nation that could afford such rampant loss of life in battle. Not only was every casualty mourned as a national loss, but the loss of so many experienced tank soldiers—most of them were veteran reservists—seriously weakened the strength of *Heyl Ha'Shirion,* or "The IDF Armored Corps," to wage the next, inevitable conflict. In economic terms, the loss of so many tanks destroyed by enemy fire was a supreme burden on a nation whose national budget was already overwhelmed by defense expenditures. The attrition of hundreds of tanks in a prolonged "conventional" war limited Israel's strategic depth by depleting reserves in only a few hours of full-scale warfare. Armored fighting machines were not custom-ordered models built to Israeli combat specifications but off-the-shelf surplus.

In heading the Merkava Project, Talik, brought into the project his years of combat experience in a wide variety of roles and combat arenas. Experience in the Golan Heights in 1967, for example, had proved that mobility and speed were no substitute for armored protection. Clearly, any Israeli design would have to be conceived with the crew's personal protection being a paramount objective and the design would have to be such that the vehicle could withstand an enormous amount of punishment without endangering the crew's lives. Since crew-protection was the overriding concern, every aspect of the tank had to fit its role; firepower would have to come second and its mobility, third. In addition, the tank would have to be large enough and sufficiently comfortable to accommodate a four-man crew through elongated hours of operational duty, and eventually combat. With Israel's limited sources restricting the number of vehicles which could be produced, the tank would have to be the best in the world.

Acceleration into the Merkava project came incidentally at the same time as Israel's production of its own indigenous fighter-bomber aircraft, the *Kfir,* or "Lion Cub." The project began in 1968, when in response to a French embargo of already paid for Mirage fighter-bombers, the Mossad obtained plans for the aircraft from a sympathetic Swiss aircraft designer. Major-General Tal had been the IDF's Deputy Chief of Staff during the 1973 War and it angered him that so many tank soldiers had died in the conflict because the IDF was not fielding as modern and uniquely suited tanks as they should have been equipped with. He used the bitter conflict as a postmortem laboratory to determine the cause for such heavy tank casualties in the Israeli ranks and what remedies—in the planned *Israeli*-produced MBT—could prevent such loss in future conflict. Through exhaustive examinations of ballistic findings, Tal and his team of tank battle experts were able to produce a working idea of what the Israeli supertank had to be like. The primary concept was to make every part of the tank play a role in the crew's protection; it became known as "spaced-armor." That would allow every physical aspect of the MBT, from fuel, ammunition, and tools, to perform a distinctive function—the spacious interior would also include the driver into the crew's compartment, removing a long-time tank crewman's psychological stigma. Tal also traveled to friendly Western nations to view the latest advances in the tank designs of the late 1970s. He witnessed prototypes of the West German Leopard, the French AMX-30, and, in Britain, an advanced look at the new Chieftain, and the American XM-1. According to foreign reports, Israeli intelligence connections had afforded Talik a glimpse of the Soviet T-72 long before it arrived in the Middle East and long before American analysts had a chance to uncover its secrets.

Major-General Tal was impressed by the Western tanks— and even by the latest Soviet offerings. But Israel was not the plush and flat fields of Germany where a believed NATO–Warsaw Pact conflagration was planned to transpire. The Merkava needed to be suited to rough terrain, mountains to the north and desert hills in the east. As the peace treaty was still a dream, the tank would also have to be a superb desert warrior. At first a wooden mock-up of the Merkava was produced and, later, the various arms producing firms in Israel were recruited for the task at hand to produce the fire-control systems, special armor plating casting, shock absorbers, and sights needed for the IDF's next generation of MBT. Speed was not an important factor, but size and security were. A behemoth of an MBT, the Merkava proved truly unique in its design; the engine was placed up front providing the crew with an additional armored protection. The tank's design incorporated a low slope configuration into the hull and a turret design to decrease the angular impact of incoming antitank shells and missiles. The tank also possessed a rear escape hatch which not only afforded the crew easily accessible evacuation means, but which could also be used to transport a few infantrymen, or keep a casualty comfortable and stable until he was transported to the battalion aid station. The large type of design utilized in the Merkava—compromising speed and mobility for protection—was in sharp contrast to the constricting size of the Soviet MBTs in Arab use. These tanks emphasized speed and mobility for the Soviet offensive doctrine of massive juggernaut attacks. The Merkava Mk I's main gun was the lethal 105mm L7 cannon, a weapon which since 1967 had destroyed thousands of Arab tanks. The primary concept behind the Merkava, however, a trait that has followed all subsequent variants, is its armor protection and resiliency. The tank's *Migun*-armor protection is a layered armor all around the tank spreading the tank's systems around the crew in such a manner that enables them to protect the crew and ammunition, in addition to their operational intention. The main example for this concept is the force brigade, located in the front of the tank. Additional contributing factors to resilience are: (1) small silhouette of the tank in the fire position, (2) lack of flammable materials in the crew chambers, and (3) storage of the heavy ammunition under the turret ring.

In May 1978, on Israel's thirtieth anniversary, the new and almighty "Chariot" was introduced in a stadium in Jerusalem during Independence Day celebrations. The unveiled Merkava Mk I was as awe-inspiring as it was mighty and revolutionary. Already, without it ever performing in combat or before the scrutiny of the press, it was labeled as the "best tank in the world." The man who took the "keys" from Talik that warm Jerusalem spring day was Colonel Avigdor Kahalani, commander of the 7th Brigade and in 1973 recipient of Israel's highest medal for valor for his now epic command of the 77th Battalion during the battle for the Valley of Tears on October 9, 1973. Although the Merkava would be stationed first atop the Golan Heights across the Purple Line from Syrian positions on the "other" side of the frontier, their first deployment in combat would be in Lebanon.

As a result of the 7th Brigade being the first IDF formation to deploy the mighty Merkava, the brigade would soon
assume the esteemed nickname of "The Chariots of Fire
Brigade." But Kahalani would not remain at the helm of
his beloved unit—he was destined to advance in rank. Prime
Minister Menachem Begin, popular among Israel's Sephar-
dic population, had been a tremendous admirer of Kahalani;
"He'll be the first Yemenite chief of staff," the prime minister was often quoted as saying. "You'll see . . . it'll be Kahalani." With Raful, his old division commander, as new chief
of staff, Kahalani was promoted to the rank of *Tat-Aluf*
(Brigadier-General) and named division commander himself. The new Brigade CO in 1980 was Colonel Eitan Kauli,
a man uniquely experienced in tank-versus-tank warfare,
and an officer who like most of his contemporaries had been
bloodied in the Valley of Tears. A soldier who learned the
rigid discipline of a tanker's life under the regime of brigade
commander Colonel Shmuel "Gorodish" Gonen, he had
fought in Sinai and the War of Attrition and was in the thick
of the choking cordite and the penetrating armor-piercing
discarding SABOT rounds of the Valley of Tears. Wounded
in the vicious fighting against the Syrians, Kauli was also
decorated for his courage under fire. He was awarded the
blue ribbon *I'tur Ha'Mofet* decoration for exemplary service
for his role as deputy battalion commander during the desperate days of hell and standoff action during the battle for
the Valley of Tears.[2] He was considered a courageous and
no-nonsense officer who expected the utmost of his men and
machines. He knew that the 7th Brigade was a unique fighting force, and that its responsibilities along Israel's north
were unique, as well.

The absorption of the Merkava MBT into the 7th Brigade's order of battle had been an important boost of morale for the "black berets" of the IDF's Armored Corps.
Traditionally, the Armored Corps did not receive many volunteers; in fact, you were volunteered into its ranks. It didn't
have the exhilaration or the esteem of pilots' course (or the
Air Force, for that matter). The cream of the conscripts,
primarily eighteen-year-old kibbutzniks, tended to volunteer
for the various *Sayerot* reconnaissance commando units or
the other special forces within the IDF order of battle, such

as Flotilla 13, the IDF/Navy's naval commandos, and the IAF's Aeromedical Evacuation Unit (IAF/AEU). Other conscripts looking for combat duty volunteered for the paratroops or the 1st Golani Infantry Brigade. Everyone left at the IDF's sprawling Conscription and Absorption Base with a medical profile worthy of combat service tended to end up in the Artillery Corps, the Combat Engineers, or tanks. Not to say that young Israeli males did not want to serve in the Armored Corps, but conditions were harsh, discipline even harsher, and leaves were few and far between; many also knew that in the eventuality of war, tank soldiers tended to become casualties at higher rates than anyone else. Nevertheless, the addition of the Merkava Mk 1 MBT was an attraction and a draw—in fact, the Armored Corps brought a Merkava to the Conscription and Absorption Base so that new conscripts could look at the hulking 60-ton personification of might and firepower through their openmouthed, wide-eyed imaginations. Virtually all of the conscripts entering the IDF in 1980 and 1981 who saw the Merkava wanted to have it as the center of their three-year military careers and actually volunteered into the Armored Corps with expressed demands to serve in the 7th (even though by 1981, the Merkava had entered service with other tank brigades). In a study conducted in 1980–81 among 2,500 conscripts to the Armored Corps, thirty-two percent stated that they "requested" to serve in the Corps as a result of the might of the tank, and an additional fifteen percent wanted to be where they were because of the honor and interest of operating a tank.[3] Most eighteen-year-old Israeli kids have a driver's license by the time they enter the IDF, but few have cars to drive. The thought of beginning one's driving career behind the throttle of a 60-ton vehicle (as opposed to Dad's white Subaru station wagon with the sticky gears) is, indeed, an attractive thought for many not looking for the exhilaration of parachuting in their military service, but still looking for a combat unit with an interesting sideline.

The Israel Defense Forces in 1982 was an army far different than the one that had fought the 1973 War. Larger, technologically advanced, and able to, for the first time in its history, strategically consider a major war being fought without Egyptian involvement. The IDF of 1982 was under

the command of one of the most popular and most courageous men to assume the post of chief of staff: Lieutenant-
General Rafael "Raful" Eitan. After all, he was the legendary 890th Paratroop Battalion commander who jumped into
the Mitla Pass in 1956; the daring 35th Paratroop Brigade
commander who took a bullet to the head in Sinai in 1967;
and the wounded divisional commander atop the Golan
Heights in 1973, who rallied the remnants of his Golan
forces, including the 7th Armored Brigade, behind him in a
desperate and successful defense in 1973. He was a decorated warrior who could lead a charge into a hail of enemy
fire as well as plan some of the most spectacular special
operations ever mounted in military history. Perhaps more
than any other Israeli chief of staff before him, or since,
Raful understood the Israeli soldier. He could be strict and
rally them to function, and yet he could sympathize with
their problems and struggles in dealing with the gargantuan
bureaucracy that is the IDF; on many occasions, he would
invite soldiers who had problems with their COs or master-
sergeants to his house in Moshav Tel Adashim for a Sabbath
leave.[4] The conscripts identified with Raful, and they knew
that he counted on them. Raful was both loved and revered.
Morale in the IDF was at an all-time high.

The 7th Armored Brigade in the spring of 1982, too, was
a far cry from the force spread out against the Syrians on
the fateful Saturday afternoon on October 6, 1973. It was a
modern fighting force by any standards—by NATO standards, by those of the Warsaw Pact, and certainly among
the levels of equipment and combat readiness of any Arab
tank outfit. The Merkava Mk I was by most standards the
best tank in the world and the one tank in service designed
to absorb the punishment of close-quarter armored warfare.
Tank officers around the world and foreign military analysts
alike were awaiting the Merkava's first baptism under fire
to see how the mighty chariot of iron fared under Soviet
ordnance. In addition to the Merkavas, the 7th Brigade
crews were considered to be the finest in the IDF (and, as
a result, many would argue, the finest in the world)—the
best trained, most intelligent, and most combat capable. The
7th Armored Brigade in 1982 could also rely on the most
effective air support in the region with the mighty Israel Air

Force bolstered in the early 1980s by the newly acquired McDonnell Douglas F-15 Eagle and General Dynamics F-16 Fighting Falcon, as well as its modified old warhorse, the F-4E Phantom. The IAF could devastate any ground target that posed problems for advancing armor formations with unprecedented accuracy and ferocity. By 1982, the 7th Brigade, like other IDF armor formations, could count on the support of the newest equation on the battlefield—the helicopter gunship. Armed with a variety of antitank guided weapons, such as the lethal American TOW ATGW, these low-level birds of prey could hug the earth along a treeline or through the inclines of a valley at a speed of 170 mph, and still hit their targets at such ranges that most tank-mounted anti-aircraft guns, like the .50 caliber heavy machine gun, would be ineffective against them. Also by 1982, the lessons of 1973 had been incorporated into *Heyl Ha'Shirion*'s order of battle. Mechanized battalions that followed the tanks into battle were armed with M113 APCs with TOW ATGWs. Infantrymen carried a wide variety of antitank weaponry in support of their armored formations, including M72 66mm LAW rockets, rifle-fired antitank grenades, and the ubiquitous RPG-7, captured in such large numbers from the Egyptians and Syrians in 1973 that they became standard issue to Israeli paratroop, infantry, and engineer forces.[5]

Because the 7th Brigade was among the first units to be equipped with the Merkava, it became known in the IDF as the Hollywood Brigade. Anyone who was anyone visiting the Jewish State made the pilgrimage to the Golan Heights to see "the" unit fielding "the" Merkava—from U.S. senators and British lawmakers to Hollywood celebrities in Israel filming a major production. Talik, the father of the Merkava, attended every showing of "his baby" along with many of the brigade's maneuvers. Although the Mk I had yet to see combat by 1982, Talik and his staff of engineers and designers were busy at work developing an Mk II variant that they hoped could be fielded soon. The word was issued to officers at the IDF's Conscription and Absorption Base (known by its treacherous Hebrew acronym of *Ba'Ku'M* for *Basis Klita U'Miyun*) to filter the best of all conscripts into the brigade.

There was, after all, tradition to maintain and there was the Merkava.

Far from the Conscription and Absorption Base on the Golan Heights, those who ended up in the 7th under Colonel Kauli's command found themselves spread out in typical security duty in April and May of 1982. Talk of war inside the base had dealt more with the Falklands conflict being fought tens of thousands of miles away than with the Syrians dug in only a few hundred yards and a no-man's-land away. Intelligence charts placed throughout the various OPs (observation posts) and bunkers illustrated the sleek silhouette of the T-72 MBT, the latest addition to the crack Syrian 1st Armored Division. Colonel Kauli thumbed through intelligence files on the T-72s performance, as well as an up-to-date version of *Jane's Armour & Artillery*, a required reference source for all senior armor officers, kept on his desk. Most war scenarios had the 7th Brigade facing off against the T-72 across the Purple Line and in the Valley of Tears, and Colonel Kauli wanted to be ready.

The 7th Brigade and its force of Merkavas would, indeed, face off against the T-72, but it would not be on the Golan. It would be in Lebanon, in the poppy fields and treacherous winding mountain roads of the notorious Beka'a Valley.

There were hints that Israel might be fighting a war inside Lebanon a year earlier, in 1981, when Palestinian and Israeli forces exchanged daily rocket and artillery fire across the embattled Lebanese frontier. It was known as the summer of the Katyushas, and the government of Israeli Prime Minister Menachem Begin and Defense Minister Ariel "Arik" Sharon were poised to rid the Palestinian guerrillas and their long-range rocket launchers from the north of Israel. Israeli air strikes, meant to deter the Palestinians, were brutally effective but they also risked a wider war with Syria. Since the end of the 1975–76 Lebanese Civil War, Syria maintained a 30,000-man garrison in Lebanon—they were mandated by the Arab League as peacekeepers, but Syrian President Assad had his own unique political agenda in a sovereign nation that Damascus referred to as "Greater Syria." Syria at first entered the Lebanese madness to save the ruling Christian minority, primarily the Maronite Phalangist militia, from the might of the heavily armed and experienced Muslim and Palestinian forces. Then, when the tide turned against the Palestinians and the Christians assumed the initiative and advantage, the Syrian Army turned against their fleeting Maronite allies. This somewhat schizophrenic involvement made perfect sense in Damascus, and it was understood in the halls of IDF HQ in Tel Aviv. Syria regarded Lebanon as its own, and it would object to any Israeli moves into the backyard of Assad's Greater Syria.

Having fought in two major wars himself, Kauli could read the impending signs of war that would soon become reality. "Soldiers have a sixth sense when it comes to impending war," reflected Brigadier-General (Res.) Elyashiv Shimshi. I "It may surprise the politicians and the public, but not the men on the line." War especially did not surprise brigade commanders. Colonel Kauli, who felt the impending signs of action in the "north," took a page out of former brigade commander Ben-Gal's play-book and set up his chart of "Days to go to war ... days to go to get the brigade ready for war." Throughout the winter months of 1981 and 1982, the 7th Armored Brigade endured a season of, what Colonel Kauli termed, "nerve-racking alert."[7] War was considered imminent that winter, and Kauli spent as much time shuttling back from Northern Command HQ to go over "new" and yet even "newer" war plans, as he did in the north and south supervising the training of his men and machines. In fact, realizing that war with the Syrians was nearing, every level of the brigade received intensified exercises and instruction—from the simple tank crew to large-scale brigade and division exercises. Leaves during this period, which extended to the spring, were few and far between for all ranks. False alarms were almost a daily occurrence—not a week went by where the brigade's personnel were not awoken from their sleep and ordered to ready their Merkavas for action. "It was," according to one 77th Battalion veteran, "a time of constant work, constant training, and terminal nail biting!" It was also a period of fluctuating emotion and adrenaline rides. Raising a soldier's psyche for war, and then having to lower it when it is only an alert can have a devastating effect on morale. Life in the brigade was becoming tense. There is a saying in virtually every army in the world— "Bored soldiers don't think." Colonel Kauli wanted his men busy. In May 1982, sensing the tension, the brigade was ordered to undergo company exercises in mountain warfare tactics—including, ominously, operations against antitank choppers. Kauli was a student of current events. The Syrians had already used their fleet of attack choppers in Lebanon months before.

It was Syrian attack-chopper sorties in Lebanon which, in fact, sealed Lebanon's fate to serve as the battleground for the next Arab-Israeli conflict. In the spring of 1981, the Syrians' 30,000-man garrison in Lebanon had squared off against the Israeli-supported Phalangist militia. The Syrians were punishing the Christians for not towing the Damascus line and for the increased brazen attacks against Syrian units throughout the country. Syrian military action was punitive, not provocative—the Syrians did not want to push the Israelis into war. Emplacement for SA-6 Gainful surface-to-air missiles were dug throughout the Beka'a Valley, scene of the most vicious Syrian-Christian combat, but never filled with the actual missile even though the areas were routinely overflown by Israeli reconnaissance aircraft.[7] Syrian retaliatory operations were viewed differently in Jerusalem, however. Even though Amman commander Major-General Yehoshua Saguy, long cautious of the ever-aggressive Israeli stand with the Christians, warned that the Phalangist-Syrian war was the doing of Phalangist leader Bashir Gemayle who was itching for the Israelis to take care of the Syrians for him, Defense Minister Ariel Sharon and IDF Chief of Staff Eitan viewed Syrian moves as a *casus belli* for future Israeli military action. They were determined not to give Damascus an inch when it came to their Lebanon policy. Lieutenant-General Eitan, in fact, recommended that IAF warplanes be despatched to blow Syrian attack choppers out of the sky.

On April 28, 1981, Raful received authorization for limited IAF air activity in support of the Christians over the Beka'a capital of Zahle, sight of much of the Syrian-Christian fighting. Two Syrian Mi-8 choppers, flying ground support missions with elements of the elite 82nd Parachute Regiment, were blown out of the skies over Zahle. The empty SA-6 emplacements were soon filled with launchers and missiles, and SCUDs based near the Syrian capital were readied for firing against northern Israel. Only a miracle, and the shuttle diplomacy of special U.S. Ambassador Philip Habib, prevented war from erupting that spring and summer. Lebanon, however, was braced for war. It was only a matter of time before a spark proved more powerful than cool heads. That flint strike came on June 3, 1982, in, of all places, the parking area of the Dorchester Hotel in London. Shlomo Argov, Israel's ambassador to Great Britain, was critically shot by three gunmen belonging to Abu Nidal's Fatah Revolutionary Council. Abu Nidal was more anti-Arafat than anti-Israel, and it is believed that he ordered the attack in order to provoke an inevitable Israeli retaliatory incursion into Lebanon, and thereby weaken his two most bitter enemies. Both the PLO and Israel fell into the Nidal trap in immediate and bloody fashion. Even though Shin Bet (Hebrew acronym for the *Sherut Ha'Bitachon Ha'Klali,* or General Security Service, the Israeli domestic counterintelligence and counterterrorist organization, similar to the American FBI and the British MI5) officials informed Prime Minister Menachem Begin and various IDF commanders that the PLO *was not* responsible for the assault in London, the IDF was ordered to attack the PLO in Beirut anyway. The IAF was dispatched for a massive bombing run against Beirut. Yasir Arafat's PLO also fell into the trap. They responded to the Israeli attacks against their headquarters with massive strikes of their own—Katyusha rocket attacks against the Galilee region of northern Israel. Israelis were forced into shelters and the reserves were mobilized. On the night of June 5, the Israeli cabinet approved Israel entering into a limited war in Lebanon. The main objective of the operation was to push Palestinian gunners out of artillery range from the Israeli frontier. It was, however, clear that the risks for a wider escalation of the conflict existed—with all of the Palestinian militias, with the Lebanese, the Syrians, and even other Arab states.

At 11:00 A.M. on the morning of June 6, 1982, the time for negotiations, shuttle diplomacy, and small-scale artillery duels had ended. Following a ferocious artillery barrage and IAF strikes against key strategic positions throughout Lebanon, a mechanized column of Israeli tanks and APCs smashed through the barbed wire fortifications along the Purple Line and invaded Lebanon. According to foreign reports, the number of Israeli troops that entered Lebanon in that massive invasion force numbered nearly 60,000 men. The initial objective of the invasion was the destruction of the PLO ministate in southern Lebanon, thus guaranteeing the security and integrity of northern Israel. It was a massive undertaking, which Israeli leaders knew would forever alter the political landscape of the area. It was one which promised to produce an incredible list of unexpected difficulties and hazards from engaging in a guerrilla-type war in a terrain of refugee camps and hillsides, to the war escalating into a full-scale regional conflict that risked the recently cemented Camp David Peace Accords with Egypt, as well as possible (inevitable) superpower involvement. The invasion also risked provoking a wider war with Syria. That was one scenario that the Israelis not only envisioned and prepared for, but secretly welcomed. The beginning of this still-unfinished Israeli involvement was called "Operation Peace for Galilee"—an innocent title for an endeavor that would forever change the military landscape of Israel.

As the divisions of tanks, APCs, and infantrymen pushed north, surrounding and then bypassing the major concentrations of Palestinian guerrilla resistance along the coastal road from Tyre to Sidon, and in the central area from Beaufort Castle to Nabatiyah, Colonel Kauli's 7th Armored Brigade sat inside their vehicles on razor's edge expecting the war to spread across the Golan Heights. Two scenarios existed where war would have come to, or through, the Golan Heights, that fateful summer. The first, called by many "The Syrian Option," had Syrian President Assad temporarily sacrificing his forces inside Lebanon by having them engage the IDF in and around Beirut as well as the Beka'a Valley, while the brunt of the Syrian Army launched a massive strike across the Golan Heights—in essence, outmaneuvering the IDF at a time when they would be committed elsewhere. The second scenario, termed "The Damascus Option," had Israeli forces inside Lebanon slicing through the Beka'a, into Syrian territory, toward the Syrian capital. President Assad had for years feared an Israeli presence in Lebanon for just that reason. The Beka'a is Syria's strategic underbelly and Achilles heel combined, according to a former Israeli colonel,[8] and Syrian moves in Lebanon have veri-

215

fied this posture as fact. According to *this* scenario, when Israeli forces would turn right in the Beka'a and proceed to the geographically advantageous western approach to Damascus, forces positioned around the capital and on the Golan Heights would have to be rushed to the Beka'a for a desperate holding action. Damascus is only a one-hour tank drive from the Beka'a Valley. Israeli forces on the Golan, in 1982 the 7th Armored Brigade, would then launch their move across the no-man's-land, and engage in a lightning pincer movement to force the Syrians to surrender and possibly negotiate a lasting peace.

IDF strategic intentions are, of course, classified top-secret. Any Israeli source would never confirm if a move on Damascus was a scenario envisioned during Operation Peace for Galilee. Yet it is known when war erupted in Lebanon in June 1982, the 7th Brigade was given strict defensive orders in their firing positions overlooking the Syrian Purple Line.[9] The 188th Barak Armored Brigade was already in the epicenter of the fighting—pushing northeast through the Beka'a's approaches for a showdown with the Syrians. Reservist units were called up, and still the 7th was standing fast. Hours after the near-fatal shots were fired in London, most units about to enter into Lebanon, mobilized for war, knew of their operational status. The 7th Brigade, however, was told to stand still and await further orders. Like most military commanders, Colonel Kauli was incensed by not being "invited to the party." Military units are created, nurtured, and prepared for participation in conflict when one is fought. A unit's participation in war is its badge of honor, and its performance in that conflict is a measure of its worth. *Not* being asked to participate in war is a black mark against a unit's abilities, and Colonel Kauli was not about to have the 7th dishonored in any way. In fact, Kauli couldn't comprehend why the 7th Brigade was the recipient of this "disrespect" in the first place. In many ways, Operation Peace of Galilee was going to be a 7th alma mater conflict: Major-General Avigdor "Yanush" Ben-Gal was a corps commander in charge of the eastern sector (commanding a corps-level force known as "Sinai Division"[10]), Brigadier-General Avigdor Kahalani was the divisional commander in the central sector, and various other former 7th officers were in charge of various General Staff and Operations Branch postings. The loyal brigade commander that he was, Kauli left his Golan HQ and went to the forward mobile Northern Command C^3 headquarters of OC Northern Command Major-General Amir Drori to lobby for work. Drori, the decorated commander of the devastated 1st Golani Infantry Brigade during the 1973 War, was far too busy for marauding brigade commanders with private agendas, but the 7th Brigade was no ordinary unit, and Colonel Kauli no ordinary brigade commander. He received one concession from the hierarchy: the 77th Battalion, commanded by Lieutenant-Colonel Dubik,[11] would be removed from its service along the Heights and attached to Brigadier-General Avigdor Kahalani's division that was tasked with the central sector.

As Colonel Kauli lobbied and politicked, the men of the 7th Brigade sat nervously by transistor radios awaiting any word—even a false rumor. On their black-and-white TV sets, situated in the battalion recreation rooms and inside some fortunate barracks, the sights of Beirut being pummeled by F-16s and Phantoms were ominous signs of a wide and new type of conflict. Nail biting was a popular activity during those confusing days, as was desperate chain smoking. Any soldier with a moment of spare time away from his post or vehicle raced to a telephone to call home, and offer tearful good-byes to parents and girlfriends. The soldiers didn't know when word would come down for mobilization, and they were determined not to go to war without speaking to their loved ones. Last good-byes, indeed, came on Friday June 4, when Kauli's work paid off. The brigade had been given an assignment. Immediately, chaos engulfed the Golan Heights base. Officers raced about with maps and canteens in hand, the field secretaries, teenage girls in uniform, held back emotion as they made the logistic arrangements for *their* men to head off to war. Tanks were placed on transporters and readied for the short ride along the oil line to the Lebanese frontier. For a few of the officers, this was nothing new. Many had been conscripts in 1973 when the "big one" was fought, and had been junior officers during Operation Litani. They had seen blood and death and knew the difference between tank warfare in its theoretical stages and the real thing on the field of battle. There were no veterans among the conscript rank and file, however. Most were eighteen-year-olds who were small children in 1973. The majority were scared, many terrified, and all experienced the gnawing anxiety of heading off to battle—the agitating of one's lower stomach, heartbeats erupting into one's throat, and the constant urge to talk to mates and crewmen. Many soldiers consider the unknown to be the soldier's worst enemy in time of war, and, in this respect, the brigade's marching orders were a bit of ironic relief.[12] Increasing the anxiety was the arrival of the reserve brigade that was replacing them atop the Golan. It was as if the new generation was about to be bloodied in this Israeli rite of passage, and those that had witnessed the horror of war, old men of thirty-five years, were to be spared. "One day you'll be like us," joked a reservist sergeant fueling a reconnaissance jeep beside a platoon of Merkava crewmen loading their gear and rations inside their vehicles. "If you live, that is!"[13]

On Sunday night, June 6, near midnight, the brigade moved out of their Golan Heights base in a long and slow-moving column. Passing Nafakh and a few battered remains of Syrian T-55s, leftovers from a decade earlier, it proceeded along the gasoline line toward Lebanon. It was a funny way to go to war. The Armored Corps had commandeered many of the brigade's M113s to carry ammunition and other supplies. With the Merkavas fastened to their transports, their crews were ferried courtesy of civilian commuter buses pressed into service. Amid seats usually reserved for shoppers and schoolchildren, and underneath advertising signs for Coca-Cola and travel agencies, the 7th Brigade went to war.

At dawn, on Monday, after six hours "on the march" (or roll, so to speak) the Merkavas' treads were clanking away on Lebanese soil. The mighty tanks had been lowered from their transporters, and the young teenagers who commanded these vehicles were no longer judged by the theoretic of war—but by survival in war. The brigade entered Lebanon through a gate that, only hours earlier, had been heavily fortified and secured against two-way traffic. As they crossed into Lebanon, the excited crewmen, witnessing the lovely

Ayun Valley filled with black smoke—the results of aerial
bombardments—found out for the first time how very hard
it is to breathe inside the confines of a flak vest when your
heart, beating at a rate of a thousand beats a second, is in
your throat. The anxiety would be premature, however. Almost two days would pass before the brigade would fire a
shot in anger.

Lots of question marks were hanging high above the Lebanon Valley: How would the Syrians react? How will the
superpowers act? What will the government in Jerusalem
decide? What is happening in the other sections? The an-
swers for those questions were out of reach for the soldiers
in the brigade's bivouac in the village of al-Marye; soldiers
cleaned their weapons, maintained their tanks, and drank
lots of coffee. Each tank had a transistor radio to keep it in
touch with the world, but the world for a soldier is the
ground where he stands and the suspicious movements a
few yards away.

Most soldiers were also listening to the brigade net to see
if they could find word on what was happening to the 77th
Battalion fighting in the central sector in the framework of
Brigadier-General Avigdor Kahalani's division. The 77th
Battalion was Kahalani's baby. It was his battalion in 1973,
and his rise to national fame in Israel following the war.
The 77th Battalion in Lebanon was the baby of Lieutenant-
Colonel Dubik, a highly regarded officer known for his no-
nonsense demeanor. "Unlike the uncertainty about the
participation of 7th Armored Brigade in the war, and which
missions would be given to it," Lieutenant-Colonel Dubik
reflected, "the battalion itself had many certain and determined things. Already at the beginning of the winter, it was
decided that the battalion would be separated from the
mother brigade and would act in the planned war in the
Marjayoun area, under the command of one of the area's
brigades. From the moment this decision was taken on, we
didn't lose any time and we planned for this war in every
possible way. It was our luck that the command of the battalion had been formed and established for a few months
prior to that, so we could dedicate all the efforts to the
central topic. Already in March, we prepared a battalion
order, very detailed with the area's larger brigade, and we

received under our command two assisting units—an infantry company from Golani and a combat engineer company. We used the winter months and the spring for combined training with them."[14] The brigade at the time was paying homage to the old saying, "Pray for peace, prepare for war!"

Colonel Kauli and his staff weren't praying for peace—they didn't want to miss the show—but they were praying that their preparations had been adequate. When Ugdah 36[15] commander Brigadier-General Kahalani ordered the 188th Barak Armored Brigade into action, he also ordered the 7th Brigade to fill the void and assume support firing positions. The brigade was still dressed up with nowhere to go, and Colonel Kauli, his command staff, and the tank crews, raised to a hair-trigger psyche with the thought of entering combat, were getting anxious.

The silence before the storm on the eastern Beka'a front contrasted sharply with the full-scale bloodletting that was going on in the other fighting sectors. Along the Mediterranean coastal sector, Brigadier-General Yitzhak Mordechai's Ugdah 91[16] was blazing a path from the border at Rosh Haniqra toward the urban center of Tyre and Sidon and their surrounding gauntlets of Palestinian refugee camps. The fighting was fierce, brutal, and often at point-blank range. "Conventional" Palestinian units, from Arafat's Yarmouk, Karameh, and Kastel brigades, found that RPGs were not just for launching at schoolbuses and Phalangist pillboxes—they penetrated the IDF M113 like a red-hot knife through a bar of butter, and they also did terrific damage to tanks. Only the Merkava was proving a nonfatal mode of transportation along the scenic Lebanese coast. Meeting Brigadier-General Mordechai's division at Sidon and around the dangerous killing confines of the Ein el-Hilweh refugee camp was an amphibious task force under the command of Brigadier-General Amos Yaron, a former special operations operator, commander of *Sayeret Mat'kal,* and at the time of the Lebanon invasion, the *Ktzin Tzanhanim Ve'Cheyl RaglimRashi* or Chief Paratroop and Infantry Officer. The amphibious task force, consisting of a bulk of the conscript 35th Paratroop Brigade and supporting armor units of Centurion MBTs, was tasked with cutting off the PLO retreat and reinforcement effort along the coast. The landing, the largest in IDF history, was made at the mouth of the Awali River and was preceded by a landing of naval commandos from Flotilla 13—the IDF/Navy's special warfare element.[17] While elements of the amphibious part, primarily the paratroopers, were called in to purify the Ein el-Hilweh camp, Sidon's largest and most volatile,[18] Brigadier-General Mordechai's tanks and infantrymen pushed directly north. Toward the prize and the objective of this latest round of bloodshed. Toward Beirut.

In the central axis route, Brigadier-General Menachem Einan's Ugdah 162[19] twisted its way up the Shouf Mountain, toward the ultrastrategic Beirut-Damascus Highway. The roadway was by far the most valuable stretch of territory in all of Lebanon; even more so, many Syrian generals would argue, than the poppy and hashish fields of the eastern Beka'a. Whoever controlled a single bottleneck along the highway connecting the Lebanese and Syrian capitals literally split the country in two—especially the southern half from the northern Beka'a and the approaches into "Greater Syria."

The fourth push, from south to east, belonged to Kahalani's Ugdah 162. This force broke into the Nabatiyah Heights, and from there cut in the direction of northwest to the town of Sidon and the Damur area. Kahalani's initial role was as a buffer to present an armored shield against any Syrian attempts to intervene in those early days of the war, in defense of Palestinian units under the gun along the coast and in the central axis. The lead elements of Kahalani's division crossed the Litani River on the British-built Akiya Bridge on Sunday morning, the first day of the war. The 188th Barak Armored Brigade detoured Nabatiyah from the west and rushed fast to the Havush bridges on the Zaharani River, in order to cross them and continue toward Sidon. Parallel to that, Kahalani ordered the Golani Infantry Brigade to remain in the Nabatiyah Heights, while sending its reconnaissance element, *Sayeret Golani,* to capture the ultrastrategic and heavily defended Beaufort Castle—a Crusader fortress that at 717 meters above sea level dominated the entire southern portion of the country and from where much of Galilee as well as the Christian enclave was visible.

Lieutenant-Colonel Dubik and the 77th Battalion were

not only unaware as to what was going on at other fronts, but exactly what was happening in their own sector as well. Dubik had studied about the fog of war at *Pu'm,* but it was a lesson he had hoped he would not have to live through. The battalion was ordered to seize the PLO stronghold at "Little Flags" at the entrance to Marjayoun, cross the Litani River, conquer terrorist strongholds neglected by IAF bombings, and proceed north up the Nabatiyah Heights. It was an armored operation—meant to deflect terrorist attention from the principal movement of the advancing Israelis. In general, this was an act of deceit, to confuse the enemy, meant to attract the terrorists' attention and get them away from the main effort, that was meant to be carried out by the 188th Barak Armored Brigade and the rest of the division's forces via the Akiya Bridge.

"At 0300," according to Dubik, "we entered Lebanon through the Weiss Gate,[20] south to the deserted airport in the Marjayoun valley, right next to Metulla. We immediately split into secondary forces, breaking through in two axes. I was on patrol axis and the battalion's deputy commander on the axis of the road to Tibanit. The engineering force, commanded by Captain Ze'ev, was ordered to open the Hardalah Bridge on the Litani River so that the axis could be used as a division movement route. We agreed that after we opened up the two axes we would meet in the village called Roman. While doing that, the Hermon Company positioned itself in the area of the 'Little Flags' fortifications, and covered up on us with tank fire, firing in the direction of Tivnit, Damaskiya, the Arnoun mountain chain and the Jermak."

The area standing in the way of the battalion's procession and the Roman Village and the entrance to the Heights was seriously mined. The Palestinians knew little about conventional combat, especially in an armored sense, but they did know how to place land mines. Concealed mines would not prove a major concern for the brigade, however, as engineers, covered by nervous tank soldiers, walked with sticks and poked the ground nervously. After all, sitting in a 60-ton vehicle gave these soldiers a sense of security that they weren't too pleased to experience. Still, however, the brigade had yet to be bloodied in combat. Some brigade officers privately thought that the unit was being kept out of the conflict as a sort of internal punishment for the glory the brigade received—justified or not—following the 1973 War.[21]

At dawn's first light on the morning of June 8, the brigade continued its advance. Looking to fight the Palestinian terrorists entrenched in the area, what Colonel Kauli's men actually found were abandoned pillboxes, a litany of land mines, explosive booby traps, and small fragmentation grenades camouflaged inside trash bins and piles of manure and underneath rocks. The area's mountainous terrain, twisting roadways, and steep inclines were pure textbook guerrilla country, but the Palestinians chose to run and flee to Damascus rather than make a stand. Their flight in many ways made the 7th Brigade tank soldiers quite happy—after all, as gung-ho as morale is supposed to be during a war, most soldiers wanted to get home in one piece. The quiet was also unnerving in an anxious sort of way for most of them, as well. According to Lieutenant Tzvi, a platoon commander, "We felt that once the shooting started, we'd be okay. Every quiet moment, however, meant that perhaps something dreadful was awaiting us."[22] Even Colonel Kauli was relieved by the quiet—"We did, however, feel fortunate that we were fighting the ghosts (and mines) and not individuals."[23]

At dusk on Tuesday, June 8, 1982, Lieutenant-Colonel Dubik's 77th Battalion was once again on the move inside the IDF's scheme of things—removed from Kahalani's division and returned to the "mother" brigade, and Major-General "Yanush" Ben-Gal's multidivision force responsible for the eastern sector. The first mission Yanush assigned to the brigade was to seize the village of El Ishiya, on the road between Dir Mims and Richan. According to intelligence reports, a Syrian tank platoon and a concentration of "infantrymen" from the PLO's Yarmouk Brigade were firmly entrenched in that area.[24] The actual strength of Syrian and Palestinian forces was not clear, but it was known that the area was not ripe for tank warfare—mountainous, with long rows of cedar and pine trees capable of concealing an RPG-wielding enemy. Even inside the bellies of the Merkava, considered by all who served it in to be the mightiest of tanks, the thought of an RPG crossfire from thick rows of trees and bushes sent shivers down the spine of every brigade soldier—from Kauli to the conscript straight out of basic training. The intelligence officer pulled out aerial photographs and schematic enlargements of the village—a small area built on a descending mountain chain, surrounded by a pine forest at its eastern-most edge. The village was divided in two by a one-lane roadway leading to the village of Richan (several kilometers away), and from it there was a "V" intersection to the right. It was a very narrow roadway, one designed for a donkey bristling with produce and spices, not a main battle tank—in fact, the road was narrower that the Merkava's width of 3.75 meters.[25] The assault force consisting of "Vulcan (or 6th) Platoon,"[26] "Zohar Company," and the "Hermon Company" were left blocking a ridge overlooking the Nabatiyah sector. Colonel Kauli would personally lead the attack. It would be his first armored charge in nearly ten years.

The cautious advance on El Ishiya commenced at 2000 hours on June 9. With Colonel Kauli's tank in the vanguard, the slow-moving column of Merkavas progressed through the narrow road, pushing away trees and other obstacles. The night was typical summer fare for Lebanon—warm, with a hint of a crisp breeze bringing in an appeasing aroma of pines from the mountains to the north and east. To the west, an orange glow of fires placed the surrounding hills inside an eerie silhouette; the sounds of sonic booms, chopper blades spinning, and artillery rounds finding their marks were inescapable—even to those wearing crewmen ballistic helmets. Kauli didn't know if the Palestinians and Syrians would pick up and run or fight, but ten meters from the village entrance the colonel would get his answer. Kauli found his Merkava the target of several bursts of 7.62mm tracer fire, and the ominous *thud, woosh* and then the blast of an RPG being fired; "the old RPG," one of Kauli's men would comment, "a sound as distinctive as a mother-in-law's roar!" One PG-7 projectile landed right underneath the chassis of Kauli's tank, and exploded in a fiery blast. The source of the fire was a building on the hill at the entrance adorned by a large Palestinian flag, and one that would receive immediate attention from Kauli's tanks. Artillery batteries nearby lit the sky with 155mm flares, and the Palestinian fire base was immersed in 105mm HE fire. Kauli had other distractions.

"Throughout the battle," according to Kauli, "the Zohar Company commander kept the communication net busy, who was in blocking in the Nabatiyah area. He drove me crazy and bugged the commander in the brigade's net, saying that it was impossible that everyone else was fighting and he was stuck in the back. Finally we told him—okay, guys, welcome to the war. He crossed the separating area between us in a mad running, and when I gave the attack order, he was already with us."

The attack force broke through the village under heavy machine gun and RPG fire, and immediately spread out through the narrow streets and alleys. Like all Lebanese villages, it was a multilevel mess made of stone houses, rock fences, and twisting passageways. Every house had the potential as a Sagger trap—every villager an intelligence agent for the Syrians or Palestinians. This was not the type of warfare that the brigade had excelled in during maneuvers in the Negev and the Golan. Tanks lost their treads amid the rubble and tanks got lost. It was impossible for Kauli to maintain visual control over his units amid the smoke and dust, and blind spots caused by buildings and hills. Kauli could have leveled the village and sorted it out later, but all IDF units were under strict orders by IDF Chief of Staff Lieutenant-General Rafel "Raful" Eitan to refrain from indiscriminate force.[27] Selected targets were shelled by the 60mm mortars in each vehicle. Kauli's tanks shelled from south to north, while Iddo and his tanks shelled from east to west. The village purification was carried out by the book—in a very orderly manner. Palestinian and Syrian resistance crumbled. In the early evening the Israeli flag was raised over El Ishiya, but before Colonel Kauli could order in infantry units to mop up the area, Yanush summoned Kauli and ordered the brigade to mount a predawn attack on the village of Richan, north of El Ishiya, which, according to aerial reconnaissance and intelligence, was full of terrorists and enemy tanks. Kauli ordered his men to sleep inside the vehicles. He got into the cannon chamber and sat with a 1:50000 map to study the axis, examine maneuvering problems, and to identify controlling areas. The preparations were exhausting, though necessary. Richan would be Hermon Company's baby.

Once again, the fog of war claimed the brigade as its victim. Yanush had assured Kauli that the IAF would soften up Richan with pinpoint air strikes an hour before the brigade's assault, but the planes attacked the wrong targets, and Richan was left virtually unscathed at the time of the attack. This was of great concern to Kauli as he gazed through his field glasses and saw the remains of a burning truck. But as the tanks entered the village, all vehicle commanders nervously caressing the triggers of their mounted FN MAG 7.62mm machine guns, the force was shocked to see civilians coming out of the houses energetically waving hello. The terrorists escaped from the village a few minutes earlier. In the forest north of the village, the brigade troopers discovered their deserted tent camp city. The brigade found dozens of 82mm mortars, tons of small arms and ammunition. Coffeepots were still steaming, and copies of the German edition of *Playboy,* perhaps gifts from visiting Red Army pupils, were found throughout the mess. Carefully rummaging through the remains of what was supposed to be Yasir Arafat's finest forces, Kauli suddenly felt a cold shock race through his body. He realized that while the rest of the IDF Task Force in Lebanon was fighting a desperate battle along the Lebanese coast, the 7th Brigade had been spared from serious action. The peace and quiet could not go on for much longer. No brigade was that lucky.

During the first two days of the fighting the eastern sector was almost entirely quiet. The IDF was set to keep a decisive military option against the Syrians, however, and was careful not to push them into battle. It was apparent that the political and military top was hesitant and in a state of disagreement as to the need to open a wide front with the Syrians. The Syrians, on their side, made public their efforts to prove they were not interested in going to war. The Syrian Chief of Staff issued explicit orders for its forces in Lebanon not to make contact with the Israeli forces. The two armies were moving toward a juggernaut, an armor-piercing impasse, and full-scale combat was inevitable. Senior brigade officers were eager for the fight. Lieutenant Ra'anan from the 82nd Battalion[28] recalls, "The entire world was at war, but the glorious Seventh Brigade, with its Merkavas, were parked like taxi cabs and its men sitting and cooking food. It was frustrating, no one was happy about the war, but when you have a well-trained force on your hand, you do want to let it be expressed in such a situation."

Syrian commanders, especially from elite unit and tank forces with close ties to President Assad's regime, were also itching for a fight and they were determined to enter the war with a quantitative advantage. The Syrians started pouring reinforcements into the eastern sector, including sending the 1st Armored Division to the area of Lake Qaroun, in the area of Kafr Maski and Kafr Qooq, and created a temporary divisional defense line protecting the approaches to Damascus from the west. Parallel to this move, the Syrians reinforced their elaborate missile setup in the Beka'a Valley with the elite 3rd Armored Division. IDF intelligence reports believed that the Syrians had moved nearly 500 tanks, including the then ultramodern Soviet T-72s, into Lebanon. When the decision was made to move against the Syrians, Yanush Ben-Gal's division received the call to break through and reach the Beirut-Damascus Axis. Chief of Staff Eitan realized that time was not on Israel's side, a ceasefire could be implemented at any time and the campaign would be pointless unless the Beirut-Damascus Highway was cut off and the Palestinians in Beirut blocked. Raful called upon his old comrade-in-arms from the Golan melee nine years earlier, Yanush, to seize the highway.

That Wednesday night Yanush's forces went on the offensive along a 25-kilometer axis through the poppy and hashish fields of the Beka'a. The main effort was in the center of the valley and along the main road and from its sides, toward Husadnabiyeh, Joub Jenin, and north. Supporting this offensive were three full IDF divisions. The action zone that was meant for Brigadier-General Emanuel Sakal's Ugdah 252[29] was not completely unknown to the IDF—they had hunted the PLO in this stretch of Fatahland since 1970. This area, known by the name of Wadi a-Time, reached up to Majd al-Anjar in the north and el-Sajar in the south. From the east it is bordered by the Hermon Mountains and in the west by the mountain chain of the Lebanon mountains. Two mountain treads dictate the area's topography—

in the north Jebel al-Arbi, and in the south Jebel a-Dahar. This area has always been thinly populated, and most of its inhabitants were concentrated in the known Druze town of Hasbaiyah.

Hasbaiyah, the capital of "Fatahland," is a large Druze town, which was destined to be the starting point for attack along the eastern front. Although reputed to be a major terrorist training and staging area, the town was conquered without a fight by the Pattons of the "Iron Footprints" Brigade,[30] already on the first evening of the war. This brigade, too, acted within the framework of Sakal's Ugdah 252. It was found out that hundreds of terrorists that lived in the town hurriedly escaped it out of fear in the first hours of the war. The two arrowheads of the brigade, that charged Hasbaiyah in a tongs movement, met in the center of the town without having to use their force at all. Following right behind the Iron Footprint Brigade toward Hasbaiyah were the APCs and Merkavas of the 7th Armored Brigade passing abandoned villages and fields. Already at 1700 hours the Romach Battalion's tanks entered the borders of Hasbaiyah, leading the brigade's line. Local civilians went out to the streets and greeted the tank soldiers waving hello. Vehicles of other units were seen here and there among the buildings. The tension melted. The residents had suffered immensely under the yoke of PLO rule. Druze and Shiite women had been repeatedly raped and abused, and the local men beaten and murdered. The Israelis were no allies, but they were saviors—albeit temporary ones. The sentiments among the locals would change in three months, but a shower of rice and flowers was more welcome than one of 7.62mm tracer and PG-7 projectiles.

Suddenly, however, explosions interrupted the peaceful atmosphere. The commander of the leading battalion, Lieutenant-Colonel Ziv, standing exposed in the turret of his Merkava, absorbed ricochets in his upper body from the unexpected barrage. His shirt was stained with blood, and fragments of his flesh strewn along the dusty top of his tank. Inside the mechanized infantry's APC, which was moving ahead of him, six other soldiers were wounded, one of them severely. "We were unable to identify where the fire was being shot from," said Ziv. "We thought at first that it was a light weaponry's fire, machine guns. Long seconds passed before we got over the astonishment. We started shooting all over. We fired without thinking, in order to get the shooters under pressure. The shooting at us did not continue, within a short time we noticed that the fire was—of all things—aircraft fire." A Syrian Air Force Sukhoi-7, firing 2.75-inch rockets, had emerged from the distance and had scored remarkably accurate shots at the Israeli column; one ricochet entered the tank from the ceiling to the floor. Commanders soon left their turrets and began firing their 7.62mm light machine guns at the escaping dot evading Israeli fire in the distance. "The IAF will get the bastard," was heard over the battalion net. "He won't make it back to Damascus."

Battalion doctors had rushed to the stalled column, and the wounded were removed to the aid station. Druze civilians, also hit in the Syrian attack, were also treated by the Israeli doctors—some even evacuated to Israel for urgent medical treatment.

Although not a single soldier had been killed in the attack, the sole Syrian Air Force fighter bomber had succeeded in halting the brigade line—a long line of tanks, APCs, and trucks. It is not an easy and simple mission to transfer such a long caravan in narrow and dark streets in the middle of the night. Ziv, the wounded battalion commander, tried to channel the brigade to a secondary road that passes in the mountain chain above the town's houses. However, this road was discovered to be useless to the Merkava's 3.7 meters of width and the vehicles were stuck one after the other in, according to one driver, "a cluster fuck of armor waiting to be ambushed." Ordnance personnel were hard at work attempting to free the roadway of the traffic jam while nonessential personnel fanned to the surrounding hills with Glilon assault rifles in hand, to prevent an ambush. Most of the officers in the unit had been school kids in October 1973 and had not witnessed the horror of the antitank ambush firsthand. They had horror stories engraved in their minds at the officers' course about what it is like to be in the epicenter of a dozen Saggers. The brigade spent close to five hours in Hasbaiyah only to bivouac on the axis close to Beit

Siniyah, about five kilometers north of the town. The men were tired and just happy to be off the road. When the sun appeared over the mountains in the east and Colonel Kauli and his officers met just after dawn they came to a frightening realization—they were smack dab in the center of a terrorist stronghold. AK-47s were found nestled next to trees, as were uniforms, food stores, and latrines.

The morning would be an active one for the unit—at dawn Romach Battalion would position itself in the head of the division's thrust toward Syrian lines. It would be the anvil of an entire offensive and likely to engage the T-72. Colonel Kauli was excited, as were Israel Military Industry officials in Tel Aviv monitoring the Merkava's deployment with incredible pride and interest.

In the meantime the 77th Battalion was sitting on the Richan-Armata axis, licking the wounds of the previous days of fighting. The men were tired and hoped for a break, but their wish did not come true. Ever since the battalion departed from the framework of Kahalani's division, it was activated as a corps reserve, and as such it was thrown naturally into the problematic battlefields as an on-call response force. On Wednesday afternoon, Yanush ordered the 77th Battalion to go to the area of Ein a-Tina to the south of Lake Qaroun, in order to assist an armored unit made up of tank school students that had suffered more than its share of casualties during its push along the central axis. The battle in Ein a-Tina was going on as part of the effort of the third arrowhead in Yanush's force, which was intended to protect the western end of the corps attack. This divisional force planned, as mentioned, to advance down in the hills of the Shouf Mountains and the bottom of the Baruch Mountain, to transfer via Ein a-Tina and to spread into two on both sides of the Lake Qaroun on the way to Kafriah and Kafr Anah.

Before noon on Wednesday a battalion-size force of tanks from an armored unit made up of tank school students left the 77th Battalion's advance and, under the command of Lieutenant-Colonel Safi Shauman, progressed at a detour movement toward Ein a-Tina. In parallel, and with no coordination, a different battalion came up from an opposite direction. The two forces charged the Syrian setup at Ein a-Tina and were stuck in a fierce firefight. Syrian antitank fire was murderous, and the Sagger crews had set up the Israeli armor into a wedge of movement where T-62s had opened up with their 115mm main armament guns. Israeli casualties were heavy.

"I gathered the commanders and I explained to them what was going on," explained Lieutenant-Colonel Dubik in an official brigade history. "Within minutes we were on our way. I took with me three doctors as well. It was obvious we would need them. While in movement on the Shabbaton Axis, Brigadier-General Amram Mitzna, the chief of staff of Yanush's corps-level force, asked me to stop the battalion at its place and go as fast as I could to Ein a-Tina with all the medical supplies I had. The armored unit made up of tank school students needed urgent medical assistance, said the head of staff. Also look for landing points for evacuation helicopters along the axis." From the tone of his voice it was clear that the situation was severe. "I raced to the target at full speed. In the meanwhile the darkness came down. In the junction of the 'Shabbaton Axis' and 'Socialism Axis,'[31] I located the battalion collection station of the brigade. The sight was hard and traumatic. The many killed and wounded were laid on stretchers along the road."

The battle for Ein a-Tina was the true modernization of limited armor war. Tanks engaged infantry and armor and then additional infantry came in to finish the job. After midnight, under the cover of an eerie orange night's sky, several IAF Bell-212 helicopters began to land in the area of the battalion collection station. The choppers unloaded a large platoon force of reconnaissance paratroopers with AK-47s in hand who were ordered to neutralize Ein a-Tina. The attack started at dawn's first light; the opening of the attack brought about the arrival of several senior officers. Together with them arrived some senior commanders. Among them was Brigadier General Yossi Peled, who got the command from the forces in the sector, including the 77th Battalion, in a force that became known as the "Special Maneuver Force." The paratroopers proved a lethal match for the Syrian antitank commandos, though the Syrians put up a determined fight.

On Thursday, at the crack of dawn, started the progress of Yanush's multidivisional corps all across the Lebanon Valley. Brigadier-General Sakal's Ugdah 252—and in it the 7th Brigade and the Iron Footprints force—moved in the eastern edge of the attack, near the Syrian border. The mission given to the division was to move along the "village axis" and conquer the small town of Rachaiya el-wadi and from there to break away to Kafr Qooq toward Kafr Yanta, on the Syrian border. On the first stage of progress the Pattons of the Iron Footprints continued to move in the divisional arrowhead. However, this time, for a change, the brigade was ordered to stop after conquering the village of Ein Ata to enable the armor men of the 7th Brigade to move to the head of the arrow and lead the division to Kafr Yanta.

Romach Battalion led the brigade advance. This veteran battalion fought in the Yom Kippur War in the northern sector of the Golan Heights and excelled in its stubborn withstanding of the Syrian attacking forces. When the IDF moved to an attack into the Syrian lands, the battalion acted as a part of the southern effort of the breakthrough forces and assisted in conquering the "enclave" and maintaining it against the Syrian-Iraqi attempts to reconquer it.

The Romach Battalion commander was Lieutenant-Colonel Ziv, a kibbutznik who, coincidentally, lived in Katzerin in the Golan Heights. Known in the vernacular as "one of the old foxes of the north," Lieutenant-Colonel Ziv was like most senior brigade officers and had served in the 1973 War; he had distinguished himself during the bitter fighting around Tel Fars. As a company commander, Lieutenant-Colonel Ziv also had been a visitor to Lebanon, a nation known as "unfriendly" to the open freedom of tank warfare that had been taught and mastered in the training scenarios of the Negev Desert and the Jordan Valley.

With Romach Battalion on point, the next unit line was the 82nd Battalion under the command of Major Dor Marcel. Dor got out of the army in 1976 as the brigade operation officer; burned out with the military society, he studied agriculture, determined to work in the kibbutzim and moshavim in the Galilee. In Israel, however, nobody truly escapes the

IDF as there is always the haunting specter of reserve duty (or, for the unhappily married, the blissful escape of a reservist stint). A few years later, after going through the battalion commander's course while in reserve service, he was convinced to return to the IDF, although the Centurions that he had mastered and cherished were retired. This time it was to the Merkavas of the 7th Armored Brigade, just in time for preparations to "Operation Peace for Galilee."

The third unit in the brigade's order of advance was an *improvised* battalion under the command of Lieutenant-Colonel Nitzan Sela, who was named in the communication network "Nomert Force." Lieutenant-Colonel Sela was a 7th Armored Brigade veteran and former commander of the 82nd Battalion during its prewar preparations in 1981. When the missile crisis was settled by the benevolent diplomatic intervention of special ambassador Philip Habib, Lieutenant-Colonel Sela left the army to go back to his kibbutz in the Jordan Valley desert. When he heard of the assassination attempt in London he immediately understood that the battalion he had primed for action would finally be sent across the frontier into Lebanon. He hurriedly called Colonel Kauli and volunteered to return to the brigade in *any* capacity.

Lieutenant-Colonel Sela's vast experience in the framework of the battalion and his deep knowledge of the small details of the planned operation and the land of the operation, were not commodities that a brigade commander forfeited without consideration and Kauli told Sela to get his gear and rifle and to head north. Unable to give him back his battalion, Kauli was, nevertheless, determined to use Sela's talents anyway. Since the 77th Battalion was pulled out of the brigade and transferred to a different sector, Kauli decided to establish an improvised battalion, which would be based on organic forces of the brigade—the mechanized infantry company from the Romach Battalion and the brigade's *Tza'ma'p* company from 82nd Battalion. The consideration leading to weakening the rest of the brigade's battalions came as a result of the special topography in Lebanon. The fact that most of the routes go through mountain areas dictates movement in lines, so that only the leading head comes into expression in contact with the air.

The Merkavas carefully pushed ahead, moving at a snail's pace to avoid any ambush or surprises in the twisting road. Although the Iron Footprints Brigade passed through the southern portion of the axis during the night, there was still a fear that the villages it went through were not totally cleared of terrorists and Syrian infantry. The intelligence messages pointed to concentrations of terrorists in the villages of Ein Horsha, Tanorah, and Beit Lahiya, and several tank platoons located in Ein Akaba. At 0900 hours the brigade reached Kafr Zeit. Colonel Kauli and Lieutenant-Colonel Hoter, the brigade deputy commander, were pressed to run fast so that the day's planned advance could be completed before the onset of darkness. Unfortunately, Lebanon made the Golan Heights look like "ideal" tank warfare terrain and the brigade was falling victims to Murphy's Law—whatever *could* slow the brigade down *was* slowing the brigade down. The Merkava was simply too big and could not fit in the village streets. A tractor had to be summoned and the narrow streets shaved in order to allow the tanks through. A small village that should have been a blur to the unit took over two hours to overcome. Perplexed villagers stared at the comical sight of brigade engineers working feverishly to produce a path wide enough to facilitate the movement of vehicles while careful not to destroy any buildings unnecessarily. "The Syrians would have blown up the village," a farmer told a tank commander. "We're not the Syrians," the young sergeant replied. In fact, the IDF was under strict orders not to destroy anything unnecessarily.

The "Village Axis" was a mountainous route that connected all the Lebanese villages in the slopes of the Lebanese side of Hermon. These villages are the highest populated areas in the entire spread and they mark the border of the desertlike area. To the east and north is dry stony ground. To the west and down are agricultural fields and greenery. The axis curved on the downhill till its end in the area of the villages of Ein Horsha and Tanura, in the lower end downhill—very deep, beyond the mountain chain of Jebel Bir Dahar. It was not terrain designed for armored warfare.

Lieutenant-Colonel Hoter encouraged the men to get *with*

the program and move the brigade as quickly as possible through the mountain routes. The topography of the axis was treacherous and one successful antitank ambush could bottleneck the brigade for a day or more. It was so different than the Golan fighting nine years earlier. Instead of being spread out along defensive ramparts, the brigade, in essence, amounted to the lead tank. Once on the road, it didn't matter if it was the 7th Brigade following behind or a thousand tanks from seven divisions. If *that* tank was *it*, *it* was responsible for keeping the pace and continuing the advance.

In the village of Ein Ata the 7th Brigade joined the Iron Footprints Brigade and conquered the place in the morning. At this stage, the 7th Brigade moved to lead the Ugdah's progress; the Iron Footprints Brigade stopped at the line of Ein Ata and started to secure the forested hill to the southeast of the village. The intention was to break the "Arafat Road" from the east to the main axis that leads from Ein Ata to Rachaiya, and therefore open an alternative way to the village axis in which the 7th Brigade was moving. This alternative road was going to have superior importance since more and more stubborn resistance was expected from the Syrian side, as the IDF got nearer and nearer to the border of Syria-Lebanon and the Syrian areas that protected the Beirut-Damascus Road. Beyond the curve of the road the soldiers in the first tanks saw a chilling sight. At the side of the road there was an upside-down Patton tank full of tar and ashes. Immediately, they felt the certainty of the war and became extremely alert. It was ten in the morning.

"We were advancing in the developing axis of the downhill," reflects Lieutenant-Colonel Ziv, "while we were sending preventive fire to the sides and washing with machine-gun fire the forests to the west of the axis. Above a controlling mountain chain on the east side of the axis some houses appeared. It was the village Ein Horsha. The village seemed entirely deserted. Suddenly, fire started from unidentified sources, from the front and the sides. The fire continued even after the front tanks passed through the village. I was disturbed by the fact that we were moving with no sufficient security of the sides as far as artillery and air force. I decided to send the mechanized infantry company under the command of Yoram into the village and purify it, so that we wouldn't be surprised on the side while we were moving or tailgated from the back. Yoram found a short search sufficient. His APCs had difficulties to maneuver in the narrow streets. Since he encountered no objection, the mechanized infantry force returned and rejoined with the brigade's line. At this point we started getting a direct fire from Syrian tanks located a rather long distance from us, in the area of Bachaifa and el-Akaba. At first we thought it was artillery, but when I went up for observation I saw the fire lights. The ranges were very large—six or seven kilometers. The fire was inaccurate but still we had a few hits, some meters away from the Merkavas moving in the axis. Since we were unable to identify the shooting tanks themselves, only the lights of the fire, I decided there was no sense in fighting in such ranges, and I commanded the line to carry on with the movement. For armor forces a mountainous axis means a definition from a tank man's point of view, and not so much a geographical definition. You define a mountainous axis as an axis in which you estimate you might have limitations in spreading the force. You cannot move with the tanks anywhere, but on the axis itself. The beginning of the axis, on the other hand, is an area where you can get off the axis, spread the vehicles, and move around the area. This is the expression of the unique thing a Merkava brigade has. While in the battle history of other brigades the Village Axis was described as a definite mountainous axis, then we estimated that the Merkavas would be able to get off the axis in the area of Beit Lahiya and move at a spread. With the mission that was given to us—to attack a Syrian armor and antitank setup in Bachaifa—there was a tremendous importance to the possibility of spreading of the Merkavas, at the beginning of the mountainous axis. Only in wide spread was it possible to efficiently attack and take advantage of the true power of the armor forces."[32]

First-Lieutenant Kobi, commander of the lead tank, was gingerly progressing on the dirt road, his progress covered with 105mm guns aimed at anything in the distance that even hinted at being a target. Colonel Kauli, in the interim, had authorized artillery strikes against Syrian positions down the road in order to occupy them as the Merkavas rolled forward. Syrian armor, including T-72s, were reported to have firing pits dug in at the approaches to the villages of Tanura and Beit Lahiya, which controlled the beginning of the axis, was dominated by scores of Syrian antitank positions. It was reported on terrorist strongholds a little north of what was referred to on the map as coordinate "Bonim 67"—the point which was defined in the coded maps as the beginning of the axis.

The artillery cover was proving to be ineffective and the tank officers moving forward felt compelled to cancel the 155mm barrage. Because of the mountainous topography, zeroing in on an accurate range was proving an impossible task to the spotters. Shells were landing long and they were falling short, but the Syrian tanks were spared. "Artillery work in a mountainous region is like eating soup with a fork," claims Major E., an instructor at the Artillery School. "Sudden rises and depressions, wind swirls and confusing valleys, make placing a one-seventy-five mm shell smack center of a target almost impossible." Without accurate artillery cover, however, the advancing Merkavas were exposed and vulnerable and the Syrians, real-estate owners in the neighborhood for a few years, had the battalion in its sights. T-55s fired first but the 100 rounds landed short. Lieutenant Kobi responded by yelling at his gunner, an award winning *Tzalaf* (sniper) to aim, lock on, and fire. He locked the Syrian tank, as it was moving on the road on its way to a different point, and fired. The tank blew up in a muffled explosion followed by a fire show; the vehicle burned like a gas station and illuminated the Syrian positions for 50 yards around.

Any hopes that the brigade advance would proceed quickly ended that afternoon when the Romach Battalion stumbled across a stretch of mountain roadway strewn with mines. A mine-clearing vehicle brought in detonated a mine and was destroyed. The entire multidivisional push was encountering delays—supplies weren't reaching forward units in one area, and in others the orders to move on were suddenly rescinded at higher levels. This was not the way the

IDF usually went to war, but this was a different sort of conflict.

As the 7th Armored Brigade was leading the eastern arrowhead, Ugdah 90 was moving in the central axis, the "Micha Axis." The division's forces reached the Hush a-Daniba stronghold, overcoming holes of mines that the Syrians and the terrorists prepared in the curves of the road.

This stage in the battle had superior importance because now the divisional arrowheads approached the first width axis in the valley—the line that connected Rachaiya to a creek in the east and the Qaroun Lake in the west. Until now the armored rows moved in length axis from south to north. Deep creeks and sand rocks separated them without any possibility of connection between them. Conquering the intersections in control of the width axis provided a possibility to concentrate all of the army force according to varying conditions and needs.

The Syrians understood very well the importance of these intersections. In the areas of Bachaifa and Kafr Mashchi, which controlled the beginning of the axis, the Syrians positioned a battalion of T-62 tanks in antitank ambush positions. From the high observation point called Ras Ashchal, Lieutenant-Colonel Hoter saw the entire battlefield spread in front of him like a chessboard. While the communication network transferred the messages of the delay of his brigade near the exploded bridge in "Bonim 67," Lieutenant-Colonel Hoter viewed with growing worry the desperate attempts of Brigadier-General Giora Lev's Ugdah 90[33] to blow up the Syrian setup in Mashchi village. "I saw the Pattons trying to break through the gridlock and now being able to do it. I saw the Syrians come up in groups of three tanks together, shooting a load of bombs and going down. They scored direct hits. Ugdah 90's tanks went on fire one after the other. I saw flames coming out of the Patton's turret. There apparently were lots of wounded. Their battalion gathering station was spread in a-Daniba and the wadi of the Hatzbani and evacuation helicopters flew constantly. At long last I was able to contact our artillery units and requested their assistance in artillery for this force who were moving toward the village Mashchi from two other directions. In this spot a Syrian battalion was holding up with a specially confident and capable commander. With the few tanks he had he succeeded in blocking an entire multiunit attack. The Syrians began an artillery barrage of their own at this point and the rain of shrapnel began splashing against the steel turrets and hulls of the Merkavas blocked up along the twisting advance route. Kauli tried to breech the mine-fields and obstacles as best he could but he realized that this unenvious predicament would get worse if the brigade didn't begin to move. The message transferred as fast as lightning among the soldiers. Its meaning was very clear to them. They all understood that too long a wait would have cost them in being hit by artillery fire, and worse—in the failure of the brigade's mission. One after the other the tanks and the APCs started passing through the improvised crossing, when each vehicle was tightening the pass and readying it for the next after him. There was someone who remembered the parting of the Red Sea, only this time, for a change, the 'Children of Israel' were chasing someone and not running away."[34]

The roadway was bypassed in favor of a wadi and slowly the brigade moved toward its next objective at Rachaiya junction. Lieutenant-Colonel Hoter was standing near the improvised crossing and sent the forces off one after the other. He was afraid all along that the Syrians would start shooting at the condensed concentration of tanks and hit them fatally. Fortunately, this did not happen. The artillery shelling was very scattered and indirect and only one soldier was wounded. The second force that crossed the wadi was the 82nd Battalion under the command of Lieutenant-Colonel Marcel Dor. From the start Kauli wanted the battalion to climb up to Ein Horsha and Tanura, detour Beit Lahiya, and open an additional brigade axis toward the enemy setups in Nachiyfa. This axis was nothing but a hill of sand and rocks. After repeatedly checking aerial photographs the commanders were not fully convinced that the battalion would indeed be able to maneuver in this difficult area. Since the gridlock had been created in the area of the destroyed bridge, the opening of the detouring axis had become critical. Once the "Bonim Axis" was opened and the mine-clearing exercise complete, Colonel Kauli opted to pour the rest of the brigade—including Dor's battalion—into that axis.

Lieutenant-Colonel Ziv's Merkavas started climbing from the wadi into the beginning of the advance when they encountered difficulties. "We started spreading on the hill area controlling from west of the axis," reflected the battalion commander, "in a way armor take control of an area. In front of us there was a tank force spread from Bachaifa to Micha Axis. The tanks were shooting at us and the tanks of Ugdah 90 as well. I located a place that seemed to me more or less suitable for armor passage and moved through it with the eight tanks of the 'Lavi Company.' I ordered the rest of the battalion's tanks to carry on and move on the axis until they reached a more passable area and then rejoin with us. While climbing on the hill to the west of the axis we found out that the hill we chose was too low and didn't enable us any observation at all toward the Syrian tanks which were standing north to us, in the area of al-Akaba. Right then I decided to jump with the tanks to another hill in the front. A deep wadi separated us from the hill. I had to decide fast whether to cross the wadi straightaway and take a chance of falling down to its bottom, or go back to the winding road and risk getting shot at from the side. I chose the short way. We drove the tanks to the downhill of the wadi, and indeed, what we feared did come true. A few minutes after we began the movement Yoad's tank, who was behind me, lost his brakes and started rolling down the wadi. He hit my tank, 'shaved' a wing and a muffler and advanced without control to the bottom of the wadi. The tank went out of order but the tank soldiers refused to evacuate it. They remained in the tank to secure it until the ordnance men came to bring it back to battle ability. The rest of the tanks carried on with movement into the wadi and started climbing the opposite downhill, but very fast, another tank was gone. This time it was Vanya's tank that spread his tread. Vanya got off the disabled tank and began running to the company commander's tank to get from him a load of tools that would enable a quick repair of the tread. He didn't manage to get very far and his tank absorbed something very strong from the side. Perhaps a missile. At that stage we didn't know what it was. Yuval, the deputy commander of the leading company, climbed with the tank to position and identified Syrian tanks in the area of Bachaifa. He hit one tank, but he was moving to another position when suddenly there was a tremendous explosion."[35]

Like hundreds before him, by being in the vanguard of his battalion's advance Lieutenant-Colonel Ziv's tank was among the first to get hit. "I felt a huge shock inside the tank. Thick smoke was all over us. I felt I was losing my balance and control over my body. I felt just like a leaf lost in the wind, the truth is I didn't identify the source of fire, I just felt the tank got a serious bang. It took less than a minute until I was able to once again control my body, but it seemed like forever. Instinctively I looked down into the tank. It seemed to me that all the tank crew were in one piece and healthy. I yelled to the driver, Dani Alfasi, to drive the tank in reverse, to get it out, and then when I looked to the sides I saw that Gadi, the loader, has disappeared. He jumped out of the tank, maybe he thought the tank was going to go up in flames. The driver did not move the tank in reverse. I looked toward him and I saw him standing and shouting, when his upper body was outside the tank and his arm was heavily bleeding. I shouted to the loader to hurry up back into the tank. The driver too returned to his tank and tried to start the engine. The tank started falling backward, but Dani managed to brake it, and then he collapsed. We carried him into the turret and I started taking care of him and putting bandages on him. Gadi, the loader, entered the driver's cell instead of him and tried to start the engine. All around us there were tank and artillery rounds falling, and the tank wouldn't start. Dangerous situation. I yelled to Gadi to try and start an emergency ignition, but even this time it didn't work. It was a while, we were already desperate, and then Gadi somehow managed to start the tank. We threw smoke grenades, and also Kobi, the company commander, created a smoke curtain, and this was how we managed to evacuate out of the fire range area and reach hiding."[36]

One of the dangers in moving into the Beka'a were the 19 Syrian SAM batteries spread out along the rift protecting Syria's vulnerable western frontier that would inhibit IAF close air support of the IDF advance. To eliminate the missiles, and much of the Syrian Air Force, the IAF launched its now legendary assault in which a combined force of unmanned drones, F-15s, and F-16s (along with F-4E Phantoms, Kfir-C-2s, and A-4 Skyhawks), supported by AWACS aircraft, blinded Syrian radars and simply decimated the antiaircraft ring; the operation, since studied by virtually every air force in the world, has since been termed "Israel's Trojan Horse." With the missiles gone, Damascus scrambled many of the Syrian Air Force's fighter wings. The air-to-air battles proved completely one-sided—in one dogfight, the IAF shot down 60 MiGs and Sukhois without losing a single aircraft. Syrian air power had been mauled, though there was one type of Syrian warplane that had been left unscathed by the "Trojan Horse": the attack helicopter.

Contrary to his premonitions about being struck by a Sagger, the culprit that hit the battalion commander's tank was a French-produced HOT Missile fired from a Gazelle chopper. The Euromissile HOT (*Haute subsonique Optiquement téléguidé tiré d'un Tube*) or high-subsonic, optically guided, tube-launched missile whose 6.6lbs of high explosive can penetrate 800mm of heavy armor was a new player on the Arab-Israeli battlefield. The Gazelles had been rumored to be flying in the area, and they were known as lethal tank killers. Silent and deadly, they could launch their arsenal of HOT missiles well beyond the range of the Israeli turret-mounted antiaircraft guns—from a distance as far away as four kilometers. The HOT missile was considered one of the best antitank missiles in the world and senior Israeli officers that had seen its effects at various air shows in Europe had hoped that they would not encounter it on the battlefield. The encounter against the HOT missile reinforced a battlefield standard that each war will introduce a weapon system that shocks and terrifies those facing it. The same held true with the Gazelles. The Aérospatiale SA 342K Gazelle is an antiarmor, armed support light helicopter first flown in 1967 though only sold to Third World armies in the late 1970s. Capable of carrying up to six HOT missiles, the Gazelle was an incredibly effective tank killer by being fast (top cruising speed of 162 miles per hour) and able to fly high (a ceiling of 13,450 feet). The French were also superb instructors and

Syrian pilots dispatched to the Gazelle program were considered among the nation's best. Just as the infantry-held antitank weaponry, the RPG and the Sagger, shocked the IDF's tank soldier in the Yom Kippur War, the antitank helicopters managed to surprise the Armored Corps in the 1982 War.

The flight of Gazelles swooped in from the east and the direction of Mount Hermon and scored direct hits on the tanks of the Iron Footprints Brigade moving on the Tuluz Axis parallel to the Village Axis. Afterward they continued west toward the Romach Battalion. In addition to the shock and anger of being hit by a 51.8lb missile slicing through the air at 537 miles per hour, the soldiers and the commanders couldn't imagine what the source of evil was. They were convinced that the Syrians were hitting them with Sagger missiles from the right flank, from the hills controlling Beit Lahiya and Tanura. Under this assumption Lieutenant-Colonel Ziv activated three efforts in parallel. First he ordered Captain Adi, Kfir Company commander, to move forward and get ready to cover up with a tank platoon toward the eastern side. At the same time he ordered the mechanized infantry platoon to evacuate the wounded from the damaged tanks and transfer them to the battalion aid and evacuation station. The Gazelles fired a total of twelve HOT missiles and managed to damage three tanks. The battalion commander himself, and with him the rest of the fit tanks of the battalion, stuck to the original mission once the attack ended and the unit was able to regain its composure—tank soldiers are trained to fight a target they can see, not one they can only hear. The tanks climbed to a high position line and started searching for the Syrian tanks in the Bachaifa area. The view was a good one. The Merkavas found seven Syrian tanks moving into different firing positions in the wake of the Gazelle attack. The T-55s were slow and not expecting a barrage of 105mm fire. In less than three minutes six Syrian tanks had been reduced to flaming coffins for their crews.

Kfir Company was organizing on the road and started moving, while firing antipersonnel rounds to the right side, toward the tents of the terrorists and the forests of Tanura. The *K'ash'a*, divisional armor officer or *Ktzin Shirion Ug-*

dati, was left in the other side of the wadi and was firing toward Tanura from his location. The area, full of forests, creeks, and numerous hiding places, was one where identifying the enemy would be difficult. The progressing company attracted the Syrian fire, however, and a pitched battle began. Antitank shells started whistling throughout the wooded area hitting trees, boulders, and tanks. The battalion crews fired smoke grenades to disguise their movement, but it wasn't long before the company's deputy commander's tank was hit. As the crew was being evacuated through the Merkava's rear door, a 100mm round hit the tank and it went up in flames. The sounds of the ammunition exploding inside the vehicle were likened to a drum solo by a madman amplified by a million loudspeakers, and the thuds and pops of detonating ordnance appeared to mesmerize many of the Israeli gunners. It was then that a second tank was hit and then a third tank; the tanks soon caught fire and burned in a blinding and choking cloud of black and acrid smoke. Brigade soldiers used to look at the Merkava as an impervious shield of fire and steel. It was a tank that was both a powerful piece of hardware and a guardian angel. They never thought that it could be penetrated and that it could burn like the Soviet tanks. It was a humbling experience that bothered everyone in the unit—from Kauli to the newest conscript out of training.

Despite the loss of three tanks and the incessant enemy fire, Romach Battalion did not let go of its original mission. Merkava gunners destroyed five more tanks at ranges of 4,000 meters. In this critical stage the 82nd Battalion's tanks were thrown into the battlefield. Lieutenant-Colonel Marcel recalls, "When it was noticed that the brigade was stuck near a destroyed bridge in Bonim Sixty-seven, we were the hope of the brigade. The plan was for us to climb in an area with a lowest passage possibility; it—in fact—was a goat road, by any standards. We received a tractor to ready the way. The idea was for us to surprise the Syrians and the terrorists from an unsuspected direction, catch positions above Tanura and against Beit Lahiya, and enable the brigade to break through in an alternate axis. According to the messages we had, there was a Syrian tank platoon set up in the area of Beit Lahiya, another platoon in el-Akaba, and another one along the route. The tanks, T-62s in a brown and green camouflage scheme, belonged to the Syrian 91st Armored Brigade—considered one of the Syrian Army's best. Mechanized infantry elements were ordered off the M113 and tasked with purifying in the area of Ein Horsha; should the units encounter resistance, then they were to seize controlling positions in the area of Ein Horsha and secure our side to the direction of Beit Lahiya. Ein Akaba was the key, as it was a piece of real estate commanding the routes north. Two hundred meters before a bridge, a stone-built remnant from the Sultan's Army, the battalion slid into the wadi and climbed up on the other side to outflank any possible ambushes and traps. The roundabout method of tank warfare was getting to the nerves of many of the commanders. If there was going to be an encounter of serious proportions, they wanted to fight it already. The move-up-and-wait method of advance was a nuisance. A few hundred meters farther up the incline, however, the silhouettes of Syrian armor became visible; gunners began identifying Syrian tanks at ranges of 3,000 meters and contact was made. The 105mm gun is lethal at close-range, though for targets up to 3,000 meters away a gunner's senses and skills are put to a test. With four targets in sight, Kauli's gunners didn't disappoint. Four T-62s were transformed into four death traps in a matter of moments.

Golan Company from 82nd Battalion drove a few hundred meters at which point the company commander's tank reached a small bridge, on which a deserted truck was standing and blocking the road; terrorists were known to booby-trap vehicles and there was some apprehension that this was a trap. The company's lead tank opted not to call in Sappers to remove the vehicle but rather charged at the truck, pushing it to the side of the road. It was here that Syrian T-62s opened up fire but their shells missed their targets. Six Syrian T-62s were destroyed in the 120-second firefight, but one T-62 managed to fire an armor-piercing round at one of the Merkavas. Ricochets were thrown toward the driver's periscope and into the cannon, but the soldiers did not abandon the vehicle.

As the last T-62 was destroyed and the damaged tank quickly attended to, a frantic message was heard over the brigade net warning of a flight of Syrian Air Force Gazelles returning to the hunting ground. Lieutenant-Colonel Marcel, playing on a hunch that Syrian commandos were monitoring the brigade's advance and calling in air strikes, guessed that they were operating in a position between Tanura and Beit Lahiya. He was confident that they were the "perpetrators" who hit *his* tanks. Therefore he decided to activate the infantry company which was joined to his battalion in order to get control over the controlling areas and secure the progress of the brigade from the side. The infantry company was a part of a battalion that had first fought under the command of the Iron Footprints Brigade and held a very important role in the conquering of Hilwa and Kafr Zeit in the eastern sector. After they finished these missions they were transferred to the framework of the 7th Brigade on the morning of June 11. Commanded by Captain Noam, the infantry company was teamed up right from the start with Lieutenant-Colonel Marcel's battalion.

Around 1200 hours, under a blistering Levantine sun, the paratroopers of Noam's company were moving along the mountain chain, sneaking toward the houses at the edge of the village of Beit Lahiya. With half a dozen Merkavas aiming their 105mm cannons toward the crest of the village, the paratroopers inched their way up the rocky slopes. Each man carried nearly 60 pounds of gear and all had dual weapons and squad roles. The *Magistim,* the FN MAG 7.62mm gunners, hurled their bodies on the hard stone ground and peered through their sights searching for any potential target. They weren't quick enough, however. Suddenly, heavy machine-gun fire was launched from concealed positions and a few paratroopers were hit and killed. The Merkavas opened fire and a full-scale battle erupted. It took nearly three hours for the paratroopers and Merkavas to secure Beit Lahiya and Tanura. It was slow and stubborn fighting. The war was nearly a week old and in the west the Israelis were seizing key ground and approaching the Lebanese capital where much of the PLO's army had escaped to. In the central sector, Israeli armor and infantry had pushed toward the Beirut-Damascus Highway. The Israel Air Force had neutralized Syrian supersonic aircraft, blowing nearly 100 of them out of the sky, but a significant ground engagement had yet to take place in the eastern sector.

At this stage of the fighting, Syrian tank units had impressed Israel's armor commanders with their tenacity and courage. Syrian commanders took advantage of the land conditions in an optimal way. It was a strong example of the tremendous influence topography had on the battle. It was possible for a handful of Syrian tanks, well-positioned and prompted to seize the initiative, to block a supposedly very forceful corps attack. The frustration and fears of Ben-Gal and Kauli increased as the battle developed and the hours passed. It was clear that if they couldn't undo the gridlock until sunset, and with an impending United Nations cease-fire, every minute was of the essence. At this juncture no one in the brigade knew, of course, that the end of the war against the Syrians was less than twenty hours away, but it was clear to everybody that the sand in the political clock was running out. Although they hadn't advanced as far into Syrian-dominated territory as would have been preferred, the 7th Brigade's eastern flank was, nonetheless, secure. Yanush, therefore, decided to dedicate Ziv's battalion to the effort of breaking the Syrian blocking action along the mountain axes and so transferred his force to Ugdah 90. The objective of the move was simple: Romach Battalion would keep the Syrian setup busy from the front, and while the Syrian tanks were dedicated in their front, their control on the Micha Axis from its eastern side would be weakened. At that time Giora's tanks would take advantage of the lighter pressure and they would at long last break through the blockage.

As Ziv's tanks assumed the vanguard, they observed several Syrian tanks in the area of Bachaifa, 2,500 meters away, and two tanks in el-Akaba, nearly 1,500 meters in range. The Syrians were not fooled. They understood that this was a delaying action and that the tanks of Ugdah 90, moving along the Micha Axis, were the main effort in this stage of the battle. The Syrians continued an incessant barrage of 115mm fire. Ziv's tank put their engines at full throttle and went up to positions overlooking the main advance and played sniper. Before midafternoon, Ziv's battalion had destroyed twelve Syrian tanks—mostly T-62s—and several BTR APCs.

Ziv's advance enabled Ugdah 90 to break the blockage and race north toward the Beirut-Damascus Highway at the easternmost approach of the Israeli advance. In the afternoon a situation was revealed in the Yanush high command position that pointed to the breakage of the Syrian setup and controlled withdrawal of the first division's forces in the sector. At 1600 hours Colonel Kauli decided to open a comprehensive brigade attack on Syrian positions in el-Akaba and Bachaifa. For this attack the Romach Battalion was returned to the brigade network and reinstated as the brigade point force. Three tank battalions were now moving north in wide assault, with Romach Battalion securing the left flank of the advance and the 82nd securing the advance's right flank. At first Kauli opted to leave the Nomert force in reserve, but at this stage the usual pressures started in the communication network. Lieutenant-Colonel Sela's men, who participated only lightly in the previous war movements, insisted on taking part in the brigade movement. At last the brigade commander agreed and positioned the Nomert force in the center of the brigade setup.

Cognizant of what was happening in his sector and throughout Lebanon's three principal fronts, namely the marauding legions of Syrian antitank commandos destroying tanks and APCs with hit-and-run RPG volleys, Kauli ordered a determined artillery barrage before issuing the "okay" for the brigade advance to commence.[37] The artillery barrage lasted 30 minutes and softened up Syrian defenses along the road to the village of el-Akaba. When the last 155mm and 175mm shells landed, Kauli issued the order of *"Kadima"* (forward) to the 82nd Battalion to charge ahead at full speed.

According to Sergeant David, a tank commander in the battalion, "In the middle of the charge I noticed the flashes of tanks from long ranges in the left side. Those were the Syrian tanks that fired at Giora's division in the Micha Axis. I decided to leave them be and carry on with my mission instead—to conquer el-Akaba. We reached the zone without any Syrian opposition. The village looked deserted and discovered two BTRs and a T-62—abandoned with the crew's personal effects still on board. Two officers grabbed their CAR-Fifteen 5.56mm assault rifles and leapt off their vehicles to see if the three vehicles were wired or part of an ambush; enemy snipers, even those armed with RPGs, always targeted officers over anyone else." While the battalion was controlling the village, a large group of civilians suddenly appeared waving a white sheet. The village *muchtar,* or senior elder, was eager to help out and informed the battalion commander and intelligence officer that the Syrians had just withdrawn from the village just a few minutes ago. Only later, when brigade and battalion intelligence officers began assembling data on the area did they find evidence that the village was not just a forward Syrian defensive area, but rather the headquarters for the 91st Armored Brigade. The Syrian brigade commander had personally managed the fighting of the entire area in the village from the *muchtar*'s home, but despite his topographical superiority, he decided to withdraw at the last minute.

At 1700 hours Lieutenant-Colonel Hoter assembled a force of Merkavas and together with Lieutenant-Colonel Itzik's paratroop battalion ventured to the village of Bachaifa to seize it and, at the same time, prevent Syrian commandos from using its high ground as a perch from where they could launch their murderous lobs of RPG and Sagger fire. As Lieutenant-Colonel Hoter noted, "We were advancing upward toward the mountain village crossing vineyards and fig orchards. The territory was rather steep, but I was certain my Merkava would manage to pass. Colonel Kauli kept calling me on the brigade net ordering me to *'Return,' 'Return,'* but I went on going regardless. We then noticed a Syrian 'Pita' on the slopes of Bachaifa; 'Pita,' the name of the Middle Eastern pocket bread, is the IDF nickname for a typical Syrian stronghold located in the approaches of a village. The stronghold was typically surrounded by an all-encompassing circular battery of guns and firing pits with infantry forces positioning themselves in the inner area of the fortifications and the supporting tanks positioned on both sides of the stronghold; this was the typical way that the Syrians organized themselves on the battlefield—first used on the Golan Heights in 1967 in order to create topographical superiority via artificial outflank defense, but in the Bachaifa zone the

Syrians did have topographical superiority anyway. The paratroopers stormed into the village and searched the alleys. They found nothing but a few burnt tank skeletons and sheep herds that were killed in the artillery hits that came before the brigade's attack; apparently, farm animals do not fair well in the destructive power of tanks fighting one another. The sight made them shiver.[38]

With Bachaifa secure, Kauli dispatched Lieutenant-Colonel Hoter and his combined force of Romach Battalion tanks and supporting red berets to finish the job in the area with the seizure of Rachaiya el-Wadi—a large Christian-Druze village that served as one of the most important centers of the Druze Rebellion against the French in the early 1920s. Rachaiya el-Wadi is what is known in Lebanon as a "drain" with many roads and routes in the Beka'a Valley all sifting through its accessible crossroads. These roads had lines west toward Lake Qaroun and east toward Kafr Qooq and Kafr Yanta, and length lines north toward Sultan Yakoub and Majdal Anjar and south toward Hasbaiyah. Rachaiya el-Wadi controlled this entire area—it was known as an "ultrastrategic" target in IDF Lebanon contingency maps. The mission to take Rachaiya el-Wadi was given to Lieutenant-Colonel Hoter's force, and he was ordered to perch his tank and paratroopers at the crossroads and prevent any Syrian counterattack to Yanush's major advance.

At night the force touched the entrance to the town. At the head of the line were three tanks and a reconnaissance APC from the infantry battalion. Following them was the paratroop battalion. The rest of the Romach Battalion's tanks waited at the entrance to the town. Lieutenant-Colonel Hoter did not want the bulk of the armor force trapped in the narrow alleyways of the village where they would be sitting ducks. Intelligence reported the presence of a Syrian tank platoon in the village.

In the morning of that Thursday as the mother brigade was attacking in the Village Axis, the 77th Battalion was progressing on the axis leading from a-Tina to Lake Qaroun. Since the hard hours of the night the battalion was transferred to the command of Brigadier-General Yossi Peled's "Special Maneuver Force." In the framework of the corps

attack on the Syrian setups in the valley, this force was ordered to be the western arrowhead which would also move
from north to south in parallel with the Ugdah 90 and
Ugdah 252. The 77th Battalion was in the vanguard—as
usual.

A few kilometers north to Ein a-Tina, on the length axis
leading toward Lake Qaroun, was located the large town of
Mash'ara. Brigade intelligence officers discovered approximately ten Syrian tanks in the town itself, some of them
hiding inside buildings parked underneath concrete poles
supporting some of the two- and three-story structures. Additional tanks were identified in a forest north of the town.
They were T-72s.

Before dawn, as only the muffled sounds of artillery were
heard in the distance, Dubik leaned over the maps and prepared the attack plan on Mash'ara. The commander of a
reserve paratroop force, Lieutenant-Colonel Nachshon
joined the prebattle meeting as well (Lieutenant-Colonel
Nachshon was an old warhorse who was a platoon commander in the battle on Jerusalem in the Six Day War and
a commander of a battalion in the battle on the town of
Suez in the Yom Kippur War, and was known in IDF circles
as an authority on built-up area fighting). After examining
the conditions of the sector, the commanders decided that
one force under the command of Dubik, the battalion commander, would break into the town in the main road and
neutralize any objection while attacking from south to north.
Zohar Battalion would lead the force and with it an engineer
platoon under the command of engineer battalion deputy
commander Ze'ev. While this force was advancing, the second force would enter the battle in which there would be
five tanks from the Vulcan Battalion and the paratroopers
deploying from APCs. This force would climb on the upper
axis, which crosses the town from south to north, parallel to
the main road. Serving as backup for this large-scale assault
on the town, a covering role was assigned to the tanks of
the Tank Commander Course, which was still at the Ein
a-Tina area "licking its wounds" from the last day's battle.
This battalion was to keep busy locating and destroying Syrian tanks in the wide area, mainly in long ranges, so that
they wouldn't interrupt the conquering of Mash'ara.

Brigadier-General Yossi Peled, the command of the multiunit force, was positioned in a high observation point, from which the entire town was spread like the palm of a hand. It was a textbook command position and Brigadier-General Peled could only hope that the battle would go according to the book. The attack commenced at 0830 hours following a brief artillery barrage. IAF jets, F-4E Phantoms, flew above the town from southeast to northwest and swooped down to bomb key points. Sonic booms of J79-GE-17A turbojet engines were heard followed by the thud claps of the 500lb bombs hitting their targets. White-and-black puffs of smoke soon rose above the town. The attack lasted a few minutes and was followed by a secondary barrage from self-propelled M109 155mm artillery pieces. Once the artillery fire subsided, the advance to Mash'ara commenced. The force was led by Zohar Company's commander's tank, Captain Eyal Liberman, and after him the battalion commander's tank. "Even before we had a chance to reach Mash'ara's first houses," recalls Dubik, "we encountered a shocking scene. Alongside the road was a burnt Merkava tank. The soldiers in the battalion were in shock as they passed the smoldering vehicle—charred a lethal coat of black. For them it was an unbelievable sight. They were used to referring to the Merkava as an insurance company. Like an indestructible thing, and suddenly, here was this burnt tank. It did something to the men, put them back into balance."[39]

The road at the entrance to the town was blocked by two Syrian tanks on fire, one next to the other; both had apparently been hit simultaneously as they failed to reposition themselves. The two tanks posed a serious threat to the advance, however, and they needed to be pushed off the road. Eyal and some of his men got off the tank and connected cables to the burning tanks; the tanks were then hooked up to one of the Merkavas and towed to the side of the road. It was a difficult task since both burning tanks generated intense heat, but the brigade-size advance couldn't wait until a fire truck could be found and the blaze extinguished. The advance into town commenced at a snail's pace. Although General Staff issued strict orders to be discriminate with deadly firepower, the 77th Battalion wasn't taking any chances with this town—not with two burnt Syrian T-72s at the approaches, and a charred Merkava at the gate to the village adorned with the corpses of the dead crew. The tanks fired a shell at each building, and the entire main street was peppered with light machine-gun fire. Throughout the slow advance, Lieutenant-Colonel Dubik received word from divisional observation points concerning the movement of the Syrian tanks. The commander of the Hermon Company, Lieutenant Moti, identified a tank among the houses and destroyed it while moving. Iddo identified a tank in the wadi at the edge of the town and destroyed it, too. Lieutenant-Colonel Dubik was concerned about Syrian armor in and around the village, but he was deterred from ordering a fast breakout of the town because of the possibility of commando Sagger teams positioned in the hills nearby. A tank, no matter how well it is concealed, gives up its position the moment its 115mm cannon unleashes a round. A Sagger is far more difficult to conceal and a "good" Sagger team, one with multiple missile sites along a ridge, can destroy dozens of tanks before it can be engaged by an infantry assault. Lieutenant-Colonel Dubik simply called in artillery and air strikes and waited until *he* was confident that the battalion's next stop was sufficiently softened up.

"The fighting in a built-up area is combined with a lot of stress," claimed Lieutenant-Colonel Dubik. "You have to move in hostile territory and you don't know what's hiding behind each house and each corner. You don't know from where you're going to get hit. We were especially worried in Lebanon because the Syrian tanks used to hide themselves underneath elevated houses where they couldn't be seen by aerial reconnaissance or routine observation posts. Only when the Merkavas rode by that particular house and we noticed that the family car wasn't parked in its spot anymore did we have to immediately face a close-quarter draw with an MBT." The advance of the Merkavas, throughout the village's main streets, was supported by paratroopers who had climbed up the hilly embankments to seek out Sagger and RPG teams.

On the whole, however, the Syrians provided only token resistance as the village was a trip wire for them to delay the Israeli advance and deploy further north to their second, and more secure, defense line in Sultan Ya'aqub, a few kilometers north. On Thursday afternoon, after a few hours of slow advancement inside Mash'ara, the force found itself outside the town, leaving behind it six smoking Syrian tanks and a few hit APCs as well. Five of the tanks were destroyed by Lieutenant Eyal Liberman's company commander's Merkava.

The advance northward continued and reached the intersection connecting the "Shabbaton Axis" leading to Jab-Jenin. At the entrance to the intersection, the battalion saw several burnt Syrian T-72 tanks; apparently they had been destroyed by IAF attack helicopters—either Bell 209 Cobras or Defender gunships. Staring at the burnt skeletons of the armor, Lieutenant-Colonel Dubik peered through his binoculars and discovered a Syrian armor line leaving Jab-Jenin and racing straight toward the Israeli advance. T-62 tanks were in the vanguard of the push followed by ten BMP-1 APCs carrying Sagger ATGWs atop their main armament 73mm gun. The Syrians had moved in order to get control of the bridge of the Litani River, in order to prevent Israel forces from passing toward Jab-Jenin. The Syrians had, however, chosen a poor time to launch an attack. The sun was in back of the 77th Battalion's armor and visibility was excellent. The dark Syrian vehicles, adorned in dazzling brown and green schemes, moved in the light grainfield like paper targets in an amusement park arcade. Lieutenant-Colonel Dubik wanted the engagement to take place at maximum ranges—this would still enable the T-62s to be blasted away by the Merkava's 105mm main gun while keeping the Merkavas out of range of the BMP Saggers. Once the Syrian tanks breached the range envelope that the battalion commander had ordered his crews to consider "the point of no return," Lieutenant-Colonel Dubik ordered his men to fire; all guns were firing AP shells sniping at the tanks and APCs. Within an hour seven of the Syrian APCs were destroyed. Some of them were on fire; others appeared to be fine, though some had plumes of black acrid smoke escaping through the 115mm main armament gun. "We could say we actually surprised ourselves," claimed the 77th Battalion commander. "In training before the war we never used to fire at such ranges, only in corps-level competition. We felt good and proud of our Merkavas in the same way that a cavalry officer in years past would feel pride for his horse. There was little time to pat one's self on the back, however. Brigadier-General Peled ordered me to seize control over the Litani River; he was afraid of counterattacks and wanted to prevent the Syrian Army to cross the Litani from east to west."[40]

At the end of the fifth day of the fighting in Lebanon the three corps were still far from completing their main mission—getting a firm hold in the Beirut-Damascus Highway. Brigadier-General Peled's force in particular, with the 77th Battalion as its spearhead, was the closest to the target. The force reached a few kilometers away from the target. Ugdah 252, in the eastern side of the corps attack, concentrated in the area of Dahar el-Achmar and was organized for the conquering of Kafr Yanta in the east on the Syria-Lebanon border. Brigadier-General Giora Lev's division in the central axis was blocked in the junction south of Sultan Ya'aqub, when its vanguard battalion got stuck in a trap. A reservist M-60 Patton battalion, made up primarily of religious seminary students, had entered into an ambush and was decimated. Scores were killed and wounded; six tank soldiers became MIAs (three of the bodies were returned years later and three remain missing to this day). Several IDF M-60 tanks, equipped with Blazer add-on reactive armor, were abandoned by their crews and ferried back to Damascus for further inspection by Soviet military intelligence. Years later, Soviet tanks would be equipped with reactive armor add-on kits of their own.

Had the battle at Sultan Yakoub gone differently, Brigadier-General Peled's forces and Ugdah 252 would have been able to gain a foothold on the Beirut-Damascus Road. At dawn on Friday, June 13, 1982, Ugdah 252—with the 7th Brigade in the vanguard—was ordered to advance to Kafr Yanta and push on in the direction of the Syrian-Lebanese border. By presenting a challenge to "Syria proper" the Israeli General Staff was determined to raise the ante of consciousness in Damascus one notch farther. Lebanon was a war that—conventionally at least—Syria couldn't win and if it didn't pull back and permit an Israeli fait accompli, the western approach to the Syrian capital, long a Syrian fear, could be realized. At this stage of the war, however, the division and the brigade were burdened by logistical problems—mainly the fueling of the tanks in the front line. The tremendous convoys which were strolling in the roads created gridlocks in the few and narrow axes and prevented the pushing of supplies to the front. Most of the tanks had no more than four or five engine hours left in their tanks, and the APCs had one to two engine hours remaining. The diesel oil tankers were stuck in the back carefully winding their way through roadways deemed secure but ripe with stragglers from PLO brigades and marauding Syrian commandos. Communication between the fighting forces and the high commands was, in essence, disconnected and the primary push with the Israeli thinking was Beirut and the destruction of the PLO.

At 0200 hours on June 13, after difficult debate, Colonel Kauli opted to wait no longer. The key for the decision was the fact that, at last, he managed to contact the high ranks stuck in the back. According to the data given to him, he decided to send the 82nd Battalion on its way with their gas tanks almost empty. He was hoping to manage and fuel his battalion at a later stage. "The mission which was ordered on us," claimed Lieutenant-Colonel Marcel, 82nd Battalion commander, "was to reach up to two kilometers south of Kafr Yanta and ambush a T-72 tank brigade which was supposed to have come from the north. Our progress way was on the 'Mazkiron Axis,' a dirt road leading from Dahar el-Ahmad toward Kafr Yanta and I knew that at the entrance to the axis, in the area of the village Dinus, there was a Syrian tank force rolling around. We moved without difficulty expecting a major engagement to transpire at any minute, but all we encountered was a BMP-1 that appeared to be lost and we destroyed it with one 105mm shot. It seemed like the Syrians were surprised by the direction of our progress, but we were learning the price of surprise as well. I had yet to learn of it, but, at the same time, the force of Merkavas moving behind us already was hit by Syrian T-72 fire."

As dawn broke, the pots of Bedouin coffee that the brigade personnel had guzzled down the night before were coming in most useful. Commanders thought of their kids waking up for school and the conscripts thought of themselves waking up next to their girlfriends. Lebanon was a horrible place to be so young, so early in the morning. The brigade entered an opening in a sharp valley separating two mound-shaped hills known as Sahal el Fukani. Alon Company led the battalion's line. Lieutenant-Colonel Marcel recalls, "We were riding in a pretty valley, pastoral landscape, among vineyards and agriculture fields. Suddenly I saw fireworks from the direction of the battalion's spearhead. It was found out that the leading company was met by ranks of the Syrian Ninety-first Tank Brigade. I spread the tank companies and the infantry and we destroyed a few trucks and APCs. It was difficult to see because the sun was shining in our eyes. At oh-four-thirty we reached an area just south of Kafr Yanta and encountered a tank platoon already set up in firing position. They fired at us and we fired back—at ranges of three thousand and four thousand kilometers. We destroyed five vehicles—tanks and APCs—and suffered no losses and then our fuel and ammo ran out."

Colonel Kauli dispatched his reservists and *Sayeret* to locate the oil tankers ahead and provide them with security as they were rushed to the fighting. Commanding the *Plugat Siyur Hativatit* was Major M.,[41] a savior to the thirsty tank battalions in Dahar el-Ahmar. In reaching the convoy and ensuring that it made it to the brigade and quickly, Major M. encountered a difficulty that would sum up some of the chaos of the Lebanon fighting—fighting the Arabs wasn't nearly as difficult as fighting the "Jews." Israeli bureaucracy spite and sometimes pure stubbornness became as significant a stumbling block as a squad of Syrian commandos. Vehicles wouldn't move out of the way, MPs refused the convoys clearance to move, and reservists, the all-knowing and all-powerful element in Israeli war who thought they knew best, felt that every war was their domain and theirs to command— no matter if the highest rank they'd ever obtained was that of private first-class. "Although we were under fire on several junctions by both Syrian special forces and Palestinian terrorists, battling the traffic and the Israelis proved great obstacles for us to cross," claimed an exasperated Major M. It took the tankers nearly twice as long to reach the 82nd

Battalion as planned, but Colonel Kauli accepted the oil tanker convoy with a sigh of relief. The refueling had to be done in slow and deliberate stages and the first to get juiced up were the reserves from Nomert Force and another company from Romach Battalion, and the paratrooper's APCs. Now he raced at their head toward Kafr Yanta, in order to replace Dor's empty tanks in their positions. It was 0700 hours and for the first time since the war started the Nomert Force found itself the spearhead of the brigade's advance. Lieutenant-Colonel Sela, the battalion commander, rushed his men to move toward Kafr Yanta.

The route that the company had to move through was a fantastic example of the beauty of the Lebanese landscape: high mountains, mountainous agriculture where the locals made the most of every centimeter of land for planting chickpeas, and winding paths that made the scenic hills appear to be impressionistic mosaics. The brigade, at first, didn't encounter any Syrian units and this didn't sit well with the unit commanders. Lieutenant-Colonel Marcel ordered in infantry forces to sweep the flanks and called in the divisional IAF liaison to bring Bell-209 Cobras to the area in order to "fly" shotgun. Moving at a pace of a kilometer an hour, the advance continued and no enemy forces were discovered. Soldiers, mainly kibbutzniks, began to pay more attention to the agricultural setup and the foliage than to the horizon where T-72s might be lurking. The city boys in the unit, those from Tel Aviv, Haifa, and Jerusalem, began enjoying the adventure as a *Tiyul,* or trip. The tension began to break—even among the officers—and joking replaced stern expressions of confidence. Suddenly, the whining sounds of incoming helicopters erupted over the pastoral landscape and the deafening blasts of explosions engulfed the column of Merkavas. An SA342 Gazelle helicopter that suddenly appeared above the peak of a mountain launched a HOT missile into the turret of the company commander's Merkava. Within 30 seconds two more tanks were hit. The Syrian Air Force SA342 Gazelles proved their lethal effectiveness. They were operating in ideal terrain conditions, hiding behind hills and tree lines. In spite of the numerous helicopter alerts which were announced throughout the brigade communication net, the Syrian pilots managed to strike again. This time, however, the tank crews reacted quickly opening fire in the direction of the helicopters; tank commanders even ordered their gunners to aim their 105mm main armament guns at the oncoming choppers—one 105mm armor piercing round managed to slice through a Gazelle and bring it down in a flurry of fire.

The Gazelles proved incredibly effective and lethal. Brigade medical teams started caring for the wounded and attending to the dead. Dr. Rahamim Ben Yosef was with the tanks of Romach Battalion at that time of the helicopter attack. "We were going up on Mazkiron Axis and then heard the desperate call for medical help in the brigade communication network. We found out that this force had severely wounded soldiers, and its regular doctors were too far from the action to be able to tend to the wounded. I took with me the battalion aid APC, and, driving scout, detoured the progressing tank convoy. We had problems locating the force until we heard the cries for help and saw the clouds of smoke. I saw the tank with the wounded driving in our direction. One of the wounded was lying on the front of the turret bleeding quite badly; all the soldiers were in shock. One of the medics from the engineer platoon that reached the tank a few minutes before me was resuscitating the wounded. He was trying to do a heart message but was concentrating on the right side of the chest in order to avoid the massive chest wound. The clinical picture was quite severe: a large wound in the area of the neck that shattered the breathing tube, and another large bleeding wound in the left chest. I tried to insert a plastic breathing pipe right into the lung but it doesn't really work. The wounded did not respond, his pupils were wide and blank. There was another wounded crewman in the tank lodged in the smoldering turret. It was a hard sight—the mortar operator was leaning on the mortar, severely wounded in his stomach and most of his fingers were shattered. With great difficulty and the assistance of another soldier, I managed to free him from the seat and get him out of the tank. The wounded had lost a lot of blood and his blood pressure was low, despite the large amount of liquids we gave him with the IV. We put in four or five liters all together. More than that was impossible to give. We rushed to evacuate the wounded to the divisional evacuation station and get them medevaced to hospital in Israel; his condition worsened fast. I wet his lips from time to time and asked him how he was feeling. His pulse was weak. I could hardly feel it. He died in our arms, even before the helicopter arrived, it was a terrible feeling. We were in shock."[42]

In all of the fighting sections, the forces were in a battle against the political clock. The commanders on both fighting sides were certain that the cease-fire would become effective shortly. Each progress toward controlling an area could have had a significant political meaning. The modern T-72 tanks of the Syrian Army's 3rd Armored Division now progressed without notice into the Israeli setup and found themselves in a trap. It was the arrowhead of the division's 81st Armored Brigade. In two hours of fighting, the 77th Battalion's Merkavas and antitank M113s armed with TOW ATGWs managed to destroy eight T-72 tanks.

Early that morning the Merkavas of 77th Battalion came out of their positions in the area of the bridge near Jab-Jenin. The mission which was given to the battalion was to lead the infantry brigade that went to conquer Jab-Jenin. At the head of this brigade's attack moved the 77th Battalion's deputy commander and the tanks of Hermon Company. The force was stopped in the previous day in the area of el-Qaroun, after destroying a few enemy tanks. Now it was on its way, advancing along the water canal leading the water of the Litani from the area near the bridge. Hermon Company's tanks were advancing fast on the pressed dirt road along the concrete canal and at 1000 hours they conquered Jab-Jenin. Immediately after that they went out and caught positions near a monastery west of the town. The Syrian forces in Sultan Ya'aqub noticed what was happening, and reacted fast. Within a few minutes Hermon Company tank soldiers identified Syrian tanks coming down from Sultan Ya'aqub in three separate charges and shelling the battalion's positions. The Merkavas immediately engaged the T-72s with barrages of 105mm launched at long ranges. The Merkavas were also firing smoke canisters from the turret-mounted 60mm mortars in order to shield the area from the fire of the Sagger team. The Merkavas were not alone in this impending confrontation. Linking up with Hermon Company was a company of Pattons from the Mahatz Brigade's Sufa Battalion. The two forces now acted as one.

Within a short time, Hermon Company managed to destroy fourteen Syrian tanks—all T-72s—and one BTR-60 APC; the Merkava mortars were remarkably accurate and had decimated the ranks of Syrian infantry racing to find cover. Tank mortars were wonderfully exact. Back in Israel, Major-General (Res.) Tal was proud. The Merkava had fought the T-72 and had won.

For the 7th Brigade, the brunt of its 1982 War ended on June 13 when a cease-fire was declared along the Beka'a Valley. The rest of the IDF continued its fight along the Beirut-Damascus Highway (following a particularly bloody battle at Ein-Zehalta) and on to Beirut. It was embroiled in sieges and massacres, controversy and quagmire.

Following the cessation of the conventional fighting, in August 1982, Colonel Kauli assumed the rank of brigadier-general and a senior field position; he retired shortly thereafter. Elements of the 7th Brigade remained in Lebanon until the Israeli withdrawal in May 1985, serving primarily along the Awali perimeter at Bater.[43] Lebanon was unlike any war that the brigade had ever fought. There was no sense of nation building ferocity, as was evident in 1948, no euphoric national victory, as was celebrated in 1967, and no back-slapping gratitude of saving the nation in a nail-biting battle of desperation, as was suffered in 1973. Operation Peace for Galilee, for lack of a better title, was an enigma—a small and ugly war that had little national support. In terms of the development of warfare, Lebanon was an important proving ground. Major-General Tal's concept of an indigenous Israeli main battle tank, one built to the very specific needs of the IDF, had been vindicated in glorious fashion. A tank that put crew safety above and beyond the demand for speed and extravagant firepower was, indeed, revolutionary, and a tremendous boost of morale for the men who fought inside these chariots of steel.[44] The IDF suffered great human losses as a result of the Lebanon war; it became a nagging scar on the soul of many senior commanders and foot soldiers alike forced to endure a tour against Hizbollah, the elements, and a close, but distant, land that had long ago lost its hold on human sanity.

Following the unit's three-year deployment to Lebanon, the Levantine landscape was no longer viewed by the men of the 7th Brigade as an escape from the doldrums of Golan service. Determination to stay away from conflict in that nation would become a part of their psyches.

The 1982 Lebanon War was not the 7th Brigade's finest hour, nor was it the IDF's shining moment—the Armored Corps had certainly seen better days. Beyond Sultan Ya'aqub, beyond Ein Zehalta, there was also the case of Colonel Eli Geva. Prior to the war, Colonel Geva was a true shining star in the IDF—destined, some had said, to be chief of staff. Decorated, charismatic, and highly capable, he was also the youngest brigade commander in IDF history. At the age of thirty-two, Colonel Geva had emerged from being a 77th Battalion officer in 1973 to the helm of the 211st Armored Brigade.[45] This brigade was charging on Syrian and PLO positions on the road to Beirut as part of Brigadier-General Yitzhak Mordechai's Ugdah 96 force that was pushing along the coastal front on the Lebanese capital. During the siege of Beirut, it was Geva's 211st Brigade that was tasked with breaking into the city along one of the most difficult axes. The first week—even two weeks—of the war had gone like most IDF operations: smoothly, even with the difficulties encountered at Sultan Ya'aqub and Ein Zehalta. But the siege of Beirut, the apparent politicization of the IDF by Prime Minister Begin and Defense Minister Sharon, and the lambasting that Israel received in the international media as a result of the assault on the Lebanese capital, initiated dissent. Colonel Geva, a soldier who had been literally brought up under fire during the War of Attrition and the 1973 War, had been raised to fight on open battlefields—not inside alleyways and city boulevards. During a commander's staff meeting before the attack, Colonel Geva decided to express his misgivings about moving in on the Lebanese capital. "This is not our fight," he told Chief of Staff Lieutenant-General Eitan. "We mustn't let ourselves be dragged into Lebanon's internal affairs." Later at another meeting with Eitan, "Going to Beirut means killing entire families."[46] He resigned his command in midwar—rather than killing innocent people, he claimed—and was subsequently fired from the IDF. The "Geva Affair" soon became one of the most controversial internal examples of dissension in IDF history and talk of the incident was forbidden among the troopers serving "in country." It remains a volatile issue in the IDF—especially in tank units.

The 1973 War had entrenched a breed of warrior into the ranks of the Armored Corps command structure that perhaps will never again be replicated by any army anywhere in the world. "Lebanon wasn't that kind of war," reflected a tank officer who had served atop the Golan Heights in 1973, "and thank God it wasn't."[47]

Postscript

In September 1993, technological and innovative ground was broken when the IDF's Quartermaster Corps' technical department came out with a novel approach to the age-old affliction of tank crewman's fatigue due to the heat and dehydration endured while serving long stretches inside the vehicle—an air-conditioned tanker's coverall.[1] The idea of IDF Armored Corps' founding father and Merkava designer Major-General (Res.) Yisrael "Talik" Tal, the one-piece coverall would circulate cool and refreshing air to virtually the entire body by means of a light, fire-resistant Nomex blend combining the circulatory apparatus found in many of the NBC (Nuclear, Biological, Chemical) warfare suits worn throughout the world. The suits would be "plugged" in to the Merkava's central air system, and a switch on the suit would allow the tank soldier to control the flow of air personally, as well as to which parts of his anatomy the greater stream of cool air is required. The suit underwent a typically grueling IDF test period, and according to Brigadier-General Michael Shaked, "The suit should enter full-scale service at the time that the Merkava Mk III enters full service." Including service with the 7th Brigade.

In studying the performance of the Merkava units in Lebanon, IDF officers and Israel Military Industries officials were impressed by what had transpired. Although the 105mm gun on the Merkava is smaller and less powerful than that found on both the T-62 and T-72, studies showed that *most* of the damage inflicted to Israeli armor (Merkavas, Centurions, and Pattons) by Syrian armor did not destroy a tank, but rather incapacitated it. The majority of Israeli tanks hit, damaged, and destroyed in Lebanon came as a result of infantry-fired antitank weapons (such as the RPG and Sagger) and helicopter-fired missiles, such as the modified Sagger (fired by the Mi-24) and the HOT missile fired by the lethal Gazelle tank-killer chopper used by the Syrian Air Force. On the Israeli side, it was found that infantry-fired antitank rounds, such as the RPG, were less of a factor in defeating Soviet-produced tanks than what turned out to be the true tank serial killer of the conflict, the TOW ATGW—especially those fired from jeeps belonging to *"Orev"* (Crow) antitank reconnaissance units and those fired from attack helicopters.[2] The tank, however, and the IDF's L7 105mm main armament gun, proved to be the true master of the battlefield. According to accounts, what made the Israeli guns so lethal, even though the Soviet-built tanks in the Syrian arsenals were of a larger caliber, was the Israel Military Industries armor-piercing, fin-stabilized, discarding sabot tungsten round. Known as the *Hetz* (Arrow) in Hebrew, the APFSDS-T was able to penetrate Syrian armor at astounding ranges of up to 5,500 meters away. That round and the training applied to Israeli tank gunners simply allowed Israeli armor to decimate enemy tanks before a fair fight could be encountered.[3] It was technology and ballistics playing a cruel fate to the Soviet-system of armor-versus-armor engagement that the Soviets had preached to Damascus.

Production on the Merkava Mk II, with its improved mobility and fire-control system commenced in 1983, and once again the 7th Brigade was the first unit to get the keys and deploy it in the field. As the Merkavas in various brigades were fighting it out against Syrian armor in the Beka'a Valley and the PLO along the coast of Beirut, Talik and his roundtable of armored warfare experts were busy at work placing the finishing touches on the next generation of Merkava—the Mk II. The lessons of the Lebanon conflict were analyzed and additions to the Merkava Mk II included a ball-and-chain configuration positioned on the rear turret for added protection against AT projectiles aimed at the sensitive crux between turret and chassis; add-on armor plates on the turret; and an advanced electronic system. Other noted improvements with the Mk II variant included increased mobility and speed, and improvement of the fire control system, the addition of special—and highly classified—armor to the turret and hull, and inclusion of an internal, commander-operated 60mm mortar. Production of Merkava Mk II continued until 1989 and the tank saw limited action in southern Lebanon—primarily on infantry support assignments against *Hizballah* terrorists armed with Saggers and RPGs.

When it came time to develop and design the Merkava Mk II, Major-General Tal and his staff of armor officers and engineers realized that Israel could not design and develop a new tank every decade or so—such a luxury was economically impossible for nation and defense industry as small as Israel's. In reality, there was no need to abandon the original Merkava design concept, either. The Mk I variant served the Armored Corps brilliantly in Lebanon and the Mk II had been a faithful tank serving in the best tank brigades in the Armored Corps' order of battle. Crews were quite fond of the Mk II's performance, and commanders had scored high points for their tank units on exercises and in maneuvers. Yet in reality, the Mk II was a stopgap upgrade of the initial version of the design, not an overall improvement. Major-General Tal wanted to build a brand-new tank on an existing platform—one incorporating improved firepower, improved mobility, and improved technology. The drawing board stage of the Mk III's development commenced several weeks after the first Mk II's rolled off the IMI factory floor in August 1983.

Looking at the changing face of the Middle Eastern military map in 1983, Major-General Tal viewed an Arab world equipping its armed forces with the world's most powerful and technologically superior MBTs on the market. The Syrians, the Iraqis, and the Iranians all fielded T-72s; the Jordanians fielded the mighty updated Chieftain (the *Khalid*); the Saudis fielded the mighty French AMX-30 and even the tiny United Arab Emirates boasted the Italian-produced OF-40. Peace existed with Egypt, but the Egyptian Army fielded thousands of T-62s and M-60s and talk was of the United States selling the Mubarak regime the mighty M-1 Abrams. These vehicles were almost exclusively equipped with newly developed armored skeletons and upgraded armor protection far superior to the type of MBTs that fought it out in the 1973 War and, indeed, in Lebanon. As a result, Major-General Tal's first point of improvement in the Mk III variant would be improved firepower and Israel's abandonment of the L7/M68 105mm rifled gun.

The L7/M68 105mm rifled gun had been, perhaps, the true unsung hero in Israel's major wars of 1967, 1973, and 1982; certainly the gun had resulted in nearly 1,000 enemy kills. Yet in spite of the new and improved APFSDS ammunition that had been specifically developed for the L7/M68, Major-General Tal realized that the time had come for the IDF to introduce a larger caliber main armament gun. Thinking of a worse-case scenario, Talik did not want Israeli brigades on the Golan Heights shooting it out with T-80s (equipped with Soviet copies of the Israeli-designed Blazer Armor) with the 105mm gun. The 120mm gun was concluded to be most suitable to the initial blueprints, though the weapon would have to be designed and built inside Israel. Initial consideration, albeit brief, centered on a sublicense arrangement with the American-produced M256 120mm gun serving on the M-1s, but this defeated the very purpose of a completely indigenously produced tank. Talik wanted every screw, every bolt, every cannon on "his" tank to be made in the Jewish State. There were other considerations behind the decision to arm the Mk III variant with a 120mm gun. Producing an indigenous gun was one thing, but an arms production industry that for years had developed, designed, and produced 105mm ammunition would now have to switch gears and begin the production of a full and advanced line of 120mm product. If a gun would be selected of the same caliber as the main American tank in U.S. Army service, the M-1, then should full-scale war once again erupt in the Middle East and the IDF forced to rely on an American arms lift, then the United States would be able to supply the IDF with plentiful stores of 120mm ammunition.

Because of the improved and enlarged caliber weapon, Talik realized that the Mk III would be forced to carry less ammunition—not only because the 120mm shells were larger but also because they required additional protection. Carrying less ammunition was a tradeoff in the eyes of the Mk III design team. If the gun would be more powerful and capable of decimating its target on the first shot, supported by an even more advanced fire-control system, then less ammunition would not specifically hinder the vehicle's battlefield performance. The 120mm ammunition would be carried in specially designed fire-retardant canisters providing the crew with an extra edge of protection should the tank's armor be penetrated by a HEAT or KE round. Studies of Israeli tanks destroyed on the battlefields of Sinai and the Golan, as well as in Lebanon in 1982, indicated that a fair percentage—too high an amount to be ignored—of the Armored Corps fatalities were from stored ammunition that detonated in the initial tank fire.

By 1983 Israel's Silicon Valley, a strip of computer research firms nestled near the northern port city of Haifa, had evolved from a small high-tech community into world players in the computer and advanced electronic field. Much of this industry, with names like Rafael, Elbit, Elscint, and El-Op, was dedicated to Israel's growing defense industry and many were enlisted with the first two Merkava variants and were called upon, again, to provide systems to the Mk III. The most important high-tech aspect of the Mk III was the fire-control system—the *Bakar Esh* as it is known in Hebrew. The Mk III's Fire-Control System was a joint venture between Elbit and El-Op and incorporated a laser range finder, a fire-control computer, and a day/night sighting system available to both the tank commander and the gunner. This new system, for the first time in IDF tank warfare history, enabled an Israeli tank to accurately fire on the move with the inclusion of a line-of-sight stabilization system for both the gunner and commander. Being able to fire on the move is a valuable addition for any tank, as it

eliminates the need to stop, search for cover and concealment, and acquire enemy targets. The high-tech aspects of
the post-1982 tanks permitted all these functions while rolling at top speeds on one's treads. This aspect of tank warfare
is most important when fighting in the vast open expanses
of the desert, and it is clear that the Mk III was designed
with Israel's next war—one fought against Iraq or Iran,
perhaps—in mind. While the IDF Armored School liked to
boast that it produced the best tank commanders in the
business and the most accurate gunners, the now legendary
Tzalafim (snipers) of 7th Brigade fame, there are factors
beyond a classroom that go into a gunner being the most
accurate that he can be. To ensure that each 120mm unleashed by the Mk III would hit its mark, the Fire-Control
System's highly advanced (and highly classified) ballistic
computer was incorporated with alphanumeric displays
showing all meteorological, climactic, and elevation movements and conditions.

Major-General Tal believed that the tank always possessed a considerable and sometimes understated edge when
faced with an infantry antitank threat (the tank—no matter
what the scenario—he believed, was always a tank's greatest
battlefield nemesis). But he realized that enemy infantry formations needed to be countered. In the Mk II version of
the Merkava, this was achieved by mounting two-turret FN
MAG 7.62mm light machine guns along with a gun-mounted
.50 caliber heavy machine gun all augmented by a turret-
interior-mounted 60mm mortar. Indeed, the mortar was one
of the most popular aspects in surveys of tank crews in units
equipped with the Mk II. While the 60mm mortar is opti-
mally used for smoke cover, 7th Brigade and 188th units
deployed to southern Lebanon during joint-security operations and retaliatory strikes have found the mortar incredibly effective in an antiinfantry role, and especially good in
launching flares. In many cases, the firing of the 60mm flare
rounds was used with great effectiveness in blinding enemy
infrared night vision equipment during nighttime strikes. It
should, however, be noted that smoke dischargers are fitted
to the exterior of the Mk III turret enabling a cloud of
protective cover at a moment's notice even if the crew is
busy firing the 60mm in an antipersonnel mission.

Beyond firepower, the second most important improvement in the Mk III variant was to be the armor protection and in this regard Major-General Tal opted to be revolutionary. Inherently frugal and practical, Israelis by nature think of equipment in two spheres of thought: "How can I use it now, and how can I improve it in the future for a minimum price?" Israelis love to tinker, love to correct, and love to add on. The Mk I version of the Merkava was a "what you see what is you get" tank, as was the Mk II; in essence, they were examples of built-in obsolescence, a symptom of the daily expanding high-tech arms race, even though more-than-capable lethal fighting systems. Major-General Tal wanted to make Mk III, his tank, permanently new and as a result designed a modular armor protection system. Instead of the traditional cast or welded armor found on most earlier tanks, the Mk III would incorporate an interior skeleton and a modular outer shell that could be removed and replaced with the latest developments in the armor technology. The new modular plates, sort of a Lego-like suit to the tank's interior, would be bolted to the tank's hull and exterior turret shell instead of being welded on or cast completely through. This pragmatic development, Tal argued, would be useful on two counts—firstly, if a breakthrough was discovered in armored steel technology, the existing exterior shell could simply be removed and replaced; secondly, and more important during war, damaged or destroyed chunks of armor could be replaced at battalion repair stations by Ordnance Corps crew—the turnaround for returning a damaged vehicle to the front could be cut from the usual forty-eight-hour frantic workload to an astounding six hours.

The first test of this design came with the *Ma'Ga'Ch 7,* the Israeli-upgraded M-60 that was suited up with a modular turret and hull reinforcement in late 1988.[4] Even though the modular design was inked into the blueprints for the Mk III as far back as 1985, little information is available on the composite nature of the modular armor as it remains one of the most closely guarded secrets in Israel. No information has been released as to spacing of the armor or the nature of its design, though it is known that the modular sheets are passive and not Blazer-type reactive armor. The foreign defense media, the army of fifth-estate reporters who were offered close access to the Merkava Mk I and Mk II, have been kept far away from a close examination of the Mk III.

Special add-on armor skirts support the upper half of the wheels and suspensions, and the engine area and the frontal turret are well-sloped to withstand a front attack by providing unique angle silhouettes. Yet the Merkava wouldn't be a Merkava if the front compartment of the tank, the frontal arc, and engine compartment, weren't protected more than the tank's other areas. If the armor is penetrated and the round manages to surpass the difficult penetration angle supported by the sloped hull and turret, the engine compartment and the stored diesel fuel provide an ample shield to prevent any conventional AT shell from entering the crew's compartment.

In the worst-case scenario when an antitank round does actually penetrate elements of the Merkava Mk III's armor, specific safety trip wires have been incorporated into the vehicle's basic design. "An ounce of prevention is worth a pound of cure in tank-versus-tank warfare," claims one senior IDF tank officer, and as a result Major-General Tal saw to it that the Mk III was equipped with a newly developed, indigenously produced, electromagnetic warning device that could alert the crew the moment their vehicle is locked on by a laser beam from an enemy tank, infantry antitank team, or even a tank-killing chopper,[5] such as the Hind or Gazelle. To minimize the chances of an in-turret fire should a round penetrate the armored protection, the volatile hydraulic system found in many Western-built tanks (including the Israeli-built Merkava Mk I and Mk II) is equipped with an electronic turret control. A high-tech and classified fire-prevention (detection and suppression) system is also built in to the Mk III version, including special round storage tubes that maintain a specifically low temperature throughout the tank's deployment to ensure the maximum integrity of the round when actually called upon for service in combat. NBC protection in the Mk III, a mighty consideration before the Gulf War in view of the heavy investment in biological and chemical agents by the Syrians, Iraqis, and Iranians, is complete when the overpressurized interior is batted down.

In contrast to comparable vehicles on the market, the

Merkava Mk I and Mk II were considered slow movers—they were large, heavy, and could never reach a speed surpassing 46 kilometers per hour. (The M-1 Abrams, for example, could reach a top speed of 72.4 kilometers per hour; Germany's Leopard 2 could hit 72 kilometers per hour; the T-72 was capable of 60 kilometers per hour, as was the Khalid.) Both tanks were built specifically for the battlefields of the Golan Heights and southern Lebanon, mountainous stretches of treacherous fighting ground where a tank weighing over 60 tons couldn't even reach high speeds without slamming into a boulder or being driven off a twisting road. Capable of firing while moving, the Mk III was a tank for a different type of warfare. Major-General Tal realized that Israel's next major war (or even protracted conflict) need not be restricted to the Valley of Tears again—or even the Beka'a Valley. The next major war would be a fast offensive war with less strategic depth than before and the need to push the battle as far away from Israel's frontiers as possible. Although the maximum speed of the Mk III remains classified, the 900 horsepower engine found in both the Mk I and Mk II versions has been considerably upgraded to a Teledyne Continental AVDS-1790-9AR 12,000hp 12-cycle, air-cooled, turbo-charged, diesel engine. To improve mobility, especially over the barren boulder-strewn wasteland of the Golan Heights and southern Lebanon, specially modified shocks have been provided for the tank's ballistic steel suspension system.

Israeli tank officers, including those who have seen the best American, British, and French tanks close up, swear that the Merkava Mk III is the finest and most powerful tank available anywhere in the world—especially when in the hands of the Israeli tank soldier. "The human touch in the tank are the hands that bring the machine from its parked state to a mobile and lethal fighting machine," claims Lieutenant-Colonel M.,[6] commander of the 188th Barak Armored Brigade's "Receive" Battalion, the first tank unit in Israel to deploy the Mk III. "The Merkava is a technologically superior tank and as a result requires the crew and commanders to provide quicker reflexes and judgment calls." As a result of the mental demands that a machine like the Mk III demands, the IDF Armored Corps did not want to place its newest, most powerful, and most expensive tank in the hands of just any soldiers. It wanted this new "baby," as the tank is referred to in Armored Corps circles, to be deployed among the most capable soldiers within the brigade. The brightest, most capable, and most motivated tank soldiers, gunners, loaders, drivers, and commanders were removed from other platoons and companies and channeled into an elite cadre of groundbreakers who would inaugurate the vehicle into the IDF's order of battle. For nearly 40 years, it had been the 7th Armored Brigade that inaugurated new tanks obtained from abroad or produced at home into the *Heyl Ha'Shirion* order of battle. The first tanks that Israel owned, the "stolen" Cromwells, were inducted into 7th Brigade service, as were Israel's first Shermans, AMX-13s, Centurions, Pattons, and Merkavas.[7] Following the 1973 War, a war that the 7th Brigade emerged from as national icons, it was felt by the IDF General Staff that the 188th Barak Brigade, an elite tank unit in its own right, had been unfairly snubbed; following the 7th Brigade's "average" performance in Lebanon in 1982, it was decided that the next major *Tzchupar* (or gift) that the IDF would offer a tank unit would go to the 188th—a unit that had suffered more than seventy-five percent casualties in 1973.

On the eve of Israel's 41st Independence Day, in a solemn ceremony on the Golan Heights, the first Merkava Mk III was handed over to Colonel Eyal, the 188th Brigade commander.

Senior tank officers, those first taught in the Patton or Centurion, are tremendous admirers of the Merkava Mk III though they still reminisce about the old days when tanks were smaller and less technological. "The Merkava might be mighty," claims Lieutenant-Colonel M., "but the Centurion had soul." Many of the soldiers of the battalion, men who had originally learned on the Centurion, disagree. "How can you argue with a 120mm main armament gun," claimed one gunner. "How can you disrespect the awesome power of a one thousand two hundred horse-power capability." Soul or no soul, the Mk III variant is but a rung on the ladder of the Merkava saga. Major-General Tal, the man who has from day one been at the epicenter of the Merkava project, is busy at work completing the details on the Mk IV. Although security around the Mk IV project has been almost hermetic, news reports in such publications as *Jane's Defense Weekly* have suggested that possible improvements could include a larger caliber gun or electrothermal weaponry. Whatever the Mk IV will carry into battle, Major-General Tal promises to soon unveil a Merkava that will once again boggle the imagination and claim to be the world's most powerful main battle tank.

Atop the Golan Heights, in the zone of operations under the responsibility of the 188th Barak Brigade, the training fields were engulfed by diesel smoke as the brigade's *Ze'evim* (Foxes) Platoon went about the task at hand of training for war in a new and ultramodern combat fighting package. The blasts of 120mm fire were deafening, as were the flashes of yellow flames emerging from targets (actually former Syrian Army T-34s and T-55s). Incorporating the Mk III into an experienced and cohesive fighting unit already trained—and expert—in handling a different tank was a challenging scenario to senior armor officers. It was not simply an exercise in learning a few new switches on a familiar system—it was learning the A-to-Zs of a completely new tank. Atop the Golan Heights, each move made by the first Mk III units were closely monitored by Armored Corps brass and representatives from the nearly 200 firms involved in the tank's production. Armored Corps officers are the staunchest salesmen and supporters of the Merkava Mk III. "It is the best tank in the region and will overwhelm any T-Seventy-two it will face in the Middle East," claimed Brigadier-General Yitzhak Rabin (no relation to the prime minister) in an interview celebrating Armored Corps Day.[8]

As the 188th Barak Brigade incorporates the Merkava Mk III into its ranks, Major-General (Res.) Tal is busy working on the next generation of "Chariot," one ready for the high-tech combat of the next century. Already, in the Mk III variant, tank warfare as Israelis have come to know it has already gone high-tech. "In the Merkava Mk III the tank commander is tasked with having an accelerated thinking process enabling him to meet all the technological options," claimed Talik, in an interview with the *Israel Defense Forces* magazine. "Because of the Mk III's ability to traverse all terrain conditions at high speeds, the commander—and crew's—element of time has increased markedly, requiring better instinctive and reactionary skills."[9] The Merkava Mk IV that Talik is currently working on promises to be a spaceship when compared to the current fleet of MBTs in the world arsenals. As a result, Brigadier-General Ami Pelnat, the chief armored officer, has engineered recruitment programs into the Armored Corps designed to attract and select fighters the same way as the IAF selects its pilots. By 1993, the last time statistics were compiled, seventy-five percent of the volunteers into the Armored Corps were suitable for command—meaning that they were of sufficient intelligence to control and command technologically advanced weapons systems. But an elite piece of machinery required equally elite crews.

Brigadier-General Pelnat, who retired from active duty in February 1994, was among the old school of tank officer who one would think would be put off by the high-tech Nintendo aspect of armored warfare today. Brigadier-General Pelnat is, perhaps, a dying breed of tank soldier. He began his career in the 7th Armored Brigade as a young soldier, eighteen-years-old and black beret, and rose through the ranks as tank commander, platoon commander, company commander, and battalion commander. Brigadier-General Pelnat was decorated for valor for his role in the Valley of Tears in the 77th Battalion, and Brigadier-General (Res.) Avigdor Kahalani referred to him as "one of the finest tank soldiers to ever serve in the IDF." He commanded a battalion in the 188th Brigade, and a reservist brigade of Merkavas that would distinguish itself in skill and ability as if it were made up of hungry conscripts. Finally, following the Lebanon War, Pelnat received command of the 7th Armored Brigade; the greatest source of pride for an armored officer is to command the brigade that started it all. Pelnat appreciated talent, as well, and realized that the Armored Corps would need talent and motivated recruits to drive the new generation of MBTs that Talik and his staff are designing. To appeal to a generation of technowarriors, Brigadier-General Pelnat opened tank unit bases to high school students. "Head-hunting" for the Sega-set.

"Ami," as his friends and comrades called Brigadier-

General Pelnat, was, however, a tank officer who believed in the domain of conventional tank warfare—thinking not shared entirely by many in the IDF General Staff. Since Lieutenant-General Mordechai Gur, the IDF Chief of Staff from 1974–1978, all subsequent chiefs of staff have been former paratroopers or reconnaissance commando officers by trade, and operators by instinct. These men were honed on small team raids deep behind enemy lines late at night, where the enemy was killed by blows to the head and garrote pulls across the jugular, and heavy firepower was a rifle-fired grenade. A battle of warfare theory and of egos soon developed in the General Staff forum between the red berets (paratroopers and commandos) and black berets (tank and artillery) and the black berets had no chance of winning in the court of Lieutenant-General Ehud Barak—IDF Chief of Staff from April 1991 to December 1994. One of the founding members of *Sayeret Mat'kal,* the General Staff Reconnaissance Unit, and the most decorated soldier in IDF history, Lieutenant-General Barak initiated an era of special operations thought that transformed the IDF for generations to come. New appointments and promotions to senior ranks were handed over to ex-paratroopers and special operations officers—not tank veterans. Former Armored Corps officers from Talik to Yanush have been quite vocal in this war between the red and black berets—it was this war that led to Brigadier-General Pelnat's retirement from the IDF. The current IDF Chief of Staff at the writing of this book, Lieutenant-General Amnon Shahak is also a red beret—a veteran and highly decorated paratroop special operations officer. Most of the new members of the general staff forum, too, are veteran reconnaissance and commando officers. It appears that as long as the covert world of the special ops operator remains "in vogue," according to one retired tank officer, armor officers and armored forces in general will remain second-class citizens.

The new special forces mode of thinking in the IDF General Staff is best reflected in the new face of the 7th Brigade's reconnaissance company—*"Pal'Sar 7."* There was a time when the brigade's reconnaissance force was made up of the unit's finest soldiers but not with commandos trained for cross-border forays where daggers and silencers would be used. Their role was to serve the parent brigade and reconnoiter terrain and provide a high-speed mobile response to enemy infantry forces. *Pal'Sar 7* was disbanded following the Buqata fiasco of the 1973 War when 24 soldiers were killed—including the company's commander. The unit was brought back to the brigade's order of battle in 1983, following the fiasco at Sultan Ya'aqub when the armored force entering the valley did not have sufficient reconnaissance information about Syrian armor deployments. *Pal'Sar 7* was not simply a reinstatement of the same, but rather a new and improved concept. The reconnaissance troopers volunteering into the unit undergo a grueling selection process, and an astounding 20 months of training. Old school armor officers consider the unit "an infantry reconnaissance force trapped in an armor brigade," but they are a statement of the changing form of tank warfare. According to Lieutenant Y.,[10] an officer in *Pal'Sar 7,* "No matter how technologically advanced the tanks become, no matter how many push buttons, laser devices, and kinetic energy ordnance is deployed, a tank will need to know what is beyond the hills up ahead and who exactly lurks at the junction three 'clicks' ahead."[11]

The face of tank warfare has changed remarkably in the years since the armored vehicles attempted to force their way up the winding road to the Latrun fortress in 1948. Israel has been the world's testing ground for the destructive power of the tank ever since. The soldiers of *Pal'Sar 7,* and the brigade officers, who stand their ground atop the Golan Heights, hope that they won't be yet another chapter in the book in the years to come.

During the 1973 War, many of the tanks in Kahalani's battalion, those that had survived the Valley of Tears bloodletting, wrote the phrase *Ha'Tachana Ha'Ba'ah Damesek!* ("Next Stop Damascus") on their tanks. The hatred against the Syrians for the surprise attack and the death and destruction that attack brought led to the desire to hit Damascus and hit it hard. Yet with peace being attempted with the PLO and solidified with Jordan, many Israelis, from the mothers of those serving in the IDF to men like Talik and Avigdor Kahalani, hope that "Next Stop Damascus" will only be uttered by train conductors on the Haifa-Damascus

Railway Line once a peace treaty is signed with Syria, or spoken by an El Al pilot prior to takeoff for the 30-minute hop from Ben-Gurion International Airport to the Syrian capital. Avigdor Kahalani is now a member of the Knesset, Israel's parliament, and during a 1993 reunion of 77th Battalion veterans atop the Golan Heights, the MK (Member of Knesset) invited Syrian commanders who he had faced in 1973 to join in the festivities. The Syrians refused.

In Israel's six major wars, nearly 17,000 soldiers have been killed in action—4,804 were tank soldiers and an astounding 1,492 tank soldiers were killed in the 1973 War alone. Too many men have been killed and maimed in Israel's battle of fire and steel. Too many stories of courage and sacrifice written.

It is a Saturday morning at a forward position for the 82nd Battalion's "H Company," and most of unit's crews are busy asleep, coming off watch, or catching up on their reading. Several soldiers are off in the synagogue, deep in Sabbath prayer; *Glilon* 5.56mm assault rifles lie at their feet, next to crewman's ballistic helmets, flak vests, and web gear. Pray for peace and prepare for war has been the motto of soldiers throughout the ages. On the Golan Heights, in the ranks of the 7th Armored Brigade, prayer and preparation are the currencies of a soldier's everyday existence.

Endnotes

Introduction

[1] Full name withheld for security considerations.

[2] Interview, Golan Heights, November 6, 1992.

[3] Virtually every veteran of the 7th Armored Brigade interviewed for this book used the expression "Quick Draw" when describing the point-blank engagements that took place in the countless small and "personal" battles fought between the Syrian and Israeli tankers during the 1973 fighting. Remarkably, in an article commemorating the 1973 War in the official newspaper of the Syrian Army (*Jaish ash'Sha'ab,* or *Popular Army*), soldiers who fought on the opposite end of the gun sight used that same term when describing the close-quarters battles.

[4] Interview, New York, January 1993.

[5] According to the reports on NBC News, many Gulf War veterans are suffering from rare and highly progressive forms of cancer that it is believed were instigated by an Iraqi chemical attack near their positions in Saudi Arabia.

[6] Christopher F. Foss, *Jane's AFV Recognition Handbook* (London: Jane's Publishing Company Ltd., 1987), p. 27.

[7] Interview, Herziliya, May 28, 1993.

[8] Aviva Bar-Am, "The Divided Time," *Jerusalem Post Magazine,* November 27, 1992, p. 24.

[1] Interview, Tel Aviv, November 25, 1992.

[2] Interview, Tel Aviv, July 1, 1994.

[3] Several of the IAF's early commanders, including the trailblazing Don Tolokowsky and Ezer Weizman, were all Spitfire pilots who fought in the Battle of Britain.

[4] Samuel M. Katz, *Follow Me! A History of Israel's Military Elite* (London: Arms and Armour Press, 1988), p. 10–12.

[5] Various Editors, *Tzava U'Bitachon A' (1948–1968): Tzahal Be'Heilo Entzyklopedia Le'Tzava Ule'Bitachon* (Tel Aviv: Revivim Publishing, 1982), p. 41.

[6] Ibid., p. 34.

[7] The phrase "push the Jews into the sea" was commonly used in Arab literature of the period, from editorials in state-run newspapers to sermons in mosques. The phrase was turned into infamous propaganda twenty years later when Egyptian President Gamel Abdel Nasser threatened to push the Jews into the sea on the eve of the June 1967 Six Day War.

[8] See Various Editors, *Tzava U'Bitachon A'* (1948–1968), p. 31.

[9] Interview with former *Rechesh* agent, Tel Aviv, June 1, 1993.

[10] Any visitor to Israel traveling the now bustling multilane highway between Tel Aviv and Jerusalem can see those Sandwich Cars along the side of the road and visible, daily memorials to those who fell in the desperate effort to supply the cut-off Jewish population of Jerusalem.

[11] Arieh Hasabiyah, *Heyl Ha'Shirion* (Tel Aviv: Revivim Publishing, 1981), p. 13.

[12] The Giva'ati Brigade deployed an elite reconnaissance battalion, the 54th (known as the *Shu'alei Shimshon,* or "Samson's Foxes"), a jeepborne assault force similar, in many ways, to Captain David Stirling's now legendary Long Range Desert Group that operated in the Western Desert, and a forerunner to the 7th Brigade's *Sayeret Shirion* of later years.

[13] See Various Editors, *Tzava U'Bitachon A'* (1948–1968), p. 43.

[14] Interview with Shlomoh Shamir, November 25, 1993, Tel Aviv.

[15] Hirsch Goodman and Shlomoh Mann, *Heyl Ha'Yam* (Tel Aviv: Revivim Publishers, 1982), p. 52.

[16] Interview with Shlomoh Shamir, November 25, 1993, Tel Aviv.

[17] Following the 1948 War, Herzog went on to serve as the IDF military attaché to the United States and Canada, head of the IDF Intelligence Branch, Israeli Ambassador to the United Nations, and the President of Israel.

[18] Aviva Bar-Am, "The Divided Time," *The Jerusalem Post Magazine,*November 27, 1992, p. 24.

[19] Chaim Herzog, *The Arab-Israeli Wars: War and Peace in the Middle East From the War of Independence to Lebanon* (London: Arms and Armour Press, 1985), p. 64.

[20] It has been reported that the element of surprise had been lost even before the attack began, as the Israeli staging area failed to adhere to secrecy and silence. According to Jordanian reports, the IDF task force used its vehicles with their headlights on full blast, and radio operators, some not familiar with the terrain or the language, violated every rule of radio security when checking their gear and positions with HQ in Tel Aviv.

[21] See Chaim Herzog, *The Arab-Israeli Wars,* p. 66.

[22] Ibid., p. 68.

[23] General (Res.) Shlomoh Shamir, *"Kravot Latrun: Shalosh He'Arot Ve'Ha'aracha,"* Ma'archot, No. 304, June 1986, p. 2.

[24] Interview, Tel Aviv, November 25, 1993.

[25] See Arieh Hasabiyah, *Heyl Ha'Shirion,* p. 22.

[26] A Muslim minority originating from the Black Sea region of Circassia, the Circassians had traditionally been an independent entity who allied themselves with whichever regional power would protect their sovereignty, way of life, and integrity. The Circassians have been conscripted into the IDF since 1954 and have served the Jewish State with incredible acts of heroism and distinction.

[27] See Arieh Hasabiyah, *Heyl Ha'Shirion,* p. 36.

[28] In 1952, as well, as a means to prepare released conscripts from the 7th Brigade for reserve duty, the IDF created the second Israeli tank brigade, the 27th (Reserve) Armored Brigade.

[29] Colonel (Res.) David Eshel, *From Meir to M-51: Sherman 3, Born In Battle,* p. 57.

[30] *"Eich Ovrim Geder-Til Be'Zachlam?"* Bamachane, April 13, 1988, p. 9.

[31] Ibid., p. 9.

[32] Interview, May 31, 1994, Tel Aviv.

[33] See Arieh Hasabiyah, *Heyl Ha'Shirion,* p. 62.

[34] Major-General (Res.) Meir Zorea, *"Ha'Shirion E'rev 'Mivtza Sinai,' "* *Ma'archot Shirion,* No. 26, July 1972, p. 8.
[35] See Arieh Hasabiyah, *Heyl Ha'Shirion,* p. 54.
[36] Ibid., p. 215.
[37] Zeev Schiff, *"A'lilot Hativa 7,"* *Ha'aretz,* October 15, 1972, p. 6C.

2

[1] Interview, Tel Aviv, November 30, 1993.
[2] Gabi Braun, *"Dan Meridor: Hu Haya Ma'Chat Kashuach,"* *Yediot Aharonot,* October 2, 1991, p. 9.
[3] Interview, Ramat Ha'Sharon, July 1, 1994.
[4] Arnan was dedicated to "Arabize" his men—European Jews, or *Ashkenazim,* were sent to the desert for some instruction by Bedouin tribal chiefs.
[5] Interview, November 24, 1992, the Knesset, Jerusalem.
[6] The other was Lieutenant Meir Har-Zion, a legendary scout and operator from Major Ariel Sharon's legendary and some say infamous Unit 101 retaliatory commando strike force.
[7] Interview, November 24, 1992, the Knesset, Jerusalem.
[8] Yosef Argaman, "New Concept In Israeli Tank Warfare," *IDF Journal,* Summer 1990, p. 12.
[9] Interview, New York City, November 11, 1994.
[10] Ibid., p. 15.
[11] Interview, New York City, November 11, 1994.
[12] *Moreshet Ha'Krav Shel Tzahal—Hativa 7 Be'Tzir Khan Yunis—Rafiah* (Tel Aviv: IDF—Chief Education Officer), No. 79, p. 5.
[13] The Ugdah also consisted of the 60th (Res.) Armored Brigade, Colonel Rafel "Raful" Eitan's conscript 35th Paratroop Brigade.
[14] See *Moreshet Ha'Krav Shel Tzahal—Hativa 7 Be'Tzir Khan Yunis—Rafiah* (Tel Aviv: IDF—Chief Education Officer), No. 79, p. 9.
[15] Interview Tel Aviv, June 14, 1994.
[16] Interview, Herziliya Industrial Zone, July 2, 1993.
[17] Interview, Herziliya Industrial Zone, July 2, 1993.
[18] See Official IDF History, p. 21.
[19] *Moreshet Ha'Krav Shel Tzahal—Hativa 7 Be'Kravot Ma'avar*

Ha'Jiradi (Tel Aviv: IDF—Chief Education Officer), No. 80, p. 1.

[20] Ibid., p. 2.

[21] Ibid., p. 2.

[22] Ibid., p. 4.

[23] Ibid., p. 5.

[24] Ibid., p. 8.

[25] Ibid., p. 8.

[26] Ibid., p. 8.

[27] Interview, Colonel Benny Michelson, IDF Historian, June 23, 1993, Tel Aviv.

[28] See, *Moreshet Ha'Krav Shel Tzahal—Hativa 7 Be'Kravot Ma'avar Ha'Jiradi* (Tel Aviv: IDF—Chief Education Officer), No. 80, p. 14.

[29] Ibid., p. 16.

[30] Ed. Aviezer Golan and Ami Shamir, *Sefer Ha'Gvura—June 1967* (Tel Aviv: Hotza'at Agufat Ha'Itonaim Tel Aviv Ve'Brit 'Olamit Shel Nitzulei Bergen-Belsen 1968), p. 50.

[31] Ibid., p. 50.

[32] Colonel Gonen, too, would grace the cover of *LIFE* in a special victory issue of the magazine.

[33] Interview, Ramat Ha'Sharon, July 1, 1994.

[34] Brigadier Syed Ali El-Edroos, *The Hashemite Arab Army 1908–1979* (Amman: The Publishing Committee, 1980). p. 443.

[35] Colonel Benny Michelson, *Operation Tofet (Inferno): Fighting East of the Jordan River March, 1968)* (Tel Aviv: IDF Military History Division), p. 14.

[36] Ibid., p. 14.

[37] Ibid., p. 15.

[38] Ibid., p. 15.

[39] Ibid., p. 17.

[40] Interview, June 14, 1994.

[41] Nir Mann, *"Kvar Be'Hatasha Nora Ha'Sagger,"* *Bamachane*, March 23, 1994, p. 33.

[42] Colonel Even served as brigade commander until June 16, 1971. He was replaced by Colonel Gabi Amir, who served as brigade commander from June 1971 to September 1972 when he was replaced by Colonel Avigdor "Yanush" Ben-Gal.

[43] According to some reports, following the 1973 War a despondent Shmuel Gonen, out of the IDF, had even threatened to kill Moshe Dayan.

3

[1] Official IDF History, *Moreshet Ha'Krav Shel Tza'ha'l: Krav Ha'Blima Shel Hativa 7 Be'Ramat Ha'Golan Be'Terem Ha'-Krav,"* No. 117, page 3.

[2] Interview, the Knesset, Jerusalem, November 19, 1992.

[3] Leslie Susser, "Israel/Jordan: The Secret Route to a Public Dialogue," *The Jerusalem Report*, August 11, 1994, p. 21.

[4] Jerry Asher with Eric Hammel, *Duel For the Golan: The 100-Hour Battle That Saved Israel* (New York: William Morrow and Company, Inc., 1987), p. 273 (Appendix A).

[5] Ibid., p. 82.

[6] Interview, Ramat Aviv, May 1993. Brigadier-General (Res.) Shimshi, a man who fought for much of his military career in the 7th Brigade, was a battalion commander in Sinai in 1973 and wrote a best-selling Hebrew-language memoir of his experiences in a book titled *Sa'ara Be'October* (*Storm in October*).

[7] It should be mentioned that Israel's Defensive Plans for Sinai, including 7th Brigade deployment in the south, are still classified top-secret by the Israel Defense Forces.

[8] Official IDF History, Volume 118, IDF Historical Branch.

[9] *"Chasifa: Kulam Be'Yachad Be'Toch Bunker Tzafuf Ve'Masriach,"* *Ma'ariv*, January 6, 1995, p. B4.

[10] Official IDF History, Volume 118, IDF Historical Branch.

[11] Identity withheld for security reasons.

[12] Interview, Jerusalem, June 1994.

[13] Interview, Jerusalem, November 1992.

[14] See Jerry Asher with Eric Hammel, *Duel for the Golan*, p. 235.

[15] Ibid., p. 273 (Appendix A).

[16] Avigdor Kahalani, *Oz 77*, (Tel Aviv: Schocken Publishing House, 1976), p. 45.

[17] Interview, Tzrifin armored base, November 1992.

[18] Major-General Hofi was a future commander of the Mossad, Israel's famed foreign intelligence service.

[19] See Jerry Asher with Eric Hammel, *Duel For the Golan*, p. 273 (Appendix A).

[20] Ibid., p. 273 (Appendix A).

[21] Interview, Latrun IDF Armored Corps Memorial, November 1992.

[22] For his role in the epic defense of the southern Golan, Colo-

nel Yitzhak Ben-Shoham was posthumously awarded the *I'tur Ha'Oz.*
[23] Arieh Hasabiyeh, *Heyl Ha'Shirion: Tzahal Be'Heilo Entziklopedia Le'Tzava U'La'Bitachon* (Tel Aviv: Revivim Publishers, 1982), pp. 201-237.
[24] Yaron London, *"Be'Chazara La'Emek Ha'Becha'a,"* Yediot Aharonot Yom Kippur, October 6, 1992, p. 3.
[25] Emanuel Rosen, *"Lama Hufkara Hativat Barak?"* Ma'ariv Sof Shavu'a, September 24, 1993, p. 24.
[26] Ariela Ringel-Hofman, *"Yanush Ve'Kahalani Lakchu Lanu Et Ha'Tehila,"* Yediot Sheva Yamim, April 8, 1994, p. 4.

4

[1] Interview, Major-General Avigdor Ben-Gal, Tel Aviv, November 1992.
[2] Arieh Hasabiyeh, *Heyl Ha'Shirion: Tzahal Be'Heilo Entzyklopedia Le'Tzava Ule'Bitachon* (Tel Aviv: Revivim Publishers, 1981), p. 234.
[3] See Arieh Hasabiyeh, *Heyl Ha'Shirion,* p. 206.
[4] Realizing the importance of military service in Israeli society, Raful even initiated a program where disadvantaged youths, those who might not have served in the IDF because of poor education, problems at home or other social ills, were conscripted into the IDF and placed in front-line combat engineering units.
[5] The IDF has always used captured weapons seized in large numbers and has even geared its military industries to support these spoils of war. Following 1967 and 1973, complete brigades were formed from former Egyptian and Syrian T-54/55 main battle tanks. The Soviet-produced AK-47 Kalachnikov 7.62mm assault rifle, the standard personal weapon of the Syrian and Egyptian armies, as well as of the Palestinian terrorist forces, were captured in such vast quantities that many of the IDF's elite reconnaissance and commando units were armed exclusively with the coveted *K'latch.* The RPG-7, however, was the most important find by the IDF, as it was powerful, easy to fire and score direct hits, and a weapon whose ammunition was in abundant supply on the battlefield since the Arabs used it as well.

[6] Interview, "Yanush" Ben-Gal, November 29, 1992, Tel Aviv.

[7] Ehud Ya'ari and Ze'ev Schiff, *Israel's Lebanon War* (New York, Morrow, 1984), p. 33.

[8] Interview with Colonel Benny Michelson, IDF HQ, Tel Aviv, May 22, 1993.

[9] Official IDF History of the 7th Brigade.

[10] See Official IDF History of 7th Armored Brigade in Operation Peace for Galilee, Israel Defense Forces, p. 23.

[11] Identity withheld for security considerations.

[12] Interview, Kibbutz Ma'agan Michael, June 3, 1993.

[13] Interview, Ramat Ha'Sharon, May 22, 1993.

[14] See Official IDF History of 7th Armored Brigade in Operation Peace for Galilee, Israel Defense Forces, p. 23.

[15] Richard A. Gabriel, *Operation Peace for Galilee: The Israel-PLO War in Lebanon* (New York: Hill and Wang, 1984), p. 75.

[16] Ibid., p. 76.

[17] Mike Eldar, *Shayetet 13: Sipurav Shel Ha'Kommando Ha'-Yami* (Tel Aviv: Ma'ariv Book Guild, 1993), p. 615.

[18] The battle for the Ein el-Hilweh camp was a block-by-block, house-by-house, room-by-room melee considered by many seasoned IDF paratroop officers to be among the most brutal in Israeli military history. The camp's defenders, mainly ideological devotees from Dr. George Habash's Popular Front for the Liberation of Palestine (PFLP) and other Syrian-controlled radical groups, fought to the death often using the camp's inhabitants as human shields.

[19] See Richard A. Gabriel, *Operation Peace for Galilee,* p. 78.

[20] Named for an Israeli soldier killed in the vicinity of a firefight with Palestinian terrorists.

[21] Interview, IDF historical officers, June 1, 1993.

[22] Interview, Haifa, June 1, 1993.

[23] See Official IDF History of 7th Armored Brigade in Operation Peace for Galilee, Israel Defense Forces, p. 23.

[24] In 1981, fearing an Israeli invasion of his fortress Lebanon during the summer of the SA-6s and the Katyushas, Arafat believed that by conventionalizing his guerrillas, he would be able to face the IDF on equal terms on the battlefield. With about 15,000 fighters, he formed three conventional brigades responsible for the territory stretching from the border with Israel to PLO headquarters in Beirut.

[25] Christopher F. Foss, *Jane's AFV Recognition Handbook* (London: Jane's Information Group, 1987), p. 27.

[26] The Hebrew letter *"Vav"* is the sixth letter of the Hebrew alphabet, and words beginning with letters owning single digit numeric value. For example, *"Zohar"* Company, beginning with the letter *Zayin,* the seventh letter, also indicates the 7th, and *"Hermon"* Company, beginning with the letter *Chet,* the eighth letter, also indicates 8th.

[27] The IDF is guided through its operational and day-to-day existence by a code called *Tohar Ha'Neshek* or "Purity of Arms." As much a moral code as a legal guideline, Purity of Arms dictates that deadly force be used only in a last resort, and that only the necessary and required force be used in any situation.

[28] The battalion is also known as the *Ga'ash* or "Rage" Battalion.

[29] Ibid., p. 78.

[30] When not wanting to release a numeric designation for their brigades, the IDF will often indicate a unit's nickname or non-numeric calling card.

[31] IDF code-names and map-coordinates for the routes.

[32] See IDF History, 7th Brigade in Lebanon, IDF Historical Branch, p. 35.

[33] See Richard A. Gabriel, *Operation Peace for Galilee,* p. 85.

[34] See IDF History, 7th Brigade in Lebanon, IDF Historical Branch, p. 35.

[35] Ibid., p. 36.

[36] Ibid., p. 38.

[37] The Syrian commandos endeared themselves in the feared hearts of Israeli forces following the 1982 invasion as fierce and highly capable warriors. Known to move about the Lebanese countryside dressed in track suits and dressed as local farmers, they were eager combatants who never shied away from a fight. Instead, they waited until the Israeli tanks were as close as possible before launching their salvos of RPGs, Saggers, and French-built Milan ATGWs.

[38] Ibid. p. 38.

[39] Ibid., p. 38.

[40] Ibid., p. 39.

[41] Identity withheld for security reasons.

[42] Ibid., p. 41.

[43] Robert Fisk, *Pity the Nation: The Abduction of Lebanon* (New York: Touchstone, 1990), p. 572.

[44] Another innovative Israeli technological concept vindicated during the fighting was Blazer, or reactive, armor. Square blocks of armor casing and explosive charge were added on the turrets and hulls of Patton and Centurion tanks—dramatically increasing their survivability. When an enemy round, be it a 120 Armor Piercing round or a PG-7 grenade, hit the box of add-on armor, the explosive charge inside the box exploded in an outward fashion and destroyed the ordnance before it could penetrate the vehicle and rip through it. Blazer armor was more like a plastic model kit than an advanced and technologically revolutionary concept. It was an add-on system of armored blocks that, once applied around a vehicle, made it virtually impervious to enemy fire. Blazer armor saved countless Israeli lives in Lebanon; many tank commanders, having survived pitched battles against Syrian and Palestinian forces, emerged from their turrets to witness that one, two, and sometimes up to five boxes had exploded. During the battle for Sultan Ya'aqub, a tank crew was captured and their disabled vehicle taken intact. It was later brought back to Moscow, where the Soviets copied the technology and applied it to their next-generation MBT—the F80.

[45] See Richard A. Gabriel, *Operation Peace for Galilee*, p. 76.

[46] Ze'ev Schiff and Ehud Ya'ari, *Israel's Lebanon War* (New York: William Morrow and Company, 1984), pp. 216–217.

[47] Interview, Ramat Ha'Sharon, June 30, 1993.

Postscript

[1] Roni Rotler, *"Chadash: Chalifa Ishit Memuzeget Le'Lochem Ba'Tank,"* *Bamachane*, September 26, 1993, p. 11.

[2] According to accounts such as Anthony H. Cordesman and Abraham R. Wagner, *The Lessons of Modern War Volume I: The Arab-Israeli Conflicts 1973–1989*, the effectiveness of the TOW was downplayed by Israeli officials in order to increase the sales potential of the Merkava.

[3] Anthony H. Cordesman and Abraham R. Wagner, *The Lessons of Modern War Volume I: The Arab-Israeli Conflicts*

1973–1989 (Boulder, Colorado: Westview Press/Mansell Publishing Limited, 1990), p. 173.

[4] David Eshel, "Merkava Mk3: Israel's New Spearhead," *Military Technology—MILTECH,* July 1989, p. 68.

[5] Ibid., p. 69.

[6] Identity withheld for security reasons.

[7] The only exception to this rule was the Soviet-built tanks captured from the Egyptians and Syrians in 1967 and 1973 and incorporated into other units.

[8] Yoav Caspi and Leah Ashat, *"Milchama Ha'Ba'ah: Yachasei Schicka Nemuchim Mi'Be'Avar,"* Bamachane, October 30, 1991, p. 54.

[9] Leak Ashat, *"Ha'Merkava Siman 4 Tehiye Kfitzat Madrega Nosefet,"* Bamachane, October 30, 1991, p. 53.

[10] Identity withheld for security reasons.

[11] Interview, June 11, 1994, Tel Aviv.

Printed in the United States
By Bookmasters